THE SKYBORN

THE
SKYBORN

PAUL COLLINS

A TOM DOHERTY ASSOCIATES BOOK
NEW YORK

THE SKYBORN

Copyright © 2005 by Paul Collins

A Starscape Book
Published by Tom Doherty Associates, LLC
175 Fifth Avenue
New York, NY 10010

www.starscapebooks.com

Library of Congress Cataloging-in-Publication Data

Collins, Paul.
    The Skyborn / Paul Collins.—1st ed.
        p.   cm.
    ISBN-13: 978-0-765-31273-0
    ISBN-10: 0-765-31273-5
    1. Human-alien encounters—Fiction.   2. Regression (Civilization)—Fiction.   I. Title.

PR9619.3.C5657S53   2005
823'.914—dc22   2005045751

First Edition: November 2005

Printed in the United States of America

0   9   8   7   6   5   4   3   2   1

ACKNOWLEDGMENTS

With thanks to Avatar Polymorph, my tech support, and my brainstormer, Randal Flynn.

THE SKYBORN

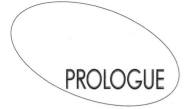

PROLOGUE

Ferrik Ramirez was dizzy. The training run in the simulator had almost blown out the safety protocols. He took a deep breath and felt his heart pounding as the buckles and straps released automatically. A red mist was rising before his eyes. If he got his hands on the idiot who had pulled that stupid stunt, he would bang his head against the bulkhead so hard he would need a gyro-compass just to find his way back to crew quarters.

He flung open the hatch and crawled out. Hearing a snort of laughter, he whirled around. Lounging in the door to the chamber was an overweight youth with limpid piggy eyes, a flattened nose like a Neanderthal's, and unruly hair that touched on non-regulation. His nickname was Tox and he was nominally Ferrik's boss. Tox laughed again, a high-pitched hee-haw that sent Ferrik's blood pressure rocketing.

"Need a change of pants, Ramirez?" Tox jeered. At the control board, an older techie grinned. Ferrik's temper went super nova and he stormed across the room.

"You could've gotten me killed, you idiot!" he yelled, throwing back a clenched fist to let him have it. "The feedback resonance on that could've fried my synapses."

Suddenly, a small skinny youth jumped between them, pushing Ferrik back. Tox was still smiling, but the smile now turned to a sneer.

"Got your little buddy here to protect you, have you, Ferrik?" The mulish laugh came again. Ferrik's fellow co-pilot, Arton, kept them apart.

Ferrik struggled to reach Tox, who blew him a kiss and made no move either to retreat or to fight back. Arton gave Ferrik a hard shove. Ferrik stumbled back, but before he could return to the fray, Arton bellowed at him. "Ferrik! Get some sense. Don't you see what he's doing? He *wants* you to hit him."

"Then we sure agree on something," Ferrik retaliated, lunging for the bigger youth again.

Arton blocked him as a tall robed figure appeared behind Tox.

"I do hope everything is in order here." It was Sub-Elder Lal Nathan, one of the few sub-elders to possess a sense of humor. Tox was so shocked he nearly swallowed his tongue. He managed to stand up straight at something approaching light speed and Ferrik was pleased to hear several joints pop. *Good,* he thought. *I hope he dislocates something, preferably his mouth.*

"Sir," said Tox, "Cadet Ferrik here attacked me, sir."

"Did he?" said Sub-Elder Nathan. "Well, he didn't do a very good job of it, since you are still standing. Now, gentlemen, I pray that you put aside your squabbles and attend me."

Ferrik took a deep breath and unclenched his fists.

Nathan closed the door behind him, as if afraid of being heard. Then he said to the shuttle crew, "I have some news. We are about to go operational."

Ferrik and the others stared, their feud forgotten. "Sir, I don't—" Ferrik began, but Nathan waved him to silence.

"I can't say more right now," the sub-elder told them, then laughed at their expressions. "Fact is, I don't know much more myself. The elders are being very . . . elder-ish . . . lately. Or, as my instructors used to say: The elders move in mysterious ways, not always for us to know."

"Sub-Elder," said Tox deferentially, "what's the big secret? Are we moving against the Earthborn scum or not? Do the elders really have some kind of secret weapon?"

Nathan's hand shot out and caught Tox on the jaw line. Tox gasped and quickly lowered his eyes. Nathan bared his teeth. "You will not speak of this, even to me, do you understand?"

Tox nodded dumbly and the smile reappeared on Nathan's boyish face, as if nothing had happened.

"There will be no more training sims," Nathan said.

Ferrik's eyes were puzzled. "But what does that mean—?"

Nathan nodded. "You will begin training in real shuttles starting tomorrow."

The three youths stared at Nathan. Arton was the first to voice their puzzlement. "But sir, all the shuttles were destroyed on landfall . . ."

"In that case, there won't be much for you to do, will there? Either way, I suggest you all get a good night's sleep."

With that he turned and left. Ferrik and Arton quickly gathered their kit and left before Tox could recover his wits enough to find some make-work for them. As it was, his deep-set eyes glowered at them as they scrambled out the hatch and headed off in the direction of the dormitories.

Half an hour later they were in the flight mess loading rehydrated food onto trays, more excited than they had felt since *Colony* had reached Earth, some two years earlier.

They found a table to themselves and almost forgot to eat as they discussed the possibilities.

"This is for real, isn't it?" Arton asked, his eyes glassy. Ferrik nodded, absently spooning something into his mouth and chewing. He had no idea what he was eating and didn't care.

"But what does it *mean?*" Ferrik wanted to know.

"What do you mean, what does it mean? It means we're going to be operational. A real shuttle crew. It means we're going into space."

Ferrik looked at him. Arton was small and wiry, with quick frenetic movements and a ferret face that always revealed exactly what he was feeling. With Arton, what you saw was what you got, which made him very easygoing and fun to hang out with.

"That's not what I'm talking about and you know it," Ferrik said.

"If Nathan were here he'd wallop you," Arton pointed out. "Do you think that's the big secret? That the shuttles weren't destroyed at all? But I don't get it. Why would that be kept a secret?"

"Maybe they were destroyed. Maybe they've been repaired."

"So why not tell everybody?"

"Because," said Ferrik, "you heard the man. The elders move in mysterious ways."

"Too frigging mysterious if you ask me," Arton said, peering at a chunk of food on his fork. He couldn't quite identify it but shoved it in his mouth anyway. Looking up, he saw that Ferrik was staring intently at him. "What?"

"Just watch what you say about the elders, Arty." He glanced around nervously. "The walls have ears, right?"

Arton nodded agreement. Sometimes they did. Sometimes electronic. Sometimes molecular. But they weren't everywhere, and they weren't always reliable after centuries of damage to the shipboard computers, to computer memory and engineering plans. "Without the elders we'd be fodder for the Earthborn scum," Arton said judicially. Then he spoilt it by winking.

"Look, *Colony* is now planet bound," Ferrik continued, as though no blasphemy had occurred. "It couldn't lift off if the elders wanted it to, no disrespect intended. Repairing and outfitting the strato shuttles is obviously a good idea. It's a big planet and there's a lot of real estate to police. But why develop an orbital capability? I mean, we just spent three hundred years up there. Why go back?"

"Isn't there any poetry in your soul, Ferrik?" Arton asked. "No romance of the spaceways? No lure to go where nobody has gone for at least two years?"

"Oh, go soak your head in a reactor tank."

"Seriously, Ferrik, I don't care why; I'm just glad I'm one of those picked to fly."

Ferrik couldn't argue with that. He was happier than he'd been in a long time and he definitely wasn't going to rock the boat, whatever that meant.

"Who says we're only going into space anyhow?" said Arton. "You think we did all those sims about what to do if we crash and have to 'live off the land' for nothing? Not to mention running into Earthborn." He shivered involuntarily.

Ferrik nodded, hoping Arton wouldn't see his own disquiet at the thought. "Yeah, I feel like I'm a walking one-man guerilla army. You know I had a dream the other night that I was . . . outside? I'm serious, dammit."

"Were you scared?"

"That's the odd part. It seemed really . . . normal."

Arton nodded, like he expected this, which irritated Ferrik. "What'd you expect? That's how the sims *work.* They rejigger the neural network, develop new neural pathways. As far as our brains are concerned, we *have* been outside."

Ferrik's appetite was rapidly leaving him. "Well, I just hope I get space duty."

Arton laughed, but nodded his agreement.

Ferrik and Arton mustered early the next morning in docking bay one, a huge arched compartment on the upper surface of *Colony,* close to its "north pole." One entire wall of the compartment, which sloped over forming part of the roof, was an enormous armor-plated hatch that could be raised in a matter of seconds, if the need arose. In all of *Colony's* three-hundred-year journey to the stars and back, none had ever done so.

Now, as a dozen trainee pilots and co-pilots—along with their astrogators and space crews—lined up in formation, they had their first glimpse of actual space shuttles. Three of them, no less. They stared in awe and with not a little apprehension at the weird craft, with their saucer-shaped pods trailing behind the giant curving two-pronged forks at their fronts. It was all very well learning to fly on simulators, but it was starting to hit each of them that soon they would have to put into practice what the sims had been preaching directly to their neocortices: the mechanics of flight, orbital as well as stratospheric, and a whole lot more. Their knowledge was far from perfect. Records had been lost, and they had too few experts to rebuild that knowledge on the long voyage between the stars. Cosmic rays had damaged the plasma computers, but as long as they did not fail too often the crew could do things with machines even when they did not quite understand how they were being done.

Suddenly an engine whined somewhere, followed by a grinding jag of noise. Slowly, the huge space door swept up and back, revealing a sky of the palest blue.

The trainees looked at one another uneasily. They had all heard the stories of how Earth's atmosphere was dangerously contaminated with pollutants, computer chip–eating bacteria, and, worse, diseases. Ferrik found himself holding his breath and others were doing the same, till Sub-Elder Nathan burst out laughing.

"Come now," he said. "An entire squad suffocating on the first day will hardly look good on my report. *Breathe.* That's an order."

When Ferrik realized that Nathan was making no effort to avoid inhaling the outside air, he tentatively breathed out and took a cautious breath. Then he sucked in a whole lungful, amazed at the sweet quality of the air. Why, you could actually taste it. He poked out his tongue, then quickly pulled it back in before anyone could see him.

The other trainees were discovering the same fact. Nathan let them take several exploratory breaths, then laughed again at their expressions.

"Earth air is perfectly safe," he said, gazing at them.

Tox scratched his head. "Begging your pardon, Sub-Elder sir, but . . . how can that be? We were told . . ."

"That if you breathe it you'll die, horribly." Nathan paced slowly back and forth in front of them, eyeing each in turn. "The ways of the elders are not for you to ponder. Suffice it to say, it is not yet time for the Skyborn to take their place upon this planet. A little dissuasion can be useful."

"Sir?" Ferrik said, but Nathan waved him to silence.

"Man your ships," said Nathan.

The teams scrambled to their pre-assigned shuttles, six to a vessel. Ferrik's crew included Prath the pilot, Tox as comm. officer, a navigator, and various flight specialists. Ferrik followed them through the hatch of a shuttle named *Procyon* and made his way forward to the bridge, where the straps wrapped him into the co-pilot's chair. Prath, a few feet away, grinned at him. Prath was a likeable fellow, slightly older than Ferrik, with wheat-colored hair and a lopsided smile that worked annoyingly well on the girls.

"I'm starting to regret that huge breakfast I had," he said.

"Me, too," said Ferrik, swallowing hard as he stared out through the forward viewscreen. The bridge contained more plasma computing gear than people—the computational requirements of managing the peculiar drive were phenomenal.

"It's just like the sim," said Tox behind them. He manned the holographic comm. panel and despite his words looked just as pale as the others.

"Yeah, sure, Tox," said Prath, "just like the sim. Remind me of that if we crash and burn."

The navigator, a rookie called Sasha, said, "Why would we crash and burn? Is something wrong?"

"He's just kidding," Ferrik said though he wasn't laughing. This was for real. If they did something wrong, if there was some kind of technical foul-up, then they really could die. Somehow, it was just like the sim and yet nothing like it at the same time.

"Computer, begin launch sequence," Prath said, all business now. His flat matter-of-fact tone immediately calmed Ferrik's nerves and he found himself automatically working through the launch steps. Indeed, several minutes slipped by without him being aware of them and he suddenly realized that the foremost shuttle had lit its torch— a term left over from the days of rocketry and not really appropriate for a gravity warp drive. It was really a combination of technologies— ones to use lasers to blast aside the air from their path, magnetic fields to hold the insulating vacuum around the craft's skin and the giant fork at the front to steer the tiny black hole before them, like a horse before an ancient carriage. When summoned into existence, the black hole, formed not of normal matter but of dark matter and invisible to human observers, could be moved around without energy loss and drag them forward in its wake, like a ship on the lip of a moving whirlpool in a terrestrial ocean, moving on, constantly on the verge of falling right in but never quite going too far. The shuttle now, suddenly, leapt out through the open hatch with astonishing speed that took Ferrik's breath away.

"Wow," said the navigator.

"Ditto that," said Prath, giving Sasha a cocky grin.

A holo image appeared next to them, its tinny voice squawking. Tox's voice answered.

"Ready, control," he acknowledged, then said to Prath, "Clear for takeoff."

"Tighten your butts," said Prath, and took them out of there.

The sides of the shuttle bay blurred past and with almost sickening speed they were outside in the air, rising rapidly into the white-flecked blue. Below them, the Earth dropped away. The tangle of ruined skyscrapers became a city and the city became a blotch on a larger landscape, which itself suddenly developed a familiar curvature. At the same time, the sky was darkening and a few moments later stars popped out.

And just like that they were in space.

The next few days were hectic. They worked heel-and-toe shifts, which meant that when they weren't flying, they were sleeping, with precious little time left over for luxuries like eating, washing, or even catching up with the news inside *Colony*.

Ferrik began to believe that that was exactly what the elders intended. They had little time, and certainly no energy, to "blab," as Tox put it, about the shuttles, or the outside air.

"Look, it's simple," Tox espoused one day. "The elders don't trust you lot. You're all as giddy as a bunch of junior cadets. This way, you've got time to shake down, get over the excitement. By the time they let you out into the real world again, all this will seem like old news."

Ferrik thought Tox had it right, but wasn't about to voice that thought. Prath on the other hand shook his head.

"You couldn't be wronger," he said.

"More wrong," corrected Ferrik.

"Yeah, what he said," said Prath. "They're not worried we're going to start talking; they're worried about something else."

"What?" Ferrik and Tox asked together.

Prath flicked his hair back. "How do I know? But the fact remains, the elders are up to something, and whatever it is, it's got a deadline. Haven't you noticed? They're in an awful hurry, and when was the last time you saw the elders hurrying over anything?"

"He's got something," said Ferrik, then wondered vaguely if they were being blasphemous. "If I have to hear one more elder tell me patience isn't just a virtue, it's a survival trait, I'll scream."

"Okay," said Tox. "So they're in a hurry. It's none of our business. Or do you two think it is?" Tox's eyes narrowed and he looked from one to the other.

"Not me," said Prath quickly. "I don't care. Just making an observation."

"Well, why don't you go and observe the line in the cafeteria? Both of you." Since seniority on board *Colony* was largely based on age (a fact that often conflicted with expertise) this technically made Tox their superior, so they took this as an order and scrambled.

As soon as they were out of sight, Prath raised his finger in a denigrating gesture. "What did we do to deserve him?" he mumbled.

"Beats me," said Ferrik. "But it must have been pretty awful."

The practical training and the long shifts were grueling but soon paid off. The crews relaxed and became proficient at flying the shuttles, not only into orbit, but also on low-altitude practice runs that had a sobering *military* feel to them along with high-altitude missions for reconnaissance purposes, mostly terrain mapping. Orbital missions involved studies of things such as global weather patterns, ocean currents, distribution of vegetation. They launched a satellite bristling with long-range scopes and communications. It was the first to reach orbit in more than a hundred and fifty years. Most of those launched in the pre-holocaust days had decayed their orbits long ago and plunged back into Earth's atmosphere, burning up in the process. A few, lodged in geosynchronous orbit or even farther out, were still to be found, though they had drifted far from their original positions. Most no longer functioned, though some could still communicate, protected by self-repairing robotics powered by huge spiderwebs made of solar energy arrays.

Part of their training also included retrieving and sometimes replacing these defective satellites, since the ones that didn't work— and didn't emit any kind of warning beacon—were a hazard to orbital traffic. Arton's shuttle had had a near miss just a week before when it shot past a dead satellite at over eighty miles a second. The kinetic energy released by such a collision would have vaporized it.

Several weeks into the missions, Prath was sweeping through an L5 orbit that took them halfway to the moon. Ferrik's sensor scope picked up an object off their port. Upon investigating they discovered it was a satellite, as they suspected. Prath brought the craft close and prepared to blast the object into its component atoms, but, finger poised over the trigger button, Ferrik stopped him. "It's transmitting," he said.

"Check your board," Prath said lazily. "Something's haywire."

Ferrik ran a diagnostic. It came up green. "Nope. It's definitely transmitting."

"That's gotta be a record," said Prath. "Three hundred years. Takes a lickin' and keeps on tickin'!"

Ferrik frowned. "There's something odd with the signature."

"Let me take a look." Ferrik transferred the data to Prath's console and after studying it for a few moments Prath gave a low whistle and looked solemnly at Ferrik.

"What do you think we should do?"

"Nothing. If these readings are right, that thing's been sitting there for two years, sending out a deep space message on a repeater loop."

"Two years. Okay, so the elders dropped it off *before* they crash-landed *Colony* on Earth. Why? And why keep so quiet about it?"

Ferrik shrugged. "You know what I think? I think it's the old message in a bottle. Remember back before landing, nobody even knew if *Colony* could take it. There was a strong possibility the retros would give out, the structural integrity of the ship wouldn't hold, any number of things. It was a miracle we made it down alive. So I think this was a kind of insurance. In case we didn't survive. Let the other skyships know what happened." He paused, thinking. "You notice it's transmitting on *all* bands? Including warp-space?"

Prath nodded. "So anybody who's still capable of listening would know by now that we made it back to Earth orbit. Except there's nobody out there listening."

"What makes you say that?"

"*Colony* received only three calls in the last one hundred and fifty years, the last over forty years ago. Let's face it, the other skyships either didn't make it or they landed, colonized, and probably reverted to a primitive state or broke up into squabbling factions. Either way, I don't figure we're going to hear from anybody soon."

Ferrik eyed the tiny pinprick of light some two hundred yards from the ship. "Maybe you're right," he said.

"Listen. I don't think we should mention this to anyone," said Prath quietly.

Everybody agreed. They left the satellite intact and continued with their mission.

A few days later, Ferrik discovered something closer to home. He had left his electropaper logbook on the bridge of his shuttle and as he was obliged to keep it updated he had rushed through dinner and a shower and hurried back to docking bay one. He retrieved his logbook and began to dictate into it, but as he returned down the main companionway toward the aft hatch he ran into a party of heavies carrying equipment and material that were shrouded in opaque plastic sheeting. One of the objects was large and bulky and had the vague shape of an antimatter fuel tank. Antihydrogen. Precious and hard to manufacture.

The heavies came to a sudden stop at Ferrik's appearance. The sergeant in charge stepped in front of him, blocking his way.

"What are you doing here, Ensign?" he demanded.

Ferrik was annoyed. This was his shuttle after all and he wasn't technically under the authority of the heavies while attached to Shuttle Command. "I could ask you the same thing, Sergeant," he said, and tried to put a peremptory tone in it. "What are you doing aboard my ship? Speak up, or I'll have to report you."

The sergeant stared at him, then suddenly grinned. "Report me, huh? And who are you going to report me to?" He looked at the other heavies, who smirked, as if they knew some joke Ferrik did not.

"Sub-Elder Nathan for a start," said Ferrik hotly.

"You're really scaring me, Ensign," the sergeant said.

Ferrik felt the first signs of alarm. He made to pass, but the sergeant stepped in front of him.

"I asked you what you're doing here, Ensign."

"None of your business, *Sergeant*. Now let me pass."

"I don't think so," said the sergeant. He signed to his men and a heavy stepped forward and deftly immobilized Ferrik. His wrist was bent at such an awkward angle that one false move would see it broken. The sergeant leaned into Ferrik's face.

"Still think it's none of my business?" He backhanded Ferrik, hard, snapping his head sideways. Ferrik turned back to face him, expressionless, his lower lip bleeding.

The sergeant raised his hand to strike again.

"Stop that!" a voice bellowed. The sergeant turned to see Sub-Elder Nathan in the companionway, his eyes dark with anger. "What do you think you're doing, Sergeant?"

The sergeant's face lost all its lines and he dropped his hand. "We found this person wandering around, sir. He wouldn't give an account of himself, so we . . ."

"So you thought you would extract one the good old-fashioned way, huh?" Nathan came forward. "Just doing your job, right?"

The sergeant nodded stonily. Nathan made flicking motions for the sergeant to step away. He was slow to move, and for a second Ferrik doubted Nathan's authority. But then the sergeant took a step to one side. His corporal let go of his hand and also stepped back.

Nathan and the sergeant locked eyes, neither giving way to the other. Finally, Nathan said, "This is Ensign Ramirez's ship. So it would seem he has some right to be here, wouldn't you agree?"

"It's off hours, sir," the sergeant said in a surly tone, his eyes unblinking. "It's off hours."

"So it is." Nathan turned to Ferrik. "Why are you here off hours, Ensign Ramirez?"

Ferrik held up his logbook. "I left this on the bridge," he said. "I needed to get it before I sacked out. Regulation one one oh five three: 'Logbooks must be signed, downloaded into storage personally on a daily basis, and be on hand at all times.' Sir."

Nathan turned back to the heavy. "See, Sergeant? He has a perfectly valid reason for being here. Now get back to work."

Nathan led Ferrik off the shuttle. He said nothing for a long time, simply walking alongside Ferrik, making the latter unaccountably nervous. Eventually, Ferrik could restrain himself no longer. "Sir, what were heavies doing aboard ship?"

"What do you think they were doing?"

"I don't know. All that stuff they were carrying . . . I guess some kind of repairs, except heavies don't handle tech stuff."

"Quite right, they don't." Nathan fell silent again. They reached an intersection and stopped. "Some advice, Ramirez. Forget what you saw. There were no heavies on your ship. You went aboard, fetched your logbook, and returned to your dorm. You met nobody."

He turned and strode away. Ferrik stared after him, sorely perplexed.

Later that night, stretched out on his bunk, Ferrik stared at the ceiling, trying to make sense of it. What had the heavies been doing on board the shuttle and why, for that matter, had Nathan come aboard after hours? It didn't compute.

"Ferrik, you awake?" came a whisper from below. Ferrik turned over onto his stomach and poked his head over the edge. Arton was in the lower bunk. He, too, was wide awake.

"What is it?" Ferrik asked in a whisper. The nearest bunk to theirs was a good ten feet away and both occupants were snoring happily.

"I've been thinking . . ."

"They have medication for that."

"Seriously, I've been thinking about what you said, and I just remembered something Lideen told me. She's engineer on *Capella*."

"You hang out with Lideen? She's pretty cute."

"Stay focused for a second, huh? She said somebody put in a new bulkhead on her shuttle, barring access to cargo hold two. There were some other changes as well, but when she asked questions she was told not to."

"Not to what?"

"Not to ask. Are you paying attention or are you thinking about Lideen?"

"I can do both, can't I?" said Ferrik.

"You? Multi-task? That'll be the day." Arton paused, then said, "What do you think it means? What's going on?"

"Any changes made to the other shuttle?"

"Not that I know of. Not yet at least."

There was a long silence. Finally, Ferrik said, "Let's keep our eyes open. But look, no more questions. To anyone. I don't know what's going on, but I don't want a visit from the heavies."

Despite trying to think through this new information, Ferrik soon fell asleep. He dreamed that the dorm was full of people and that somebody was tugging his arm. He woke to find it was partly true. There were three men standing in the shadows by his bed, and one of them—a stern-faced man—was tugging his arm. Stern-face gave him a nasty grin while one of the others reached past him and jabbed a small flat device against Ferrik's arm. There was a sharp hiss that stung and almost at once Ferrik felt the world drop away.

He woke slowly and tried to look around, but his head ached and his eyes itched as if every pollen known to Mankind had been sprung on him. He knuckled his eyes and sat up, wincing with pain. Where was he? The Shuttle Command dorm room high up in *Colony* had been replaced by a tent-like module and low flexi cots, on one of which he lay. Filthy canvas flapped in what must be a wind, though he'd never felt more than a gentle breeze in his entire life. He suddenly sneezed and wiped his nose on his sleeve.

It wasn't till he tried sitting up that he realized how incapacitated he felt. Every muscle in his body reacted sluggishly as he struggled to put his feet on the ground. He sneezed again, and it dawned on him that only really sick people sneezed. Unless you were Earthborn and immune to the virus. His mind reeled with sudden comprehension. He had been deliberately contaminated. But he hadn't transgressed. He'd done nothing to deserve this!

One section of the canvas wall whipped aside and a large hairless man, well muscled and tanned, strode in and regarded him with what seemed like good humor.

"Where . . . where am I?" Ferrik croaked.

"Where?" the man repeated. "Where, indeed. But if I were you,

I'd be asking, 'Who am I?' And the answer to that would be: 'Nobody. Nobody at all.'" The man snorted at his own joke.

Ferrik looked past the grinning face to the gap in the tent wall. Beyond the opening was a vista of tangled metal and crumbled stone walls, buildings, and an endless sea of mud.

Ferrik stared, aghast. He was outside *Colony.* He was on the surface.

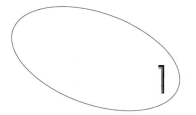

1

Sarah sat on a pine-covered hill looking down at the ragged, malnour-ished group that had arrived at her camp that morning. There were about sixty of them. Too many, really, for her people to handle. They seemed peaceful enough in a bedraggled sort of a way, though a cou-ple of them looked like they could be trouble.

She had come up the hill to be alone with her grief and felt almost angry that she now had to deal with these newcomers. *He's dying,* came the thought. She tried to push it away. The premature-aging disease, progeria, had wiped out many of her friends, would wipe out many more. Sarah stared around her at Sherbrooke Forest, which stretched away in all directions, and noted the odd silence. Was she being stalked? She almost hoped it was that, she felt such an impotent rage building in her. *He's so young!* But the silence had a different feel to it.

Even the sky, even the wind, were still, as if the whole world were holding its breath. *Waiting for him to die?* Drifting up from what they rather jokingly called the "town square" were the uncertain voices of the family. It reminded her of a time two years earlier when the giant skyworld *Colony* had first landed and Sarah had stumbled on—and adopted—a member of its crew, cast away to die. Then, too, there had been many arguments for and against admitting the newcomer to the ranks of the family.

It would be no different this time. Charity never begins at home.

Back then, Sarah's family had been a small band of twelve ragged kids eking out an existence in a post-holocaust city; now, it was a thriving population of one hundred and eighty men, women, and children.

They had fought hard every inch of the way from Melbourne to the Dandenongs, and paid for it. At times it seemed everything was against them: hunger, nature, rival gangs, the ever-present threat of the Skyborn, even their own ignorance.

But that was the past. Now they had a working farm that provided food and safety and the only home many of them had known. They had a water mill for grinding corn and wheat, and which supplied water via a network of bamboo pipes; a large pond system they had stocked with fish, and corrals of wild boar, sheep, and goats; they lived in cabins made from sunbaked mud and straw bricks, rather than the old portable huts; and they even had a burgeoning network of trade with other local communities, which supplemented their crops and provided them with a smattering of finished goods, such as pots and pans. And the size of the family deterred even the most persistent of predatory gangs. They had built a shortwave radio transmitter with a former colonist's help, and were in touch with other communities across the continent and, more recently, New Zealand, or Aotearoa as they now preferred to call it.

The radio was manned twenty-four hours a day, mostly by Denton, who had surrendered to an already obsessive-compulsive personality trait. If *Colony* ever mounted a full-scale attack on the Earthborn, the outposts would warn them. They had also retrieved from the city her prized possession: a library. Schooling was now a compulsory activity, not only for children but for the older kids, too. There was so much to learn. Or relearn.

Sarah looked over to the radio shack, listening for something. She could see Denton with his earphones plugged in, as alert as ever. It was unlikely the outposts could have been overrun; they were too cleverly hidden. And Sarah prided herself on expecting the unexpected. Or trying to. Though she hadn't foreseen the newcomers.

No. Her unease had another source. Con was dying.

She struck a fist against her thigh in sheer frustration, blinking back tears. Con would not last the week. He would die, twenty-one years old, not of wounds sustained in battle, not of the pox, which sometimes reappeared, but of plain indecent old age. And there was nothing Sarah could do about it. Sooner or later most of them would succumb to the "disease." Some, like Sarah and her sister, would be spared, having had the good luck to have an ancestor whose DNA had reasserted its right to a decent lifespan, more in keeping with the biblical three-score-and-ten than the now prevalent one-score-and-make-a-will.

Sound returned with a suddenness that made Sarah think it was she who had been holding her breath, not the world around her. She heard a humming, like giant bees, rising and falling through the ghost gums. Or was it more wasp-like, and sinister? Sarah moved down the hill to the warning bell but did not ring it immediately, in case she was wrong. Already the settlement had been raised three times for no good reason and with each false alarm their reaction time lengthened, and that could spell disaster. Sarah leaned against the pole, cocking an ear to the distant whine of motors.

Within the thickly wooded forest there was indeed a pursuit in progress. Sarah's right-hand man, former Skyborn, Welkin Quinn, gave his cruiser full revs. The ancient one-man aerial cruiser screamed manically around giant boles. Its modular shape crashed through ferny brakes and piles of dead leaves, causing them to explode upward in the slipstream. He leaned with the bike between flowering gums, dodged boulders, and presented as hard a target as possible.

He rarely chanced a look behind him. At the speed he was traveling, one split second of carelessness could wind up in disaster. When he did quickly look around, all he saw was a blur as the other three cruisers closed in on him.

It was more than the sound of the high-pitched cruisers that caused him dread. The enemy was now within firing range. Evasive action in such a wooded forest was too dangerous. He veered to the left of a towering eucalypt and almost ran into its neighbor. He weaved and swerved, but no maneuver he tried could shake them.

He was clearly being shepherded, and there was nothing he could do about it. He eased the throttle as the closest pursuer drew level with him. He could easily have taken out the enemy cruiser, but the delay would have brought his own ruin as well.

A second cruiser roared above him; the other dived below. Bracketed, he banked to the left and realized his mistake a second too late. The aerial net bucked and rocked and collapsed within itself, entangling him. Its ropes ran taut and left him suspended twenty feet above the ground.

Welkin cut the whining motor and wiped the sweat from his goggles.

The three cruisers circled him like frenzied bees around a hive. The riders, Gillian, Harry, and Elab, howled with laughter. "Eyes open!" Harry shouted above the noise, punching the air in triumph.

Welkin shrugged resignedly. At least he had nearly beaten them back to base. And in better time than any of the others in training. He made a motion with his hands, admitting defeat.

His team holstered their weapons and landed. The Earthborn were always taught that the enemy was never defeated, not until they were dead or weaponless.

Gillian hung back slightly as Harry and Elab untangled ropes and helped Welkin out of the net. Welkin's eyes met Gillian's briefly and both glanced away hurriedly. "Remember what Sarah always says," said Elab. " 'Your opponent's best move reveals *your* best move.' Therefore, you shouldn't have gone where we wanted you to go."

"I could've taken you out," Welkin said good-naturedly. "I had a laserlite strapped to my thigh."

Harry laughed. "Gillian and Elab had you covered. But you wouldn't have noticed; you had your head in the sand."

Welkin joined in the laughter. "Yeah, right. Like you guys weren't wetting your pants trying to keep up."

Welkin's radio crackled with life. "That you, Welkin?"

"Sarah," Welkin responded. "We've just finished a training run with the aerial net. I almost made it home."

"Didn't!" Elab called above Welkin's boast.

Welkin grinned, but that soon faded. Sarah's voice sounded strained. "We've finished practice anyway. Sarah? Everything all right? Is Con—?"

The silence lengthened. The four looked at one another.

"Con's okay," Sarah said. "I'd like you guys to get back here. We have visitors."

The team's faces darkened. "On our way," Welkin said.

They dismantled the aerial net and throttled their cruisers back to the farm.

Welkin could see at first glimpse why Sarah had sounded so concerned. The newcomers would easily stretch their resources. Although survival of the family in part depended on numbers, they could only take in so many at a time. And this group looked big enough to be a family all by themselves.

Leaving the cruisers beneath temporary camouflage netting, the four Committee members found Sarah at Con's bedside. At Welkin's look, Efi—the family's doctor—shook her head.

"He just slipped into a coma," she said. "I don't think he'll wake again." She hurried out, too distressed to say more.

Welkin sat down heavily in a chair. "I shouldn't have gone today."

Sarah put a hand on his arm. "He *told* you to go, Welkin. It was his way of saying the safety of the family is more important than anything or anybody."

Welkin clamped his jaw shut, his eyes shining. Sarah said quietly, "Make your goodbyes, everybody, then come to my hut. The family has business to settle."

After she left, they each took hold of Con's limp, cool hand and remembered times they had spent together, good times, funny times, even ribald times.

Welkin waited till last, then grasped Con's hand tightly. "I remember that when I was alone and lost you were one of those who took me in and gave me a new family, and a new life. I remember that you shared with me and fought and bled with me." He bowed his head a moment, too choked to speak. Then he looked up again. "I remember that you saved my life in the fighting at Fern Tree Gully. And I remember that you were always my friend."

He knelt down, pressing his forehead to Con's for a brief moment, then stood and hurried out. Gillian kissed Con as Efi returned to watch over him.

They gathered a few minutes later in Sarah's hut. She was talking to three members of the new family. They were thin and harried looking, but with Welkin's trained eyes he recognized whipcord muscles flexing beneath their emaciated flesh.

When Sarah saw Welkin and the others she excused herself and joined them.

"They seem to have been on hard times," Welkin said.

"The way they're getting stuck into that tucker," Gillian agreed.

They walked a distance before Sarah said, "The group back there, that's Tolk, with the blond hair, Fish in the middle, and Angela." She glanced at the forest that swept down the slopes to the foothills. "Sounds like they're in a bad way."

"Better them then us," said Elab.

Sarah clucked her tongue. "I'm more inclined to be charitable, but unless they can look after themselves, we can't help them."

Gillian's mouth set. Before she could say anything, Welkin said, "It's a Committee decision."

Gillian looked away.

"You're right, of course," Sarah sighed. She didn't really have the energy for this. She kept thinking about Con. "Call the others in, would you, Welkin? We'd better get this sorted before our guests get too settled."

The Committee comprised ten leading members of Sarah's family. There were five Skyborn, Welkin, his sister Lucida, Efi, Harry, and Elab. The others were Earthborn: Sarah, her sister Gillian, the stuttering Budge, and Denton. Con, who had been the family's journal holder, would have to be replaced.

It was no surprise to anyone that Gillian was the first to speak.

"It's a big ask. No one took *us* in." She stared defiantly at the other Committee members.

Denton gazed at his feet, oddly embarrassed by this straightforward assessment. Sarah indicated something behind Gillian. Gillian got an uncomfortable feeling and turned to find Tolk at the door. Damn. How long had he been standing there? What had he heard?

Saying "sorry" wasn't among Gillian's virtues. She scowled and bulldozed ahead. "Let's just weigh up all the facts, that's all I'm say-ing. This isn't the time to get soft and sentimental."

She looked down, avoiding Tolk's eyes.

"We'll understand if you don't want us," Tolk said softly. He seemed not to care that all eyes were on him.

Sarah made no response, except to study him. He was bedraggled like the others, and painfully thin, ribs showing through slashes in his tatty tunic. He also seemed nervous, or shy, which was at odds with the fact that he was the leader of some sixty people. He was barely eighteen.

Welkin knocked on the table to be heard. "Whether we want you isn't the issue," he said. "We've managed to avoid food shortages by careful planning and intensive farming. Feeding such a large group of people would place a severe burden on our own community."

"We can hunt as well as anyone," Tolk said quickly. "And we'd work real hard."

Welkin nodded, weighing up his words. "That would help, but maybe not enough."

Sarah rapped the table. "One lousy harvest and we'd be in serious trouble. The snows up here—they're bad. We simply don't have enough stored away to accommodate so many people."

Tolk hung his head. When he looked up, his eyes glistened. "I un-derstand. I told my people this when we first decided to travel up here. But the old ones said joining a large community would be our only chance for survival. We're not really fighters, you see." He looked back briefly over his shoulder. "There are lots of gangs out there. They're picking us off, one by one."

"We're sorry," Sarah said, genuinely. "Had the situation been re-versed, we would have sought to join your group. But now, we need maneuverability, too. We're just not equipped to handle so many peo-ple. It could compromise us."

Tolk turned to go. "The only one who seems to want us is the Prophet."

He had only taken two steps when he heard a sharp knock on the table. Welkin called him back sharply. "You've come into contact with the Prophet?"

"Yeah." He made the meeting sound inconsequential. "He wanted to *assimilate* our group, but we decided against it."

"And he just let you go?" Sarah asked.

Tolk hesitated. "Not exactly." He took them all in at a glance and rested his attention on Sarah. "Why do you sound so surprised?"

Welkin knocked the table before Sarah could answer. "We've heard of the Prophet. He's some kind of religious zealot who absorbs smaller groups or kills them if they refuse. Earth history is full of such fanatics."

Tolk stepped back into the doorway. "I don't know about history," he said. "Maybe we were bigger than most groups he'd come across. I guess he figured we were an even match for him. We'd heard of him anyway, so we were forewarned. We played along like we wanted to join him. He sat some of us down and gave us his spiel, you know? His political philosophy, as he calls it."

"And then you just walked?" Welkin said.

"We split in the middle of the night. Killed a few of his people who followed. After that, he left us alone, sort of."

Sarah knuckled the table. "Fanatics like the Prophet never leave people alone, Tolk. They stamp them into the ground till there's no trace of them left."

Tolk nodded. "Maybe. It's one of the reasons we wanted to join your community." He looked at all of them then. "You people think you're safe because you're established and have good fighters." He shook his head. "Let me tell you, no one's safe from him. He's building a force. God's Army, he calls it."

Gillian dispensed with the protocol of knocking. They always did when an agenda turned into a full-on discussion. "Degenerates will flock to anything or anyone in times of crisis."

Tolk smiled fleetingly. "And why not? He offers the homeless somewhere to sleep, safety, and food. The way the world is right now, that's a pretty attractive offer."

"And yet you walked out on it?" Lucida persisted.

"We didn't care for his 'message.'"

"Which is?" Sarah asked.

"He calls his people the 'Collective,' says it's an old Russian term.

He preaches that the Collective is more important than the individual, that the individual is alone and vulnerable and has no identity or existence except as part of a larger group. Only the group endures; only the group is truly important."

"Joining them might have put you out of a job," Sarah said pointedly.

"I'm okay with that," Tolk said, shrugging. "But my family doesn't want to lose complete autonomy, any more than yours would. To the Prophet, everything has to be done in the name of the group, the Collective. The 'whole' confers immortality, because even if one individual dies, it doesn't matter; his or her contribution to the Collective will live on forever. Life after death. But this can only be achieved if each unit submerges itself and its own needs and its ego to that of the Collective. The will of the Collective is all that matters."

Sarah sighed heavily. "Totalitarian fanaticism at its best," she said. "Based on a belief in divine destiny, and no doubt the divinity rather conveniently resides in the Prophet himself . . ."

"Something like that," Tolk said. "Look, I'd better get back to my group. We have some ailing children that need attention. I'll leave you to your meeting."

They waited till Tolk had left before resuming the discussion.

Gillian rapped the table, looking around at the others. "Some things don't add up here. Call me a cynic, but I need a few things explained."

"We can't be too harsh on them, Gillian," Lucida said.

"And we don't want to be a bleeding-hearts society, either," Gillian replied, her voice rising.

"Keep it calm," Sarah cautioned.

Gillian took a deep breath. "Okay. Tolk said earlier that his people are hunters. If that's true, why are they so malnourished?"

"I wondered that, too," Welkin said.

"They might not be very good at it," Sarah pointed out. "Or maybe somebody isn't giving them much of a chance to hunt. They don't have cruisers to rustle up the odd mob of kangaroos. I remember when we were living in the city, we sometimes had no time to gather food. It was dog-eat-dog back there. Remember?"

Gillian and half the Committee remembered the bad times in the ravaged city only too well. Ferals, Bruick's jabbers, hoboes, and the Skyborn. Life was hard and often short.

"All right, but I'm still not convinced," Gillian said. "He said they weren't fighters. Now if that's true, why would the Prophet have considered them such worthy opponents? I mean, if they're as harmless as he's making out, they would've been a walkover for the Prophet, wouldn't they?"

"Your point being?" Lucida said.

Gillian gritted her teeth. "He's lying." Her voice rose with exasperation. "He's hiding something—something he doesn't want us to know."

"Nobody wants to make herself look useless," Sarah said, but it was plain that Gillian's words were hitting home.

"Third point," Gillian said, holding up three fingers. "Did I mishear something to do with 'units' being a euphemism for people in that speech of his? It was almost as though he believed in that stuff himself."

"Wait a minute. Are you saying he's a . . . a spy for the Prophet?" Lucida said.

"I'm saying we need to be careful," Gillian said. "He doesn't ring true as the poor harassed refugee. And if you lot fell for that phony 'I have to look after the children now' stunt, I'm very disappointed in you all."

Sarah became thoughtful. "I must admit I was surprised by his vocabulary. For someone who doesn't know history, he seemed quite eloquent talking about Russia—a country from the past—and communism."

Everyone started speaking at once. Efi, Elab, and Denton began a heated three-way discussion, while Lucida tried to explain to Gillian why she was wrong. The other members of the Committee sat quietly waiting for some order to return.

When Sarah thought the discussion had gone on long enough she banged the table three times. The others fell silent.

"I think we're going to need Tolk and his people," she said. A murmur sprang up, but Sarah motioned for silence again. "Some of you may not know, or remember, the history of the last war. Much has been lost, but one thing is still known: It was started by a religious-based dictatorship. One in which the individual was subordinated in every way possible to the will of the State and the monster that ran it." She paused. This echo from the past and all the horrors it contained could be seen on every face. "I don't see much difference between the political philosophy of that dictatorship and the Prophet's. Nor in their aims . . ."

The temperature in the room seemed to drop.

Sarah stood. "'Those who do not remember the past are condemned to relive it,'" she quoted, expelling her breath in a shaky sigh. "It's my firm belief that history is about to repeat itself here in the hills of the Dandenongs."

"And we can stop it," Welkin said, standing also. "But we'll need all the help we can get."

Gillian leaned back in her seat. "And if they can't feed themselves because they're lousy 'hunters'?"

"So we go into rationing mode," Sarah said. "We've done it before." She raised her eyebrows at Elab, Denton, Budge, and Harry. "You've all been quiet. What are your thoughts?"

Budge spoke for all of them. "There's a m-m-marauding band out there. It's l-l-large, may-maybe as big as Bruick's j-j-jabbers when we finally b-b-beat them—"

"—With the Skyborn's help," Gillian cut in.

"Yes, with—with their help," Budge agreed. "Buh-but the thing is, Gillian, we could've taken the-them out back in Melbourne, when they were only a small group. In tuh-the end, Bruick some . . . how made a deal with *Colony*, and the next thi-ing we knew Bruick had himself the stockade and im-munity from attack. We all know we shou-should have wiped him out wuh-when he was a nobody."

"So it's like Sarah said," Welkin put in. "We need all the able-bodied defenders we can get if there's going to be a war." Before anyone could object to his use of the word "war," he added, "We're the largest community among the Earthborn right now. And make no mistake, if the Prophet is half as crazy and ruthless as he sounds, he will come for us and there *will* be war. One that will take away everything we've fought so hard to get. And everyone we care about."

"A show of hands?" Sarah said, putting hers up. "I vote they stay and we take sensible precautions." She glanced at Gillian. "Keep your enemies near."

The vote was almost unanimous. Gillian was the only dissenter.

"Carried." Sarah noticed Gillian's grim expression. "Sorry, Gillian. Just remember when we first found Welkin. If everyone had thought like you do, and some did, there'd be no Skyborn in our ranks right now."

Sarah wasn't point scoring. Without the help of renegade Skyborn, their people would have had no technology, no radio transmitter, no knowledge of laserlites or cruisers. None of the materials that had protected them from attack and helped them survive the rigors of this past year.

Gillian flicked a look at Welkin, which he found unreadable. "I'm fine with the decision," she said. "Just don't come crying to me when Tolk's lot show their true colors, that's all."

Everybody jumped when Patrick O'Shannessey suddenly barged into the room. He was sweat-stained and bleeding. He'd been on a long-range patrol and no one expected him back for at least another day.

"Ye'd better all come quick," he panted. "We got ourselves a prisoner. He needs medical attention, fast—he's in a bad way. Oh, did I mention he's from *Colony?*"

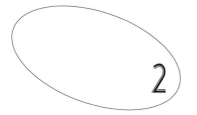

2

A small crowd had gathered around the injured Skyborn. It wasn't often that Earthborn got to see a current colonist up close—some in fact had never done so.

"Not much different from us," one of Tolk's people said, plainly disappointed that the man didn't have two horns and a tail (as was rumored among the youngest Earthborn).

"No, we're not," Welkin said pointedly. "And right now this one needs help." He maneuvered the kid away. The injured colonist's uniform was torn and bloodstained.

"Okay, people," Harry called out. "This isn't a circus. Let's clear the place." He looked meaningfully at the kids from Tolk's group. "Sarah's over there, organizing where you folks will be sleeping tonight."

They slowly filed out, giving Welkin and Efi room to move.

"What'd you think?" Patrick asked Efi. "It's bad, is it not?"

Efi felt for the man's pulse. "*Eiparhi elpitha.* He's burning up with fever." She rummaged through her field kit, pulling out clean cloth and a variety of jars, some filled with desiccated substances, others with pale fluids. She sent one of the younger boys to find a paperbark tree and tear off strips of the pliant papyrus-like bark, explaining that it helped sterilize wounds and kept infection at bay. Then she started mashing herbs for an oral antibiotic.

"Infection kills more people than injuries," she explained as she worked. "I just wish we had Skyborn medicines."

Welkin took on a thoughtful look at her words; a shadow fell across him as he was bent over the injured Skyborn. He looked up into the face of a big sneering kid from Tolk's group. He recognized him as a youth called Fish, supposedly Tolk's right-hand man.

"Stay back," Welkin said, and returned his attention to the Skyborn, who seemed oddly familiar. He was small and wiry. Checking his utilities, Welkin found an ID tag. Its holographic DNA representation spun around the tiny face, his name below in 3-D UV letters. "Arton Haberd," Welkin said in surprise.

"A friend of yours?" Fish said behind Welkin.

Welkin pocketed the flashing ID tag and stood up. "I thought I said Sarah was looking after you people." He wasn't used to having his authority disregarded. Committee people carried weight in the family.

"That Skyborn," Fish said. "He should be killed. That's what his kind did to my brother and sister. Them and their fancy weapons." He went to spit on the comatose man, but Welkin stepped into his line of fire.

"Not all Skyborn are butchers," Welkin said. "I don't know where you're from, but around here, orders are obeyed. And we don't kill unarmed people."

"Orders?" Fish looked behind him. Several of his friends fanned out. One of them laughed.

Welkin tensed. He had to set an example, quickly. The problem was, what *kind* of example he set would probably have long-term repercussions. He had two choices: a *violent* example, or a *diplomatic* one. He was sure he could take out Fish, but he also knew that to do so would be to tear apart the embryonic federation of families they had just voted on. He sighed inwardly. Sarah had been a good teacher. Too good, perhaps. "We need the Skyborn alive," he said evenly. "That way, we gain intelligence on what *Colony* is up to. Dead, he's of no use to us."

"Alive he's just another enemy," Fish sneered. He took Welkin's diplomacy as a sign of weakness and strutted before his posse.

Patrick stood then. He and his sister Mira were not Committee, although they were in line to be. He had no compunction about being tactful. "Did ye not hear what Committeeman Welkin said?" He leaned forward, almost touching Fish's nose with his own. Patrick was far more powerful, and several times more intimidating, than Fish. The latter knew he had suddenly bitten off more than he could chew.

The pair stood in a silent tableau, eyes unblinking. Some of Sarah's people came over to watch the drama unfold.

It was Fish who backed down. He wasn't stupid enough to mess with Patrick O'Shannessey. Few people were.

Patrick glared at Fish's posse. "I heard the boss tell you people to go over there," he said, pointing to Sarah and Tolk. "Now *go!*"

Fish laughed uneasily, though he was moving away at the time. "We mightn't want to stay—not with Earthborn scum sleepin' with the enemy."

"That'd suit me just fine, boyo," Patrick said. He watched them move off. When they reached Tolk, Fish drew him away, nodding toward Welkin and the others.

"Let it go," Welkin said. "They're new. They're not used to the rules yet."

"Oh, I'd say that one's a real slow learner," Patrick said.

Efi stood up. "*Sta heria tou theou tora.* I've done what I can. We'll need to take him over to the infirmary. *Ston diabolo!* These blowflies just love the smell of blood."

Once they had the Skyborn settled down, most of them joined Sarah and the others. Finding room for Tolk's people proved harder than it had at first seemed. There was insufficient shelter, and it necessitated vacating some shacks and doubling up in others. Altogether Sarah's family was not pleased at being burdened by Tolk's people.

Sarah said as much that night during dinner.

"And don't say 'I told you so,'" she said to Gillian. "Half the decisions we make, people don't like. When we move from here, everyone's going to moan. But if we stay here overlong, *Colony* will be on us like a ton of bricks."

"Where'd you find Arton, anyway?" Harry asked, spooning a huge amount of mashed potato into his mouth. He then managed to shove in a spoonful of peas as well.

It was Mira O'Shannessey who answered. "We were on our way

home. A flash flood took our food pack, so we came back sooner than we planned. We almost missed him. I think he was calling out in delirium. Anyway, he'd crashed his cruiser. Judging by the broken branches he'd fallen some twenty feet. Cruiser must've clipped the tree. I figure he was maxing the gyros when he hit."

"Ouch," Gillian said.

Lucida leaned forward. "What sort of stuff was he saying?"

"Words we've never heard," Patrick said. "Prioriny—prio—?" He grimaced at his ignorance, seeking help from Mira, who merely shook her head. "Shite," he said lamely.

"Doesn't really matter," Lucida said. "Maybe he's a runaway. If he is, he'll be a good man to have on side."

"Unless he's a plant," Gillian said.

"He'd be pretty dedicated to run headfirst into a tree and nearly get himself killed," Sarah said.

"Accidents happen," Gillian pointed out.

"We can only wait and see," Sarah said. "Either way, it's too early for guessing. But we'll take precautions. Double the guard on him." She thought back to the trouble Welkin had had with Fish. She didn't want to admit it to Gillian, but she was having second thoughts about Tolk's people now. All of a sudden they were being hit with some hard choices. She wondered if they had reached the end of them.

"We already have a double guard," Gillian grumbled. "Welkin's inside the infirmary. Seems like he doesn't want to miss a word the Skyborn says. Mind you, the poor bugger is pretty out of it and probably will be the rest of the night."

Sarah nodded and let the conversation wash over her. She found it hard to concentrate, knowing that Con was lying in a coma not fifty feet from where she sat. Nevertheless, she tried to focus. Welkin obviously wanted the latest Intel on *Colony,* but the kid had been abandoned by his "family," and she suspected he somehow needed reassurance that some of them still remembered him and that his escape and renegade status hadn't cost them dearly. No matter which way you cut it, she thought, he and the others were Skyborn. They'd left childhood friends behind, and mentors, too, who had been as close to him and Lucida as parents. That was a wagonload of betrayal to cope with.

Sarah blinked. They were all waiting for her to answer a question. "Sorry? I vegged out there for a second."

"What do you think Fish was on about this afternoon?" Gillian asked. "He seemed dead set on causing trouble over the Skyborn."

"They'd already made up their minds on that score," Harry said. "But I think it's jealousy, pure and simple. See, us Skyborn are incredibly valuable. We're smart, we're technologically developed, we're also a lot handsomer than you lot, and we've got a more developed sense of humor . . ." Lucida threw a blob of mashed potato at him, amidst general hoots and groans. The potato hit him on the chin. He didn't even blink. He wiped it off and licked his fingers. "Hey, your potato tastes better than mine. What gives?"

Sarah forked the last of her food into her mouth and swallowed. "Ignoring Harry's interesting theory, we need to remember that any group that survives out here does so because it's developed a pretty tight group identity, a team spirit, I guess. Well, that team spirit can flip into mob mentality in the blink of an eye. Or it can be nudged. I think Fish was nudging, looking for a weakness, a chance to create chaos and dissension. Either he's angling for Tolk's job; he could dislike Tolk's passive approach; he isn't the kind of bloke who *asks*; or he's what he seems to be, just another useless troublemaker." She pushed her chair back. "I figure he'll push us again before their lot settles down into our way of thinking."

She got up from the table, stifled a grimace. "I'm heading over to the infirmary." She picked up a plate and dished some stew into it. "I'll take this to Welkin." She left no doubt in anyone's mind that she wanted time alone.

If not for the alert guard on the infirmary door, Sarah might have thought something was amiss. She closed the door behind her, and felt uneasy. The silence reminded her of death. She quickly checked on Con, but he was still in his coma, his condition unchanged. She continued through to the back room.

"You okay, Welkin?"

Welkin stirred at her voice. "Sure. Just thinking."

Sarah let go of the breath that she had been holding. "I couldn't see you for a moment. Why don't you fire up the oil lamp?" She went over to him and rested a hand on his shoulder.

"I've seen all I need to," he said quietly. "And the oil's running low."

She set the food down on a table, then lit the lamp. Welkin barely acknowledged the food. "Take a look at the back of Arton's neck, under the ear," he said.

"Head wound?"

Welkin shook his head. "His neural jack's been surgically removed. Not a very neat job, either. Not up to *Colony*'s standards. And it's not that recent." Welkin frowned. "Something's wrong."

"He's burning up, that's for sure," Sarah said, checking his temperature. She rinsed a rag in a bowl and mopped the colonist's forehead.

"More than that," Welkin said. "He's delirious. Keeps muttering about something . . ." He sat on the floor and rested his head against the bunk. "I'll stay with him the night. I want to be here if he becomes lucid."

Sarah nodded, decided not to dig further for now. Welkin clearly was worried about something, but she knew better than to press him prematurely. "Call me if you need to." She started to leave, then stopped.

"What's going on between you and Gillian?"

Welkin reacted. "Nothing's going on."

"Maybe that's the problem." Sarah suppressed a smile. "You want to talk about it?"

He shook his head.

"Have it your way. If you change your mind, you know where to find me."

She left. Welkin scowled softly. He should have said something. Sarah had way more experience at relationships than he did and, besides that, she was a girl. That had to count for something. The problem as he saw it had started not long after they'd defeated Bruick's jabbers. He'd gotten it into his head that he and Gillian were an item. But the first time he'd put his arm around her she'd blown up at him.

Accused him of treating her like she was his property, that she had no say in the thing.

He had been . . . flabbergasted. She had settled down a bit after that, and had tried to explain. But that hadn't made it any better.

"I've always thought of you like a . . . like you were my brother."

"Brother?" His heart dropped to his knees, the hurt plain to see.

Her voice softened. "Welkin, we can't—it wouldn't be fair. Just because Sarah is exempt from the progeria doesn't mean I am. You could live another sixty years. I probably won't last six." She sighed. "Can't we just be friends?"

His heart crash-landed like a lead weight somewhere around his ankles. Rock bottom. "Friends?" He suppressed the quaver in his voice. "Sure. That'd be great." He snapped petulantly, "Fine."

Since that conversation Gillian had been true to her words. She had acted toward Welkin as if he were her brother, sometimes her big brother, sometimes her little brother, who needed scolding from time to time. He put up with it because it was Gillian and because, as the months passed and the ache in his heart failed to subside, he came to know how he truly felt about her. But instead of making matters better, it made them worse. When she was around he was almost unbearably awkward and clumsy, as if his arms and legs had grown several feet longer. He bumped into things, dropped things, and lost the train of his thoughts. He found a definition of his complaint in one of Sarah's old books; apparently, he was . . . in love.

Or he had a brain tumor. The symptoms sounded a bit similar. Both were incurable.

Some time after Sarah left the infirmary, Welkin fell into a disgruntled sleep, waking suddenly when Arton muttered something. "Arton? It's me, Welkin Quinn. You're safe."

Arton's eyes opened slowly, but his gaze was disturbingly vacant. His jaw moved and Welkin leaned close, trying to catch the whisper-fine words.

". . . he's crazy, I tell you."

"Who is?" Welkin asked. "Who's crazy?"

Arton's fevered eyes swiveled toward Welkin. "Jamieson . . ."

"Elder Jamieson—?"

Arton jerked his head aside in delirium, then swung it back loosely, as though his neck were broken. Welkin dabbed the colonist's face with the damp cloth. His skin was hot and his eyes had a feverish gleam. Welkin's own temperature was rising: Mention of Jamieson was enough to do that. The elder was a fundamentalist, one of the old breed that harbored a deep resentment against the Earthborn. He was also responsible for banishing Welkin from *Colony*.

"His eyes . . . his eyes, spae him . . . don't you see what he sees? . . . mega-death . . . mad as a missile."

Welkin leaned over to catch the mumbled words. "Arton? Tell me more. Has Jamieson gone horizon crazy?"

Arton's face relaxed then and his eyes seemed to focus. "Who are you?"

Welkin hesitated. Any of the colonists who had been taken in by the Earthborn were obviously renegades—less than vermin, fit only to be exterminated by *Colony*. "I'm a friend," he said after a short silence. "Someone you can trust. We saved you from the crash. Do you remember crashing into the tree?"

But even before Welkin had finished speaking, Arton's eyes had glazed over and his head lolled to one side.

Welkin sat in silence for a while, then started to slowly pace the room. He felt uneasy, not just with Arton's words, but something else, something that prickled his skin. Sounds outside the window made him start, deepening his unease. Before the hour was up he was so edgy he knew he had to get Arton out of the infirmary. Mira was on guard outside. She was more than adequate for the job, but Welkin had learnt to follow his gut instincts. Much as he loved the family, he knew that even his own friends could become pretty irrational when it came to Skyborn from *Colony*.

He hastily packed everything Efi had told him that Arton might need in an emergency, then called out to Mira. She came immediately, covering the room with her laserlite.

"Whoa!" Welkin said. "I just need a hand with him. I don't feel comfortable with him here. Everyone knows he's in the infirmary. I . . . I've got a bad feeling." It sounded lame now that he had to put it into words, but to his surprise Mira just nodded. Gut feelings worked for her.

"Paddy's two doors down," she said. She took Arton's arm across her shoulder and Welkin took the other. "There's no lock on the door, as you know."

"Won't need one," Welkin said, as they moved toward the door. "If no one knows he's been shifted, anywhere will be safer than here."

He peered through the slightly open door. "Now's as good a time as any. Let's go."

Together they half carried, half dragged Arton out the door, into a sharp left turn, then twenty feet to Patrick's hut. They were inside with the door shut before the burly Irishman could demand who was there.

Patrick took little persuading to sleep in the infirmary for the night. He left in the fervent hope that the "heathens" would try to break in before morning. Mira went back to her guard duty outside the infirmary, keeping up appearances.

An hour passed so quickly that Welkin was barely aware that he had fallen asleep. He only woke when he was suddenly gripped by the wrist. He jerked awake to find Arton's startled eyes on him.

"Run—prion diffusion—!"

Welkin groped for words. "Prion? What's that?"

Arton's body stiffened. Although weak from his injuries, he managed to lift his head from the straw pillow. "Put them in the isolator. Just do it, you fool."

Welkin's skin goosed. It was the urgency in Arton's voice more than anything that made his heart thump. "What's happening, Arton? Try to think." He gently shifted Arton's elbows, easing the man back down to the bed.

Arton shook his head as though unaware of Welkin's presence. "They've identified the reverse transcriptase enzyme? *Already?* That means all they have to do is hijack the right RNA messenger gene? Space!"

Welkin sat back and listened well into the morning. Incoherent rambling it might have been, but Arton's broken sentences began to make terrible sense.

. . .

Welkin woke to a mob of voices. They swept past the hut like a wave, then found their focus two huts away. There they gathered, their demands threatening, angry.

Welkin pulled aside the hessian sacking from the window. Daylight flooded in, blinding him. By the time he adjusted his vision, Sarah and several others had added their own voices to the mob's.

Arton's eyes were closed, but his face had lost some of its rawness from the day before. Welkin pulled on his fur buskins, but hesitated at the door. He went back to the window and listened.

Sarah was flanked by Elab, Patrick, and Mira O'Shannessey. She had her hands raised, trying to bring some calm to the unruly gaggle.

"He's the enemy," someone yelled, and others joined in, chanting, fueling the anger of the group.

A small knot of people ran from surrounding huts and Welkin sighed with relief. Committee members and others from their group now joined Sarah on the infirmary veranda. Flanked by the new arrivals, Sarah finally commanded a semblance of order.

"What exactly is this?" she said. Her voice was clear, authoritative, and cut cleanly through the remaining strident voices.

A youth pushed his way forward. It was Fish, Welkin saw. Several of his group shouldered their way through the gathering, like heavies from *Colony,* Welkin realized with a start. An elder with heavies to enforce his rule.

"Hand over the colonist," Fish demanded. He looked to either side of him, acknowledging his support.

"You think we're not taking good care of him?" Sarah asked. This brought a round of laughter from her family.

"We'll take good care of him," Fish said. "String him up like his lot did to some of us."

A chorus of approval rose from his own ranks. Bolstered by the support, Fish strode to the bottom of the steps. He stood on the first step and turned his back to Sarah.

"There's a war going on and we're being slaughtered. We can't have Skyborn in our ranks." He glanced over his shoulder and stared at Sarah. "Next thing you know, we'll be breeding with them."

Sarah waited for the audience to quieten. "Your ignorance surprises me," she said quietly, so that only Fish and his minders could hear her. Louder, she said, "We have a wasting disease. How many people do you know live past twenty?"

"You have!" Fish accused.

Several assenting voices rose in anger.

Welkin clenched his jaw. He saw Sarah telling her own people something. Probably not to retaliate. His mind made up, he went to the door and shut it quietly behind him.

"I have," Sarah agreed. "And so do the Skyborn. If you can't learn something from that fact then I can't help you." She indicated Efi and Elab. "The Skyborn are just like us—three hundred years in space hasn't turned them into aliens."

"Just murderers," Fish spat.

But even now his support was less vocal.

Sarah spread her hands, taking in the compound. "Everything you see here is attributable to the Skyborn. Without their help we would still be in Melbourne, just another homeless band trying to survive. Now we have a thriving community."

She took two steps down and towered over Fish. "What is it with you people that you hate so much?"

"It's them or us," Fish said emphatically. "You're aiding and abetting the enemy. That's treason."

"You're wrong," Welkin said. He drove through Fish's people like a wedge. He detoured around the steps and jumped up to the veranda.

"This place is crawling with the enemy," Fish said.

Welkin frowned. "Perhaps it is—but I don't think it's the Skyborn." Before Fish could retaliate, Welkin added, "One of the things that the Skyborn can tell you about is history. Most of which you seem to have forgotten." He held up a hand to stem the inevitable response. "The injured colonist is a prisoner of war. There are rules on treating POWs. That's what being civilized means . . . having *rules* that you obey even when you don't agree with them."

"*Your* rules," Fish said. "Rules which your people don't abide by."

By now most of Sarah's people had gathered around the newcomers. "My rules are those held by this community," Welkin said, looking out at his family. "I suggest that you people have a good think about your own values, and ours. If they're too far apart, maybe you had best leave."

"Maybe we will," Fish said. He flicked his head and strode off across the compound, his followers close behind him.

Welkin wiped a sleeve across his forehead. It came away damp.

"You're becoming quite good at standing up for yourself," Sarah said. "For a moment there I thought we were going to have to knock some sense into him."

"Save your energy for later, Sarah." Welkin paused to clear his thoughts. "*Colony* has a secret weapon. Arton's not making a lot of sense, but I know this much: They're going all out to get us this time. And it's going to be swift and ruthless."

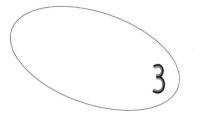

3

While Sarah was organizing an urgent Committee meeting, Welkin detailed a guard for Arton. "Shoot to kill if any of those people even dare to come through that door," he told Patrick and Mira.

"We'll gladly do that, Welkin me boy," Patrick said.

Mira looked up from mopping Arton's forehead. "His fever's broke. He'll pull through with luck. Even that gash on his arm isn't so festered."

Welkin nodded. "If he says anything, write it down. Anything at all, even if it sounds like gibberish. It could be more important than you think. We'll try to decipher it later."

By the time Welkin arrived at the main hut the Committee was seated around the table. Present were Sarah, Gillian, Lucida, Harry, Elab, Efi, and Budge. Denton was at the radio shack.

"We were just apologizing to Gillian," Sarah said to him. "Maybe we should have just told Tolk and his people to move out right at the beginning."

"It's never too late," Welkin said. "Speaking of Tolk, I didn't see him or the other one—Angela?—just now."

Efi rapped the table, then realized the informality of the meeting. "*Signomi.* Maybe Fish is trying to form a splinter group."

"Or maybe while we were all occupied, Tolk and a few of his people were searching for Arton," Welkin suggested. "Don't worry. The O'Shannesseys have the situation well in hand."

"Okay," Sarah said. "What did you get out of the colonist—sorry—Arton?"

Welkin hesitated. This had to be done just right. Too much was at stake. "*Colony* plans to launch something called 'Cleansweep.' I couldn't make too much sense of what he was saying, but it sounds like"—he kept his voice calm—"biological warfare."

The sudden silence was broken only by children's voices as they played outside. "What are we talking about here?" Sarah asked. "Some kind of virus? How would they infect us?"

"Efi?" Welkin said.

"*Colony* scientists developed a plague that could wipe out hostile alien species—in case they needed to cleanse a planet for terraforming. *Theimame.* That stuff was in the data banks as ancient research. The moment we knew we were returning to Earth, further research was dropped."

"But surely any virus they were working on would be harmful to *all* humans? I mean, it's not as though we're two distinct species." Sarah tried to keep her whirling thoughts in order.

Efi bit her lower lip. "*Poios kseri?* I can't remember much of that stuff, but the virus was extremely deadly. A planet the size of Earth could be sprayed within a day."

"Making Earth totally uninhabitable to the Skyborn as well as us, surely?" Gillian said.

"They have their world on board *Colony,*" Efi said. "And you can bet that if that's their plan then by now *Colony* is hermetically sealed and able to withstand any biological threat from without."

"Great," Sarah said. "Just great. They've been away for three centuries, so what's another decade or so? They'll just wait it out."

Elab banged his hand against the table before alarm could sweep through the Committee. Everyone jumped. Elab grinned. "And just to make you all feel much worse, the plague could have a short lifespan. Something that eradicates itself within a week. Just long enough to kill anything humanoid."

"So why haven't they spread this plague already?" Sarah said.

"Could be several reasons," Welkin said. "As we know, their surface shuttles were all destroyed on landing. So it's not possible to spread the virus globally. They could suit up and spread it with cruisers, but unless they scored a direct hit on a settlement, it would be pointless. And perhaps you're right, Sarah, they haven't done it because that's not what 'Cleansweep' is all about. Thirdly, one thing I am sure about is that *Colony* is now divided in its ranks. One camp wants peace with the Earthborn and to return to one of its original tenets, that is, to terraform a planet. The other camp, ruled by the elders, is moving ahead quickly with their 'Cleansweep' program."

"So the warring factions are hindering one another?" Sarah said.

"Sounds like it to me," Welkin said. "But it's hard to tell."

"It could explain why they haven't been hounding us too much lately," Gillian suggested.

"It fits." Welkin looked over to Lucida, who hadn't said a word. "The elders have no need to take part in piddling skirmishes when they know they'll have us all soon enough."

"Luckily for us, Arton was in the appeasement group," Lucida said.

Sarah raised querying eyebrows.

Lucida made a face. "It seems to me that if we can use Arton as a bridge between his faction and us, then we'll be reunited. If we had an elder in the infirmary right now, all we'd have is trouble."

"Without meaning to cause problems," Elab said, wiping his nose, "if we had a referendum, the vote would swing to let sleeping dogs lie—leave *Colony* alone and perhaps they'll leave us alone, like they have been doing."

"Pah, pah, n-now w-we know the rea-son f-for that," Budge said.

"Space!" Lucida exclaimed. "I've just thought of something. It mightn't be related, but one of the newcomers—remember Travis? He was captured by *Colony* troopers about six months ago but escaped recently."

"The one who has night terrors?" Gillian said.

"That's him," Lucida acknowledged. "He can't remember much of his time on *Colony*, which suggests he was drugged. But there are two unsettling facts: *One,* he has a series of circular puncture marks on his back and legs, obviously from a biopsy needle."

"And the second?" Sarah asked.

Lucida frowned. "They kept him alive for five months. Instead of just killing him."

"This biological warfare business," Gillian said worriedly. "You don't think they injected him with something, do you?"

Lucida closed her eyes for a quick prayer. "Efi?"

Efi shook her head. "*Ohi.* Not unless it's time-coded."

"You are joking?" Sarah said, shifting uneasily in her chair.

"It'd be simple enough," Efi said, candidly. "Introduce an immature virus, wait for it to gestate, then . . . outbreak in plague proportions."

"We could all be sitting time bombs?" Gillian said.

Welkin rapped the table loudly. "Okay, everyone, let's just drop this talk of viruses, okay?" He had to call for silence. "When it comes down to it, we need to get aboard *Colony* and find out what's going on firsthand . . ."

Sarah interjected before he could continue. "Infiltrate *Colony* now and the two opposing factions on board might unite to fight the common foe."

"So you suggest we sit back and see what happens?" Harry said.

"Hold on," Welkin said. "This much I do know. Arton might be delirious, but he *laughed* at the idea that *Colony* has forgotten about the Earthborn. They have internal problems, but the elders are ruthless in exterminating agitators. Remember, their main objective is genocide. We have to gain access to *Colony,* and to do that, we need to get on board."

Sarah shook her head. "Too dangerous, Welkin. I don't want to risk anyone on a suicide mission. And especially not one of you. And it would have to be a Skyborn if anyone had a chance of getting through their defenses." She shook her head emphatically. "It's not on."

"I have to disagree," Welkin countered her. "Let's have a vote."

Sarah sat back, puzzled. Welkin didn't have a hope of getting that vote carried. As he was chief of security, any loss of confidence would see him walk from the room.

Which he did when the vote was in Sarah's favor. He stopped at the door and made a show of disappointment. "I've done my best. I figured you guys would get behind me on this one."

"Welkin," Harry said. "It can't be done. We all know how impregnable *Colony* is. No one's just going to walk in there without a fight. No one."

"Maybe you're right," Welkin replied. "I'd better get back to Arton."

"Welkin?" Sarah said as he opened the door. "We've made an executive decision. You'll adhere to it, won't you?"

"I'm Committee," he said, and closed the door behind him. He took a deep breath. They would leave him alone now. Time enough to gather what he needed. He thought back to Sarah's look, the almost imperceptible change to her mouth, as though she had suddenly seen straight through him. He waved off his doubt. Nothing he could do about that. As long as he was careful, no one would be any the wiser that he was gone until it was too late.

He made his way to the hut where Patrick and Mira had Arton. "So what's the Committee come up with?" Patrick asked.

Welkin forced his voice to be steady. "I lost a vote of confidence. Seems like everyone just wants to sit back and see what happens." He nodded to Mira. "How's our patient?"

Mira glanced down at Arton. "He's been sleeping, mostly." She handed Welkin some yellowed paper. Unable to decipher her smudged scrawl, he said, "Perhaps it's best you tell me what he's been saying."

"It's all there on the paper," Mira said. She snatched it from his hand and Patrick laughed.

She whirled on her brother. "At least I can write."

Welkin would have ruffled her hair in camaraderie, but Mira wasn't the type to respond to fraternal affection.

"It says," she said, squinting in the half light, " 'more training runs . . . three ready . . . not safe, not safe . . . why me? I didn't do anything. Where's Ferrik?' " She looked up and glared at Patrick. "I see nothing difficult with that, Welkin." She handed the piece of paper back to Welkin, almost challenging him to dispute her.

"Who's Ferrik, I wonder?" Welkin took the paper and stared down at it. The writing seemed to contain more than what Mira had read out. "Nothing else?"

"I would have written it down, wouldn't I?" Mira said icily.

"I guess you would have at that," Welkin said. "But it doesn't make much sense, except the part about Ferrik. Plainly that's a friend and something's happened to him. I'd like to know what 'three ready' means, though." Welkin scratched the stubble on his chin. "And training runs? That might be some kind of delivery system . . ."

Patrick shook his head. "He was rambling. Tossing and turning like he was wrestling with demons."

Welkin folded the piece of paper and stashed it in his fatigue pocket. "I'll send someone over to relieve you guys. You've done a great job, thanks."

He left by the back door. The Committee meeting had finished and despite a cold reception, Welkin was pleased that Efi and Lucida actually volunteered to look after Arton. That problem solved, he headed for the cruiser shed.

The family had twelve cruisers, five of which needed overhauling. Of the remaining seven, only three were functioning, the others being regarded as "iffy." Spare parts being at a premium, the Earthborn were reluctant to cannibalize anything remotely looking like a cruiser. Arton had crashed his own cruiser—the mangled wreck was at least good for spare parts, but not a rebuild.

Welkin tinkered around for most of the afternoon. Meshing the parts was easy, as they had tiny devices built into their modular components that fused, unfused, and cleaned themselves. By early evening he had test-ridden the three cruisers. There was no room for mechanical mishaps for what he had in mind.

The following two days passed in a whirl. Tolk's people kept pretty much to themselves in a tented satellite area next to the settlement. An uneasy truce existed between the two groups, one that Welkin sensed more than saw, since he kept to himself. Arton's fever had broken, but even in moments of lucidity, he remained suspicious. Try as he might, Welkin could get no more information from him.

"You're one of them, now," Arton said one morning.

Soon after he was rescued by Sarah, Welkin had known that he had more in common with the Earthborn than he did with his own people. Now he simply replied, "We're all part of the same race, Arton." He had promptly left then, knowing better than to debate with a brainwashed Skyborn.

By the third day, Welkin was reasonably satisfied that he was prepared to put his plan into action. Then he ran into Gillian. She'd been looking for him.

"Look, I'm kinda busy right now," he said stiffly.

"You're up to something."

He stopped, forced himself to relax. "You're right. I am up to something."

"Well, are you going to share, or not?"

"The Committee needs to be convinced and the best way is to get more out of Arton. He's getting better every day, but Tolk's people—especially Fish—are also getting more and more vocal about having him here. He's in danger."

Gillian nodded suddenly. "So you want to move him?"

Welkin hated lying but knew he had to. Too much was at stake. "That's the plan."

"Why didn't you say something? I could have helped."

He shrugged. "I don't know."

Gillian stiffened slightly. "You don't want me involved, do you?"

"It's not that, Gillian. It's just . . ." He shrugged again.

"I thought we were friends."

He turned and stared at her then. "Yeah. That's right. *Friends.*"

Gillian reddened. "You've been pretty much avoiding me these last few months. Except for training practice and Committee meetings I hardly ever see you anymore." She sounded hurt.

His heart leapt, but he squelched the feeling. He'd made that mistake before, reading too much into a situation. "I've been busy," he said.

"Everybody's busy, but they still make time to hang out with friends."

There was that word again, needle sharp, like a nerve being plucked. "Look, I'm sorry. I'll try to make time; it's just . . ."

"Oh, please, don't make an effort on my behalf." She turned on her heel and walked off. He had a fleeting glimpse of her face, as she flashed a look back at him, eyes watery, but it was so incongruous that he quickly convinced himself he'd imagined it.

The next day, after a night of fitful dreams in which Gillian frequently threw her arms around him and admitted what a fool she'd been, Welkin rose as the dawn chorus began. Galahs, rainbow parrots, myriad sulfur-crested cockatoos, and some fifty other species welcomed the new day in their usual screeching manner. He threw cold water on his face and gazed at his haggard expression in a cracked mirror.

Careful not to make his own brand of noise, Welkin skirted the guards whom he had positioned the night before. For security's sake, no one other than Welkin knew where the guards were stationed on their nightly roster.

Welkin had been apprehensive about "inadvertently" leaving the cruisers unguarded—they were the family's most prized possessions, commandeered from the Skyborn—but absconding with a cruiser would have been impossible with a guard on duty.

The crunching of gravel as he moved toward the cruiser shed sounded like pistol shots to him. He crept into the hay barn by climbing an external ladder and entering via the loft. He had previously oiled the hinges on the big gable doors so they swung open silently at his urging. Scanning the former stables for signs of movement, he swung down on a hoist chain.

"I thought it a bit strange when I found no one patrolling the area," someone said.

Welkin's heart missed a beat. "Harry. Space, man. You nearly gave me a heart attack."

Harry stepped out of the shadows. "You nearly gave *me* one. I figured whoever was on duty had been killed by Tolk's people. When I heard someone out back I didn't know whether to rouse the family or just start shooting."

"Well, you did the right thing," Welkin said sheepishly.

"You're going to *Colony,* aren't you?"

Welkin's jaw tightened. He had obviously been careless.

"No one else knows," Harry said. "If that's what you're worried about. I just thought it a bit strange how you've been avoiding everyone lately. And spending time in here, alone."

"This thing has to be done, Harry. You know that," Welkin said. "Like Sarah said, only a Skyborn stands a chance of infiltrating *Colony.*"

Harry put his hands up defensively. "Hey, I'm not arguing. I'm with you, spaceboy."

Welkin reached the cruiser he had prepared. "Then why didn't you speak up at the meeting? Everyone turned on me."

Harry grinned. "Come on, Welkin. We did the same psych programs on *Colony*. That's the way you planned it. So the family wasn't split. Wouldn't be surprised if the others knew it, too. You've never walked out of a meeting just because the vote's gone against you."

"Maybe," Welkin conceded. He looked about the hay barn. "Don't suppose you can stand guard on the cruisers till the morning shift comes on?"

"Nice try," Harry said, straddling a cruiser.

"No way," Welkin said. "One's company; two's a crowd."

Harry shook his head. " 'Two's company; three's a crowd.' I believe that's how it goes."

"Whatever, doesn't matter," Welkin said. "One might just sneak past their defenses. Two's almost impossible."

Harry checked the plutonium canister. The powerpak's holo indicator flickered a little but showed it half charged. There was a reserve canister, too, which could double as a portable energy device. "Enough to get me there and back."

"You're not coming," Welkin said emphatically.

"Try and stop me," Harry said, equally insistent.

It seemed to Welkin that the light outside had suddenly intensified, as though a full hour had passed since he had entered the shed. "I don't have time for this, Harry. If we lose two cruisers, Sarah's going to . . . there's no telling what she'll do."

Harry pressed the ignition stud on minimum revs. The gyros hissed sibilantly. A fine film of dust lit up through the shaft of daylight from the window. "If she were here now? She'd be doing exactly what I am, and you know it, Welkin."

Welkin fired up his own cruiser and opened up the vertical valves. The cruiser ascended, clearing the straw-strewn ground by inches. "All right," he granted. "But I'm in charge."

Harry grinned. "You're the boss, Boss."

They revved the vertical valves and rose to the hayloft. Within seconds they were through the gable doors. Once clear of the scrubland surrounding the settlement, they nailed the throttles and darted through the trees like night demons.

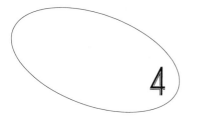

4

Sarah emerged from the infirmary after seeing Con, tears streaming down her cheeks. A moment later Gillian appeared out of the shadows. They exchanged a hug. Losing someone dear never was easy, especially to an insidious disease like progeria.

Suddenly Efi threw open the infirmary door and rushed over to them. "Sarah, there's something I think you should hear," she babbled excitedly. *"Ande re! Gligora!"* She stopped momentarily, smacking her forehead. "Sorry. Come quickly. Arton thinks, that is, oh, you'd better come hear it for yourself. It's about the progeria."

Puzzled, Sarah and Gillian followed Efi back inside.

"It sounds to me as if the elders have decoded the entire Earthborn genome."

Sarah stared at her, trying to understand. "I'm sorry, Efi. I can't think straight right now. What are you talking about?"

"Signomi," Efi said, exasperated. "Sorry. I'm so excited. Sarah, whatever the elders are planning, it requires an intimate knowledge of Earthborn DNA. Including the junk DNA and *all* mutations."

A light seemed to go on in Sarah's head. "The progeria?" she said, almost holding her breath.

Efi nodded, then said gently, "Sarah, you're hurting me."

Sarah looked down and realized she was gripping Efi's arm, white-knuckled.

.　　.　　.

Welkin's annoyance soon subsided. Sharing the mission somehow made the dangers ahead seem much more bearable. Besides, it was hard to feel anything but exhilaration while cruising. With the wind gushing past his ears, and the staccato *flick flick flick* as the cruiser passed the heavy boles of the forest, he felt powerful, almost invincible. The thought made him rev down. It was due to the Skyborn's perceived invulnerability that the Earthborn had scored the cruisers in the first place.

When a clear patch of forest presented itself, Welkin looked around for Harry. He was over to his right, slightly higher up among the branches. What Welkin saw next nearly took his breath away. A cruiser dive-bombed from above the forest canopy. Welkin revved the gyros so they screamed for a moment.

Harry intuitively dived, heeding the warning.

Welkin held up a finger and pointed skyward.

They immediately broke away from each other, presenting diverging targets. It was almost inconceivable that *Colony* troopers were this far east. But Welkin knew from experience that the elders were out to eradicate the Earthborn. Maybe their pursuer was the vanguard of Arton's "Cleansweep."

At this thought Welkin gave the throttle a full turn, while Harry skimmed bracken away to his left, then veered for a denser patch of woodland. If their pursuer was in fact part of a large force, someone had to warn Sarah. Welkin signaled Harry, who banked hard and fell in behind him as they entered thick forest again.

Their pursuer sideslipped sharply, losing height, gyros screeching at the sudden drop in altitude, the gyros' vacuum-insulated supercooled containment units straining and the cruisers' computers cutting in to avert disaster. Welkin cursed beneath his breath. The cruiser had followed them almost as though the rider could read their minds.

Welkin caught sight of it sporadically as they tore through the middle terrace of the forest. It wasn't till now that he noticed something odd. The cruiser seemed to be carrying two people. At the speed they were traveling, it was hard to tell more than that. Troopers never doubled up, not unless they had been ambushed, or a cruiser had been damaged beyond immediate repair. Come to that, troopers never scouted solo. Far too dangerous in this terrain.

He eased back on the throttle. Harry screamed past, a look of sudden panic on his face. If they were to beat the troopers back to the settlement, now was not the time to take on their opponents. Only skill and daring would achieve that. Harry looped around.

Their pursuers revved back the moment they saw Harry peel away. Welkin groaned. It was Sarah, with Gillian riding pillion. Welkin eased back on the vertical throttle and powered down to the ground. Harry completed a circuit and came in from behind the settling cruisers.

The screaming gyros died when the three cruisers settled onto the fecund ground. Welkin's immediate anger was replaced by despondency. How could he have been so careless? Was the entire family in on this?

He turned to Harry accusingly.

"Don't look at me," he said. "I only found out about your plan half an hour ago." Welkin looked questioningly at Sarah.

"It's not in your nature to be so moody," Sarah said. She climbed off the cruiser. "You led us a merry chase," she added. "We had to break the rules and climb above the trees."

"I was trying to be inconspicuous," Welkin said.

"Well," Sarah said. "Never mind all that. You did catch us on the hop. I figured you'd make your break during the night. But when I saw you'd left—"

"—the cruiser barn unguarded . . ." Welkin finished lamely. He looked over at Gillian, who seemed to be glowering at him.

"Yeah," Gillian said tightly. "Nice *plan.*"

Sensing what she referred to as a "situation," Sarah quickly said, "Harry being there was a surprise. Almost threw us off. We figured he was the guard, but had slept in. We settled back down—then Gillian saw the hayloft doors wide open."

"Now that that's settled," Harry said, "what next?"

"I'm going ahead with this," Welkin said. He stared at them defiantly, gripping the cruiser's throttle to emphasize his resolve.

Sarah glanced at his white knuckles. "Right now I don't have a say in what you do. I left the Committee a letter. I've resigned," she said.

Gillian nodded. "Ditto."

"You can't resign," Welkin scoffed. "You *are* the Committee. The main members, anyway."

"The others will cope," Sarah said. "Tolk and his people are moving on. With him out of the way, there shouldn't be any problems, bar the usual, that is. Besides, I have . . . other reasons for wanting to come." Her voice dropped to a hoarse whisper. "And Con died a short time ago."

Nobody said anything for a long moment; then Sarah wiped her eyes, and managed a wan smile. "He'd have been all for this, you know," she said.

"Yeah, but the great lunk would've let us go off and take all the risks," said Harry.

They laughed. That was Con, all right. The levity seemed to make things better.

Sarah said, "So we're going with you." She considered telling them the news regarding *Colony*'s decoding of the Earthborn genome and all that it might mean, but stopped herself. Raising hopes that might yet turn out false was not her way.

Welkin sat back. "None of you wanted anything to do with my plan the other day. If you'd spoken up then, we could have planned this a whole lot better."

Gillian snorted. "No, you planned on a one-man show, Welkin. What were you thinking?"

"What was *I* thinking?"

"Heaven forbid that you should care about anyone but your—"

Sarah intervened. "We're here now; that's what matters. We're a small enough group to be unobtrusive. This is your show, Welkin. How do you want to play it?"

Resigned, Welkin simply said, "By ear."

"By ear it is," Sarah said. She hit the cruiser's ignition stud. "We'd better get out of here before someone else decides to join the party."

"Not much hope of that," Welkin muttered. "These are the only serviceable cruisers."

"Gillian?" Sarah said. "You coming?"

Gillian moodily climbed on her cruiser. Welkin had half hoped she would ride behind him.

They covered the miles rapidly. Welkin led the way with Harry bringing up the rear. Sarah and Gillian rode flank, alternating from left to right. They had taken a circuitous route to Melbourne, so that it wasn't till late morning that they skimmed low across the Merri Creek. Its murky water held many dangers, including half-submerged tree stumps, rusting car wrecks, and the occasional demented and mutilated remnants of industrial robots unable to understand the world that had survived the great destructions of war. But this close to Melbourne it was still safer than trying to crawl their way through dense scrub that hadn't been cleared, unless by natural disaster, for more than a hundred and fifty years. Although there was always the risk of being seen by the naked eye, the creek had now cut a deep gully through the land, so that for the most part, it was beneath the radar nets set up by *Colony*.

They rocketed beneath overarching bridges and causeways, their exhaust kicking up white licks of water from the creek. They powered down at Dights Falls, where the creek joined the Yarra River.

Once a roaring rapids, Dights Falls was now little more than a gently gurgling waterfall. Landslides, dams, and other obstructions had trapped much of the mountain water from both the creek and the river.

Welkin landed first. He chose a spot where creeping lantana was thinning over the rocks. It was as close to cover as he dared go. There was no telling what the vegetation hid. Too far out in the open and they were exposed. He was glad that the others came in behind him, silently acknowledging him as the leader of this expedition.

When the last cruiser fell silent, he said, "This is about as close to the city as we can get without drawing attention to ourselves."

The group looked wearily south-west. Central Melbourne was a good day's trek away on foot, barring any incidents. But everyone knew that Welkin was right. *Colony* cruisers often swept along here. The last remnants of the smaller tribes were yet to be fully flushed out. It was all that had saved the family from *Colony*'s full attention in the early days of its migration.

From the family's time in Melbourne, they knew there were tribes on the outskirts of the city that they had never even met—nor wanted to on this occasion.

"Gillian?" Welkin said, indicating the tangled ground cover. She lifted it up like netting, and Welkin eased the cruiser beneath it. When the three cruisers were stowed away, Welkin hunkered down and crept beneath the mat of vegetation.

"Not bad camouflage, eh?" he said cheerily.

"Urgh!" Gillian said. "Apart from the bugs and stuff. Hope there's no snakes under here."

"Bound to be," Harry joked. "This close to the water. Seasons are all shot to pieces, but I reckon April is still snake season." He unslung his laserlite. "The very thought of snake is making me hungry."

"Charred's nice," Gillian said. "Just watch where you're pointing that thing if a snake starts winding itself around your leg."

Sarah pulled a rollpack from her cruiser and rested her head against it. "I think a good rest before nightfall is in order."

"We mightn't get a chance later," Welkin agreed. He looked over at Gillian, but she seemed preoccupied bedding down on the other side of the cruisers. He shoved his feelings away and curled up on his rollpack.

"Looks like I volunteer for first guard duty," Harry said, looking down at his companions.

"Last man standing," Gillian said.

Welkin was about to jibe her, but thought better of it. It seemed that he had only just put his head down when he awakened. He opened his startled eyes to see Harry kneeling over him.

Harry pointed urgently.

Welkin blinked, then focused to where Harry was pointing. He couldn't see much beyond the cruisers and the overhanging foliage, but he did hear a sharp snapping sound, as though a dry twig had been broken.

Welkin roused Sarah and Gillian and they became instantly alert.

"How many?" Gillian queried.

"Four, five," Harry guessed. "Hard to tell. They came from across the Merri. Almost as though they knew we were here."

"Might've seen us land," Sarah guessed. "Are they ferals?"

Harry shook his head. "No ornaments that I could see. Shaved heads. Tatty loose clothing—not bound up in rags like the ferals."

"I'd say cave clan," Gillian said. She had never come into contact with the tribe herself, but an old Aboriginal mentor by the name of Mundine had told her about them. It might have been an urban myth, but according to Mundine, there were more drains and passages beneath Melbourne than there had been roads on top. Some had been reused as communication and automation conduits. When the holocaust finally arrived, those caught underground—cave clans, derros, criminals—came away pretty much unscathed. Whole new religions started up, inspired by the sheer providence of survival, so the people stayed put, breeding new civilizations of subterraneans who rarely surfaced topside.

Sarah grunted. "Sewer dwellers." She started ticking off scurrying figures on her fingers. When she'd exhausted both hands twice over she gave up. "I think I've counted about twenty, Harry," she said tightly.

"Twenty-eight and counting," Gillian said, fondling her laserlite. "They're thick on the ground." She squinted. "Like ants around a picnic table."

"We could make a dash for it on the cruisers," Harry said.

"Too dangerous," Welkin said, feeling his authority erode. No matter how hard he fought against the idea, he knew Sarah was the natural leader in this new situation. "Anyone seen weapons? Sarah?"

"Bows, knives," Sarah mumbled. "Usual stuff. They'll wait till dark, then rush us. Unless we take the fight to them earlier."

"According to Mundine," Gillian said, "they've mutated down there in the drains. Can't stand daylight, but can see better than rats in the dark."

Welkin looked behind them. "They can't come in from the bank. So it'll be a frontal attack."

"They could try burning us out," Harry said. "Some of this lantana is tinder dry."

"If they torched us then we'd need to risk the cruisers," Sarah said.

"Only they'll be prepared for that. Besides, even cave clans must know the value of cruisers. Burning us out would simply be an outside risk. Welkin?"

Welkin shifted uncomfortably. "If they've got any sense they'll just fire arrows at us from a distance until there's no resistance." He scrambled away to the left and gently lifted the ground cover. "I say we spread out. Wait for them to make the first move, then hit them with everything we have."

"Sounds good to me," Sarah said. "Get as far away from the cruisers as possible. It's not as if the idiots know how to fly them." She pursed her lips. "Just in case." She removed the shielded powerpak canister from its bracing lock. The others quickly disabled the other cruisers.

"This is costing us time," Gillian said, pocketing her powerpak. "What say they figure on starving us out?"

"They only have till dawn," Harry reminded her. "It's a wonder they haven't already attacked."

"Which could mean they're not entirely stupid," Sarah said. "Never underestimate the enemy."

"Right," Welkin said. "Let's move out quietly."

Although it was only late afternoon, the sun was occluded by smog-laden clouds and an eerie red-hued twilight fell on them. They were spread out a hundred feet to either side of the cruisers when the initial attack came.

It was so sudden that Welkin heard, rather than saw, the barrage of arrows that zipped into the lantana. Suddenly, dark figures were running helter-skelter across the rocky embankment.

There were at least thirty of them, Welkin saw. That was the risk of waiting for the attack. Word would have spread that three cruisers had landed at Dights Falls and were easy pickings. Such a prize would have been a magnet few could resist.

Their adrenaline-charged war cry had little effect on the veteran skirmishers. Confrontations with Bruick's jabbers and a host of warring tribes had prepared them against psychological warfare.

The defenders let the first few attackers scamper across the rock-strewn ground to their cruisers, waited till they crouched to go under the dense lantana, then took them out in a sudden lethal cross-fire.

Welkin depressed the firing stud and watched a youth drop dead across the lantana. Others flopped to the ground as laserlite fire tore into the crouching figures.

Now arrows began cutting into the ragged line of foliage. Somewhere to Welkin's left he heard a loud grunt. Who had followed him? Gillian? Harry? It didn't matter. Someone was hurt. He crawled across the dank soil, oblivious to the arrows that sought him.

"Harry?" Concern choked his voice. Harry was clutching his arm. An arrow shaft protruded between his fingers.

"Stings like hell," Harry gasped.

"Tell me about it," Welkin said, remembering his own leg wound the year before. He pushed Harry's hand up to his mouth. "Take a grip of the cuff in your mouth," he said.

Harry bit down on the cloth.

"They used to barb these things," Welkin said, prior to pulling on the shaft. He tugged hard and it came out easily.

"Freakin' space!" Harry cried.

Welkin threw the splintered wood aside and smirked. "Either it got you on a ricochet, or the arrowheads are blunt. It barely scratched you."

"There's a gaping hole in my arm," Harry gasped.

"It just nicked you," Welkin said. He knew exactly what Harry was feeling. Those arrows *hurt*. And sometimes they were poisoned. He staunched the wound with a wad of cloth, then tied a clean rag around the torn flesh. "Efi will need to take a look at it later. Take some of her antibiotic cordial."

"Are you kidding?" Harry asked. "I'm going to gargle with the stuff."

An arrow skittered past Welkin's foot and he dragged his leg back under cover.

"They've spotted me, Harry. Stay put; I'll be back." He slithered away across the ground, hoping to draw enemy fire.

Another arrow spun off the ground, kicking up gravel. Welkin pushed forward until he became so entangled in the creeper that he could go no farther. He pulled out his knife and cut away at the cling-ing vine.

More arrows winged past, one clipping his jacket. He spun around at a sudden sound and grunted in surprise.

Welkin barely saw the enraged caver who had launched himself at him. The impact threw him backward. He slashed at the writhing youth with his knife, sure the knife was sinking into flesh. Down, down, down he plunged the blade, but still the youth kept pound-ing him.

The caver scrambled on top of Welkin, arms windmilling, his pal-lid face close to Welkin's. Their eyes locked for a moment, and for one horrendous moment, Welkin thought that he'd been attacked by a mutant. The caver's black pupils took up most of his eyes, so that the white was a thin border framing the black.

The caver plunged down and Welkin cried out when the youth's mouth found his ear.

Welkin left the knife in the youth's back and tried dragging his head back. He pulled at the youth's shaved head, and when that didn't work, he found the man's eyes and sank his thumbs into them.

The caver screeched and pulled back and Welkin delivered a solid left hook. His opponent slumped across him.

Welkin pushed the inert body from him and dabbed at his ear. Not much blood—only a surface wound. He got up and looked at his knife embedded in the youth's back. There was no blood and the blade had hardly pierced the clothing.

Taking a deep breath, Welkin knelt beside him. On closer inspec-tion he saw that the youth had been wearing some sort of lightweight body armor, only it had been put on backward. Not trusting anyone to fasten the straps, he had been content with wearing it backward—at least he could tie it on without help.

Plucking his knife from the caver's back and sheathing it, Welkin crawled toward the open track. He scanned the immediate area through the laserlite's scanner. The rocks were strewn with dark lumps—bodies, Welkin realized. No sign of life whatsoever. For a brief moment, he felt elated. Then alarm overrode his elation. What if

Sarah and Gillian had also been killed? It was as quiet as space out there.

He slithered along the gravel, keeping to the ragged edge of vegetation. Finally he heard movement to his left. "Harry?"

"What took you so long?" Harry forced a smile. "I hope Sarah or Gillian packed some of Efi's herbs. This is stinging like all get-out."

"Does it hurt to move?"

"You're not leaving me here again," Harry said. Clutching his arm, he crab-crawled alongside Welkin, who held up the canopy of vine to ease Harry's passage.

"Gillian should be about here," Welkin said. He looked out at the broad expanse of the Merri Creek. It seemed too tranquil a place to die in. "Gillian?" he called. Then louder, "Gillian!"

Harry tugged Welkin's arm, knowing his anxiety could get them killed. "Maybe she changed position, like we did. Once the cavers zeroed her."

But Welkin was starting to have a bad feeling. It was getting darker by the second and he couldn't see anything. Where was Gillian? Where was Sarah? He needed to do something. He stretched his cramping leg. "I have to stand up, Harry. Keep me covered, okay?"

"Don't do anything rash," Harry said. He flicked up the night scanner, seeking heat images. The cooling bodies barely registered.

Welkin gave him the thumbs-up and stood. He moved away from Harry's position in case he drew attention. He hadn't realized how far he had moved from the cruisers. At one point he almost doubled back, figuring he'd missed them. Since no one had called out to him, he reasoned, with rising dread, that the others must be dead.

He was about to throw caution to the wind when Harry's scanner picked up thermals. He jabbed his finger toward some thicket.

The mass of ground cover farther ahead moved like a breaking wave. Two shapes moved from beneath it.

"You'll bring down the elders if you keep making that noise," Sarah warned jovially enough. She turned and said in a lower voice, "All's clear."

Welkin expelled a deep breath, hiding his panic. "I thought you guys were back there," he said, pointing stupidly. "We were more spread out than I'd thought."

"Cavers must've made the same mistake," Gillian said. She raised her laserlite and scanned the banks. The dark shapes blotting the terrain like speed bumps no longer registered on her scanner, which measured life signs more subtle than just body heat, such as the regular movement of a human diaphragm.

Gillian saw the red smear on Welkin's ear. "Where's Harry?" she said, suddenly tense.

"He's all right," Welkin replied. He dabbed at his own wound, annoyed that Gillian seemed more worried about Harry than him. It was an uncharitable thought and he pushed it away.

"I'm not all right," Harry said grumpily from the dark. "Neither would you be if those cavers had stuck you with a bloody great arrow."

Sarah pulled his hand away from the wound. "Not much blood by the look of it."

"It still *hurts*," Harry said.

"You Skyborn have a low pain threshold," Sarah said, ignoring Harry's grinding teeth. "Beats me how you thought you were going to colonize alien worlds."

"Hey," said Welkin, "don't blame the rest of us 'cause Harry's such a baby."

Harry kicked at him, but Welkin skipped out of the way, grinning. Sarah removed Harry's bandage and replaced it with a small pre-fabricated poultice that she had packed in case of such emergencies. "Herbs aren't as powerful when they're not fresh, but this should stop the inflammation and keep out the germs," she said.

"Glad to hear it," Harry mumbled, peering worriedly at the bandage as if he could actually spot germs trying to sneak under the edges of it. Back on *Colony*, bacterial infection simply wasn't an issue. "Give me a medivac scan and knit patch anytime."

"Maybe later," Sarah said, laughing lightly. *Colony*'s equipment would never be at their disposal. She handed Welkin a precious plaster for his ear, but he didn't take it.

"Blood's already stopped," he said. He was standing very close to Gillian. His breath came out in wisps of white in the cooling air. He badly wanted to touch her, to apologize for everything that had gone wrong between them. Instead, lamely, he said, "See anything?"

"Looks like we got them all," Gillian said, lowering the laserlite. "Shame, really. They're a good buffer against *Colony*. Doesn't do us any good to kill them."

"Nor them us," Welkin reminded her. "But they're so stupid and scared there's no talking to them."

Gillian uttered an exclamation and brought her laserlite back up. The sudden movement kicked the others into action. They fell into a defensive crouch.

Gillian sighted along her laserlite. "I think it's a caver," she said. "He couldn't have heard us—seems a little disoriented. But not for long . . ."

"Hold it," Welkin said. He raised his laserlite and picked out the green image that was staggering into the dark. "I think that's the one that tried to bash my brains out."

"You going to drill him before he gets away?" Gillian's infrared tracking beam was scribbling on the caver's back. "He'll bring more of his mates."

Welkin turned to Sarah. "He had on body armor. There might be an old army supply cache somewhere around here. With a little persuasion he might tell us where."

Sarah reached out and averted Gillian's aim. "If Welkin's right, then we need him alive. Those places are treasure troves."

"Works for me." She turned to Welkin. "You want to fetch him or shall I?"

Welkin passed his laserlite to Sarah. Checking his sheathed knife, he took off at a jog. He was back within minutes. The caver hung like a trapped rag doll in Welkin's firm grip. But what he lacked in size he made up for in anger.

"Leggo of me," he hissed, struggling frantically. Welkin simply tightened his armlock and the youth gasped.

"Gillian," Sarah said. "Stand watch. There could be more of them out there." She turned to the prisoner. "We're going to have a little chat, you and me." She glanced at Welkin, checking that he didn't mind. He seemed happy enough restraining the caver.

"You're a pack of murderers." The caver's voice was unusually loud and guttural.

"He needs a wash," Sarah said to no one in particular. "I seem to remember we were resting here—peaceably—till you attacked us."

The caver ignored this. He shoved back at Welkin, trying to head-butt him.

"We know who you people are," the caver said. "You're the easterners. Think you're a cut above everyone else. But you're no better than the filth from *Colony*."

Harry grasped the caver's ear.

"No need for that," Sarah said, but Harry ignored her. He pushed his face close to the caver's, oblivious to both the man's raw anger and his bad breath.

"It's been a while since we tasted you lot," Harry said. "There's not much flesh on you, of course." He looked around and winked at the others, then swung back to the caver. "And you reek of sewage, you little scab. A good dip in the creek'll fix that."

The team went along with Harry's pantomime and looked on hungrily.

"Start the fire, Gillian," Harry said, his eyes not leaving the caver's.

"Start the fire," Sarah chanted, as though it were a ritual. Gillian and Welkin caught on and they repeated the mantra several times before Harry continued.

"We're not easterners, see. We eat easterners for breakfast. Spit 'em out real easy like. We're your worst nightmare. Gillian? How's that fire going?" He let go of the caver's ear and unsheathed his hunting knife. He ran his tongue down the blade as though slightly crazed. "No hair to scalp," he said clinically.

The caver kicked back against Welkin, but the Skyborn applied more pressure, lifting the man off the ground so that his legs found no purchase. Powerless, they wriggled as though he were being hanged. Welkin didn't let him down till he stilled.

"Kill me and the lot of you won't last the night," he gurgled.

Sarah took over from Harry. She made a show of pushing him

away and he taunted her with his knife. "I get first cut." She glared at the others as though seeking a challenge.

"First cut!" they chorused, ritualistically.

"Now that that's settled . . . are you threatening us, weasel?" The caver stared fixedly at Sarah's lips and shivered.

"You got anything you want to tell us?" she asked. " 'Cause right now you're more use to us dead than alive . . ."

His eyes widened and suddenly he was blurting everything he knew. "Troopers. They got some sorta sonic net. Drains at night, like, but comes back on strong at daybreak. Get caught inside the net is worse than havin' your eardrums bust. Sends animals crazy with fear, but they survive. Us? We can't get outta the zone quick enough. Troopers come down and pick us off. Sods don't even land their cruisers. Just hover and slaughter us while we're helpless."

Sarah grunted. "This net, where's it at? It has to be powered somehow—solar, perhaps. And why isn't it everywhere?"

The caver relaxed slightly. Gillian was still busily collecting twigs for a fire, but the caver now realized that he was worth something to these people. "They're mobile units. They place them all over the joint. No telling where they are till it's too late."

"Are they underground, too?" Welkin demanded.

"They don't work too well underground." The caver smiled at a thought. "The troopers aren't subbies. Don't like the dark or the small spaces."

Sarah took in the darkened horizon. The orange glow from *Colony*'s lights pierced the western skyline. There was nothing the caver could tell her about the Skyborn. "You seem to know a lot about these sonic nets."

"Been caught on the edge of one, once. Nearly sent me crazy."

"And a bit deaf," Sarah hazarded a guess. "You're lip-reading, yeah?"

"I can hear, sort of," the caver muttered. "Everything comes through with a roaring sound."

"You speak louder than you need to, it's a dead set giveaway," Sarah said. "What's your name?"

The caver hesitated. "Trilocide. Folk call me Cide for short."

Sarah looked over the youth's shoulder. "Ease up a little, Welkin. Cide's had enough things go wrong, without getting his arm busted."

Welkin eased the pressure, and Cide sighed noisily. He still gripped Welkin's forearms as though trying to relieve the pressure from around his throat.

Sarah looked at Welkin and Harry. "Any ideas on this sonic net stuff?"

Welkin nodded. "They're neural nets. Thin bands of neural disrupters. They were originally designed as handheld weapons." He paused in thought. "They can't penetrate density—well, they can, but it muffles the frequency so it's not as effective."

Sarah turned Cide's head and repeated what Welkin had said.

"I don't know tech-talk, but I know a way past the nets."

"By river? Or the sewers?" Sarah guessed.

Sarah considered Welkin and Harry. The Skyborn weren't partial to darkness or cramped spaces. As they were brought up in constant light, the dark was something that only deep space held. And deep space was death.

Welkin turned Cide's head around. "The body armor. Where did you get it? Was it an army dump?"

Cide looked up from Welkin's lips and smirked. "Got this off a body. All the dumps around here are long gone. *Colony* destroyed any that we missed." He turned to the others. "I can get you into the city. That's all that's on offer. Not through the *sewers*—that's scum territory—but the storm water drains."

"We've been in drains before," Welkin said, addressing Harry. "And we have powerpaks, now."

"It's your call," Harry said. "So long as the tunnels aren't too small. I hate crawling in all that stuff."

"What's in it for me?" Cide asked as an afterthought.

"Isn't your life enough?" Gillian said. Her face was now illuminated by a powerpak. Something in the way the light played on the contours of her face made Cide decide that was enough.

"There's nothing here for me now anyway," he said. "You've killed everyone I know."

"Not everyone," Sarah said, walking behind the caver. "Not by a long shot." Her voice dropped. "We'll need to find another hiding spot for the cruisers." She looked over at the far bank of the Yarra River. "The rest of Cide's friends are probably watching us right now."

They dragged the cruisers out and fired up. Gillian went pillion with Harry, and Cide went with Sarah.

"How am I supposed to hold on with my hands tied behind my back?" the caver demanded.

Sarah jerked her head, forcing Cide to pull back from her ear. "If you think I'm having you on the back with them untied you're crazier than a cut snake. We could leave you here, trussed up. Then again, feral cats might take a shine to some fresh meat."

Cide's face lifted in faint hope. "Leave me if you want. I won't be going nowhere."

"Nice try," Sarah said. She hit the ignition stud.

They flew in single formation, sticking to the middle of the Yarra until it widened into a huge basin of naturally dammed water. They saw all manner of detritus clogging its passage: nanodiamond furniture frames, fallen trees, rusting pipes, broken holoscreens, and myriad plastic fragments.

It took half an hour to find a spot farther downriver where Welkin figured the cruisers would be safe—somewhere far enough away so that any spies wouldn't hear the gyros cut out, but close enough to make the walk back to the falls manageable. Even so, it took a further hour and a half cutting their way through the mangroves and sinking to their knees in the treacherous mud that at times tried sucking them down. Welkin only untied Cide's hands after he slipped on a rock and nearly drowned when his foot became snared by a submerged branch.

At last they arrived at the runoff from Dights Falls. "Okay, caver," Welkin said. "Here's where you earn your keep. Lead on. And remember, one false move, one booby-trap—if any of our team gets killed, you're gone. Understood?"

"You think I care about dying?" he sneered. He stopped so suddenly that the others turned as one. "I don't—I've lived with death all my life. But I'll take you to where you want to go. Just don't expect me to hang around when the troopers find you."

Something in the way Cide tried to attract their attention made Sarah stop. "Hold it," she hissed.

They pushed back into the shrubs. Welkin cupped Cide's mouth with his hand and dragged him down. He struggled for a moment, then relaxed.

The ridge by the falls was crawling with scurrying figures. It was too dark to see clearly, but their intent was obvious.

Welkin shoved Cide to Gillian and sighted through his laserlite. After a moment he brought it down. "Stripping the dead," he said. "Keep close, guys. We don't want that lot following us down here."

"Where's the outlet, Cide?" Sarah said. "And any more little tricks like that and so help me I'll gut you."

Cide cast a lingering look toward the ridge. It might as well have been on the distant horizon so far as escape or rescue was concerned.

"Well?" Sarah prompted. "The drain!" Her voice had a thin edge.

"There's a track leading to it. There," he said, pointing to a bank beyond a patch of marshland.

"After you," Sarah said, prodding him forward.

They trudged across the mangrove swamp. Each step threatened to suck them down into the mud. Finally they clambered up the bank. Reeds and shrubs covered their passage from prying eyes. Faint voices drifted down from the ridge, some jubilant at finding a precious item, others wretched at missing it, some challenging the lucky ones.

The storm water outlet had long since fallen into decay. Someone had once attempted to hide the exit with corrugated iron, but it now lay rusting and covered by bracken.

Welkin was about to push Cide through when a sound like a freight train came straight at them. "Cover," he snapped, grappling Cide to the ground.

The team flattened themselves against the bank. Welkin barely covered Cide's mouth in time.

A scantily clad clansman on a skateboard rocketed out of the drain. Like a ski jumper of two centuries before, he flew from the lip of the drain and landed on the bank.

"Yayayayyayyaya!" he screamed.

Three more jabbering cavers followed him, each landing smoothly and continuing on down the embankment until their wheels sank into the mud. The group each squatted and in the same motion collected their boards and kept moving across a small tributary.

Cide writhed beneath Welkin's grip. The Skyborn dug his forefinger into the cavity beneath the caver's earlobe and he froze.

The team didn't move until the skateboarders were lost to sight.

"You're a foolish kid, Cide," Sarah said, bending, her nose less than an inch from his face. "If they'd so much as turned around just then they'd all be dead meat."

Cide edged back when Welkin released him. "The drains are full of subbies."

"Then you'd better hope that we don't come across too many of them, hadn't you?" She yanked him from the ground. "Hold your breath, guys." She crouched by the ragged hole in the grille and pushed Cide through it. The others followed blindly behind.

"The smell's worse than anything in the lower decks of *Colony*," Harry said, almost gagging. He took one last gulp of fresh air before entering.

"Don't worry, Harry," Gillian joked. "It only gets worse. And hey, *this* is a storm water drain, not a sewer."

They didn't light their powerpaks until they were well away from the mouth of the outlet. The crumbling piping continually leaked muddy water so that individual drips formed one long cacophony.

Welkin tried to decipher some of the graffiti. He mouthed one of the scrawled words. "Schm . . . moozle." He blinked, utterly confused.

Sarah and Gillian smirked. "It's what happens when things go wrong," Sarah elucidated. "A *shemozzle*."

"I don't see why anyone would want to write that," Welkin said. "It's just a waste of time."

"Time's one thing most people have plenty of," Sarah reminded him. "I have a book of graffiti back at camp—before the holocaust, the graffiti artists were a lot more talented. Brightened up the dullest buildings for a while. By the end it was kids in chameleon suits against police flybot cameras and smart itch dust. Some of the kids got so into graffiti they learnt to scribble their names on Web sites. Tagged them with virtual spray paint."

They trudged along through a trickle of brownish water. Their progress through the mire created new smells as they broke crusted sludge. Wave after wave of insects—mostly mosquitoes, Sarah claimed—rose *en masse* at their intrusion. They soon gave up slapping at them; rather they fluttered their hands to deter them.

Welkin stamped ahead of Cide and held his powerpak beneath his face, illuminating crumbling controls for defunct automated systems and other reminders of a time long ago. "How long does this drain go on for? Not all the way to the city?"

Cide nodded slightly. "Sort of. A couple of miles long and sometimes deeper than a hundred feet. But length and depth don't matter down there. There's the underground monorail system that runs alongside it. The drain's blocked further down—was an overflow for a flood canal. Burst its banks and storm water surged the main chamber."

Sarah's skin prickled with doubt. "This is becoming a maze. I bet people get lost down here."

"Going gets easier when we hit the main system," Cide said. "Mostly been cleaned out by tribes over the years. Sort of neutral territory from the Skyborn."

"Odd that *Colony*'s not discovered it yet," Welkin said.

"They have, but for the main part, you people don't like draining," Cide replied, addressing Harry as well. He had obviously recognized their powerful legs and heavier-than-usual build.

"Don't get cocky," Welkin said, then realized Cide couldn't hear too well. He brought the caver's face around. "Don't get cocky," he repeated, overenunciating each word. "We're as accustomed to the dark now as you are. As for *Colony*, they don't need to send troopers down here. Renegades like the jabbers do deals with them. It wouldn't surprise me if gangs of them don't come down here and seal off the exits.

They'd wipe out your entire community. You'd be like rabbits down a hole with nowhere to go."

Cide sucked noisily on his tongue. "Well, it ain't happened yet."

"It will," Welkin said. He looked up at the ruptured red clay piping. "Perfect place to test out a virus."

Gillian kept to the lip of the pipe, barely skirting the sludge. "There's virus enough down here without needing to test anything new." Welkin nodded, eyeing Gillian's back.

"We turn left here at the juncture," Cide said. "Through the grille. It's rusted to hell and back, but opens."

Crosswinds blew eerily through the juncture. They had to be near the surface here. Besides the wind, the water had been trickling against them, indicating they had been steadily climbing for some time. Welkin knew little of storm water drains, but he had constantly checked the waterline of each new section they entered. According to the tiny dots of flotsam stuck to the rough sandstone walls, the drains never flooded above shoulder height. Still, that left little room for survival if a storm surge swept them away.

Welkin had a sudden odd feeling, like they were being watched. He raised his powerpak. The light brought squeals of dismay as rats the size of tomcats scattered into the dark.

Gillian looked quickly about, grunted. "Ergh."

The walls were crawling with cockroaches, their tiny antennae quivering. In contrast, on the floor was a pile of rusted tiny robots, many-limbed and long-decayed. Welkin lowered his powerpak. Somehow not seeing the insects made him feel much more comfortable about being down there. At least their rusty simulacrums were stilled.

He stared at the T-junction. Every instinct told him to follow the main pipe, but judging by the relatively clear ground, this was the more trodden path. The grille had been worn smooth in places by overuse.

"Sarah?" he called. The darkness was eroding his confidence.

Sarah waded through the water, no longer worried about what might lie beneath the surface. Memories of the old days were coming back. She joined Welkin at the mouth of the tunnel, which slanted down into darkness at a steep but still manageable angle.

"Cide—you know the routine," Sarah said. She pulled at the grille and it swung open noisily.

Welkin nudged Cide forward with the stock of his laserlite.

They left the main pipeline at a crouch and entered the small tributary pipe. It was an overflow of some kind and although it was in pretty good condition, they soon realized that no one would use this pipe as a main thoroughfare. Stalactites hung from the roof like drips of glue frozen in time. They reminded Welkin of a horror vid he had once seen on *Colony* of a monster's mouth as it opened wide to devour its prey.

Welkin was about to call a halt when Cide leapt sideways. Sarah dived forward, caught the caver's body armor but lost her grip. He darted away like a rat fleeing a trap. The others gathered around the rock-bored tunnel.

"After him or not?" Sarah looked at Welkin. This was still his show—his first leadership.

It was dark and claustrophobic—the two uppermost fears the Skyborn dreaded, followed by the contrast of space madness from the immensity of the void and now, more recently, fear of the horizon, that strange aspect of planetary life that divided the deck of the Earth from itself and gave the illusion of spreading out forever, with only the merest hint that you were actually riding a gigantic *sphere*. Welkin turned to Harry. He was a veteran of the lower decks, and had long since defeated his fears, his demons. Even so, the aperture was small, and he was nursing an injury. The tunnels were a maze in which they could easily become lost. Welkin looked back the way they had come. Too many diverging tunnels and pipes. No way would they find their way back to Dights Falls.

Without further thought, Welkin forged into Cide's escape tunnel. The others crammed in after him.

This smaller path had never been used for drainage. Someone had chiseled it out of the bedrock to form an emergency exit from the main drainage system. A rope had been attached to an iron ring pin at the entrance. Shielding their heads against the jagged rocks, they gripped the rope and abseiled down backward. Sometimes stumbling over calcite stalagmites, they descended until they heard voices. A great many of them, some querulous, others chanting. Suddenly the chanting stopped.

Welkin stepped out of the tunnel and onto a platform. He had seen enough underground monorail systems to know what they were. The entire network of monorail pylons and wires hung in a gnarled tangle between the pedestrian paths. Up ahead a broken carriage hung like a Christmas decoration in the mouth of the tunnel.

"Out, quick," Welkin said, and quickly stepped sideways when the others caught up with him. "Cut the light."

They fanned out along the platform with their laserlites tucked firmly against their shoulders. Cavers rarely had firepower, but as the family knew, their accuracy with arrows was daunting. A roaring fire some fifty yards away threw back the darkness. Smoke hung like a storm cloud near the roof. Inert but still sparkling nanodiamond light globes overhead were jewel-like reminders of a distant past when this station was a bustling metropolis of commerce, full of commuters parking their compressed-air bicycles or rushing out of automated minibuses powered by hydrogen engines or plutonium powerpaks.

Cide had picked his way through the tangled wires and struts and had reached the next platform. He was pointing animatedly in their direction.

Then inexplicably someone slashed a blade against Cide's throat. He dropped like a severed marionette and there was a mad scrabble to claim his body armor.

"Ohmigod," Sarah muttered at the suddenness of the youth's death.

A splinter group of cavers now gathered, mustering the courage to lope across the two-lane carriageway and face almost certain death.

Welkin couldn't make out individual faces, but one thing struck him as odd: Most of this group had some object strapped around their heads like an extra appendage. Then he realized what it was: an archaic miner's torch, as though it were an icon of cultural significance.

Welkin switched his attention to the edge of the main group. "Over to the left," he said uncertainly. "They've got someone strung up."

Sarah joined him. "Looks like they're set to roast him over a spit," she said. She couldn't tell from this distance, but judging from the man's size, he looked like a Skyborn. Sarah bit her lip. "One of your people, Welkin."

Something clinked and skittered off across the broken tiles. A *shuriken*. Another one sliced the air and struck the wall behind her. Others became snarled by the fallen cables. Sarah back stepped across the platform. The sharp-edged bits of rusted steel weren't lethal, or powerful at this range, but they were sometimes poisoned.

Welkin looked back at the gaping hole in the wall. If they made a break for it up there, the cavers were bound to know a way to cut them off. He looked at their numbers—he would never have guessed so many Earthborn would be underground. To fight or run?

The cavers surged forward, taking the decision from Welkin.

Laserlite fire spat across the platforms. The first wave of cavers toppled forward, several pitching down onto the causeway. But others kept coming. Some were already pushing their way through the maze of cabling.

Harry and Gillian faced left and right along the platform and took out the leaders. An arrow shattered against the wall beside Welkin's head, showering him with splinters and chips of ceramic tiling.

"Sarah. No!" Welkin yelled.

But Sarah had already leapt down on to the causeway and was sprinting across the mounds of refuge that littered the tracks. She swung up to the next platform and made for the hapless Skyborn.

Welkin swung around and took out two pursuers. A third skidded on some litter and somehow recovered in time to lunge for Sarah. The two bodies fell in a tangle. The uncertain light made it hard to follow what happened next.

"No!" Welkin cried, and frantically pushed past Gillian.

"Cover him," Harry snapped.

Gillian let off several shots as other cavers made for the grappling figures. The chamber was now a constant roar of agitated voices.

Gillian wanted to stand firm—knew it was the right thing to do—but their position had become untenable. Arrows rained on them from the mouth of the main tunnel. There was no shelter here other than a fallen sign that read: "Victoria Park."

"We're outta here," she said.

Harry covered her as she ducked down onto the causeway and scrabbled through the obstructions. Harry followed, then tripped, but scrabbled up at a run. Arrows zinged and thrummed between them. Safely on the next platform, they caught up with Welkin.

"Sarah?" Gillian demanded.

"She's okay," Welkin panted. He held a bloodied knife in his hands.

"It's all right," Gillian said, shaking him. "Come on; they're after us." She pulled Welkin by his jacket. Up ahead they saw that Sarah had cut the Skyborn from the pole. Harry and Sarah had him slung across their shoulders and were dragging him down a long-defunct escalator well.

"Shouldn't we be going up?" Welkin wondered.

"There'll be other exits," Gillian said.

They barreled down the worn steps. Rocks and other hurled projectiles followed them down into the iron stairwell.

When they reached the bottom, Welkin turned and squeezed off three shots up the stairs. "Go, go, go!" he snapped at Gillian.

A body tumbled down the steps, but that didn't deter their pursuers. They surged down the stairwell like lemmings bent on suicide.

Welkin turned and ran.

Gillian was ahead, almost camouflaged against the olive green–tiled wall.

"Go!" Welkin screamed at her. The cavers' screams of anger were close behind.

"Cave-in," Gillian panted. "There's been a friggin' cave-in. It's not serious, but we need time." She punched the laserlite stock into her shoulder and shot a volley at the cavers as they stormed into the thoroughfare. The red pulses lit up the darkened tunnel like a strobe light. Several bodies crumpled, but the impetus of the crowd pushed the foremost cavers forward.

They roared as they came.

A fall of dust filled the air, cutting visibility to a couple of feet.

"The whole place looks as though it's about to come down!" Gillian shouted.

"The roof," Welkin said with sudden inspiration. He flicked the laserlite's setting and fired a sustained pulse into the ceiling. Gillian fired another pulsar into the billowing dust, then aimed a continuous burst into the roof.

Several cavers staggered through the dust, taking them by surprise.

"Welkin!" Gillian cried.

Too late. Welkin went down amidst a flurry of blows.

Gillian barely had time to see him disappear beneath an assailant when someone charged into her. She fell back, bounced from the wall, and by reflex alone struck out with the stock of her laserlite. The lightweight weapon glanced off the caver's cheek, hardly checking him. They, too, fell, scratching and punching in the clogging dust. Gillian swore as teeth bit into her shoulder.

Suddenly a rumbling echoed in the confined space. It gained in volume until it drowned out the noise of the frenzied mob. Dust bucketed down; then an avalanche rocked the length of the tunnel.

Gillian kicked backward frantically. Someone had grabbed her feet, was dragging her away. Then rough hands clutched her tunic and hauled her up.

"Don't. It's me!" Welkin screamed.

Then Harry was there, gasping for breath. "Up the stairs. We're through." Nearly blinded, he waved Gillian past, then helped Welkin. He'd been cut above the eye, and blood was streaming down his dirt-caked face.

They staggered over fallen rocks, clambered over the rubble of the cave-in, and belly-crawled through a narrow gap between the collapsed walls.

Gillian went first. She could see the orange flickering of the underground fire. A hand reached down and pulled her through.

"I'm stuck," Harry cursed.

Welkin pushed up against him and began clawing at the packed earth. Gillian shoved her hand through the fissure. Harry gripped it and with Welkin pushing behind, he squeezed through the gap.

Welkin fishtailed up through the hole, then gasped as someone grabbed his legs.

"I've got 'im," a gruff voice crowed. "I've got 'im."

But the next second the entire tunnel roof fell in and the voice was cut short.

Welkin kicked away the hand that was still clutching his leg. It hung on tenaciously, then spasmed and went limp. He yanked his foot back, groaning with fatigue and claustrophobia.

He clawed his way up onto the platform and buckled over, gasping for air. A uniformed hologram flickered into life, jarred into animation by the tunnel collapse, and a word balloon darted around its head. PLEASE PRODUCE YOUR E-TICKET. Welkin stopped, awestruck at this ancient Earth technology come to life.

"Forget it," Sarah said at his side. "We've got no time." She pulled him along after her. "This whole place is unstable. It's back up the way we came. C'mon—I need a hand with Ferrik."

They dodged through a shower of hurled rocks and joined the others by the ruptured wall.

"Ferrik?" Welkin panted, frowning. He knew the name from somewhere but right now couldn't think where he had heard it.

"The trooper." She misunderstood Welkin's reaction, at least in part. "Couldn't leave him to die. Are you all right with that?"

Welkin had pretty unpleasant memories of the troopers, but that was ancient history. The puzzle of the man's name was uppermost in his mind as he nodded. "Fine. You did what you had to." Then something else occurred to him. "But Sarah, he's not a regular. Those clothes are . . . I don't know what he was, but he's not a regular . . ."

"What are you saying?"

"Maybe he's a spy, a plant . . . Just be careful."

"Quite a risk he's taking."

Gillian butted in. "We should have left him," she said.

"Then we'd be no better than these animals," Sarah said.

Tiles fell from the wrecked dome, exploding on impact like cluster bombs. Caver survivors began regrouping on Platform Two, but they seemed too disorganized to do anything but shout obscenities and throw rocks. Those with bows now seemed reluctant to lose their precious arrows.

"Make it snappy," Sarah said as she sidestepped a thrown stone. The throwers jeered. She guarded the tunnel mouth as the team clawed their way up the incline. A *shuriken* thrown from too great a distance spun lazily through the air. It clattered at Sarah's feet. She didn't retaliate.

They hauled themselves up by pulling on jutting rocks and pushing against the sides of the roughly hewn tunnel. It was obviously an escape path from the extant sewer system and was not intended as a path from the station.

Gillian and Welkin assisted Ferrik between them. He was of average height but strongly built, like most genetically engineered Skyborn—their training for Earth missions had begun years earlier. Added to that, they had all been raised in a gravity field half again that of Earth normal in preparation for life on Tau Ceti's third planet, a world significantly larger than Old Terra. Ferrik had obviously been tortured, and despite his strength, the ordeal had left him weak and confused.

When they broke through into the drain, Sarah called a halt, activating her powerpak so that it illuminated the decrepit tunnel—the others left theirs off to conserve energy. Sarah and Welkin conferred quietly for a few moments, exchanging grim looks. This was now officially a joint leadership mission. It had deviated too far from Welkin's original intention of a solo expedition to *Colony*. Success would rest on Sarah's experienced leadership.

She took a deep breath. "I'm not sure what's worse—the dust down there or the disgusting smell in here. Right. Harry, make sure no one's stupid enough to follow us. Ferrik, we need to talk." She nodded to Welkin and Gillian to accompany them.

Ferrik eyed Welkin apprehensively.

"Never mind him," Sarah said. "We're all friends here. We could've let them roast you down there, but we're not all cannibals. Have you got that?"

The Skyborn looked puzzled for a moment. Either Sarah's English had improved since she had met the other Skyborn, or the colonists had studied the Earthborn's degenerated language. Either way, he deciphered Sarah's speech more easily than Welkin had on his first meeting. "Got it," Ferrik said. "What happened to you?" he asked Welkin.

Welkin mistook his query and touched his ear. "It's nothing. You get used to it. Arrows in the leg are worse."

Sarah snorted. "I think he means what happened to the nice clean-cut Skyborn kid who could barely stand on uneven ground when the elders ditched him overboard on a suicide mission." She affectionately ruffled Welkin's shaggy hair—something she hadn't done since day one. "The best thing Welkin did for *Colony* was leave it. Best thing for us, too."

Ferrik grimaced, struggling with a decision. He forced a tight smile and eyed Welkin. Neither his gaze nor his words were unfriendly, but he was not yet prepared to give much away. "Was it the best thing?" he asked, genuinely curious. "You look half starved. And your face, those marks—"

"Scars," said Welkin. "I'm like that all over." He suddenly laughed at himself, a bright, quick laugh, for he realized he was actually proud of his battle scars. How far he had come since that day Sarah found him. "You get used to it. The elders won't have you back on *Colony* now. You know that, don't you? You've been 'regrettably' contaminated." His voice was almost bitter for a second. "Like me."

Ferrik blinked, trying to absorb everything that had happened to him. He hadn't fully come to terms with the implications of his predicament yet. Uncertainty showed on his face; everything that had transpired since waking in the canvas module flashed through his mind. That had been three long weeks ago. Events before that were another life altogether. "You're right," he said, hanging his head for a moment. He raised it slowly, a bitter gleam in his eye. "I trained for Earth Mission from the day I was born. I was supposed to be a *pilot,* up there." He jerked his thumb at the ceiling, meaning the sky and space. "And now I suppose I'll spend the rest of my life crawling around in tunnels."

Gillian's eyes flashed with irritation and she started to say something, but Sarah placed a hand on her arm. "How you spend your life, Ferrik, will be up to you," she said. "You've been trained to think like a Skyborn, just as Welkin was. Now you need to start thinking like an Earthborn. I don't know why you ended up out here, but you need to adjust and you need to do it fast."

"To live amongst savages? To die of horrible diseases?" he mumbled, lost in momentary thought.

Sarah clicked her fingers and Ferrik brought his head back up.

"Welkin is still here, Ferrik. Disease can be treated, and we're not all savages. You should also know that Welkin and Harry aren't the only Skyborn who have joined us." At Ferrik's evident surprise, she said, "Don't worry; I'm not asking you to swear blood brotherhood. But just so we don't misunderstand each other, I see a big difference between Skyborn who are trained to kill and those the elders have brainwashed into believing the Earthborn are simply diseased savages. Which are you?"

"I've never killed anybody, till today," Ferrik said, looking down at his hands as if they didn't belong to him. "And those I killed were trying to kill me. And they were savages."

"You fell in with the wrong company," Sarah said. "The cave clans are every bit the monsters the elders warned you about. But they're in the minority." She met his gaze. "Just remember who saved your neck down there."

Ferrik's look was frank and open and Sarah found herself liking the kid. He said, in a tone that was thoughtful rather than challenging, "You must need something from me. Is that why you saved me?"

"Why, you ungrateful—" Gillian began.

"Gillian, put a sock in it," Sarah said. "Ordinarily, he'd be right, by the politics of most Earthborn as well as of *Colony* itself. It's been a long time since sheer altruism had good press. But here it is, Ferrik: I saved you because I wouldn't let anybody die so barbarically. Do you understand?" Ferrik nodded. "Good. Harry? We're on the move." She turned and walked away.

"You're just going to let me go?" Ferrik asked, suddenly confused. These savages were not acting the way they were supposed to, the way the elders had taught him they would. Maybe it was some kind of trick to lull his suspicions. He calculated his chances of making it down here on his own. They didn't look good.

"Go, stay, curl up and die, or come with us, it's your choice," Sarah said. "That's what we give you that the elders don't. Freedom of choice."

"Sarah?" Gillian shot a warning look at her.

"The last place he'll go is *Colony*," Sarah replied, reading her sister's concern. "The cavers back there will finally pluck up enough courage to come looking for us. If Ferrik wants to stay, fine. They'll waste time on him first—and by then we'll be long gone."

"I'll need a weapon," Ferrik hedged.

Sarah laughed, more at the look of disbelief on the others' faces than from Ferrik's audacity. "You've got Buckley's chance. In Skyborn terminology, 'Negative on that request.'"

Harry, Welkin, and Gillian shouldered their laserlites and pushed on in single file through the tunnel. Sarah fell in behind them. "Good luck," she said without turning.

"Hold on," Ferrik said. "With a laserlite I'll last longer—give your team a better chance of putting distance between us."

"Nice try," Sarah said over her shoulder.

"Isn't there anything you need?" Ferrik called.

"Not unless you know how to get into *Colony*." They kept going.

"It's a mistake leaving him," Welkin said, his voice muffled by a storm surge in an adjacent drain.

"Somehow I don't think we will be," Sarah said. "Right now he's confused, but he's not stupid."

"I hope you're right," Welkin said. "And I hope it doesn't occur to him to trade us for his rehabilitation."

Sarah smiled. "How did you get to be so cynical?"

"Must be the company I keep."

"Must be."

They had gone less than a few hundred feet when Ferrik called out, "All right. I'll do a deal."

Sarah turned slowly. "I doubt there's anything you have that we need."

"I was with the perimeter patrol. I know my way around the boundary matrix—how to penetrate its defenses. And I know how to get back to the monorail system. This drain leads to an old reservoir.

Beyond it you're in Penitent territory. You don't want to mess with them."

Harry called from the front of the column. "I don't know about the rest of that stuff, but security changes procedure every day, Sarah. Especially when they lose a component—that is, personnel."

Ferrik looked at his wrist, forgetting the cavers had stolen his timer. "They took me less than six hours ago. No one'll know for sure that I'm missing yet. Security's automated on a random sequence," he said, ignoring Harry's frown. "Has been for months."

Sarah's tongue parted her lips as she thought this through. "Why should we trust you?"

"Those animals back there will hunt me down like space demons." He tramped through ankle-deep water. "I won't last five minutes."

"You're right there," Sarah agreed. "But maybe I've changed my mind." She looked evenly at the Skyborn among her team. Their faces were gaunt in the spectral light. "I know you people pretty well. And I know from experience that Skyborn don't just switch sides at the drop of a hat. It takes days, even weeks grappling with your conscience to betray the elders' doctrine. What makes you so special, Ferrik? Think fast—I don't give second chances."

"Like I said—"

"You lied," Sarah said impatiently. A noise echoed along the drain. "Quick about it," she prompted. "My patience just paid out."

Ferrik winced as a rumble of voices grew louder. "All right. The truth. I've only been with the perimeter patrol for three weeks. Before that, I was . . . I was a pilot. Then something . . . I'm not sure what happened. I was grabbed in the middle of the night and I woke up with a patrol, outside *Colony*. Since then I've been stumbling from one disaster to the next. It's all crazy. Yesterday I was part of a team that got cut off in caver territory, but instead of sneaking out they just opened fire on the first cavers we came across. Then the others came."

"Why'd they start a fight?"

"I don't know. Nothing came through from Central Command. We were connected via neural net and ringphone. What they did was suicidal. We didn't stand a chance."

"Survivors?" Sarah said.

"I think so. They were guarding the cruisers. I managed to patch through a warning, but the heathens were everywhere. I think two of my patrol got away. They're on foot. The cavers—there are more of them than we were told. Not that they gave us much Intel."

"If they make it back to *Colony* before we do, the security matrix'll get changed. Right?"

"That's routine," Ferrik said.

Welkin was puzzled. "If you were part of this perimeter team, what were you doing so deep in the field?"

"I don't know," said Ferrik. "Orders came through and we were all reassigned. There's something going on, some big push, and we were part of it, but I tell you I don't know what the plan is. You know the elders; everything is on a strict need-to-know basis. Period."

"Sounds like some kind of death squad to me," said Welkin. "Locating key opposition groups and eliminating them, maybe. Is that right?"

"All I was told was that we had to scout out the caver territory and report back, unseen," Ferrik said. "It's not like we exterminate every Earthborn that comes along. Space, I've seen troopers *dealing* with Earthborn. Swapping valuables for information. Medicine, stuff like that."

"Anything you gave the cavers would've been tainted somehow," Sarah said. Ferrik shook his head. He couldn't answer that. Sarah went on, "And when you were finished with them, you would've wiped them out like you did Bruick's jabbers up at the Stockade."

"What in Space is a jabber?" Ferrik's puzzlement seemed genuine, but Sarah could not afford the luxury of trusting anyone outside her team.

"Maybe you *are* the new chum you're trying to make out you are, and maybe you're not," she said. "As for the jabbers, your people did us all a favor. But in the process a lot of my family died." She stopped, marshaling her thoughts. "What were the cavers offering in return for your 'priceless' wares?"

"They were cleaning out the monorail system," Ferrik said. "A mostly mopping-up operation. The monorail people are pretty disorganized. Loners, freebooters."

"Cleaning them out?" Sarah queried. "Not of dirt, obviously. But of other Earthborn. Cleaning out the underground in advance of . . . what?"

Ferrik looked anxiously behind him. The cavers were close now, scuttling along like a pack of marauding rats on the scent. Their voices were indistinct, like twittering birds, but their intent was far more deadly.

"The monorail system apparently spreads throughout central Victoria. I wasn't briefed on the operation—but we all heard the rumors. Some kind of medical experiment."

"Right," Sarah said. "Ferrik, you go point. Welkin? If he so much as makes a wrong move, nail him." Welkin nodded, hefting his laserlite. "And, Ferrik?" she added.

The Skyborn paused.

"On the evolutionary scale? I don't put *Colony's* Skyborn too far above the cavers. Remember that."

Ferrik squeezed past the others and took the lead.

They began to run. Despite his injuries, Ferrik moved quickly and nimbly.

Enhanced bioengineering, Sarah thought as she forced herself to keep up with the others. *They've created mutated humans . . . machines.*

Despite the glow of the bobbing powerpaks, they ran their hands over ruptured piping to feel ahead for ceiling obstructions. Without the powerpaks Sarah knew they wouldn't last an hour. The thought gave her some hope. Their pursuers had no such help—though Cide's exceptional night vision had robbed her of certainty. Once they turned off from the main drain, she hoped the cavers would have less hope of finding them. But right now, they seemed uncomfortably close.

They had traveled what seemed a considerable distance when at last Ferrik signaled a halt. The team bunched together in single file. Up ahead, Welkin gasped in wonder.

"What's happening?" Sarah called from the rear. She heard dripping water as someone hauled themselves out of the drain.

Gillian ignited her powerpak and moved forward. Suddenly the team found themselves in a tall vaulted cavern. Towering columns of lichened stone disappeared into the dark recesses of the chamber. Tree roots pierced the sandstone walls like petrified snakes, questing down into the ground in search of long-lost water.

"Keep back," Welkin said. They were on the edge of a crumbling concrete ledge, supported by intact geometrical pillars made of carbon whiskers. Below was a body of water that went on for as far as the powerpak's light reached. "No telling how deep this is," he added.

Harry climbed some rungs and joined Ferrik on the grilled walkway. The others followed him, glad to be out of the backbreaking drain.

"What is this place?" Harry wondered.

"I heard my team leader say it was once a processing plant," Ferrik said. "Purifying water, maybe." He looked about the cavern. The walls themselves seemed to sweat water. Perhaps some sort of bioengineering device, still functioning. "It's so ancient there's no telling what it was used for."

Something in the way he spoke and acted made Sarah anxious. He wasn't looking about the chamber in awe, or even with curiosity. He was more concerned with something unseen.

"What's up?" she asked.

"I don't know. . . . Something," Ferrik said. "I have a bad feeling."

"Down there," Welkin said suddenly.

As one they brought their laserlites to bear on the water. Welkin directed his light to the water's edge. Moored against a bollard was an aluminum dinghy.

"Maybe it belongs to the cavers," Gillian guessed.

Sarah looked across at Gillian. "I doubt it."

"These catacombs are supposed to be crawling with Earthborn," Ferrik said. "Sects, mostly. Fanatics. Ferals and cavers worry at them, but they're growing stronger all the time."

"While they're able," Sarah said. "Or until *Colony* finds a way of flushing the rats from the drains. All right, guys. Eyes open." She took two steps before coming to a sudden stop. "Hold it." She tensed. It was hard to hear above the myriad sounds of dripping water, but she was sure she had heard a noise from the opposite bank. "Cavers?"

"There will be soon," Gillian said from the storm-water drain.

"They're coming fast." She joined the others, spooked. "They're making a helluva noise. Sounds like they're the ones being chased."

"Okay, move out," Sarah said. "Ferrik?"

The Skyborn moved off at a ground-eating lope. Their footsteps clanged as they put as much distance between themselves and their pursuers as they could. Cries of pain came from behind. Whatever was happening back in the storm-water drain, it was something they wanted no part of.

Ferrik took a flight of stairs four at a time. Sarah and Gillian stumbled after him, trying to maintain his pace but lacking his engineered stamina. He waited at the edge of the powerpak's light until the team caught up.

"Keep moving," Sarah wheezed.

"We can't," Ferrik said. "Look." He angled her powerpak upward.

Sarah followed the beam. On a balcony above them a line of ghostly pale faces peered down. Behind her she heard a splash. When she turned around, Ferrik was gone. She mentally shrugged and returned her gaze to the silent watchers. She couldn't see any weapons, but judging by their impassive faces, they felt in no way threatened by her team.

"Something's happening," Welkin said, pulling Sarah down with him behind the buckled railing. The others ducked for cover, too.

Above, several men were twirling their arms in the air as though about to lasso something. They suddenly straightened their arms.

Several loud thuds echoed in the chamber, followed by screams and splashes.

"Whatever they're doing, they're not aiming at us," Sarah observed.

A barrage of projectiles soared down at the carriageway behind them. There were more splashes and curses as cavers crashed into the water.

"Well, I'll be," Sarah murmured. "Slingshots."

"And they're pretty accurate with them," Harry said. His statement was punctuated by several more screams. Retaliatory arrows smacked into the rock face.

Movement below drew their attention to the broad expanse of water, where several cavers were splashing frantically. Then a barrage of rocks rained into the flailing men. Within seconds only eddying ripples marked where the cavers had disappeared beneath the water.

"Ferrik knew what he was doing," Gillian said. "Sarah, let's get out of here."

Sarah cut the air with her hand. "Wait a minute. These people haven't attacked us yet." She turned to Welkin. "Any ideas?"

Welkin wiped perspiration from his brow. "There's nowhere else to go. They've got us trapped up here, if that's what they want."

"We're not exactly defenseless," Harry said, gripping his laserlite. Gillian, too, clutched hers.

More pale faces emerged from a storm-water drain. It seemed to Welkin at that moment that an entire subterranean race had suddenly oozed up from every hidden crack and crevasse and was now waiting for them to do something.

Waiting, perhaps, for them to make one false move.

"Easy does it," Sarah said. "Keep your hands where they can see them. We're sitting ducks right now. Shoulder your laserlites, guys. No sudden movements."

Welkin led them slowly back to the landing below. There was no sign of Ferrik. Apart from the sound of their passage, and the almost rhythmic dripping water, the cavern was ominously quiet.

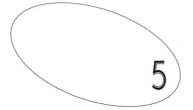

5

By the time they reached the bottom of the stairs, a small group had gathered on the landing. They looked almost monastic in their dark cowled cloaks, which were fastened by cord around their waists. Every one of the group had their hands crossed and covered by their voluminous sleeves.

"We thank you," Sarah said. She looked from one to the other, uncertain whom she should be addressing. "Who's in charge here?"

Every member of the group bowed. Finally one of them spoke. He was a tall, gaunt man with emaciated cheeks and a blotchy complexion.

Sarah locked eyes with him. He was the oldest Earthborn she had met. Due to the wasting disease, most died before their twenty-first birthday.

"We are the Penitent," he said. "I am Jacob." Welkin looked from Sarah back to Jacob. He was about to say something, but the man raised his hand for silence. "All shall be revealed. But first, we must depart." He looked around the cavern where moments before his people had rained death on the cavers. "I fear a member of your group led you into a trap. There is no escape from this chamber unless you know the secret paths."

"Ferrik," Sarah said between gritted teeth. Louder, she said, "We're grateful for your help."

The Penitent ignored her, but nodded curtly to Welkin. He then indicated that they should follow him.

They soon lost track of the turns and fissures they traversed. At times Welkin guessed they were going around in circles, but he tried to put such thoughts aside. After all, hadn't these people rescued them from the cavers? He wanted desperately to talk to Sarah about Ferrik. If what he had said about *Colony*'s security was true, then they needed to breach it as soon as possible, or they never would. But Sarah had simply put her finger to her lips. Maybe she knew what was on his mind; maybe she was playing it by ear. In any case, there was little they could do right now but follow these Penitent, unless they wanted a fight, and unfortunately, they were heavily outnumbered. Perhaps Sarah planned to enlist their help in reaching *Colony*? To do that she would have to gain their trust. Welkin let it go. There would be time enough when they reached the Penitent camp to adjust their plans. He hoped.

It took only a half hour to reach their destination. Their first sight of it was from a ledge high above the settlement. The terrace had been worn smooth by the passage of many feet, indicating that these people had been established here for quite some time. Braziers illuminated the vast chamber with flickering orange light. Guttering sconces dotted around the walls added to the sepulchral sight.

"Well I'll be," Sarah whispered. "They might be a chauvinistic lot, but it looks like they've got a giant underground railway system down here. It's not Flinders Street," she said, turning quizzically to Gillian.

Her sister creased her brow in thought. "There must have been dozens that we never knew about. Remember that map you once showed me? It seemed like the whole of Melbourne was riddled with places like this."

"But I always figured they were inaccessible," Sarah pondered. She signed to them to keep their voices down.

"Apparently not," Harry said quietly. Peering over the edge, he judged there to be about a hundred individuals in this settlement. "Plus more out scouting, I bet," he said. "And look at all those corrugated iron sheds. They must have an army down there."

"Certainly enough for a crusade," Sarah said.

They heard a solitary drumbeat as they wound their way down the cliff face. Moaning drifted up to meet them, but Jacob said it was merely the wind through the tunnels. To Welkin, it sounded more like many tortured souls than any act of nature.

When they reached level ground, Jacob assigned two of his people to show their visitors a hut where they might clean up before a feast.

Welkin was about to decline his kind offer when Sarah shook her head. "Thank you for your hospitality, Jacob," she said quickly. "Are you the leader of these people? We should get together and discuss our problems. We might be able to help one another."

Jacob turned to Welkin, his face obscured by his hood. "The master requests a brief audience with you." He indicated the others. "Meanwhile your friends will be well accommodated."

Welkin looked quickly to Sarah for guidance. "We'll be fine," she said. "Give our regards."

Welkin recognized Sarah's quick humor. With a wave he followed Jacob toward a double-storied building.

Welkin was escorted back to the others some time later. He had much to think on. His team rose from their hessian straw mats when he closed the door behind him. "No lock," he said. "But then, a solid kick would knock the whole thing down."

Gillian joined him by the window. He gave her a quick look, then gazed back outside. The Penitent seemed peaceful enough, but it was rare in this world to find anybody who did not have an agenda and who did not distrust strangers.

"Food and drink and comfortable sleeping mats," Gillian said. "But if they think we're staying they have another think coming, right?"

"They left us with our laserlites," Harry said. "That must mean something."

"Sure does," Sarah said. "Either they're completely stupid or they're not afraid of our weaponry." Welkin said nothing; he stayed by the window, seemingly oblivious.

"Maybe they just know we couldn't get out of here if we tried," Gillian suggested.

Welkin let the conversation wash over him. The Penitent, when not accosting strangers in dark passageways, seemed friendly. They went about the business of living the same as everyone else: They cooked and ate and talked and slept. He watched some children playing, noting that their game, which involved hopping across squares drawn on the ground, was obviously quite ancient, since it was also common on board *Colony.*

It was all very reassuring.

"Hey you," Sarah said, shaking Welkin playfully. "You find them strange?"

They *were* strange. Deathly pale and gaunt, never venturing out into the sunlight or the fresh air. Indeed, the Old Penitent had hinted that their tribal myths blamed the Sun and the Moon for the destruction of the Earth and the degradation of humanity.

"Are we safe here?" he mused aloud.

Sarah gazed around at the Penitent as they went about their business, answered the question that wasn't quite a question. "I don't know. What did you find out from talking to the 'master'?"

"Bits and pieces," said Welkin. He thought back to the disturbing conversation that he had had with Jacob's superior, Matthew.

"You know that we come in peace," he had said, and Matthew smiled and waved his hands dismissively.

"You have been sent to us," he said, nodding his ancient head. Ghoulishly pale in the flickering torchlight, he patted Welkin's arm paternally. "You are in our care and we will not shirk our obligation. Fear not, for does He not protect you as He protects us?" The Penitent made a ritual signing at the mention of "He."

"'He' is your leader?" asked Welkin cautiously, not wishing to offend.

Matthew smiled beatifically. "He Whom we worship"—he made the signing again, a complex pentagram sketched out in the air—"is both Many and One. He cannot die, as befits a leader, and His children are therefore immortal."

Welkin considered this carefully. "Are you His children?"

Matthew looked mildly shocked. "We? We are nothing. We abase ourselves before Him and pray for His forbearance."

"Where does He live?"

Matthew looked at him with something like pity in his eyes. "He is everywhere, my son. When the time is ripe, He is everywhere. Is this not known to your brethren?"

Welkin decided to dodge that one. "Many things have been forgotten, Matthew. Many things."

The Penitent sighed. "That is the truth."

The memory of this conversation made Welkin uneasy. Born and bred in the scientifically advanced culture of *Colony,* he was uncomfortable with what he thought of as mystical mumbo jumbo. It was even possible that on some odd level he felt the man was speaking a kind of heresy . . . a heresy against science, against the brightness of the human intellect . . . entwining it, as here, in dark and distasteful myths.

Coming back to Sarah's question, he smiled at his misgivings, and repeated as much as he could. "In short, I learnt nothing."

Sarah mulled that over. "We'll need time to digest it. Meanwhile, I'll take the first watch."

However, before they could bed down for the "night" they were summoned to a celebration. Matthew explained that it was their custom to welcome strangers and to call upon His benediction.

"He will shine on your travels," said the old man. The celebration was held in the main station office where Welkin had met Matthew. The large building gazed upon a barbaric festival in which scores of Penitent painted their faces in ancient and cabalistic designs and danced with total abandon, usually after imbibing copious amounts of an acrid beverage called *pecane.*

To Welkin's surprise, and confusion, Gillian stayed close to him, their shoulders brushing as they sat on the concrete floor. He shot quick sidelong glances at her, trying to interpret this. Was she just being friendly again? Or apprehensive? Maybe she didn't even register the physical contact, though Welkin wondered how that could be. Each time they touched, a kind of electricity shot through him. After an hour of this the muscles in his back and side ached as he strove to hold himself perfectly still, not allowing himself to move a fraction of an inch closer to Gillian, or pull away. That way he could measure exactly the number of contacts and know with certainty it was she who made them.

During this, the Penitent happily plied everyone with food and drink and frequently asked for comments on the dancing ability of various members of the tribe. The celebration lasted for hours.

Stumbling from exhaustion, they were led back to their shed. Sarah propped herself against the door to keep watch, but hardly had the others closed their eyes than hers, too, slid shut and her chin dropped to her chest.

Some indefinable time later, Welkin tried to open his eyes but couldn't. They seemed gummed up. He wanted to rub them, pry them open, but somebody was sitting on his arms.

"Get off," he muttered, and realized he couldn't move. His eyes opened then and at first he could make out little, as images swam to and fro before his blurry vision. He blinked several times and suddenly everything snapped into focus.

Matthew was gazing down at him. Welkin's head whipped back and forth, taking in the situation. The rest of his team were also bound tightly hand and foot to the subway rails.

Welkin stared back at Matthew.

"What's going on?" he demanded. Behind the old man were a score of Penitent, all abasing themselves on their knees. At the sound of his voice they cried out in great sorrow, offering profuse apologies.

"He came to us in the night and asked for your souls. We could not refuse," said the old man. He seemed genuinely sorry. The others were coming round.

"You drugged us," Welkin accused. "You knew then."

"We suspected."

Sarah tensed, but her hands and feet were securely bound. She raised her head, mind in overdrive.

Harry shouted, "Let us go. We haven't harmed you."

The chanting Penitent climbed off their knees and their voices rose. "O Thou Who art Many and One, we call upon Thee for mercy and understanding. We who are Fallen and accursed pray for Thy blessing."

"Bless us, Great One, for we are reborn in man's disguise," cried Matthew in pure joy.

"Consume us, O Great One, that we may partake in Your Glory!" The chant swelled: "The Fallen fell, and found their fate; the Fallen fell, and found their fate; the Fallen fell, and found their fate . . . O Blessed be the Fateful One . . ."

Their voices died away. They turned and scurried into the shadows. Gillian strained vainly against her bonds.

Matthew wrung his hands in anguish and gave Gillian a look of such profound pity that for the first time she was genuinely scared.

"Be patient. He shall come for you soon. It will all be over quickly." Matthew turned and fled after the others, but Welkin called out after him and he stopped and stared back.

"Who is *He*? *What* is He?" Welkin demanded.

That same pitying look. "I have told you, my son. He is the Many and the One. He lives in the Pulse, in the Blood and the Heat. He comes to this place of Accursed Darkness when He chooses, or when we—the Penitent, His fallen children—need to be punished."

Matthew cupped a hand to his ear and his eyes widened in alarm. Then quite suddenly he hurried away.

"Anybody else unhappy with this situation?" asked Harry, trying to keep his voice level.

"Shut up, Harry," said Gillian.

"Can anybody get loose?" Sarah asked. "Try. I don't know what's supposed to happen next, but I don't want to be here when it does."

"Me neither," said Gillian.

But try as they might, none could so much as loosen a single limb, let alone get a hand free. Nor could they reach to sink their teeth into any of the ropes binding them.

Panting, they took a brief rest. "I'm open to ideas," Sarah said. "Anyone?"

"Wait a minute. I felt something," said Welkin, frowning. The others fell quiet, listening. But there was no sound to be heard.

"Do you think they've left us out for the cavers?" asked Gillian.

"Not a hope in Space," said Welkin. "We saw what the Penitent did to the cavers."

"Quiet a second," said Harry. "I think I felt it, too."

"What?" asked Sarah.

"That."

There was a sound now. Faint, almost subsonic. But it grew, became a humming in the rails. Welkin and Harry looked at each other.

"It can't be," said Harry.

"Can't be what?" asked Gillian, exasperated.

"We know it's not a sub-train," said Welkin.

"Unless the elders have repaired part of the system," said Harry, straining to gaze down the tunnel in the direction from which the humming seemed to be coming. "Maybe *Colony*'s done some deal with these crazies."

"The rails are definitely vibrating," Harry said worriedly.

"They're more warped than Matthew," Sarah said. "It's not a train."

The sound and vibration grew. Before long it was felt in the ground, too. "Okay, it's probably not the monorail," Harry said, pulling harder at his bonds.

Sprinkles of dirt fell from the ceiling as the noise grew. "Can anyone see anything?" Sarah called.

Harry sniffed the air. "No, but I can smell something."

"Me, too," said Gillian.

Harry frowned. "It's pungent . . . musky . . . some kind of animal smell." He craned his neck to look at the others. Fear was in his eyes. "There's some kind of animal coming."

"Steady up," Sarah said. "Nothing's that huge."

Suddenly the sound hit them, hugely amplified, as if whatever was approaching had just turned a bend in one of the tunnels. It was a high-pitched chittering noise. Harry strained to see into the nearest tunnel.

"Space!" he exclaimed.

A dark tide was sweeping toward them. Gillian caught sight of it and moaned.

"What is it?" Welkin asked, unable to see from where he was.

"Rats," Gillian wailed.

"But that's crazy. Rats couldn't make the ground shake . . . unless . . ."

"Unless there are thousands of them," finished Harry tonelessly.

Welkin closed his eyes. "The Many and the One."

"I hate rats," Gillian said, squirming.

Sarah put in a Herculean effort to break loose, but the ties held fast.

Suddenly the vanguard raced into the cavern. It was evident that these weren't just any rats. Not only were they the size of tomcats, but their eyes glittered with a malevolent intelligence.

"What *are* they?" Harry asked.

"Mutants?" Sarah wondered. "Some genetic experiment gone wrong? The ancients' work?"

The forerunners fell upon them, snapping and clawing at their faces and limbs. Welkin and the others squirmed and writhed, trying to throw the rats off, but their bonds gave them little room to maneuver.

Screams and cries of pain filled the cavern along with the insane squealing of the rats. It was pandemonium. The main host had nearly reached the cavern.

"Gillian?" cried Welkin.

"I'm still here," she yelled as she whipped her head sideways, slamming a rat away.

Welkin thrashed about. His life couldn't end like this. There had to be a way out.

The multitudes erupted into the cavern and swept toward them. The cacophony filled the station. It was at that moment that a new sound started, although none of the family heard it at first. It was the hiss of a laserlite on full spread.

Through the squirming, snapping bodies Welkin could just make out Ferrik on the platform above them, fanning the deadly beam of a laserlite into the packed ranks of the rats. From the terrible screeches and screams it sounded as if he was slaughtering them in droves.

Whatever he was doing, it gave the team a momentary reprieve. The rats pulled back, as if to reevaluate, though that couldn't be right. Ferrik jumped down, quickly slashed Sarah's bonds and handed her the knife, then leapt back to the platform and continued firing at the rodents.

Sarah freed the others, knifing several rats as they clung tenaciously to Welkin's boots. "Quick now!" she screamed. "Make for Ferrik."

They all scrabbled toward the Skyborn.

"Back that way," he said, pointing. He kicked at a bundle of gear at his feet. "You'll be needing this lot. Move it."

Welkin hesitated. All his instincts told him not to trust the Skyborn. But here he was, rescuing them from certain death. And offering them their laserlites and utility packs. The others scrambled for their gear, slung it over their shoulders, and fled into the tunnel that Ferrik had indicated.

The Skyborn waved Welkin away brusquely. "Powerpak's almost gone. Go, or we're both going to die."

But Welkin shook his head. "We'll all make it." He snatched the last utility belt from the ground and clipped it around his waist. Someone hadn't collected their laserlite, so Welkin took it.

At that moment Ferrik's laserlite spluttered and died. The Skyborn switched it to flashlight mode and broke into a run, lighting the way. "Keep up," he shouted.

Welkin kept pace until they reached the others, where Ferrik took the lead. Welkin turned at the tunnel and sprayed the horde of scurrying rats with laserlite fire. His own powerpak was registering low, so he ceased fire and sprinted after the others. Behind them, with a kind of collective roar, the rats surged forward in furious pursuit.

The race through the twisted and debris-filled tunnels was a nightmare. They plowed into obstructions hanging from the ceiling and tripped over obstacles almost invisible in the gloom. And all the time that awful churning sound of death was snapping and snarling at their heels.

Suddenly, by accident, they burst into a shunting yard where the Penitent had gathered. They seemed to be in some kind of trance, swaying to and fro like a massive wave. Many were holding tallow candles, their tiny flames winking in the darkness, illuminating individual faces in golden light. The fugitives slowed, almost stopped, at the unexpected spectacle. The Penitent in turn froze in mid-movement and stared back at them.

Then the noise reached them, and the smell.

The Penitent let out a collective moan. Matthew had been addressing his congregation from an open cargo carriage. He staggered a few steps as though unable to comprehend what he was seeing. "What have you done?" he asked, but no one heard him.

"I don't think we're too welcome here," Welkin said. "Keep going."

They charged through the shunting yard unimpeded. Over intact nanodiamond rails they vaulted, through gutted carriages, at other times stumbling over loose detritus. They were almost through the yard when the Penitent sank to their knees and started to chant a prayer.

Behind them, the rats swarmed in, and within seconds the yard was awash with the snarling brutes. The kneeling Penitent were just as swiftly covered in a mass of crawling, writhing, and biting rodents, yet they made no move to escape or fight back, but went on chanting, sometimes in high, piercing screeches that ended suddenly.

Fear drove the fugitives on, for it soon became apparent that a large body of the vermin had struck off after them. Several times the pursuing rodents tried to outflank them, and once they were cut off, till Gillian spotted a storm drain high on the wall to their left.

They scrambled up, hoping that the mutants weren't clever enough to herd them into a trap. But the drain was clear and they pelted along it at a stoop. At one point they crossed a natural fissure-like tunnel that was strewn with bones, a sure sign of their pursuers' destructive passage. The sight of such carnage drove them on with renewed vigor.

Some time later, having left behind all sight and smell of the creatures, Welkin called a halt and they came to a panting stop at an intersection. They were all past exhaustion, even Ferrik. He leaned his laserlite against a long-disused exit ladder. Despite the powerpak's depletion, it still produced a meager light.

While the others collapsed and noisily sucked air, Sarah went over to the Skyborn and squatted beside him. She put a hand on his arm and he looked back at her, confused, and perhaps scared. The terrible finality of knowing he could never go home was beginning to sink in. "Thanks for coming back," she said, panting. "We owe you big-time."

He stared back at her. Slowing his ragged breathing, he said, "I didn't lead you into a trap back there. I just dived into the water when

I saw we'd walked into an ambush. You saved my life. Guess we're even," he finished lamely.

Sarah grinned uncertainly. "Fair enough," she said, placing a hand over her erratically pumping heart. It hadn't had such a good workout in a long time. "So what are your intentions?"

"Meaning?"

"Well, you know where we're going. Are you coming with us? Or are you going to stay out here? I figure you're not going to warn your superiors that we're coming, since you just saved our lives."

Ferrik looked around him. None of the others were paying any attention to the conversation, or to him. It went against everything he had ever been taught about the Earthborn. "I truly have no idea." His hands hung over his knees and his head slumped, as if now, in the absence of clear action and danger, he felt the sense of loss and purposelessness most keenly.

Sarah knew she would have to make the decision for him. He had been conditioned to take orders. But she also knew that she had to do it right.

"Gather round," she called to the others.

Ferrik immediately tensed, wondering if he was about to be betrayed, but Sarah had already placed a hand lightly on his shoulder, and was offering the universal peace sign: a smile.

The others gathered themselves up. Almost ritualistically they squatted in a semi-circle around the pair, as though knowing what was expected of them.

Sarah poured some water from a canteen into a metal cup and held it in both hands, reverentially. "This man seeks membership into the family," she intoned. Her eyes flicked toward Welkin.

He knew the procedure and did not question Sarah's decision to initiate it. "Is he fit?"

"He is fit," said Sarah.

"Will he serve?" asked Welkin in a droning voice.

"He will serve."

"Has he spilt blood for the family?"

"He has spilt blood for the family."

"Then," said Welkin, aware of the power of ritual in all their lives, "let him be joined with us."

"So shall it be," said Sarah, and she took a sip of water from the cup. She then passed it to Welkin, who did the same, and so on to Harry and Gillian, who, taking their cue from Welkin, did likewise. Finally, Gillian passed it to Ferrik and the youth took it from her and she saw that his hands were shaking and that he looked almost frightened.

"I will join the family," he said simply, and drank the rest of the water.

"He is now our brother," said Sarah, and the others repeated this. Ferrik smiled hesitantly. The lost look was gone and Sarah felt instinctively that they could trust him now with their lives.

Gillian punched his arm playfully. "Thanks for coming back for us."

He nodded, too overcome to reply. Today he had lost one family, but now he had found another and they had welcomed him.

Harry stood and stretched. "What the hell were those things? I mean, maybe they're mutations, but where did they come from? How in space did they evolve like that?"

Welkin frowned. " 'They live in the Pulse,' Matthew said. 'In the Blood and the Heat.' "

"Classic gobbledygook," Harry said.

"Maybe not," Welkin told him. He suddenly slapped his forehead. "Don't you see?"

"All I see is somebody hitting himself in the head," Harry joked.

Welkin went on. "The rats must come from *Colony*. New gods, from the lower decks. That's what he meant by the Pulse. Listen, the generators on *Colony* are massive and they're buried at the center of the ship. Their rhythmic vibration fills every part of *Colony*. You don't even notice it till you've been away and come back."

"And the Blood and the Heat?" Sarah said, leaning forward intently.

"I think that means the warmth that *Colony* provides, and the food sources available there. But also it explains the rats' changes. *Colony*'s crash-landing must have damaged some of the ship's antimatter–ion drive generators, leaking radiation. The plasma inhibitors would shield it from the rest of *Colony*, but if some of the rats had nested in the drench vats . . ."

Harry nodded. "Makes sense, although perhaps *Colony* was breeding them . . ."

Ferrik sifted through his memory. "I know the vats were producing native animals for reintegration. The radiation would have wrecked the computers controlling the vats. The rats got in the vats and the new generation were remade, well, wrong. That could explain those . . . things. But that's irrelevant. What it does tell us is that now we have a way in."

They all looked at him. "What about the perimeter?"

He shook his head. "That's a lot riskier," he said. "They might not have changed the security codes, but then again, they might have. Besides, the perimeter is the perimeter. It is the most closely watched part of *Colony*. But there are large sections of *Colony* that are now underground due to the crash impact. Some of these must lead into the lower decks where we—that is, the elders—still can't penetrate."

"There are still lower deckers around putting up a fight?" Gillian asked.

Ferrik rolled up a sleeve, showing an ugly puckered scar. "What they lack in weaponry they make up for in determination. They're pretty good fighters."

"That rat trail we crossed," said Welkin. "All we have to do is trace it back to its source."

"Is that all?" asked Harry. "We just go wandering along Rat Highway and when we run into the little buggers we say, 'Oh, we've just got some business with the skyworld that spawned you . . .' "

Welkin threw a handful of dirt at him. Harry ducked, but his words made sense.

"Harry's right," said Gillian. "We have to be careful." She touched the smooth walls of the drainage system, then looked up at the rusting ladder. It led nowhere, for the ceiling aperture had long since collapsed. "They get our scent and we're as good as gone."

"Something Matthew said . . . I think the rat invasion is a regular event," said Welkin. "So they probably don't return to the ship straightaway."

"You hope," said Harry.

"Well, we've all got laserlites this time and we've got spare powerpaks." He winced the moment he said that. He hadn't offered Ferrik a powerpak for his depleted laserlite. It wasn't that he didn't trust the Skyborn, but old habits died hard. If Ferrik noticed the slip, he didn't show it.

Sarah stood up. "Then we're wasting time. Let's move out."

With a groan the others got to their feet, checked their weapons, and shouldered their packs. Ferrik handed his laserlite to Gillian. "I gather this one's yours?"

Gillian took it, flipped out the spent powerpak, and snapped in a new one. "Good as new. Thanks."

Welkin took point, leading the way. Sarah and Ferrik brought up the rear.

"Eyes open," Sarah warned.

The pungent odor of rodents hit them when they were within a few hundred yards of Rat Highway. They paused to listen but heard nothing. Welkin moved cautiously ahead to reconnoiter. After several long moments he returned and signaled them to follow him.

They found the highway still deserted except for the occasional rodent corpse and copious droppings. The smell in the fissure tunnel was intense and sickening. Harry lost what little food was in his stomach almost right away and Gillian came close to losing hers.

Sarah stayed well in the rear to give the others as much time as possible if the rat horde should reappear. But nothing happened, except that they hit a snag that at first threatened to stump them.

The fissure moved straight toward *Colony* like an arrow and quite possibly had been caused by the crash itself rather than some subsequent earth movement, though small quakes weren't unknown.

At one point, part of the ceiling had collapsed, but a small gap had been left—or excavated—near the top. They enlarged this and continued on their way after blocking it behind them.

Welkin rubbed his hands free of grit and dirt. "I doubt that'll hold them for long if they decide to come back," he said.

Sarah coughed; their excavations had clogged the air with dust. "I'm not an expert on rats, but from what little I do know, all underground creatures have numerous exits and entrances. At best it'll only slow them down."

"That'll do me," Harry said, spluttering like the others.

After they followed the fissure for more than a mile it suddenly widened into a small cavern. Looming above them was the crumpled and pitted hull of *Colony*.

The Skyborn among them, Ferrik, Welkin, and Harry, stood as though mesmerized, looking up at the tortured slab of permasteel. It had until recently been their home, where they had been trained above all to defend the skyworld beyond question. Yet here they were about to breach its hull like common thieves.

Gillian was about to say something, but Sarah shook her head. She had seen that look of awe on the faces of the Skyborn before when confronted with their birthplace. She let them have their moment of reflection.

Welkin was the first to break from his reverie. He saw Gillian staring at him quizzically and laughed it off. "She doesn't look too invincible right now, does she?"

"The Mighty always fall, Welkin," Sarah said. "It's a given." She turned to Harry. "Time's short," she reminded him.

At first glance the cavern seemed like a dead end, but a quick reconnoiter revealed half a dozen small tunnels hidden within the ruptured rock face, some slashing through the floor. Only two or three of them were large enough for humans to make any kind of quick getaway through.

However, that wasn't what they had come for. While the others stood an uneasy watch Welkin and Sarah explored the hull.

Finally Welkin called Sarah over. "There's a tear here," he said, poking his hand through.

Sarah followed the line of the rupture. The opening was about ten inches wide and twice that height. "It must take those rat things hours to get through that and assemble on the other side."

"Maybe they've started their own colony out here," Welkin quipped.

"Just what we need, another tribe of semi-intelligent creatures." She stood back from the gash. "We'll have to burn our way through."

Welkin's shoulders slumped. "Sarah, it's at least seven inches thick. We'd run out of powerpaks long before getting through."

"Let's just blow it," said Ferrik, who had come up behind them. He opened his rucksack and pulled out a small timed device, obviously an explosive.

"Where'd you get that?" Sarah asked suspiciously.

"When the Penitent attacked us they fought over our gear—weapons mostly. Heathens killed more of themselves than they did us squabbling over it." He stopped a moment, remembering the slaughter. "Matthew managed to stop a riot and demanded what was left." He hefted the small device. "I found it stashed with your gear."

"The gods are smiling on us," said Sarah. Ferrik offered her the bomb, but she declined and motioned for him to deploy it.

"How big an explosion?" Welkin asked.

"We don't want to be standing here when it blows," Ferrik said. "The hull is permasteel and even though it's cracked here and space-weathered, it'll still need a kick and a half."

Welkin eyed the ceiling. "We likely to bring anything else down?"

Ferrik followed his gaze. "It's a shaped charge. This one is designed to blast open doors and bulkheads, so most of the explosive force should be focused straight in and—"

"Straight out," Welkin finished for him. Such incendiaries had never been needed when he served on *Colony*. Rupture the hull in the main cruise cabin and the entire craft would be placed in jeopardy. He realized with a start that a whole lot of weaponry must have been developed since his departure.

"Set it," said Sarah.

Ferrik flipped open a cover and pushed the button inside. "Two-minute fuse," he said.

"Listen up, everybody," said Welkin, raising his voice. "Take cover. Watch out for falling debris. And when we get inside, assume somebody heard us knocking and is coming to see what's going on."

"They might be some of our people," Harry said.

Welkin looked anxiously at Ferrik. "The people we knew would all be gone now," he said.

To break the awkward silence Ferrik looked at the timer. "Ninety seconds and counting," he announced.

"Eyes open," Sarah said, ushering them to take cover.

When the incendiary went off, it made an almost disappointingly small detonation. Not even a real explosion, thought Welkin, more an impressive *whoosh* and a great flash of intense light, almost like an arc welder, only brighter. They were fortunate that Ferrik had warned them to close their eyes; the intense light would have easily seared their retinas.

No matter how small the device had been, it worked. When the dust cleared there was a hole in the side of the burnished hull the size of a large hatchway.

"Guess we just made life for the rats a whole lot easier," Harry observed.

"Don't expect 'em to say thanks," said Gillian.

Welkin clutched his laserlite. "Here we go."

They stepped in single file through the newly blasted breach and into the lower decks of *Colony*.

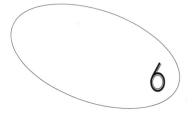

6

Sarah tilted her head back, nostrils flaring. "What's that awful smell?" Before anyone could answer, she let loose an almighty sneeze.

Ferrik started. Sneezes aboard *Colony* were non-existent.

Welkin snorted. "It's good clean *Colony* air." He looked about in wonder. "Main ducts down here would've been terminated, but cond-ox still gets pumped through the ship's osmotic pores."

"In case someone gets trapped in a cabin, or a section shuts down?" Sarah said from the rear.

"Everything needs to breathe," Welkin said mysteriously.

"Give me good clean Earth air anytime," Sarah said, sniffing.

"That stuff we Skyborn almost gag on when we first breathe it?" Harry joked.

"The very same," Sarah said.

"Okay, everyone," Welkin said. "We need a little quiet now. When I say the walls have ears, I mean it literally."

Dim red lights glowed into life, spaced at intervals, testament to the wondrous engineering of a bygone time. No one was on the other side to greet them, but they took no chances. Welkin assigned Gillian and Sarah to flanking duties while Ferrik brought up the rear. The Skyborn was sweating visibly. Welkin wondered whether it was be-cause he was back on board *Colony* and knew what the elders would do to him if they caught him, or because he was in the dreaded territory of his childhood nightmares. The lower decks were to the Skyborn what hell, with all its fire and brimstone, was to the Earthborn.

Welkin cautiously led the way through the twisted compacted corridors. Like Harry he had spent some time in the lower decks, but not as much; he motioned Harry to join him and together they charted a way through the topsy-turvy landscape.

Yet even Harry was disoriented. At least half the decks were concertinaed and the rest had endured massive structural dislocation. Walls had buckled and twisted and there were no level floors or straight corridors. Indeed, floors and ceilings often nearly met, even in the passable corridors, leaving narrow gaps to squeeze through. Bulkheads leaned together to form inverted "V"-shaped passageways. Metal walls and machinery and weight-bearing diamondoid columns had ruptured, sculpting the landscape into a mass of tangled jagged metal and plastic like some deadly Sargasso. Adding to the underwater effect, optical wires and plasma cables dangled from the ceiling and walls like trailing kelp. The only thing missing was the sharks, and Welkin felt sure they would be encountered soon enough.

"Eyes open," he hissed as Gillian slipped and cried out. "Watch what you're doing back there." He paused until the echo died. Stepping with stealth, he waved the others forward, but not without noting Gillian's scowl.

Electrical discharges from ravaged conduits rained sparks on them and somewhere water tanks had ruptured so that they swished through several inches of runoff. Welkin wondered what electrocution felt like. *Colony* was way beyond electrics, but he knew lower deckers would scavenge any energy source they could to survive.

Traversing the wrecked arteries of *Colony* soon took its toll. Cut, bruised, and weary, they stopped to rest and eat twice before they eventually made contact with others. When they did, it was not quite in the way Welkin had envisaged.

They had just spent an hour climbing down the face of a chamber that had been created by some kind of intensely hot explosion. The result had blasted a great spherical hole in the lower decks, which had also fused much of the surrounding metal. Welkin wondered if someone could have set off a small tactical nuke. He hated to think of the radiation dose they were getting if that was the case. Or perhaps a minuscule container of antimatter had ruptured.

The chamber looked like some outlandish ant's nest. The fusing had left many pieces of metal jutting in all directions while others had melted and formed wonderful shapes that were also razor sharp. Harry cut his hand quite badly on one and had to be patched up while the entire party was suspended some two hundred feet up the side of the "bubble," as Gillian called it.

When they finally reached solid decking, or the bottom of the bubble, they moved out across the base toward what looked like a tunnel entrance on the other side. Suddenly Welkin stopped.

"Nobody move," he said, barely above a whisper.

The others froze, and turned slowly to look at him. "I don't think the floor is—"

With a deafening screech the floor gave way and they dropped into some kind of shaft. The bigger sections of flooring stuck in the opening, but Welkin and the others plunged downward. Death seemed imminent, but the shaft curved to the left, slowing their descent, dumping them out onto some kind of plastic ceiling slab, which promptly collapsed under their weight.

They dropped some ten feet into the middle of a brightly lit cavern and hit the floor with an assortment of grunts and groans.

Welkin was the first to scramble up. "Everyone okay?" he called.

"Welkin." Gillian's voice made it abundantly clear that something was wrong.

Welkin followed her gaze. They had landed in someone's burrow. And they weren't alone.

Even in the artificial light of the laserlites, Welkin could see that they were surrounded by a group of lower deckers. They had the look of half-starved ferals—tattered clothing, pale scabrous skin. Many of them seemed dazed, too exhausted to even care that a group of people had just fallen in on them.

The family automatically swung their weapons around, but the burrow dwellers made no move to attack them. Welkin lowered his laserlite and stared around. He quickly realized that these emaciated people had themselves been in some kind of battle and were in no state to fight.

The family relaxed their guard and shouldered their weapons. Then Harry suddenly strode through the dust-clogged air, hand outstretched.

"Clifford? Sorry for dropping in uninvited."

One of the walking scarecrows peered at him; then a big grin broke across his blackened face and he stumbled forward to meet Harry. They embraced, pounding each other's backs.

"Harry? Is that you, you old space dog? I knew you were too mean to kill." He turned exuberantly to his people. "It's Harry. One of the Forgotten. One of the Originals who escaped Earthside."

Murmurs snaked around the chamber. Despite their emaciated appearance and fatigue, the lower deckers broke into cheers and rushed forward to embrace the family.

They must think we've come to rescue them, Sarah thought. She tried not to stare at the injuries and grief-swollen eyes, and blocked out their hacking coughs. *So much misery, so much death.* Then she remembered that some of these people had probably never seen Earthborn before. They had been trapped down here for a long time.

"Okay, everyone, just pull back. Give these people air," Clifford called out. He clapped his hands for attention. "I said back off!" He pushed one or two away from the family.

Reluctantly they regrouped just out of reach. A woman cradling a crying baby simply sat at Sarah's feet, staring forlornly up at the well-fed Earthborn.

Sarah crouched down and ran the back of her hand across the baby's soft skin.

The mother suddenly handed the baby to Sarah, who felt awkward and irrationally scared she might drop the incredibly fragile thing. But she was also profoundly stirred. The baby's eyes fixed her with a look that must be as old as the human race itself. She blinked rapidly, and her eyes filled with tears.

Someone laughed good-naturedly and suddenly everyone was talking.

Clifford clapped for silence. He was beaming in all directions at once and his emaciated face actually seemed to glow. "Listen up, everyone," he yelled. When they had hushed sufficiently, he pointed at Harry, grinning. "Now, you've got some explaining to do, mister. Where in Space have you been? And how did you get back here?"

"It's a *long* story," said Harry. "These are my friends, my family." He quickly introduced the others, and mentioned other members of that original Skyborn party who had escaped with him. Clifford vaguely knew of Elab and Efi, but they had been members back then of warring lower-deck tribes. Harry then gave the lower deckers a potted history of their escape and their trek to freedom.

When he had finished, Welkin indicated the walking wounded and the bodies covered with scabs. "What about your people, Clifford? What happened here?" he asked.

"Drench rats," said Clifford. And he told them that after the crash, while the elders had patrols out sealing all the cracks they could find in *Colony*'s hull below level five, and killing any lower deckers they came across, the rats living outside in the old subway system had found easy access to the lower decks and an endless supply of food: thousands of dead and dying bodies sandwiched in the wreckage where only something the size of a rodent could get at them. The rat population quickly swelled. They had found rat heaven: heating, water, and food. It wasn't long before they had built a super nest inside one of the vat chambers intended for genetically engineering animals from the zoo banks. Then the first altered rats had appeared. Smart, adaptable, aggressive, and able to manipulate their environment. The vats, damaged, had produced cunning monsters.

It made life in the lower decks even more precarious at first, yet since the first changelings had appeared the rats had tended to leave the lower deckers alone, as if they somehow understood that life inside *Colony* was a delicately balanced ecosystem, which shouldn't be disturbed. Instead, they periodically swarmed out through the hull and through the old underground network, bringing back further supplies of food, which they stored away until their next swarming.

"Why don't you escape outside?" Welkin asked.

"Some do," said Clifford. "But either they never come back or else those that do tell frightful tales of cavers and ferals, the Penitent, or the endless *Colony* patrols that carbonize them without hesitation." He looked at his ragged crew. "This is pretty much all that's left of the lower deckers, Harry." He looked up at the gaping hole in the ceiling. "Some hermits survive outside our group, but they're mostly newbies who don't trust us."

Hearing this, Ferrik said, "The elders are still throwing dissidents down here. Orders are to kill them and dump them through the bulkheads. But they're not always killed."

Clifford started. Despite Ferrik's ragged appearance, he still wore a patrolman's uniform—and no one, but no one, was thrown into the lower decks in their uniform. "You've got an upper decker in your group?"

A low angry murmur rose from the lower deckers. Sarah nonchalantly rested her hand on her hip, ready to swing her laserlite around and up.

"He's with us," Harry said bluntly. "He's family now. And you heard what he said. They're supposed to kill dissidents, but more and more heavies are disobeying orders."

"The only reason they don't kill us is because they want us to live in terror till we're killed by the savages belowdecks," a woman scoffed.

Clifford desperately wanted to believe something positive. "He's your guide, right? You guys have come down here looking for us?"

"Clifford!" the woman reproached. She was the mother of his child. Clifford waved her to keep quiet and turned expectantly back to Harry.

But the Skyborn's face was grave. Welkin answered for him. "It's not as easy as that. The elders still control *Colony,* but there's growing dissent, not only from the heavies but right across the skyworld."

"I see," Clifford said. He glanced at his partner, and the child who was now staring google-eyed at Sarah. "We can't last much longer down here. We're spent. The elders have thrown everything at us lately. A newbie said that everyone above deck has had their jack removed. A few of us still have ours, but I doubt we're wired into the system anymore."

"We know about that—and need to find out more," Welkin said.

He sought Sarah's silent approval to continue and after a brief hesitation she nodded for him to go on. She was now fighting Gillian for the baby's attention. "Listen, there's a place you can go," he said. "And there are ways to avoid tribal Earthborn . . ."

He briefly told them about the farm and the family and all that they had managed to achieve in the face of great opposition and danger. Clifford and those who had come close to listen became excited at this news, but it was clear that they were in no condition to travel right away, nor could they find the farm without a guide.

Clifford eyed Harry and Welkin. "What I haven't figured out yet is why you people are here."

"That's easy," Welkin said. "We have to get to the upper decks."

"Then you're either space crazy or you're dreaming, I can't work out which. Either way, you're ill-equipped," Clifford said frankly.

"There aren't enough of us to attack *Colony*," Welkin said. "We don't have the weapons, or the will." He flicked a look at the other family members, especially Harry. "The smaller the group the harder it is to detect infiltrators."

Sarah spoke up. "The elders are designing some kind of weapon of mass destruction. We believe it's biological. A virus . . ."

Clifford nodded sourly. "A newbie we rescued said something about that. We didn't want to believe him, but . . ." He waved over a short blond-haired man with narrow features and lively eyes. "This is Lal Nathan. He was a sub-elder working in the upper levels. At least, he was, until he and Jamieson's daughter became too friendly."

Lal grinned. He was an instantly likeable fellow with a cheeky look. He was also the unlikeliest sub-elder that Welkin had ever met. Then again, he had been stripped of his elite uniform, and now wore discarded remnants. Poverty humbled anyone.

Then Ferrik pushed his way through the crowd. "Sub-Elder Nathan? Is that you?"

The former sub-elder shrugged. "Don't go calling me names, Ensign. You don't look too spaceworthy yourself."

Sarah squeezed Ferrik's arm gently. "We need information right now, Ferrik."

trance. "Long ago. Lucida, too." His eyes roved about, settled on a door. "In there. We used to meet our parents."

Harry started. "You knew your parents?"

Welkin nodded. "We were close. I don't know why we were different." He moved to a table that sat in the middle of the room and gently reached out and touched it, almost as if it might give him an electric shock. Then his fingers went to a notch in the corner and he caressed it.

"I did this. When I was about four years old. I threw something at my sister and she ducked and it broke the table. Mother was furious." Then he gave a light laugh. "Not about the table. Because I nearly brained my sister."

His eyes glistened and he blinked several times rapidly.

"Welkin," said Harry softly. "We can't stay here."

Welkin moved quickly to the other door, opened it, and peered in. Memories unspooled from some long-ago tape, giving him flickering fragmentary glimpses, like a holovid that had shorted out. He heard his mother making a joke, his father laughing; he saw himself and Lucida doing chores, homework, bickering, crying . . . Then suddenly the corridor doorway burst open and heavies shouldered inside the tiny apartment. There were harsh shouts, orders, and someone cursed in the saddest, softest way that Welkin had ever heard.

He whirled quickly, but the corridor door stood innocently open, no heavies in sight; the horror that unfolded here was just his child's memory of it. He came back to the shuddering present, the more mature Welkin still shivering from the child's nightmare of long ago.

"You okay?"

Welkin opened his mouth to answer, but his mouth was dry. He gave Harry a nod and took a deep breath.

"They found out," he said. "They broke in and took us to be rehabilitated, me and Lucida. We never saw them again. We never saw our parents again." His chest felt like it was being squeezed in a vise. "They said later that Mother died of the age plague. We never found out what happened to Father, just that he died, too . . ."

Harry gave him an awkward hug. That simple human touch restored Welkin to the here and now. He smiled weakly.

"We need to get going," he said. "Ferrik must be freaking."

Harry grinned. "No argument there." He exited. Welkin followed more slowly, feeling as he did so that he was leaving behind more than just a dusty abandoned apartment.

Outside, Welkin carefully closed the door, eyed it a moment longer, then turned and headed briskly down the corridor. Harry and Ferrik fell in beside him and for a while none of them said anything.

It was shortly after this that they found a crew locker room. The lockers were stacked in neat rows like plastic dominoes. Welkin stared at them and felt an unreasoning hatred build inside him. He hated their uniformity, which repeated itself endlessly throughout *Colony;* he hated the *cold inhuman precision* that was embodied in everything on board the skyship, every tiniest detail, unlike the messy, chaotic *human* world of the Earthborn. He wanted to lash out and destroy the careful order of the locker room. And, he realized, not just the locker room.

He forced himself to remain calm; the feeling passed. Perhaps the Earth needed some of this order. Perhaps the Earthborn needed to work toward some compromise with it, not just bring it down. Not just destroy.

The lockers were finger-coded and required living blood pulse. Welkin looked to Ferrik. "Are they keyed back to Control?" he asked him. There had been no need for such security measures before, but things had obviously changed.

Ferrik knelt, feeling around the code pad. "I doubt it. They wouldn't expect infiltration up at this level."

Welkin pulled out his laserlite pistol. Cutting the lockers open was easy, but then security would know the room had been breached. On the spur of the moment he decided to open dozens of lockers. It took several minutes to cut them open. Then selecting three suitable uniforms, they threw the contents of the lockers across the deck. At least *Colony* wouldn't know exactly which uniforms were missing. Not in a hurry, anyway.

Ferrik pulled on a polished boot. "Shame there weren't any captain uniforms in here. I always wanted to be a captain, just like Sobol."

"Sobol?" Welkin said, sliding a watch onto his wrist.

"Not *like* him as such," Ferrik corrected. "Just someone with a bit of power," he finished lamely.

Harry eyed the uniform he had found. "At least you're not one of the perimeter guards anymore. Knowing our luck, our own people might've taken a piece out of us, thinking we're contaminated." He kept some personal effects in case he was stopped and questioned.

"Ever the optimist," Welkin said, smoothing out his own engineer second class uniform. "As for me, I've jumped several ranks. Goodbye, Ensign Quinn," he said, pushing the tabs of the jacket together.

"And I'm a nobody in Component Supply," Harry said.

They were nervous at first as they struck out, but after they had passed several *Colony* personnel without incident they knew their impersonations worked. Passing a communications office, they came upon a mess hall full of noisy gossiping workers. Pausing, they took a deep breath, then stepped inside and looked around. It was almost like coming "home"—a home they hadn't visited in a long time. It seemed familiar yet oddly alien at the same time. The hall was very spacious, quite capable of accommodating two hundred hungry people at more than two dozen tables. The food shelves and dispensaries lined one wall while at the far end were a series of booths where people could watch holovid news and features. Nearby were several lounges and airpool tables, light-colored balls hissing quietly, their minijets twirling them slowly above the table deck, waiting to be hit by those wishing to relax.

Harry said, "Okay, I'll leave you to it. I'm going back to that communications office. If my skills aren't too rusty, I'll tap into the ship's comm.net. Wish me luck."

"You got it," Welkin said. "But take Ferrik with you. I'll mingle with these people. Meet me back in here as soon as you're done. Anything goes wrong and we rendezvous back at the shaft in exactly three hours. Got it?"

They split up. Welkin filled a tray with food at the auto serve. Nutrient rich but processed, the food on his plate looked about as appetizing as month-old vomit. There was a time when he would never have thought that food grown in the filthy, diseased earth of his homeworld would seem so superior to *Colony* food.

He moved toward a small group of red-eyed maintenance men who had obviously just come off shift. They wouldn't be too observant, and ranked lower than Welkin in his engineer's uniform. They were a safe source of information. If there was such a thing.

He was nearly at the group's table when he spotted someone he knew. The man—Rodin—was in the act of rising from a table around which sat a dozen fellow officers. In another second he would be standing and the moment he lifted his eyes he would see Welkin. So Welkin did the only thing he could think of. He sat down in the first available chair and stared down at his tray.

An attractive ensign in the next seat turned to him. "You look like you're hiding from someone."

Welkin nearly froze. Instead, he forced himself to smile. "Actually, I am," he said, covering his face with the flat of his hand. "Gambling debt. You know how it is."

The ensign looked perplexed for a moment. "No, I don't gamble."

"It's not much," Welkin said, looking around, seeking an excuse to move on. "I just hate confrontation."

"That accent," the ensign said, following Rodin's progress through the mess until he left the hall. Her frown deepened. "You've been spending too much time outside." When she gripped his arm Welkin almost jumped out of the seat. "I know!" she exclaimed, her eyes going wide. "You're with Special Operations. I bet I'm right."

Welkin smiled faintly. "Only you don't bet, right?" He carefully extricated his arm from her hand. "You know too much already, okay? I'm here undercover, so don't make a scene. Just keep your voice down."

The ensign clasped her hands and smiled hesitantly. A rumor had spread that the heavies were impersonating the lower ranks in an attempt to penetrate the Doves. Special Operations were almost as bad as the heavies. It didn't pay to mess with them. You could wind up as rebel bait for less.

"I'm not really ready to pay up my debt," Welkin continued with their previous conversation.

"I might have to report you," she said, forcing a wider smile to cover her rising panic.

Welkin saw that Rodin had gone. He expelled a sigh of relief.

"I see I'm not the only one who's worried," she said, misconstruing the sigh. She held out her hand—fingers spread—as was *Colony* formal protocol for shaking hands. "Fona. Hydroponics assistant."

He placed his palm against hers and they linked. "Athol. Field engineer."

"Ahhh." She clenched Welkin's hand a moment longer than was necessary and quickly released it when she realized her error. She didn't know whether to get up and leave or to stay seated. Either could offend the agent sitting next to her. How did she always get caught up in this sort of stuff?

Welkin felt pleasure at her confusion. She didn't know whether the conversation he was having with her was real or he was actually a Special Operations agent who was sticking to his fake identity. In any event she was backpedaling at a rate of knots.

"I wondered about the suntan," she said, sticking to the dialogue that she thought was expected of her. Disregarding all knowledge of his true identity, she added, "So you've been outside? Is it as hostile as they say?"

"I get out when I have to, you know?"

"So you're part of the extermination sweeps? Do they use engineers on those?"

He was startled by her candor. He'd forgotten how casually he himself had once spoken of exterminating Earthborn "scum."

"No. Actually . . ." He paused for dramatic effect and leaned closer. "I shouldn't be telling you this, but I'm part of a top-secret long-range expedition. The elders have been sending out Specials since just after we landed." He looked around quickly, as if checking for eavesdroppers. She leaned even closer and gazed at him in a conspiratorial fashion. "To tell you the truth, I've been out for the last eight months. I just got back five days ago, and I've been stuck in decontamination ever since."

She pulled back then, eyeing him with alarm. "You're . . . clean . . . aren't you?"

He managed a short laugh. "They scoped me and rayed me till I was inside out. I'm clean as a whistle. Most of that contamination guff is just propaganda anyway. Don't believe everything you hear."

"Oh, I don't. I try to stay objective. But tell me more." She pulled back in sudden alarm. "Only if it doesn't breach any rules."

"I'm busting with this stuff I've been through," he said, holding his hand over his mouth. "I desperately need to confide in someone." He thought for a moment while Fona's mouth gaped in open admiration. "I've got it. I'll tell you everything, but how about a trade?"

She looked at him quizzically. "A trade?"

"Yeah. I'm kind of out of date. Lots of things have changed around here since I was sent out. What's going on? The boffins down in decon wouldn't tell me a thing."

She suddenly reached over and brushed her fingers over his neural jack. She laughed at herself. "You know, for a moment I thought you were just stringing me a line about being Special Operations, but I guess you're for real. Okay. Deal."

She glanced around the room. "Why don't we go somewhere quieter? There're some booths at the back and we can get some juice."

As they left the table, Fona looked back at Welkin's full tray. "You're not hungry?"

"Just for news right now," he said. "After what I've been living on these past months, I don't think I could stomach good old *Colony* food."

"You poor thing," the hydroponics assistant said.

After selecting their drinks they retired to one of the secluded booths at the back. "Trade for trade, but I warn you," Fona said, "I want ground-level details! The real dirt."

"Your head will be *soiled,* I promise," Welkin said. "You first."

"Space! I hardly know where to begin. All right, the order to remove the neural jacks . . ." And she told him everything, or at least everything that a lowly hydroponics assistant would know, or might surmise, with a few intriguing nuggets of information thrown in that she had picked up from her friend, Holga, who worked as a clerk in Political Engineering.

"You know, Holga never told me anything about her department sending people Earthside."

"That's politics for you," Welkin said. "Keep everyone in the dark and pull as many swifties as possible."

Fona pouted. "A bit harsh, but true. And say, you have a real funny turn of phrase. You must have been in real deep Earthside."

"You're telling the story," Welkin reminded her.

Life on *Colony* had changed. The directive from above to have all neural jacks removed had come suddenly and, seemingly, without warning. Yet for a while afterward many pinpointed the "breakout" from the lower decks as the "inciting incident," claiming that the elders feared that some of the Skyborn sentenced to the lower decks might try to reinfiltrate *Colony*. If they did so, their neural jacks could help them paralyze the ship. With their customary overreaction, the elders ordered that all neural jacks—except those belonging to elders and selected personnel—should be removed "for the safety of the ship and its crew." Defending this extremely unpopular move, they quickly pointed out that infiltrators—even Earthborn scum!—could easily coerce an otherwise loyal member of the crew into using his or her neural link to cast *Colony* into chaos.

The surgical removals were hurriedly and sometimes inexpertly carried out. It was rumored that dozens of crew members died from infections that set in afterward and there were more grumblings from the crew, but these seemed to settle down. In reality they went underground.

The move by the elders had polarized the Skyborn, bringing to the surface long-held resentments and disagreements, suppressed till now.

Thus the Doves were formed. No one really knew who they were, since they kept their membership secret, but they wasted no time in issuing their own political statements, posting leaflets around the ship, sending out wholesale e-mails and virtuals over the intranet system, and even, on occasion, hacking into the elder-sanctioned holovid news.

Indeed, much of what Fona had to say was an unedited rendition of the latest Doves' propaganda. She even fished out one of their leaflets, complete with a moving image, a rotating *Colony* prior to its damage, still pristine. She slipped it to Welkin beneath the table. He shoved it in his pocket for a later, detailed viewing.

"I don't believe in any of that stuff they preach," she quickly informed Welkin. "I just think you people should be aware what's happening on board, that's all."

"Appreciated," Welkin said, squeezing Fona's hand. He waved her on.

According to the Doves, the elders were increasingly taking on a siege mentality, fearing that their centralized power base was being undermined; in consequence, life on *Colony* was becoming more regimented, more controlled from above; surveillance was on the increase; more Hawks—the opposing camp—were being recruited into the ranks of the heavies. Unpleasant "incidents" were escalating; rationing had been introduced on some items, all of which only served to intensify the social pressures within *Colony*. The latest Dove pamphlet noted that the consumption of alcohol, psychoactives, and virtual fantasies was up fivefold and—a little known or acknowledged fact aboard the ship—so were suicides.

Welkin asked what the Doves' agenda was. Fona set her jaw. "They want out, Athol. They want to make peace with the Earthborn." She shuddered, despite her obvious sympathy with the Doves. "And to start colonizing Earth and, you know, have a normal life. People are sick of being cooped up in here when there's a whole planet out there, just waiting for them. But they say the elders are scared. Scared they'll lose control over *Colony* and the rest of us."

"The planet Earth's history is riddled with dictators," Welkin said, urging her on. Just then he saw Harry loitering by the food dispensers. He was in for a shock if he ordered any.

Fona went on to tell Welkin more or less important news, but then she stalled, and a look of momentary horror crossed her face.

Welkin frowned. "You were saying?"

"You're not a Hawk, are you? I mean, what I've been saying, it's just what I've heard. I don't personally believe in any of that stuff."

Thinking fast, Welkin stood. A way out of telling her anything had suddenly presented itself. "It was good to meet a like-minded person, Fona," he said, staring into her eyes. "When the time comes, you'll be safe. I'll make sure of that."

He got up from the booth and moved away quickly. He knew she hadn't moved a muscle by the time he reached the corridor.

Welkin beckoned Harry and Ferrik and they strode purposefully toward the communications office.

They had been just as busy as Welkin. "We've set up a special comm.link that only we can access any time we want by jacking into the ship's system," Harry said. "Messages are automatically encrypted, then decrypted by our neural implants. I couldn't find out much of what's going on. There are stand-alone plasma computer nodes that seem to be used for Special Operations. All references to them are heavily encoded and booby-trapped. We only just narrowly avoided setting off a ship-wide alarm. Their AI firewall is hungry."

Harry's face was pale; even so, Welkin got the impression that infiltrating *Colony*'s network had been scarier than he was letting on. Ferrik quickly told Welkin how to access the special comm.link and the double-blind codes.

Welkin handed Harry the pamphlet issued by the Doves and proceded to fill them in on what he had found out. "Take the pamphlet back to Sarah. Tell her to set up a forward base inside the ventilation shaft up here. You need to find a way so she can hook into the comm.system from there and monitor any news, especially the general security channels. Can you do that?"

Harry looked thoughtful for a moment, then slowly nodded. "Yeah, shouldn't be a problem. Will take a little time. What are you two going to do?"

"Dig deeper. We'll report in at . . ." He glanced at his watch. "Twenty-two hundred. That gives us six hours."

"Eyes open." Harry hurried away.

Ferrik looked at Welkin. "Where to?"

"I think we need to have a long talk with an elder, or someone in authority. Somebody who won't be immediately missed."

Ferrik thought for a moment. "Anyone in particular? An officer perhaps?"

"Yeah. One who works higher up. The closer they are to Jamieson or Tobias, the better."

"You're reaching for the clouds now," Ferrik said. "But sure. I've got nothing to lose."

Welkin stopped Ferrik from moving off. "Just remember there's a whole new world called Earthside out there. Believe me, it's not worth losing."

"Maybe," Ferrik said.

They found a public turbolift and rode it to level eight. There were thirty-five levels, but to go any higher via the turbolift would be to invite suspicion. They moved up the next ten levels by the emergency stairways.

"I hardly knew these existed on *Colony*," Welkin said.

"The stairwells were mainly a precaution against a crash-landing on Tau Ceti III," Ferrik said, keeping pace with Welkin. He refused to hold the rail as he ascended the stairs, but it was clear to Welkin that Ferrik had never used the stairs, either. "Emergency drills up and down these things used to be carried out regularly."

"Obviously before our time," Welkin said.

The unusual mode of travel exacted a cost. They were puffing and sweating before they had gone halfway. Neither of them was unfit, but the odd gait forced them to use muscles they didn't know they had.

Then they ran into trouble. Ferrik was slightly in front, taking the next bend, when he suddenly ducked and fell backward right into Welkin. Welkin caught him, then realized Ferrik wasn't hurt; he had a finger to his lips and frantically gestured Welkin back down the steps. They retreated quickly down to the previous landing.

"What's up? Somebody coming?"

Ferrik shook his head. "Motion monitor," he said.

"Did it see you?"

"We got lucky. It was scoping the other way."

"What's a security camera doing here?" Welkin asked, puzzled.

"They've been going up all over the place lately," Ferrik told him. "No real pattern to their locations, but it's all part of whatever the elders are up to. For some reason, they're getting more paranoid. Maybe the Doves are hurting them more than they let on."

"How do we get around it?"

"We don't. But there's another stairwell in Sector G."

Welkin frowned. "That means crossing about five hundred yards of corridor, some of it pretty public if I remember."

Ferrik nodded. "It's your call."

Welkin thought for a moment, then motioned Ferrik to follow him. They went down two levels and Welkin stopped at a nondescript panel set in the wall. He removed a power screwdriver from his kit and unzipped the screws, removing the panel. Inside was a crude console, used by maintenance workers to monitor the condition of the local network. The controls, sensing his presence, reconfigured themselves.

"What good's that?" Ferrik asked.

"It's made a communication jack for me." He patched into the ship's comm.link and sought Harry's patch. To his surprise, Sarah came online.

"You guys got that working fast," he said.

Sarah's head and shoulders appeared in 3-D. She grinned. "We got lucky. Harry found a redundant communication conduit in the ventilation shaft one floor up. He tapped into it."

"It can't be traced?" asked Welkin.

"He says not immediately, unless someone's looking for it," said Sarah. "Apparently automatic virus checks have a twenty-four-hour cycle."

"If we're at the end of that cycle we could be compromised," Welkin said.

Sarah went off holo and came straight back. "Harry says he's patched in a rotating something or other. So long as we aren't active for more than three minutes we're safe. Where are you guys now?"

Welkin told her, then asked to speak to Harry. He appeared in holo and Welkin explained what he wanted. "I'll see what I can do," he said. They broke the link, aware of the three-minute communication limit.

Ferrik nodded in admiration. "So Harry turns it off and we sneak past. Simple and neat."

The comm.link reactivated and Harry came back on the screen. "Sorry, Welkin, no can do. Any modal change will be logged into the system and I figure we don't need that kind of attention."

Welkin thought hard. He really didn't want to risk the public corridors any more than he had to and the stairs would take them exactly where they needed to go. Then he had an idea. The board he was jacked into had sparked it.

"What happens if you run a routine maintenance diagnostic on the stairwell security system?"

There was a long pause, then a chuckle. "Well, for one thing, somebody will get a roasting," Harry said, "and for another, the detectors will shut down automatically for . . . let me see . . . Looks like about twelve seconds. Nice one, Welkin."

"Okay. Synchronize watches." They did so. "And commence diagnostic one minute from now. Mark that and counting."

"Good luck," said Harry. "Signing off." The holo dispersed. Welkin removed the jack and quickly replaced the panel. Then he and Ferrik got into position. Twelve seconds was more than enough time to get past the monitor and up to the next level. They hoped the elders weren't sufficiently paranoid to mount a second camera on the next landing.

Welkin counted down in a whisper. Finally he said, "Five-four-three-two-one-and zero-zero plus one-zero plus two and GO!" They scrambled around the bend and raced up the next set of stairs, their tired leg muscles protesting at the effort. They darted beneath the monitor, which was reassuringly still, and started up the next set. Welkin was still counting softly, "Zero plus eight—zero plus nine—zero plus ten—zero . . ."

They whipped around the next turn, out of the monitor's field of vision, and froze. Welkin did the last two counts silently, using his fingers to indicate to Ferrik. They waited a few more seconds, but nothing happened and they quietly continued up the stairwell.

Finally they reached level nineteen. From here they made their way to a distribution bay. It was a large space filled with cruisers, maintenance rigs, automated cranes and gantries, robot forklifts, launch platforms, and wheeled containers. It offered innumerable places to hide and to lie in ambush.

For the next hour or so they lay low, scoping out the new territory.

They saw several likely targets come and go, but each one was accompanied by assistants or heavies. It was almost as though *Colony* had been put on high alert.

"This doesn't feel right," Ferrik said after a while.

Welkin pictured the heavies who had just left the bay. "Maybe you're feeling uneasy about turning on *Colony?*"

"I'm not 'turning' on anyone," Ferrik snapped, then shook his head in apology.

"It's all right," Welkin said. "I went through the same thing when the Earthborn captured me. I tried to run every chance I got. If anyone but Sarah had found me I would've been carved up on the spot. She had a fight on her hands to stop her family from doing just that."

Ferrik looked at him. "And why did you side with them? It made you the most hated Skyborn in *Colony*'s history."

Welkin winced. His mouth suddenly felt dry. "I didn't know that."

"I figured not," Ferrik said. "On the other hand, being on the elders' Most Wanted list also made you something of a hero in certain groups."

"You're joking," Welkin said.

" 'Joking,' " Ferrik mused. "The Earthborn use that term a lot. I wonder if the rest of us lost our sense of humor somewhere out among the stars."

"I think we can put the blame for that at the elders' door," Welkin said. "They made a grim situation a whole lot grimmer. There were other choices." He didn't like to think of the way he and his sister were brought up on *Colony,* made to think that family and parents were wrong, even sinful. The elders had a lot to answer for. "So we're famous?"

"I've heard that certain radical groups study you and your sister," Ferrik said, keeping watch on the bay doors. "Elders do, too, of course. Trying to learn why Skyborn would turn into what they call 'degenerate traitors.' Sorry, no offence meant. But Sub-Elder Nathan once said there's a fifty-terabyte file on you and it was growing."

"Guess I should feel flattered."

"Yeah, somebody's even making a sim-movie of you."

For a second Welkin thought he was serious, then laughed at his own moment of vanity. "Oh, go soak your head," he said. Then, in a different tone: "I didn't have a choice, you know. I was found guilty of treason by the law of association. Harry had said things he shouldn't have, so I was arrested and sent out on a sham mission. Even if I'd escaped the ambush and made it back to *Colony* I would've been burnt down. Others were. *Colony* used us as guinea pigs. Actually, it was more like how miners in the old days used canaries in the mines to test for poisonous gas. It worked, but it used up a lot of canaries."

" 'Eliminate the worms and the core stays whole,' " Ferrik recited an elder dictum, then snorted in contempt. "Part of the heavies' charter is to keep the 'core' pure."

"That might've worked in space," Welkin said, "but there's no room for it here on Earth."

Ferrik shrugged. "I've seen documentary evidence the Earthborn are slaughtering one another across the planet. Seems to be their chief pastime."

"I mean the 'new' Earth," Welkin said. "The one we're building."

"You think you'll make it in your lifetime?" Ferrik asked.

"Who knows? Miracles happen," Welkin said. "Who would ever have thought I'd be trying to kidnap elders? And I'll bet you didn't think one day you'd be chatting to a degenerate traitor on board *Colony*."

"That's affirmative," Ferrik said. After a moment's pause, he sat up. "We could be waiting here an entire period before someone comes by. Let's go up a level, see if it's busier."

Welkin was staring at two aerial transport flyers in the process of being rebuilt. "The elders have been busy," he said.

Ferrik followed his gaze. "So?"

"I seem to remember," said Welkin, "that flying crews often forget to wipe the local plasma computer node when they disembark or finish a shift."

Ferrik agreed. "It's a serious offence, but it happens."

"Maybe we don't need someone after all."

"I'm with you," said Ferrik. They checked that the way was clear, then began to belly-crawl to the nearest flyer. They had to stop once when an elder and two maintenance officers passed close by. They overheard a snatch of conversation. One of the officials was blathering. "It's not my team's fault that we're behind schedule. If Supply did their job properly, my people wouldn't need to improvise and alter components. We'd meet the deadline." The official stopped. "Where are you taking us?"

The elder's eyes widened. "Are you questioning my authority?"

The official hurried forward. "Of course not, Elder, sir." He waved at the two flyers. "It's just that work is way behind and—"

They passed out of hearing. "Sounds like they're having major problems," Ferrik said. "It'll explain why nothing much is going on in here."

"They'll be having more problems if I have my way," Welkin confirmed.

They continued their slow, cautious crawl toward the nearest flyer. Shortly, they were lying beneath it. Welkin put his ear to the hull, more feeling for vibrations than listening for sounds. Finally he whispered, "I think she's empty. Come on."

They wriggled to the entrance, took a quick look around, then jumped to their feet and leapt into the hatch. Ferrik closed it behind them.

They both breathed out. Welkin turned to the piloting console. He jacked into the ship's comm.link and got Harry again. He quickly explained their plans, then signed off. He and Ferrik studied the on-board computer. "Sure could use Harry here," Welkin said. "Look, see what you can download. I might just play saboteur for a little while."

"Sure." Ferrik watched Welkin slither up into the other flyer before dropping into the comm. officer's chair and swinging the keypad into position. A 3-D holograph materialized above the holovid, a matrix of burnished red lines spreading into flight plans.

Welkin explored the second vessel from stem to stern, looking in particular for signs of retrofitting. He was hoping that the nature of the modifications might confirm or dispel his worst fears.

Although there had been substantial refitting within the flyer, none of it was conclusive proof that the elders planned some kind of genocide on the Earthborn. He quickly altered several reconfigurable matrix boards into garble and deleted flight programs. It wouldn't take an experienced molecular software engineer long to sort out the mess, but without explosives there wasn't much else he could do. Considering there was some kind of deadline, and apparently a shortage in Supply, perhaps he had in fact created more damage than he thought.

After he had inflicted similar damage to the flight control computer situated at the back of the bay, Welkin returned to Ferrik.

"Any luck?"

Ferrik looked up. "I've located a number of sub-systems embedded in the general listing 'Delivery Mechanism,' but I'm a little wary of hacking too much—a lot of gear has been rigged with explosive software firewalls. Literally explosive. Even the flyer engineers tread carefully around this stuff."

Welkin sighed. "Everything I've found is circumstantial."

"Guess we go back to Plan A."

"Looks like it," Welkin said glumly. He wasn't happy about the idea of kidnapping someone. No matter what they found out, they would, afterward, have to face the difficult task of neutralizing the captive. And any way you looked at it, that seemed like cold-blooded murder. But it would have to be done. They could not afford loose ends. Too much was at stake.

"Let's do it," he said. They cautiously opened the hatch and peered out. Checking that the way was clear, Ferrik stepped out, dropping out of sight immediately and squirming beneath the flyer.

Welkin tampered with the flyer's cockpit and joined Ferrik. There they waited for long seconds, listening for any hue and cry. But none came.

They retraced their steps and didn't breathe easy again until they had regained their original place of concealment.

And there they waited. It was nearly two hours before they spotted a lone harried-looking officer, clipdeck in hand, crossing the hangar floor. Even as they were trying to decide how to spring their trap, he walked into it. They suddenly stood up on either side of him and he blinked at them, puzzled rather than scared.

Mistaking them for the two maintenance officers recently seconded by the elder, he said, "Where were you hiding? No matter. I'll need to report it, though. Follow me."

Instead, they jumped him. Ferrik deftly wrapped his forearm around the officer's neck and squeezed.

"We want him alive," Welkin said as the man's eyes bulged.

The next moment Ferrik was dragging the unconscious man across the deck. "I've put him out for a moment," he said as Welkin picked up his legs and swung him behind a crate.

"You'll have to teach me that trick," Welkin said, looking dubiously at the unconscious officer. "You sure he's not dead?"

"Hold on a few seconds longer and they don't get back up," Ferrik said. "Give this one a minute or so."

True to Ferrik's word, the officer gained consciousness moments later. He glared around at them and opened his mouth to speak. Welkin pointed a laserlite pistol at his head. He closed his mouth.

"Good," said Welkin. "You learn fast. Now, we have some questions for you."

"And we have some for you," someone said behind them. They turned slowly to discover that they were surrounded by silent, grim-faced heavies wearing blood-red brassards on their sleeves. There were at least a dozen of them.

The leader stared at Welkin with undisguised contempt. "This one's mine," he said. Then pointing to Ferrik he added, "The other's yours."

"Been fraternizing with Earthborn scum, have you, Welkin?" The man leading the heavies was no other than the head of security, Harlan Gibbs. He brought his hand up, activating a security ring on his third finger and aiming a fine mist that shot out at Welkin and Ferrik. They lost consciousness.

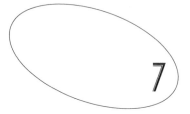

7

A fist smashed into Welkin's head, slamming it sideways. Blood arced from his mouth, spattering the wall. Welkin poked around in his mouth with his tongue. The sharp metallic tang of blood made him feel sick. There was no throbbing pain yet; adrenaline was clamping down on that.

"Clean off that mess," said Harlan Gibbs. A pale, nervous assistant sprang to obey, ordering a robot vac across the wall's surface. Welkin drooped in the chair, stalling for time and acting more dazed than he was. His bonds were expertly bound with clampfiber, but one of his hands was ever so slightly loose. He started working at it.

"Welcome back, Welkin," said Gibbs genially. "If you find yourself experiencing *déjà vu* any time about now, rest assured that you have good reason for it."

He grabbed Welkin by the hair and jerked his head backward. Welkin was forced to stare up into Gibbs's heavily lidded eyes. This close, his face looked drawn, almost skeletal, compared with how Welkin remembered it. Even his voice rasped.

"Where are your friends? How many of them are there?" Gibbs demanded.

"There are only two of us."

Gibbs backhanded him sharply. Welkin stifled a groan. "Negative," said Gibbs. "You will answer my questions truthfully."

Welkin noted the robes Gibbs was wearing. They were somewhat tatty and stained; they even looked slept in. Welkin had a suspicion that Gibbs was no longer in favor with the elders.

"I don't recognize your authority, nor does anyone else from what I hear."

Gibbs stood back as though he had been struck. He raised his hand to strike Welkin's face, then stopped himself with a visible effort. "Rebels of your ilk never do," he said. "At first."

Gibbs squeezed Welkin's jaw and jerked his head around. "So let's have a little chat, you and me. You've been off having adventures with those dirty diseased Earthborn scum. Probably breeding with them, too, right?" He winced in disgust. "But something brought you back here. Elders Jamieson and Tobias think your sudden reappearance means nothing. But I know otherwise. Things are coming to a head. *Colony* is divided. Jamieson's Final Solution approaches. And all of a sudden, you and your little deviate friends pop up. Coincidence? I think not. Harmless? No. When is a disease ever harmless? And be assured, Welkin, you and your kind are a disease, one that I will root out if it takes the rest of my life."

"But it's not going to take the rest of your life, is it, Gibbs?" Welkin said.

Spittle flecked Gibbs's lips and his eyes shone like glazed marbles. He stared at Welkin blankly.

"I mean, the Final Solution will take care of the Earthborn problem, right?" he continued. Gibbs didn't move a muscle. "Your delivery systems are nearly ready. You just need to solve the final prion problem."

Gibbs pulled back and fleeting alarm crossed his face. "You know nothing of this," he said, reclaiming his composure. "You can't."

"There you go again," said Welkin, "underestimating the 'enemy.'"

Gibbs started to pace. "It couldn't possibly do you any good, knowing," he said, more to himself than to Welkin. "The targeting mechanism is irreversible. Besides, what are you doing here, if you know so much?"

He stopped pacing and his hand lashed out, slapping Welkin hard across the face. It stung, but Welkin clenched his mouth shut, stifling the shock. He thought fleetingly of Ferrik and hoped he was holding out. At least Gibbs was talkative—there were worse moods he could be in.

"*Colony* is cracking up," Welkin said, as calmly as he could manage around a rapidly swelling mouth.

"So you have spies amongst us?" Gibbs said. "I've long thought so. Indeed, I've tried telling the elders, but they dismiss my fears as paranoia. But, I will tell you this, Welkin: They're scared. Not of you or the Earthborn maggots crawling around out there with you. They're scared of *Colony*. They sense that power is trickling through their fingers. They understand history. They know that it is nearly impossible to contain a situation such as this. They're an oligarchy now, and they want to stay that way—the fewer in charge the better. So drastic measures are called for. How to contain the 'contagion' within *Colony*? How to maintain their power? How to reunite the Skyborn under their rule and forever remove the temptation of the Outside?" He paused, licking his dry lips. "An awkward situation, don't you think? A puzzle with no apparent solution. But of course, there is one. Turn Earthside into a raging cauldron of sickness and despair. Then let some of the Doves venture out . . . let them come running back as their organs dissolve and their eyeballs bleed and their skin peels off. Let all inside see this and then all the problems they face will evaporate. Quite elegant, don't you think?"

"Quite mad was my first thought."

"Of course, my problem is a little different," said Gibbs pleasantly. "How do I make myself indispensable to the new reunification of *Colony*?"

"This ought to be good," said Welkin.

"Why, through you, of course. And the confession you're going to make. Let me see, I would imagine you have at least two dozen spies embedded within *Colony*. An entire network of terrorist cells, just waiting to be activated for the day when you and your heathen friends can kill the elders and take control of *Colony* yourself."

"You amaze me," said Welkin. "Nothing like scaring them where they scare most."

"Exactly. You know, Welkin, it's a pity we're on opposite sides. I could use someone like you. One who sees straight to the heart of the matter. A shame you've been contaminated. Idealism is such a difficult disease to eradicate." He paused, dragging over an instrument tray. The devices on it belonged more to a medieval torture chamber than to this brightly lit room. Welkin paled. "I think I shall have to get a little messy. Please accept my apologies in advance."

Welkin redoubled his efforts to loosen the clampfiber on his right hand. He could almost slide his hand out now. Just a little more . . .

There was a knock at the door. Gibbs grunted irritably. "Come." A man bowed in, handing Gibbs a message cube. He dismissed the man, placed a fingertip to the cube, and waited for it to check his skin DNA. He read the holo message that appeared, scowling. As he turned, Welkin threw a laser scalpel like a dart. Gibbs reacted but not fast enough. The scalpel seared a deep gouge across his cheek. He howled in shock and stumbled back.

"Restrain him," he yelled at his assistant. Welkin had freed his arm and seized another scalpel from the instrument tray. A neat flick of the scalpel severed the remaining clampfiber that bound him. The assistant rushed him. Welkin slashed him in the shoulder and kicked him in the groin. He shrieked and collided with the instrument trolley, which skittered across the room.

"Help!" yelled Gibbs. Just as Welkin jumped to his feet the door burst open and several heavies barged in, lasers leveled.

Welkin slowly lowered his hand. With three laserlites directed at him, he dropped the still-live scalpel. Gibbs, still clutching his blistered cheek, rushed for safety. He stopped at the door. "Take him and the other traitor to the generator room. Wait for me."

The heavies grabbed Welkin and dragged him from the room.

When Welkin saw Ferrik he regretted his rash attempt to escape. The Skyborn had received a more severe beating. One eye was nearly closed shut; he was covered in cuts and contusions, and winced every time he took a step. Nevertheless, when he saw Welkin he greeted him with a characteristic smile.

"We've got them on the run," he said.

Welkin smiled. "Yeah, they're really worried now."

"Shut up," snapped a heavy.

"Or what?" asked Welkin. "You'll kill us?"

For answer, the heavy jabbed him in the ribs. Excruciating pain shocked through him, but he did not cry out.

They were taken into a large chamber that was connected by a long access corridor to the ship's generators. No doubt their bodies would go into one of the plasma chutes, and some of their molecules would fuel the hyperfast plasma computers for an hour or two.

The heavies placed Welkin and Ferrik against a wall, and stood back. They held their laserlites across their chests as Gibbs came in, a blood-soaked permaheal covering his cheek.

Ferrik whistled softly. "You should never have been a Systec. You're a heavy through and through. Welkin, next time, though, cut his jugular, huh?"

"You got it, Ferrik."

Gibbs eyed them. "This is the last time I believe we shall meet," he grated. He signaled his lieutenant, who promptly ordered his men to shoulder their weapons and take aim.

"We'll be seeing you in hell, Gibbs," Welkin said.

"A quaint Earth expression," Gibbs said. "I prefer deep space."

The lieutenant looked to his superior for the final signal. Gibbs raised his hand, held it there for a dramatic moment, then brought it down hard. The heavy turned to give his men the order to fire.

The order had hardly left his lips when the chamber's two exits imploded, filling the air with smoke. Out of the smoke came a barrage of laserlite fire, raking through the ranks of the heavies, dropping them almost faster than they could return the fire. Gibbs took a pulse in one eye, which exploded with a pop. His face congealed like a fried egg and he collapsed.

Within moments the air was filled with the sharp reek of ozone. Welkin and Ferrik had dropped into a crouch as soon as the doors blew in. Now out of the smoke several men wearing infrared goggles surged across the deck to them.

"Come with us," one of them said. And, still trussed, they were hustled from the room.

Outside, they broke into a fast trot. Their rescuers ripped away their goggles, revealing a band of seasoned veterans who moved with the precision of a military unit. They met no one and eventually reached a cul-de-sac where Welkin and Ferrik were untied, then blindfolded.

What followed was a nightmare journey that was as painful as it was disorienting. Many times they stabbed themselves on jagged pieces of metal, stubbed their toes on obstacles, and banged their heads on unseen obstructions. *Colony* was no longer the smooth cocoon of Welkin's childhood.

Their rescuers—if that was what they were—apologized several times but did not slow the pace. They climbed up ladders, scrambled over debris, edged beneath what felt like collapsed ceilings, squirming along on their backs, before jumping to their feet again and running at a crouch through squat-high tunnels or corridors.

Eventually, completely out of breath and bleeding from dozens of tiny cuts and jabs, they came to a stop. The blindfolds were removed and the leader of the group handed them food and water.

"My name is Theo," he said. He was large, intense, and quietly spoken, with a thin, wispy beard. He had the kind of innate authority and grim determination that makes leaders, the kind that never have to raise their voice or repeat an order twice. Welkin was warily impressed. "We lost a man back there," Theo told him. "His name was Tenin. I hope rescuing you was worth it."

"I hope so, too," Welkin answered. "But for what it's worth, I'm sorry."

Theo acknowledged Welkin's words; then they were on the move again. The blindfolds were not used this time and Welkin and Ferrik made lighter work of the next stage of the journey, which wasn't, in any case, of great duration.

They reached an enclave via a service vent. "Brighter than a thousand suns," the rebel called enigmatically.

Someone acknowledged the password and Theo waved them through a grille before pulling it firmly into place behind them.

Welkin hesitated on the threshold. More than sixty people had taken up a militaristic residence. He had no idea where they were, but the place looked like a perfect hideout, easily defended, with a number of bolt-holes in case of trouble or overwhelming opposition.

Theo led them into a small room. Cups of juluval juice were passed around; then Theo directed them to take seats. He introduced them to his lieutenant, a barrel-chested, bearded giant named Hatch, whose hair and beard were a flaming red. "Like my temper," he said, then guffawed as if he'd made a grand joke.

"You know who I am?" Theo asked.

"I'd say you're the leader of the Doves," said Welkin. Theo nodded. "We've heard of you," Welkin went on. He turned a full three hundred and sixty degrees, not quite believing what he was seeing. He hadn't seen so many adults in one group for more than two years. Only his Earthside experiences saved him from intimidation. "Are there many cells like this?"

Theo shook his head. "Don't be fooled. There are still relatively few of us in active operation, but we have 'passive' members all across *Colony*, even amongst the Hawks themselves, which is how we found you. But before we go any further, why don't you tell me why you've come back? I hope it's not an acute case of homesickness."

Oddly enough, Welkin suspected that homesickness had been somewhere in the back of his mind when he first started planning this venture, but he kept that to himself. Otherwise, he told Theo everything. At the end, Theo nodded slowly. "We've heard rumors of a doomsday weapon to be used against the Earthborn. We're sympathetic, but the bottom line is, it's not our problem. Unless you can help us."

Welkin spread his hands. "We'll help any way we can, but I think you're wrong when you say it's not your problem. For one thing, most of the outside is controlled by the Earthborn. They're acclimatized to the dangers and diseases out there, whereas the Skyborn aren't."

"You think we want to go outside?" asked Theo.

"I think you need to, if you're going to have a future," said Welkin. "*Colony* is a closed system, not just in terms of energy and food supply, but also in terms of its ideas, its gene pool, and ultimately its very culture. Closed systems are inherently unstable, except in exceptional circumstances."

"We've done okay for three centuries, or perhaps the elders intend to generate an 'exceptional circumstance,'" Theo said.

"It still won't work, not in the long term. You need to leave *Colony*, and your chances of survival will be greatly enhanced by a pact with the Earthborn, especially if *Colony* continues to be a source of conflict."

Welkin suddenly smiled. "We have a large community. We're farming the land, setting up trade networks with local communities, and we've started redomesticating cattle, sheep, goats, and horses."

Theo leaned forward. "You have horses?" he said eagerly. A look of boyish wonder crossed his face. "I thought they'd be extinct by now. It's always been a dream of mine to see them . . . maybe even, you know, ride one."

"We ride them sometimes," Welkin said, stretching the truth. "But right now our priority is to survive. *Colony*'s presence isn't making it easy. And remember, wipe out the Earthborn, and you risk losing everything alongside them. Including the animals. *Colony*'s drench vats are malfunctioning, so its DNA zoo is useless. Right now *Colony* has two enemies. Her attention is divided and so is her ability to strike effectively. While she goes after us, you have a chance of hitting her from behind. Surely you, of all people, understand this."

Theo eased back. "Okay, you've got my attention. What else?"

"Any weapon that can be used selectively against the Earthborn can be used against your people. Gibbs said as much." One of Sarah's sayings came to him. "Your enemy's best move is your best move. If that's true, then any weapon that the elders set great store by should be of no less importance to you."

Theo suddenly grinned. "You play chess?" Welkin nodded. "King's knight to bishop three."

"Unorthodox player, huh?" said Welkin. "I like that."

"So let's do something unorthodox," said Theo, and held out his hand. Welkin took it and they maintained the grip for a long moment.

"Done," said Theo. He reached out and clasped Ferrik's hand as well.

"So what's on your mind?" asked Ferrik.

"Welkin contacts his people. This will need much planning. I'm not willing to commit a large force, but I believe our goal can be achieved with stealth and subterfuge. What you might call *infiltration*."

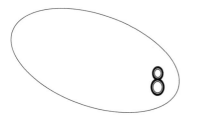

8

Theo wouldn't let anyone leave until things settled down within *Colony*. The slaying of Harlan Gibbs and the heavies had thrown the entire Skyborn population into turmoil. Squads of troopers had been withdrawn from Earthside duties and brought back on board to flush out the perpetrators of the atrocity. Welkin also assumed, and rightly as it turned out, that his sabotage of the two flyers had been detected.

The next day Theo sent a team of three people to escort Ferrik and Welkin back to where Sarah, Gillian, and Harry were hiding. They arrived back at the sanctuary two hours later, all dressed in stolen uniforms.

Sarah hugged Welkin. "We were worried for you. Alarms were screaming around the clock."

"I was worried about myself for a while there," Welkin said. "Hey, great uniform. I see you've been demoted, though."

Sarah looked at her epaulettes. "Oh, I don't know. Maintenance third class can't be too bad."

"Don't believe it," Welkin said. "They supervise the human waste chutes and the recyclers."

Sarah sniffed the uniform. "I thought it was a bit on the nose." She saw Ferrik smiling. "And I don't believe a word you're saying."

Welkin looked at Gillian and said, "Hiya."

He was expecting a similar greeting. She gave him a nod but otherwise seemed oddly distant.

Sarah saw the exchange. "So, apart from becoming a joker, what else has been happening?"

Welkin explained everything that had happened since he and Ferrik left Harry. Ferrik had discovered that his entire squad had been killed in the caver ambush, and as he was the sole survivor, now with the Earthborn, it had been decreed by the elders that he had led the squad into the ambush. He was now a "degenerate traitor" to his people. He tried to make light of it, but it was clear that it hurt him deeply. Harry's comment, "Join the club," did not help.

The next twenty-four hours were difficult for Welkin. Gillian barely said a word to him, perhaps as a result of their confrontation some days before. By contrast, there was an instant chemistry between Sarah and Theo, a meeting of equals . . . and more. They managed to find plenty of excuses to spend time in each other's company. And why not? Theo was the first man Sarah had met who was older than she. Welkin should have been happy for Sarah, but the ease with which the two acknowledged their attraction for each other threw Welkin's own relationship with Gillian into stark contrast.

That evening Harry found Welkin moping in a corner by himself, watching Gillian across the room as she chatted gaily to one of Theo's lieutenants.

Harry sat beside him, his eyes straying to the pair across the gloomy chamber. "Nice night for a bit of romance, huh?" he said, chewing on some food liberated from *Colony*'s mess.

"Is it night?" said Welkin. He looked around the sanctuary. "Why bother keeping track of time in this place?"

"Just talk to her," Harry said. "Tell her how you feel."

Welkin hung his head. "I can't."

"You can; you just don't want to. Or you're scared."

Welkin looked sideways at Harry. "You're right. I'm scared."

Harry nudged him. "Want my advice?"

"No."

"The way I see it—"

"*No.*"

"—is like this: Taking the short-term problem first, because the

long-term problem is way too difficult for the likes of me to comprehend, Gillian's all het up at you because you didn't confide in her
about your secret expedition. In fact, you confided in your old buddy
and pal, Harry . . ."

"You know that's not true," Welkin said indignantly. "You stumbled on my plans in your usual clumsy flat-footed way."

"As I was saying," Harry went on, "from her angle, you confided in
me, not *her,* which means you kind of left her out of the loop just when
you guys were getting closer, which translated means she should have
been the *first* person you included in the loop. So naturally she feels *ex-
cluded,* which makes her then feel unwanted and, worse, superfluous,
not to mention angry, since if something happened to you it would af-
fect her enormously. All of which you completely disregarded in your
usual ham-fisted and insensitive fashion. . . ."

"Are you finished?"

"I was just getting started."

"Okay, already. I get the picture." Welkin swallowed his annoyance. "So what do I do? And by the way, it's the long-term problem
I'm interested in."

Harry sighed. "Relationships aren't difficult, Welkin. We just
make them that way. *Talk* to her."

"Talk?"

"Yeah, you know, *communicate.* Trust me, it solves most problems.
She's over there chatting up that guy just to annoy you. She's probably
hating every syllable she utters. I bet she's churning up inside like you
wouldn't believe."

"She looks pretty happy to me," Welkin mumbled.

"That's just on the outside. In reality, she's probably telling him
off because he hasn't tied his shoelaces the Earthborn way. You should
have heard her earlier. She laid into one of the Doves because he
couldn't understand a word she was saying. One of their top guys
comes along then and brushes her off, saying the Earthborn have cor-
rupted the language so much it's easier to speak Japanese."

Welkin smiled at that. He remembered briefly how Sarah had
sounded to him at first. The Earthborn managed to clip their "ings"
and leave letters out of words for speed's sake. When they spoke fast,

their words ran into one another at such a rate it might as well have been a foreign language.

"What are you waiting for?" Harry persisted.

Welkin watched Gillian and the lieutenant glumly. "Maybe you're right. But I'll have to wait for the right moment."

Harry stood up. "Don't wait too long. There's never a 'right' moment."

"What does that mean?"

"Nothing," he said, and walked off, humming.

Welkin called after him, "I hate you sometimes, Harry."

"I know," Harry called back, unperturbed.

Theo's people—especially the red-bearded giant, Hatch, who had once been a heavy—had an inexhaustible energy that left Welkin drained. He had rarely seen such enthusiasm from Skyborn. Theo's planning proceeded almost non-stop. It seemed that his spies had reported some time ago that a secret weapon was being developed in guarded labs high up in restricted elder territory. But something had changed about a month ago. Some new intelligence had been received and the top-priority program had suddenly gone into high acceleration amidst a lot of fervid—almost *religious*—excitement among the elders. Theo didn't know why, but it worried him. He said as much to Welkin and Sarah.

Welkin was meditative. "Anything that makes the elders happy can't be good for us."

"Okay," said Sarah. "They're happy. We still have to see what's in those labs."

"Storming them isn't an option," said Hatch, tugging at his beard.

Theo nodded. "He's right. Each level has its own checkpoint where neural IDs are taken. It's a shame the elders had everyone's neural jacks removed. Obviously, they foresaw this kind of civil unrest." He stopped at the look on Sarah's face. "What?"

He then noticed that Welkin and Harry were grinning.

"Am I missing something?" Theo asked.

Welkin turned his head and lifted a fringe of hair to reveal his still-intact neural connection. Theo stared at it, then looked at Harry. "You too?" Harry nodded.

Theo sat back. "Well, well . . . they say the gods love the underdog. Seems to me the elders were a little premature when they ditched you guys overboard."

"And there are more of us out there than you know," Welkin said.

Theo snorted. "It certainly explains why they're searching for you two so aggressively."

"Here we are," Welkin said, beaming.

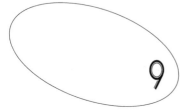

9

A three-dimensional schematic was suspended above a table, rotating as Theo pointed a lightrod. Everybody gazed at the holomap as he explained some modifications.

"Since touchdown the elders have instituted a program of rebuilding and restructuring. A lot of the internal topography of *Colony* has been altered. New bulkheads have been built, new passageways created, old ones cut off, sometimes even isolated. Space, the bottom levels are so mangled they can't repair themselves and we can hardly penetrate them. It boils down to simple paranoia. It's now much more difficult for any opposing force to move smoothly and quickly through *Colony* to any of the critical systems, such as navigation, engine room, and plasma computers. But they also unintentionally created a kind of maze in which there are now numerous 'overlooked' passages. Admittedly, some of them aren't much bigger than a rat's track, but . . . ."

He stopped, looking at Welkin and the others. "Is there a problem?" he asked.

Welkin flinched. "No problem. Just try to leave rats out of this, okay?"

Theo was amused. "Anything you say. The bottom line is this: We can penetrate to the heart of certain areas without arousing suspicion and effect fast getaways. One of those areas is the sub-elder dormitory on level sixteen."

"And why do we want to go there?" asked Welkin.

Theo's face was grave. "Let's just say it's a good place to make connections."

It was night, internal ship's time. The family accompanied a small squad of Doves under Theo's command. They were rigged for rapid travel and moved swiftly and silently along empty corridors. The overhead lights were out and Welkin noticed that the ceiling cameras did not swivel and track their passage.

"It's like a ghost ship," Welkin said, vaguely remembering vids of old Earth films like *The Marie Celeste* and *Ghosts of the Titanic*.

"We uploaded a computer worm into the surveillance system," Theo told him. "As far as the security system is concerned, these corridors are terminated. We're practically invisible."

"Practically?"

"Some areas are so hot they have double, sometimes triple, levels of surveillance. We haven't figured those out yet." He added, "Welkin, I know you were Systec Class, but forget most of what you know about *Colony*. You're way out of date and technology's moved on without you, okay?"

"You've done fine by us," Sarah said quickly for Welkin's benefit. "All you Skyborn have."

Theo stopped and looked back at Welkin and Harry. "You *have* done well. You've been a thorn in the side of the elders since the day you left *Colony*. But right now, the elders have stuff in their labs that we don't even know about. I'm just saying, be careful. They may have found stuff here on Earth that means their tech abilities are greater, even if their understanding's limited. And they have imagination."

"Understood," Welkin said.

Theo wired himself into a neural navigator. Its schematic gave their exact location and how to traverse *Colony*'s innards to reach their preferred destination. Theo had already told the system that he knew their destination could be reached in a much more efficient and desirable manner. He studied the image, then highlighted his preferred route in green neon.

They reached a crossroads. Theo went forward, checked the way was clear, then motioned the others to follow him. He darted across the intersection and the entire squad joined him as one. Welkin was impressed by their discipline. If he could acclimatize a squad like this to the outside they would make a formidable fighting force.

They came to a dead end. Old schematic technology did that sometimes if it wasn't updated. One of Theo's men deftly uncrypted a maintenance plate on the wall and told it to unseal. "These tubes network the entire ship. They have maximum security, but we've looped some of them," Theo explained.

One by one they clambered in. The casing was clamped shut from the inside and they moved out at a low crouch. The flooring underneath was metal grating that clanged softly with each padded footfall. The walls were lined with thermal-clad conduit and long-redundant power cables. Theo's headpiece illuminated the way.

Sarah tugged at Welkin's uniform. "You once said that *Colony* was like a giant living embryo. Everything worked on microtech and nanotechnology or something."

Welkin stepped over some conduit. "Your point?"

"This stuff, wires and everything," Sarah said, exasperated. "Even *we* had this technology when *Colony* left Earth."

Welkin almost laughed out loud. "*Colony* almost *lives*," he said. "It even repairs itself when damaged—computers, drives—*everything* is self-repairing. These wires are leftovers from the founding crew, who insisted that no matter what technological leaps 'Man' made, we should always have this archaic backup." He frowned in thought. "A bit like when computers were first popularized. People still clung to hardcopies in case of emergencies."

"But these pipes look new; they can't possibly be three hundred years old."

"*Colony* is a mixture of microelectromagnetic systems, exotic materials, and intelligent nanomaterials—materials powered by mechanical nanorod logic computing—and also of course our scattered quantum and plasma computing systems. For example, cleaner bots scour *Colony* looking for any sign of decay and automatically either fix it or alert Control that deterioration has been detected. If only we had more Skyborn, if we'd had millions of Skyborn, if our older population hadn't been decimated . . . we could have maintained it all, but we lost—a lot. Complexity's hard to maintain in a closed system, and cosmic rays did so much more damage than we thought possible. Deep space can be dangerous."

Sarah shook her head. "But still, it's amazing," she said. "What next, I wonder?"

"The Earth," Welkin replied. "But not if we can help it."

Now and then other tubes branched off to the left or right, and some even opened out at their feet, dropping down to tubes on lower levels, while others shot straight up to the next floor. Welkin realized that if Theo had had more techs at his disposal, the tubes would have given him near total access to the ship. Of course, if the elders didn't know that, they had to be stupid. And stupid they weren't.

Welkin was right behind Theo when he suddenly stopped and gave the hand signal for absolute silence. Welkin reflexively passed it on. The next second, everyone was frozen in mid-step, hardly daring to breathe. Then came the sound of voices, heart-stoppingly close.

Heavy footfalls pounded the permasteel decking, *clunk, clunk, clunk* . . . Welkin couldn't quite pinpoint where they were coming from, then with a lurch of his stomach realized they were directly underneath him. He had been about to step across a vertical shaft that dropped straight down for a dozen dizzying stories. Suddenly, on the level twenty feet below him, the head of a man appeared as he stepped across the shaft and disappeared. Then a second man came into view. He actually stopped with one foot across the shaft, gazing down. He gobbed a ball of saliva and watched it fall.

"Hey, Peterson, check this out."

The faint voice of the other man came back. "I got no time for games," he answered sourly. "Get a move on."

But the spitter did not move. If he so much as lifted his head a few inches he would see Welkin standing above him. Welkin's worst fears were realized. The man's head started to tilt back. Welkin stifled a gasp.

"I said, get a move on," snapped Peterson, his voice muffled with distance. The spitter scowled, stepped across the shaft, and was gone. Welkin slowly exhaled. Then Theo issued the signal to move on.

Half an hour later they reached a spot that looked no different from all the other spots they had passed. Welkin didn't have a clue how Theo knew where he was, but he seemed confident enough. More hand signals directed the squad members to various duties or positions. Theo took him and the others aside and spoke in tight whispers.

"We five are going to rappel down this next shaft and then exit the tubes. We will be at the rear of one of the dormitories used for sub-elder shift workers. The shifts are two days on and two days off. My men have been monitoring their rosters and we have selected two prime candidates. All being well, we will shortly have two hostages."

They followed him to the shaft and rappelled after him, then squeezed through one of the hatchways. As he had said, they were in a large dimly lit chamber in which they could hear two men snoring softly.

Theo bade the others to stay where they were, weapons at the ready. Then he moved forward toward two bunks. Other shadows, coming from different parts of the room, also converged on the sleeping figures.

A moment later there were the muffled sounds of a struggle, then sudden silence. Theo returned, and gave them the thumbs-up.

At that same moment a door behind them opened and a man stepped through, yawning. He sized up the situation instantly and turned to flee. But Welkin was faster. Experience living Earthside had honed his reflexes. He launched at the man in a dive and tackled him to the ground. Harry and Sarah were on him just as quickly, pinning him to the floor and stifling any attempt to cry for help.

Theo came up and quickly injected the man with a hypo gun that hissed as it pumped sedative into his arm. He slumped instantly. One of Theo's people bound him with ezyclips and Welkin slung him on his shoulder, fireman fashion.

Theo grinned. "You guys are fast," he said. "Glad I brought you along for the ride."

Moments later they were safely back inside the maintenance shafts. But "safely" turned out to be somewhat premature. Whether someone else had turned up to inquire for the missing men or some unseen camera had monitored events inside the sleeping chamber, an alarm had gone out. One of Theo's men, whose job it was to monitor *Colony*'s ship-wide comm.system, hurried forward shortly after they returned to the shafts. Welkin heard his urgent whispered exchange. "They're searching for us," he said. "And they've got a pretty good idea who and where we are."

"How long before they zero our position?" Theo asked.

The man shook his head. "Not less than five minutes, not more than ten, or else they're clumsier than I think they are."

"I'm not about to count on them making mistakes," said Theo. "Pass the word. Trinity. Move it." The man darted away and Welkin heard him hissing instructions.

"Trinity?" Welkin asked Theo as he came up to them.

"Means we split into three groups and take different routes home. Your lot's coming with me. Stay close."

"What about the prisoners?"

"They'll be taken care of," Theo said ominously.

With that he headed out at a fast dog trot. Welkin and the others fell in behind and did their best to keep up. It was clear Theo knew these disused corridors and shafts like the back of his hand. He led them for three or four hundred yards along a collapsed corridor, one wall leaning in at a drunken angle. The floor was covered in loose debris, which made rapid movement difficult and precarious.

Welkin was starting to think that Theo was making a grave tactical error. Everything he had done so far since reentering the shafts was pretty predictable. But maybe, Welkin thought shortly, that was the point. That was when Theo led them to the top of a vertical shaft in which ladder rungs disappeared down into shadows.

Here he halted for a brief moment, letting everyone catch their breath. "We're going to climb down so far we'll be completely beneath their search parameters. But I warn you, it isn't going to be easy."

With that he started down. It wasn't long before Welkin knew— with painful precision—exactly what Theo had meant by not being easy. Within just a few minutes his arms felt like they were being pulled out of their sockets and he could tell by the low moans and curses of the others that they were faring no better. The act of climbing, up or down, exercised muscles seldom put to much hard labor, and now they screamed in protest at the torment.

But there was no stopping. A hundred feet they climbed down, then two hundred, then three hundred. Welkin's fingers were numb and his arms and legs shook like Jell-O. A mist of pain filled his head and he tried not to think of anything beyond transferring his hand to the next rung down, letting a foot fall like a sodden lump to the lower rung. He would never have believed that the simple act of descending a ladder could be so grueling and so painful.

Suddenly, the man above him cried out, and fell. He crashed into Welkin and Welkin felt his own grip being torn from the rungs. The man fell past him and plummeted down the shaft. His scream cannoned up and down the confined space. Welkin frantically tried to keep his grip, but his numbed hands could barely make a fist, let alone hold on to anything. Then he felt an arm grab him around the waist and pull him back to the ladder. It was Theo.

Welkin clung on desperately, breathing hard. He didn't think he could go much farther. Theo must have realized this, for he called out softly. "We're nearly there," he said. "Twenty feet." To Welkin he said, "You okay?"

Welkin nodded. "Sure," he wheezed. "Keep going."

They continued on down and it was more like thirty feet, Welkin thought, but they finally came abreast of a horizontal shaft into which they gratefully climbed.

Welkin and the others collapsed, barely able to move. Theo squatted beside Welkin. "My men train at this," he said. "It's one of our standard escape tactics. Sorry I had to put you through that."

"The man who fell . . . who was he?"

"A recent recruit," Theo said, and a shadow passed across his face. "He never had a chance to practice for this kind of thing, either."

"I'm sorry," said Welkin, but Theo dismissed his apology with a wave. Welkin understood. This was war, and in war there were casualties.

"How long before you can move?" Theo asked.

Welkin gave a hoarse laugh. "How about a month?" he said. "Space, I don't think I could lift my hand even if my life depended on it."

"We'll hole up here for an hour, then move out. Everybody get some rest. We'll do the return journey in easy stages, staying wide of the elders' net."

"Suits me," said Welkin, closing his eyes.

Back in sanctuary, some four hours later, Theo administered an anti-sedative to each of the unconscious sub-elders, who had been brought to the sanctuary via other routes. Within moments the captives were wide-awake, and quite indignant that they had been kidnapped.

"You'll pay for this outrage," one of them said.

"But not before you pay for the atrocities that you have committed," Theo told him.

The man's eyes gleamed fanatically. "The elders know all that goes on within *Colony*." He struggled vainly against the binding around his wrists. It constricted even as he fought against it. "What do you want with us?"

Theo spoke up. "Your neural IDs and authorization codes."

The man slumped against the bulkhead and laughed. "They're useless to you, you fool."

One of the others snorted. "You've been in the lower decks for too long. You'd need neural jacks to use them."

"Welkin? Harry?" said Theo. They obliged by revealing their jacks to the three prisoners. The men fell silent; then the most senior of the three got an odd look of intense pain on his face before it went slack.

Theo frowned. "What's with him?"

Welkin's eyes went wide. "Ohmistars."

He grabbed the man's jaw, forced it open. A torrent of blood poured out along with his mangled tongue.

"Quick. Get a medkit!" yelled Welkin. Theo rushed away and re-turned two minutes later with the kit, but it was clear from Welkin's expression that it was too late. The man was dead.

The other two now had wads of clothing jammed in their mouths to stop them from imitating their superior.

Sarah shook her head, puzzled. "The injury wasn't life threatening. I don't understand."

Theo explained, "It isn't, by itself. But they've been conditioned to . . . self-destruct if you like. To trigger it they need to suffer some kind of intense self-inflicted pain or injury."

"Can we still retrieve his codes?" she asked.

Theo shook his head. "If we had the equipment set up, maybe. There's a window of about an hour, often a lot less. Depends on several variables, like ambient temperature, age, health. Lucky for us you nabbed these other fellows."

"Let's get on with it before we lose them as well," Welkin said.

Theo nodded agreement. "I would have liked to talk to them first, but you're right." He pulled out his hypo gun and sedated the prisoners.

Strapped to gurneys and tranquilized, the two remaining sub-elders slept peacefully, unaware of the equipment trays wheeling themselves up alongside them by command. Nearby, on two identical gurneys, lay Welkin and Harry.

A neurologist called Paschoff signaled the team of techs to hook the sub-elders up to the portable plasma computer cube he was operating at a nearby desk. A moment later he gazed at its projected holo-screen, moved his fingers against the icons floating in the air, and muttered, "Yes!"

The others crowded about him.

"We have neural synch," he said. "I'm penetrating their outer defenses, and here come the protection algorithms." He almost flinched. "Nasty critters," he said pensively. He studiously touched away at the virtual icons, making odd faces and muttering to himself. Then his face cleared. "Okay, I'm in. Their IDs and codes are naked to me. Duplicating them and downloading." He looked surprised that everyone was just standing around looking at him. "Hook up our dynamic duo. Do I have to hold your hands every bit of the way?"

The techs hooked into Welkin's and Harry's neural jacks. Both flinched although neither could feel the download.

A progress bar appeared on the holo field. "Transfer begun," said Paschoff, eyes fixed on the flowing holo data.

Welkin stared straight up at the ceiling. He was feeling odd. The ceiling started to ooze, changing shape and color.

"You fellows might experience upload leakage. Strange images, auditory feedback . . . all perfectly normal. If you start feeling seasick that's also okay," Paschoff said absently.

"Okay for you maybe," Harry muttered.

The upload seemed to take an eternity. Finally the computer cube tersely announced the job complete and Paschoff wiped perspiration from his forehead. "I'd like to welcome our two newest sub-elders to the ranks of Godhood."

Welkin tried to sit up but slumped back, dizzy and disoriented. Paschoff assisted him and he forced himself to sit up and stay up.

"This will help," Paschoff said, handing Welkin and Harry a juvo drink enriched with salts and electrolytes.

"You boys are in for some *fun*," Paschoff said with uncharacteristic flippancy. Welkin and Harry, now starting to experience sickening headaches, glared at the man.

"You're a sick man if you think this is fun," Harry groaned, holding his head.

After several hours of intense planning, Sarah, Gillian, and Ferrik returned to the lower decks with Theo to enlist the aid of the nether rebels in a possible raid into elder territory. Theo went along to help train and organize them and familiarize them with the new layout of the upper decks and the best way to penetrate them and move around. They would also need more sophisticated weapons. Their current arsenal was mostly cannibalized or at best gleaned from brief encounters with heavies.

Before they left, Welkin found himself alone for a moment with Gillian. He took the bit between his teeth and blurted out that they needed to talk.

Gillian eyed him. "So you got Harry's lecture, too?"

Welkin, tensed for any kind of response other than this, burst out laughing, then looked at her sheepishly. "Yeah."

"Somebody oughta do something about him."

"Laser-knitting his mouth shut might help."

"Nah, he'd just write loads of notes."

Welkin snorted. Why was it so easy to talk about Harry and not about themselves or their feelings?

"Look," he began haltingly, "things are going to get pretty hot around here, and"—Welkin could feel her breath on his face; a thrill of electricity shot through him—"and one of us might not come back."

"I know."

He swallowed. "I don't want to be friends."

He felt her sigh like a light breeze. "I know."

"I want . . . more than that." There, he'd said it. Unbelievable. He quickly looked down at his feet, unable to meet her eyes.

"Welkin . . ." He looked up, was shocked to see that her eyes were wet. She shook her head, as if angry at herself. "I don't feel that way about you; I don't—"

She hurried off.

"But—"

She was already gone.

Welkin and Harry, dressed in the uniforms and robes of sub-elders, waited until nightfall, when the ship's lighting was in downtime. The plan was that Theo and Hatch would escort them to the entrance of the first restricted levels of elder territory.

"There's just one stumbling block," Theo said.

Harry groaned. "Don't tell me," he said. "We have to grab Elder Jamieson himself."

"Not quite."

"That's a relief," Harry said. "That man turns me to mush just by looking at me."

"He's mortal like the rest of us," Theo said seriously. "No, I'm referring to the levels immediately below the restricted level. They've recently been upgraded and turned into a kind of buffer zone. No one gets in or out without being heavily scrutinized. Facial recognition programs. Verification of documents. DNA skin samples, blood pulse, mitochondrial DNA cross-checking. The works. Standard stuff but actually more difficult for us to penetrate."

Harry frowned. "Let me get this straight. We've actually solved the harder problem of gaining access to the restricted levels, but we can't get to them because they've using *easier* security methods?"

"Unusual, sure. They've got guys in the buffer zone who know everyone by sight. That's their job. And if they don't know you, you're dead. That's kind of hard to get around without some pretty fancy programmable masks. Not that you two couldn't use a little cosmetic help, but we don't have the materials in our inventory."

With a huge effort, Welkin pushed his personal pain aside and concentrated on what Theo was saying. "You didn't bring us this far for nothing. You've got a plan."

"I've always got a plan," Theo said. "It's just that some are more humanly possible and nicer than others."

"My head hurts already," said Harry. "Fire away."

"I kind of thought I'd surprise you."

"Fine. Lead on. I love surprises."

"I don't," said Welkin.

They moved through disused companionways and utilized several access shafts and crawl spaces to reach a point near the outer hull of the skyship. The circuitous route helped them avoid detection, but Welkin was confused. He didn't have the greatest sense of direction, but it seemed to him they had swung wide of most of the points that gave any kind of access to the upper and lower levels. Indeed, the spot Theo had taken them to was a sort of dead end. If they were caught here, they would be trapped.

"The next two stages are going to be difficult and dangerous," Theo said to Welkin and Harry. Hatch nodded in agreement. "Whatever you do, don't make any noise."

Hatch fished around in the backpack he carried and brought out a small electronic device trailing wires. He attached this to a circular "plug" in the bulkhead wall, which, Welkin noted, actually had a slight curvature. He realized that this wall was part of the inner hull. The plug, which might have been an odd kind of hatch, had no handles or any means of operation. Hatch produced some putty and stuck the bare ends of the wires against the plug's surface, forming a triangle. He then worked the device, frowning as various figures appeared on a small digital screen. The device emitted soft harmonic sounds.

Whatever Hatch was doing, it was not quick work. It was forty minutes later before he suddenly muttered, "Yes!" under his breath and the plug screwed itself deeper into the wall, then swung away, revealing a narrow vertical space sandwiched between the inner bulkhead hull and what must be the exterior hull of *Colony*.

Hatch had already detached his device. At Welkin's and Harry's inquisitive looks, he said, "These are special hatches. Command doesn't want just anybody opening them. Too dangerous, especially in space. So they made 'em so they work on harmonics. Each hatch responds to a specific set of musical notes, and they keep changin' 'em, to confuse people. It's just a matter of running all the possible combinations, and gettin' lucky. We got lucky."

"That's why we call him 'Hatch,'" said Theo.

"Are we going in there?" Harry asked dubiously, eyeing the dark, claustrophobic space.

"Oh, it gets better; trust me," said Theo. He bent over and squirmed into the hatchway, then pulled himself through. His voice came softly to them. "Whatever you do, don't step on any of the sensors."

"Sensors?" Harry squeaked. "What sensors? What does a sensor look like?"

Hatch winked at Theo. "You'll know 'em when you see 'em. In you go now," he said cheerfully.

Feeling cornered, Harry reluctantly climbed through the hatch and into the great curved "gap" between the inner and outer hulls of *Colony*. Beneath his feet there was nothing but dark space that he imagined curved out and down to the ship's "equator," then in again.

When Welkin was also inside, Hatch replaced the "plug," reassuring them that the harmonic code would not be changed anytime in the next forty-eight hours.

But Harry wasn't listening. He said, somewhat nervously, "What happens if we slip?" They were standing on thick I-beams that both held the two hulls apart and secured them. They were spaced at ten-foot intervals and although it wasn't easy they could be used for climbing and "walking." The gaps between them, however, were still dark and frightening.

Theo pointed. "If you're lucky, you'll come up against one of these beams. If not, it's a *loooooong* way to the bottom. And this isn't the hard part yet."

"It isn't?" Harry's voice was thin.

"Uh-uh."

Theo moved them out. He led the way, followed by Harry, then Welkin, while Hatch brought up the rear. Despite his bulk and his appearance of awkwardness, Hatch proved to be as nimble as a sanitation minibot. By comparison, Welkin and Harry felt like clod-footed junior cadets.

They traveled like this for more than an hour, always moving at an incline, gaining height as they moved. The hardest part was at the start. They each wore a headlamp that glowed softly, but its main function wasn't so much to illuminate the way as to reveal the presence of sensors. The "sensors" turned out to be infrared laser beams, invisible to the naked eye, but some component of the light from the lamps exposed the beams. Then it was a matter of going up or over or even squeezing beneath them. The network of beams would allow small objects to pass through, since the engineers who designed them didn't want the alarms going off every time a rat took a sightseeing tour.

That was one problem. In the beginning, however, just reaching for a new handhold, then forcing oneself to take that daunting, hesitant step across what *felt* like a bottomless pit, was nerve-racking enough, but it got worse long before it got better.

Within ten minutes they were drenched in sweat. Harry was starting to wonder why he had volunteered for this mission, then remembered that he hadn't. He had had the "luck," if you could call it that, of still having a neural jack. The thought of having it removed, which had unnerved him earlier, now seemed attractive.

For an hour they moved steadily and stealthily between the hulls, then suddenly came to an abrupt dead end. Directly above their heads was a solid "ceiling" of permasteel that joined the two hulls. Theo said it formed an unbroken ring that circled the entire ship and that there were six of these rings, all parallel to the ship's equator, and set at intervals from one another.

"So how do we get through it?" Welkin asked.

"We don't."

"But we're still not high enough, are we?"

"Not yet," said Theo.

"And the answer to this riddle is...?"

Theo said nothing and Welkin became aware that Hatch was at work once more with his harmonic device. But this time he was doing something at the outer hull.

Welkin stared. "You're not serious, are you?"

"Wait and see," Theo said. Welkin edged closer, peering over Hatch's shoulder. He had already connected the device to a small electronic lock on the extraordinarily thick hatch of what must be an airlock. The airlock was the thickness of the space between the hulls but looked as if it protruded farther in both directions.

Within a couple of minutes there was a hissing noise as pressures equalized and Hatch unscrewed a manual wheel lock in the center of the hatch, then pushed his hand through a protective membrane and yanked the whole thing open. As his hand pulled out, the membrane re-formed. Inside, there was a space barely large enough for two of them and certainly only big enough for one person wearing a space suit.

"Welkin, we'll go first," said Theo, and the two of them squeezed into the space. Theo operated the controls inside and the outer door popped open, letting in a shaft of bright moonlight. Immediately outside the exterior door was a narrow metal catwalk with no guardrail. Welkin glanced down and wished he hadn't. It was several hundred feet to the earth below. Theo motioned him aside and shut the door. Moments later Hatch and Harry appeared. Harry's eyes went wide at the drop that greeted him, but he said nothing. His shoulder wound had been itching, and when he took a look at it, it was festering. He only hoped he could hold out till someone looked at it.

"You dampen the telltale?" Theo asked Hatch, who nodded.

"Nothin' will show up on their boards."

"Good. Now listen," he said to Welkin and Harry. "You need to lean close to the ship. Move slowly. Watch where you put your foot. A hundred yards from here we have to climb to the next catwalk. The angle of the hull here makes it easy. Your biggest danger is that a gust of wind will blow you off. Okay, let's go. Oh, just in case, if you do fall, don't scream on the way down, huh?"

He started off. Harry said to Welkin in low tones, "Considerate guy."

Welkin knew exactly how Harry felt. He felt far more exposed now than he had inside the skin of the hull. Here he could *see* the danger. Space, he could feel it. One false step and he would go sliding down on the hull till he got to the equator, whereupon he would shoot out into space. *Next stop, mother Earth.*

They soon reached the point where they had to move up to the next catwalk. The ladder "rungs" were recessed into the hull and using them was more like climbing a hillside than using a ladder. And it was fairly easy. At least there was something to grab hold of, Welkin thought, and that was a big improvement over the narrow, dizzying catwalk.

They made it to the next catwalk and moved along this for about two hundred feet. The only difficulty was when they encountered a lit porthole and had to inch past it on their bellies. It meant that they had to look down rather more than either Welkin or Harry wanted to. But once past that, the rest was clear sailing.

Theo took them to another airlock and this time they went straight through to the passageway, rather than going via the inter-hull space. They were past the buffer zone and not far from the elders' restricted area.

As they took a brief breather, Harry asked Theo about the climb they had just made. "I thought you said that was the really hard part?"

"You didn't think so?"

"Not really," said Harry. "To tell you the truth, crawling between the hulls spooked me a whole lot more."

"I don't like heights." Theo's voice was unsteady.

"Me neither," said Hatch.

Five minutes later they were inside a maintenance shaft, peering out through a grille. A pile of crates was stacked in front of the aperture, but by straining they could just see around the edge to the entrance of the first level of restricted territory, where two heavies slumped, half asleep, in a pretense of guard mount.

"That doesn't seem right," said Hatch.

"Explain," said Theo.

Having been trained as a heavy, Hatch could not comprehend that two of his own elite brethren would be so negligent. Seeing them slouching in their chairs made his skin crawl. He gestured at them, as though his answer was self-explanatory.

"You might be right," Theo said. "And then again, the obvious effectiveness of the buffer zone may be responsible. What do you two think? It's your necks."

Welkin and Harry discussed it briefly but decided that they had come this far and that no one knew of any other way to get the information they needed. They said brief goodbyes to Theo and Hatch, who neutralized the grille matrix. They squirmed out on their bellies, keeping the pile of crates between themselves and the resting guards. A few moments later, after straightening their uniforms, they strode openly toward the checkpoint, employing the ancient ruse of boldness with a dash of arrogance thrown in.

The guards snapped to full alert when Welkin's outraged voice bawled them out. "What's the meaning of this?"

They fumbled for their weapons, and jumped to blinking attention, eyes straight to front.

"You call this security? Is this what the elders expect from you? Answer me."

"It won't happen again, Sub-Elder," one of them said tightly.

Despite their initial reaction to his sudden appearance, Welkin's confidence slipped. These were elite heavies, selected to protect some of *Colony*'s top-ranking personnel. He pushed on nonetheless. "You're right about that," he said, and stepped close to the man so that their noses were only inches apart. "How would you like to be transferred to an Earthside patrol? I hear the fatality rate is exceedingly high."

The man swallowed but said nothing.

"Leave them be this time," Harry said, bored. "Elder Jamieson is waiting for us."

Welkin continued to stare at the heavy. He worked his mouth as though chewing on thought itself. Finally he stepped back, straightened his robe. "Consider yourself on report. One more infraction like this and . . . let me just say there are worse things than being sent outside. Much worse."

Heart hammering, he turned on his heel and strode over to the security lock and jacked in as if he did the same tired thing every day. Next to him, Harry did the same. Both held their breath. This was the critical moment. In less than a second they would know if Paschoff had done his job correctly or not. If he hadn't, Welkin was sure the heavy he had just verbally abused would find it immensely gratifying to jump him.

When the lock said "authorized" Welkin almost collapsed with relief. He turned the slump into a peremptory gesture of irritation. "Space! Why do these things take so long?"

The airlock door irised open and they stepped inside. As the air cycled through, they realized the pressure was dropping slightly. It was a good sign, though a scary one. Biohazard labs always had negative air pressure so that if a leak occurred air rushed *in,* stopping any bacterial or viral agents from rushing *out.*

Beyond the airlock was what appeared to be a changing room. As they stepped into it two plastic-wrapped packages slid down a tube. Inside were white coveralls. Shrugging, Welkin and Harry put them on. The garments fitted themselves to size.

"I feel as though I've finally earned my official uniform," Harry said smugly. Wearing fresh adjustable clothing every day was something he could easily get used to.

"Don't get too comfortable," Welkin said, as though reading his mind.

"That's right," Harry jibed. "Go and spoil one of my few pleasures."

Moments later they were moving down a central passageway, their feet clanging softly on the metal grilled deck. The passageway was dimly lit, yet on either side, behind transparent diamondoid panels, row after row of laboratory alcoves contained benches, above which moved bright, almost garish, spotlights.

Numerous technicians and scientists, all clad in protective coveralls, sat at benches or tables, their eyes glued to photon tunneling microscopes, or hologram screens giving readouts from particle distribution analyzers.

Three large, cumbersome devices filled one lab almost entirely. It made Welkin swell with anger. All this technology bent on destruction, rather than building a better Earth.

Harry nudged Welkin. "G-MMSD. Genetic Manipulation through Miniature Synchrotron Device."

Welkin nodded. "Some biological lab." As if to underscore this point, they next passed a larger alcove containing dozens of *Colony's* cloned rhesus monkeys. The walls here were clearly soundproofed, as no noise from the primates penetrated beyond the glass wall.

As they watched, scientists drew blood from several monkeys while a technician stamped a biopsy gun into the thigh of a monkey strapped to a bench top. The monkey's mouth opened wide in indignation, as it strained against its bonds.

"I don't like this," said Welkin.

"So where to from here?" Harry asked in a whisper.

"Up," said Welkin. He instinctively knew that the most closely guarded secret of all would be on the topmost level, the one most difficult to reach. The only problem was that entry to each new level was blocked by yet another checkpoint and security lock. Presumably, at some point, their neural IDs and codes would no longer authorize them to ascend.

"And then we'll have some explaining to do," said Harry.

Each time they reached a checkpoint and jacked in they began to sweat and exchange nervous glances. At any second they expected warning klaxons to blare and to hear the heavy tromp of approaching heavies.

But nothing untoward happened.

On level twenty-eight they saw two Earthborn women, shackled in chains, being dragged into a laboratory. The prisoners screamed and pleaded, but the heavies treated them no better than they did the monkeys. Welkin clenched his fists in impotent rage. The stakes of their mission were too high to jeopardize.

As they approached the final checkpoint, both Welkin and Harry had serious misgivings. It seemed highly unlikely that just anybody could gain entry to the final level. If anything was going to go wrong, then this was it.

And they were right.

The pair was only a few yards from the checkpoint, which, like the others inside the restricted area, was not manned by heavies, when the airlock door irised open and a man stepped out. He glanced casually at Welkin and went to go past, then did a double take. He opened his mouth to yell, but Welkin's reflexes were fast. His hand chopped out, catching the man in the larynx. The man gurgled deep in his throat and dropped to his knees, gasping for breath.

Welkin and Harry quickly assured themselves that no one had seen anything, then grabbed the man and dragged him into a nearby storage cavity.

Still clutching his throat but breathing a little easier now, the man stared around at his captors. "How are you, Zubin?" Welkin asked.

Zubin's jaw tightened. "Sorry about the jab," Welkin added, "but I figured you were about to seriously inconvenience us."

"Nice running into an old classmate," Harry said, smiling.

"What's happened to you?" Zubin gasped. Both were thought to be rebels, and their now-unguarded accents were almost unintelligible to him. His abhorrence was obvious.

"More to the point, what has happened to *you*?" Harry asked.

Zubin recovered quickly from his initial shock. "You've got a nerve coming back here," he said hoarsely. "They'll kill you; you know that, don't you?"

"If I were you, I'd be more worried about my own skin," Harry told him.

Zubin clearly hadn't been thinking along those lines. Being a sub-elder with good prospects of making elder-hood soon tended to breed a kind of conceit that one was untouchable. Besides, if this pair had intended to kill him, they would have done so by now.

"What are you doing here?" he asked with feigned deference.

Welkin suddenly realized that Zubin might prove quite useful. Even his natural arrogance could possibly be turned to their advantage.

"We're going upstairs," Welkin said.

Zubin sneered. "Not a chance," he said. "You must have stolen neural IDs and authorization codes to get this far, but they won't work on the executive level."

"And why's that?"

"Because it's very unlikely that you have the proper codes to gain access and because unless you've stolen an eyeball or two—" He stopped, realizing his mistake.

"Retinal scanners," Welkin said.

"Afraid so," said Zubin, recovering. "For living eyeballs, and the rest of the body, too. But I tell you what, Welkin, just for old times' sake, let me go and I'll give you fifteen minutes' head start. You can't ask fairer than that."

Welkin reacted in surprise. "You'd let us go?"

"I am a valuable asset to the elders," he said, assuming an air of superiority. "My loss or incapacitation would set back the program by several weeks, possibly even longer."

"You must be a Big Guy up there," Harry hedged.

"There are few molecular biochemists of my skill," Zubin granted.

"No doubt," Welkin said. "Get on your feet."

"What are you doing?"

"What are *we* doing?" Welkin amended. "You're going to conduct us safely upstairs."

"Upstairs?" Zubin said, confused at the colloquialism. Then, "I will do no such thing. Besides, I don't have authorization." His face blanched. "They'll fry the three of us."

Welkin clasped Zubin's head to either side of his eyes, and dug his thumbs into the man's temples. He gazed levelly at Zubin. "Nice try, you little weasel. We'll take your eyeball with us, and test it ourselves." He shifted his thumbs to Zubin's eyes.

Zubin struggled, but Harry pushed him up against the wall. "Wait!" Zubin squealed.

"Changed your mind already?" asked Harry.

Zubin seemed to be trying to get himself under control. "You can take my eyes and chop off my thumb—though you need them with blood pulse—but you can't imitate my voice."

Welkin gave Harry a querying look. Harry said, "We can drag you back to the lower decks. I'm sure they've got a voice simulator down there."

Zubin sagged. "All right, I'll come. But you've just signed all our death warrants."

"We'll see about that," Welkin said. "Do as you're told and make no false moves and we'll live through this. Otherwise . . ." Welkin left it hanging.

"This will ruin me," Zubin said, slumping lower. "All the good work I've done. A life's work—gone because of you."

"It's not so bad Earthside," Harry said. "We could use someone with your skills. Now keep quiet."

"I'd never—"

Harry shoved the man forward. "Stow it. The people out there are each worth ten of you."

Welkin checked that the coast was clear and they stepped out into the corridor and approached the checkpoint. "Now do your bit," Welkin said.

Zubin input his authorization codes and ID. "This won't work," he said, pulling back.

"Stage one authorized," said the checkpoint.

Welkin rammed Zubin's head against the mask of the retina scanner. "Open your eyes or you never will again."

Harry looked uneasy for a moment. He surreptitiously pointed to Zubin's tongue.

Welkin took his meaning. One chomp on his tongue and he'd be dead just like the sub-elder. But he didn't think Zubin had it in him to kill himself. Not when there was a chance of escaping his inferior captors.

He was right.

Zubin opened his eyes and pressed his face to the "mask" of the retinal scanner. He placed his splayed hand across the palm imprint pad.

"Say whatever you have to," Welkin said.

Zubin coughed, trying to clear his throat. "Nightingale flock," he said hoarsely.

Considering the state-of-the-art technology, the computerized security system took its time verifying Zubin's second-stage authorization. Welkin wondered for a frightening second whether the system took into account perspiration from accessing personnel, facial flushing, or even whether there was a deck pressure analyzer underfoot. Could it even sense Zubin's fear through a surreptitious neural scan?

Tense moments passed; then the airlock dilated and the three men stepped through. Presently they were within the changing room. Here bio-isolation suits hung from the ceiling in individual rigs.

"You have to put these on," Zubin said. Quickly, the three climbed into suits, then Zubin, flanked on either side, stepped into the elders' most restricted area.

Initially, there seemed little to tell it apart from the three levels immediately below, but there were differences, some more subtle than others. Obviously, everybody was wearing a formfitting bio-isolation suit for one. This proved a godsend, as it effectively concealed Welkin's and Harry's identity from the casual scrutiny of those they passed and especially any more intimate acquaintances.

The more subtle signs were harder to quantify, but Welkin decided that there was a charged feeling up here in the inner sanctum, as if the personnel knew they were engaged in life-or-death activities. There were also more heavies around, patrolling the corridors, shepherding lab monkeys and Earthborn, and generally lending the entire floor a feeling that the elders were ever vigilant.

A gruesome experiment was under way in one chamber. An Earthborn and a heavy were squatting inside a hermetically sealed chamber. Suddenly, the Earthborn started to bleed from the eyes, ears, and nose. Moments later he vomited and his bowels discharged. He screamed and started writhing on the floor. The heavy backed away, clinically aghast, but otherwise unconcerned with his proximity to his screaming prisoner.

"What's going on in there?" Welkin asked, almost absorbed. Zubin didn't answer.

Appalled by the sight, they retreated from the view field. Welkin had placed a knife in an external pocket. He pulled it out, flicked open the blade, and pressed it against Zubin's bio-isolation suit.

"Talk," Welkin rasped.

Zubin licked his lips nervously but shook his head. "Go ahead," he said. "I'm immune, just like you saw. All Skyborn are." He might have laughed then, but for the set of Welkin's mouth, and his glaring eyes. "But you two aren't inoculated, are you?"

Welkin stared at him. "This is an interesting complex you've got here, Zubin. My guess is that it houses a number of nasty little viruses. Ebola, Lassa, Marburg, hantavirus . . . Am I right?"

Zubin clenched his mouth shut.

"I suppose you're immune to all of them?" Welkin asked pleasantly. "Okay. Then you have nothing to lose."

He flexed his arm as if to stab through Zubin's suit.

"Wait. I'll tell you," Zubin said quickly.

"Make it quick," Harry said close to Zubin's ear. Two techs walked by and Harry laughed, pointing at the view deck where the now-dead Earthborn was being hefted onto a trolley for an autopsy. The technicians followed his finger, mumbled something, and kept walking.

"Go on," Welkin urged. "And remember, you're the first to go if we get found out. So help my stars, you'll be the first to die."

Zubin gently guided the knifepoint from his abdomen. "We've . . . found a way to . . . to cleanse the planet of Earthborn."

"How?"

"You saw it. The elders have taken an ancient Earth virus, Marburg, and modified it to kill Earthborn only. The elders discovered that the Earthborn have several genes no longer possessed by the Skyborn, as a side effect of some of the Skyborn's genetic modifications preventing disease and local Earthside mutations. We've managed to alter the mechanism by which Marburg locks onto a target cell. This is a protein which we no longer produce but which those extra Earthborn genes do. All Skyborn bar a few unfortunate throwbacks are immune. The delivery device is a reconstructed RNA messenger gene—RNA copies from DNA in cells, to make the proteins from the DNA 'blueprints'—spliced together with what's called a prion. It's an adaptable cellular mechanism gone out of control and capable of spreading catastrophe in the body."

"Space, *why?*" asked Harry.

"Why do you think? It eradicates the Earthborn *en masse* but leaves the land and other biological entities untouched."

Welkin shook his head, thinking this through. "That's just part of it," he decided. "Their other agenda is to keep all Skyborn locked up inside *Colony* where they can maintain complete control."

"They wouldn't do that," Zubin scoffed. "And how could they? There's already enough dissension within the ship."

"You've just seen how," Welkin told him. "A few holovids full of people dying like that fellow back there and *nobody* will want to leave this place."

"You have no idea what you're saying," Zubin said. "Your mind's been poisoned by the Earthborn. There are at least forty of us sub-elders who know the truth. How would they—?"

He stopped, staring at them.

"That's right," Welkin asked. "You're all expendable."

"That's Earthborn propaganda," Zubin said. But his words sounded hollow. "They wouldn't terminate us. We're the next generation of elders."

Exasperated, Harry grabbed Zubin by the arm. "*They* themselves are the next generation, Zubin. And maybe the next one after that. You think they want a pack of upstarts taking over control? You're space crazy if you think that's going to happen. When did one of them last die? Can you tell me that?"

Welkin said, "As soon as this work is completed the entire sub-elder stratum will be terminated. Maybe they'll infect you with Ebola or something, then put you on the holovids for the edification of the rest of the Skyborn. The elders are never wasteful."

Zubin hovered between belief and disbelief. Then something occurred to him. "That's a pack of lies," he said.

"Don't believe it," Harry said.

"You're wrong," Zubin said more firmly. "Circumstances have changed. We're not alone anymore. Besides, you're right; the elders aren't wasteful. No one's indispensable, but I've saved them years by identifying the original Earthborn genes."

"Proud, are you?" Welkin said. "Proud of what you did to that helpless Earthborn back there?"

Zubin's mouth set. "That 'helpless' Earthborn probably died a lot quicker than the rest of you will," he said.

"Why, you—" Harry clutched Zubin by the throat.

Welkin pulled his hand away. "Explain, Zubin."

Zubin gained his composure. "Because the day after tomorrow is D-day. And I don't have to tell you what 'D' stands for."

"The day after tomorrow," Welkin said numbly. It was a moment of introspection that cost him dearly.

Zubin slammed his forehead into Welkin's nose.

Welkin's head snapped back and he rocketed into the wall and slid down.

"Welkin!" Harry screamed. He swung a punch, but too late. Zubin weaved past Harry's left hook and counter-punched him. Harry staggered back into a defensive crouch, but vital seconds had passed.

Before either Welkin or Harry fully realized what had happened, Zubin was halfway down the corridor calling for help.

Harry pulled Welkin to his feet. "Forget those airlocks," he snapped. "There'll be a ship-wide lockdown in place already." He dragged Welkin with him back along the corridor. "We've got to get out of here *fast*."

Guided by Harry, Welkin jogged behind him. His nose was a searing concentration of blood and pain.

10

Welkin and Harry raced into an airlock, ordered the bio-isolation suits to loosen apart in distress mode, and cycled through. They made the next airlock, one level down, without interruption. Here also they managed to cycle through without being intercepted.

"Where is everyone?" Welkin mumbled.

"If I lay my hands on that weasel . . ." Harry said.

"We got too complacent," Welkin said, having finally stemmed the flow of blood. "Stars, that hurts."

Harry gave Welkin's nose a cursory glance. "Your nose is on the other side of your face. It hurts *me* just looking at it."

Welkin glowered at Harry. "How'd Zubin manage to trick us like that?"

"That's what elders are made of, remember," Harry said. "Cunning and deceit. They're corporate top dogs riding on the backs of lesser mortals."

"And he's only just learning," Welkin grated. Then he clicked his fingers. "Got it!"

"What?"

Welkin took a deep breath. "It helps if I breathe through my mouth."

"Oh."

"Not that," Welkin said. "They're afraid of what we might do up here, afraid we might unleash some unpleasant little viruses."

"Then we should stay?" Harry said, halting.

Welkin wasn't so sure. "They could easily pipe the virus through here, trapping us," he said. "Why else has everyone cleared out?"

They encountered no one as they went back down to the lower levels. It seemed as though a silent evacuation signal had been sent to all the personnel.

"We've got to hurry," Welkin said.

But Harry slowed down. "Wait a minute," he said. "They could easily close the airlocks on us, but they haven't. They've left them wide open."

They had reached the last of the restricted levels now. Welkin exhaled noisily. None of this made sense, but he was in no mood to decipher it.

"I hear voices," Harry said. He swung into what appeared to be a rec room. While Harry guarded the door Welkin inspected the room for other means of escape. "One way in and one way out," he said after a quick inspection.

"There's a comm.system," Harry said, indicating it.

Welkin went over it and jacked in. Typing in the link that Harry had installed earlier, he felt a surge of relief when Sarah answered.

"Well, you two sure stirred up the hornet's nest," she said. Then her face lost its animation. "You're hurt."

"Never mind," Welkin said. "What's been happening?"

"The elders have established martial law and a strict curfew. No one's allowed out in the main corridors. Theo's managed to jam their automatic shutdown, but only some levels are responding. Heavies are stationed at all main access areas. It's like they're expecting a mass revolt."

"Don't tell me," Welkin said. "They're saying that 'armed and dangerous rebels have infiltrated *Colony*. Don't be alarmed; the situation is well in hand.'"

"Pretty much so," Sarah said. "Your *face,* Welkin?"

Theo's voice suddenly came on the line. "Welkin? You there?"

"I'm not going anywhere at the moment," Welkin said. His nose was throbbing now that the adrenaline had stopped rushing.

"I've got your position on holo. Are you in immediate danger?"

Welkin looked over at Harry. His face was drawn. "What can I tell you? It's not an ideal picnic spot," he replied.

"Can you hold out a while longer?"

"We have a pistol between us. Maybe we can keep them out of the cabin for a bit."

"My Doves can't make a move without being identified and I'm not sure numbers are what count right now. We're closer than you think. When you hear a commotion, head for the airlock at the end of the corridor. Can you do that?"

"It's heavily guarded," said Welkin. "Pun intended."

"We'll take care of the heavies. Good luck."

"You too, Theo." Welkin unjacked from the comm.link. He quickly explained to Harry the plan, or lack of it.

"Any second they're about to make a systematic sweep," Harry said. "And this is about the third cabin they'll hit." He scanned the room for surveillance chips. "And to make matters worse, they'd just have to know we're in here."

"The very fact they haven't moved from that airlock must mean something," Welkin said.

"But what?" Harry stepped back inside the cabin and closed the door. He pointed his laser pistol at the control panel and looked at Welkin for confirmation.

"I wouldn't lock us in yet."

"Just say when," Harry said.

Theo, Gillian, and Hatch hurried down a long corridor. They were heavily armed, and the former heavy carried small cluster grenades in bandoliers over his shoulders.

Theo believed that a small three-person rescue attempt stood a greater chance of success than a full frontal assault. He had wanted to take his own people only, but Gillian had insisted on going along. It was, after all, Welkin trapped in there.

They made good time to the point where Welkin and Harry had separated from their own escort. From here they could see that the checkpoint had been reinforced with more heavies and that others were in the act of wheeling a miniature gravity wave amplification cannon.

It was a truly drastic piece of ordnance to use inside the ship. The gravity waves were so large as to be almost undetectable, but the cannon caught onto a part of their string structure and flung them back and forth until they were strong enough to be released and wreak havoc, emitting a beam of deadly crumpling effects.

"Space," said Theo. "The elders must seriously be spooked."

"Best we not give them time to set that critter up," said Hatch. Theo agreed.

"Ready?" Theo asked them. The other two nodded. "Okay, Hatch, I want smoke and noise and lots of bodies." He readied his night amplifying visor. "Let's make it fast."

Hatch smiled grimly. He deliberately focused on what he was doing. He had few friends within the heavy ranks, familiarity being something that was not encouraged among the elders' elite soldiery. Still, Hatch did not want to know whom he was about to kill. Selecting specific grenades, he locked them into a cluster rig, and popped the rig into a launcher and took aim. There was a soft *whoosh* and the cluster of grenades sailed right into the midst of the heavies.

A heavy screamed a warning, but the voice disappeared beneath a mushrooming sound that shook the air.

Dense smoke filled the corridor and several heavies lit up like pyres; others were coughing, almost blinded. Theo goggled down and the others followed suit.

"Too easy," Theo said worriedly, but they were committed now. "Move it," he shouted. They rushed forward. The heavies, represented as green masses through the shields, fell to the rebels' firepower. Theo deftly attached an explosive to the airlock and set the timer for eight seconds.

The three scurried back through the billowing smoke. Alarms were sounding shrilly. The airlock exploded spectacularly. Due to the negative air pressure most of the blast was drawn inward, decimating the packed ranks of heavies on the other side.

Even as Theo, Gillian, and Hatch moved closer, they could see laserlite fire on the other side. "Careful," Theo said. "Our boys might be coming through."

Shields down, they moved through the smoke. In the confusion heavies came at them blindly, easy targets. Attacked on two fronts, some fired blindly into their own ranks. The command to cease fire came too late, even for the speaker.

"Welkin? Harry? *Come on!*" yelled Theo.

Welkin and Harry were within twenty feet of the airlock but running blind with hands touching the walls for guidance through the smoke. Welkin shoved Harry forward, covering for him as best he could. Harry stumbled over several bodies and crawled the rest of the way to their rescuers.

Welkin was about to dash for the lock when Theo's team came under sudden attack from their flank.

"Space," Harry swore, ducking. A large band of heavies in riot gear and vision shields charged up the wide passage to their left. Others ran at them from the passage to their right.

"Welkin. It's an ambush!" Harry coughed; then his eyes went wide. A sniper was crouching and was taking a careful aim at Theo.

Harry yelled a warning and shoved Theo aside, taking the laserlite pulse full in the shoulder. He fell and didn't get up. Gillian stared numbly, then looked up at Welkin, who was still trapped inside the lock. Their eyes met for a moment.

Laserlite fire punctured the gloom like tracers, some ricocheting along the smooth walls like skipping fireflies.

"Theo, get them out of here!" Welkin shouted over the noise. He shot Gillian one lingering look, then turned and ran back the way he had come, disappearing into the haze of drifting smoke and making Theo's choice simpler.

"Pull back," Theo ordered.

"No," said Gillian. "We can't just leave him."

"Pull back now, soldier."

Gillian gritted her teeth and grabbed Harry's arms along with Theo and stumbled back to cover, firing one-handed as they retreated. Hatch unloaded a dozen cluster grenades right into the midst of both advancing bands of heavies. They had turned a bend in the corridor when the corridor blossomed orange and black.

Slowed by having to drag Harry's body along behind them, they finally reached a maintenance tube in the rear wall. Hatch booby-trapped the door with the reminder of his cluster grenades. Sweating, he followed the others into the tube, which he clipped shut before hurrying to catch up with the others.

A while later they all came to a panting stop in a small junction. Gillian checked Harry for life signs. She hung her head, refusing to believe he was dead.

"I'm sorry about your friend," Theo said. "He saved my life and I won't forget that. Ever."

Gillian looked up. There were tears in her eyes. "He believed in this," she said quietly.

"This?"

Gillian nodded. "He believed that if Earthborn and Skyborn were to survive they had to do it together."

Theo laid a hand on her arm. "That's a fine thing to die for," he said. Gillian nodded again and covered her face with her hands.

"Say," whispered a hoarse voice, "who's the funeral for?"

Gillian whirled. Harry was staring fixedly at her. His skin was pasty and he was clearly in pain, but he was alive. She wanted to thump him but settled for hugging him instead. He winced. "Ugh, that hurts."

She looked scornfully at the neat hole in his shoulder. "Don't be a baby."

Harry gently eased her away and peered at the hole. "What do you know? They cauterized my arrow wound."

Welkin found an unlikely hiding place in what at first seemed a miniature zoo. It was full of cages and pens crammed with animals, no doubt destined for biological testing. Heavies had already swept the vicinity twice, but each time the animals set up such a ruckus that the heavies were sufficiently distracted. But his luck could not possibly hold out. He knew that this level was a hermetically sealed unit, completely cut off from the rest of *Colony*. There were no maintenance tubes or ventilation shafts that crossed over, no turbolifts or stairways. There wasn't even an external porthole.

Welkin had just finished wiping congealed blood from his face when a livestock tech came in. Welkin barely managed to slip behind a utensil-laden trolley before the man did a circuit of the room. He looked around suspiciously, as though he shouldn't be there, or perhaps he had been warned that a rebel was on the loose. He was wearing the ubiquitous coveralls as well as a visored cap, which marked him as one of lower and more menial status. He was about Welkin's size, too.

Welkin stayed hidden until the tech came within range; then he struck. Or tried to. The tech sensed his presence and instinctively sprang back as Welkin came at him. Too late Welkin realized that this was no ordinary livestock tech.

The man launched forward with a jab kick. But for Welkin's and Sarah's unarmed combat training, the man's foot would have seriously disabled him. Instead, Welkin swept the foot to one side and flattened himself against the deck for a leg sweep. He snapped his straightened leg around and swept the man's foot from under him.

Welkin wasn't sure what happened next. The man fell, but seemed to be back on his feet in an instant. The man's foot lashed out in a crescent kick, striking Welkin's forehead. He screamed out as more pain flooded his head. Clutching desperately at the legs of the trolley, he pulled with all his might and swung it in front of him.

The trolley jarred as the man ran full into it. The castors thumped back into Welkin's shins and he yelped. He rolled away from the trolley, expecting instant retaliation, but none came. Opening his eyes against the blinding pain, he realized his adversary was comatose on the deck.

Welkin hobbled over to the man and rolled him onto his back. His head lolled. "Broken neck?" Welkin shook his head in disbelief. He kicked the body, expecting the man to leap back into life. When he didn't, Welkin riffled through the man's belongings and recovered a micro laser. Not a weapon that a lowly livestock tech would carry. Then the man's holo ID tag completed the puzzle. Jordie Ryan was a senior heavy attached to undercover surveillance. The most hated of the heavies, for they were elite spies. An excellent choice for impersonation, since he would be virtually unknown, as part of his ongoing cover. Welkin took the ID and got to work.

Moments later he had on Ryan's coveralls and peaked cap. He dragged the body to a waste disposal chute and piled a stack of uniforms over it. With luck it would buy him enough time to think things through. Despite the pain in his leg and his head injuries, he pulled his shoulders back and stepped brazenly into the main passageway. Then an image of the submissive livestock tech, à la Jordie Ryan, struck him. This current persona did nothing brazenly. Quickly he fell into a more submissive posture: He hunched his shoulders, studied the floor, and shuffled along as if he expected to be kicked at any moment. The visored cap hid his face quite effectively. The charade had obviously worked for Jordie Ryan.

Welkin passed several groups of heavies who consistently either ignored him or brusquely ordered him aside. He would flatten himself against the wall as they jogged past, keeping his eyes down, his whole manner servile. Luckily, other crew members also studiously ignored him. He was now a member of the invisible underclass.

I'm getting good at this, Welkin thought, and then rebuked himself sharply: *Remember what landed you in this mess in the first place. Don't get cocky.*

He shuffled up the passageway, veered into a cross corridor, and found what he was looking for: a small, empty lab with a comm. panel. Quickly he stepped inside and made sure he was alone. He would have to jack in. It was a big risk, but he needed Intel, and fast.

Theo and Gillian bandaged Harry's wound and gave him a sedative. He winced but wasn't in as much pain as before. That done, Gillian straightened up.

"You're lucky the wound's cauterized. But we still have to get you to Sarah," she said.

"You're going back for Welkin, then?" Theo asked. Gillian nodded. "You'll need my help," he said.

Theo led Gillian and Hatch and Harry by a short route to a ventilation shaft that gave access to a large dark chamber above. They scrambled up a buckled ladder and squeezed through an opening.

Hands reached out and helped Harry through. Gillian was startled to find Sarah waiting there. Theo quickly filled Sarah in on what had happened. Gillian said nothing, but Sarah could tell by her sister's expressionless face that she was worried about Welkin.

She forced a smile. "We'll get him back," she said. Gillian nodded, not trusting herself to speak.

Welkin grumbled. There was so much traffic on the line that he was having a hard time getting through. Worse, there was some kind of jamming going on. The comm.system refused to link to the secret frequency. He tried switching to another band, inputting the frequency again. Almost instantly Sarah's voice came online.

"Welkin. Thank God you're okay. Where are you?"

"Level fifteen," he said. "I'm still mobile."

"Okay. We've got to get you out of there," she said.

"The others made it back all right?" Welkin asked.

"They winged Harry," she said. "But it seems he's as chirpy as ever, dammit."

Welkin closed his eyes in relief. "That's Harry all right, as thick-skinned as they come." In the background, muffled, he could hear Harry protest the slur on his character.

"How's Gillian?"

"She's fine. She sends her love."

"Really?" Pain like a fist surged back, gripping his chest.

"You hold on, Welkin."

"I don't want anybody else taking chances for me," said Welkin.

"We're not leaving you there."

"I'll figure something out," he said.

Theo took over then. "Welkin, this isn't about you. We can't let you fall into the elders' hands. You know too much." He looked away from the holovid for a moment. Sarah said something about lights, and Theo nodded.

"Stay handy, okay?" Theo said.

Welkin understood that to mean he should be somewhere close to the bulkhead. "What are you going to do?"

"Give them nightmares," Sarah said off holo.

The holovid flat-lined. He stared at the now-dormant holo stage, wondering what she meant. Several minutes passed and he grew edgier. He couldn't just wait here. He had to do something. But what? As though in answer the lights flickered, then died. Almost immediately he heard terrified screams, and soon a low keening started up.

Welkin whistled softly. Sarah was smart. If there was one thing that could blow the fuses of almost every Skyborn it was complete and utter darkness . . . the darkness of space . . . of death . . .

Then, in the distance, there was a muffled explosion followed by the pounding of many feet. Welkin felt a moment of elation before something crashed into the back of his head. He spun lazily around and saw a triumphant Zubin standing over him. Then he sank into his own darkness.

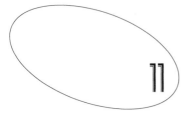

11

Gillian came awake suddenly. She had dozed off and now stared up into her sister's face. "We're ready," Sarah told her.

Gillian frowned, disoriented from the quick nap. "Who's ready?"

"We are," came a voice from the gloom. Ferrik stepped into the light and suddenly Gillian realized there were dozens of people crowding up behind him, all waiting patiently in the darkness, all lower deckers, Clifford's people. Gaunt, pale, but *ready*. She gazed at them in amazement.

"When did they—?"

A comm.panel beeped. Sarah addressed the holovid but without the visuals. "Where are you?" she asked. Exchanging a few short sentences with the speaker, she turned to the others.

Ferrik shook his head. "Is that a good idea?" he asked. "The entrance will be crawling with heavies. And what did you mean when you said 'nightmares'?"

Sarah smiled. "Just this." She reached over and pressed a pad on the comm.panel. Nothing seemed to happen at first, but then myriad lights across the rest of *Colony* shut down.

Sarah's powerpak lit up. "Come on," she said. The door irised out and they charged into the gloom.

A huge explosion rocked the deck. The handful of heavies that had managed to overcome their instinctive fear of the darkness and find lights were knocked off their feet. Smoke and whizzing shrapnel filled the air as a stampede of bodies poured through the non-existent airlock.

The lower deckers, wielding makeshift weapons and a long-nursed hatred of the "softies" from the upper decks, went on a rampage, dealing with any *Colony* opposition they could find. Sarah and her team searched for Welkin. They found nearly a dozen Earthborn imprisoned in cells, freed them, and sent them back down the ranks to a place of safety.

Sarah had to stop Clifford's people from blowing the upper level, where the deadliest biohazard strains were kept. She and Hatch and Ferrik—heavily armed—donned bio-isolation suits and used a captured officer to access the security lock and retinal scanner. They entered the upper level carrying a heavy sack.

Ten minutes later they were back. Sarah was carrying several CRCs (compact replay cubes). She zipped them into her jacket. Gillian was beside herself. They still hadn't found Welkin.

"What are those for?" she asked, referring to the CRCs. Talking seemed to take her mind off other matters.

"A gift," Sarah said cryptically. "Too late for Con, but not the others. So no one else has to die."

Gillian's eyes went wide. "You think they found a cure for the progeria?"

"No, but I think they might have laid the groundwork for one without meaning to."

They located a command console in Elder Tobias's office. Gillian—almost frantic with worry—left with Theo to conduct her own search for Welkin. Meanwhile, Ferrik hacked into several programs showing a schematic of the next level. He gave Hatch a nod and pulled out a transceiver and spoke a coded word.

Instantly, a dozen charges went off on the upper level, flaring with a magnesium brightness and exploding in an inferno of flame.

"What on Earth—?" exclaimed Sarah.

"Incendiary bombs," Hatch explained. "The entire level will be incinerated."

Sarah pulled back from the holovid. The picture looked so real she could almost feel the searing heat. "What if something gets out?"

"No way. These little babies consume all the available oxygen and suck in everything. Besides that, they produce a heat in excess of fifteen hundred degrees centigrade. Not even a microbe will live through it."

"Won't it damage the lab?" asked Sarah.

"No," said Ferrik. "All biohazard labs are designed to self-incinerate their contents if the need arises. We would have used their own emergency system, but it was too complicated."

Sarah turned her attention back to the holovid. The inferno continued. Metal tables and computers melted and nothing escaped the maelstrom. She turned away when trapped research personnel became human torches. Ferrik quickly cut the audio.

Welkin was having a dream. Something wet and squishy was pressed against his face. He couldn't work out what it was.

He opened his eyes to see Sarah and Theo. Gillian, teary-eyed, was dabbing a wet cloth at his face.

She made a tiny sound in her throat when she saw he was awake and threw her arms around him. "It's okay," he said, pressing his face into her hair. "I'm here. I'm back . . ." He couldn't believe this was happening; maybe she was delirious.

Gillian suddenly straightened and slapped him across the scalp, the only part of his body not injured.

Welkin smarted and stared at her in surprise. "Ouch." Gillian was smiling and still blinking back tears, which was confusing.

"Does this mean we're not friends anymore?" he asked cautiously.

"Can't friends slobber over friends?" said Gillian. He shrugged, which hurt, and decided this was a big improvement, whatever it meant—or didn't.

Then Sarah grinned and thumped him on the arm. It seemed everyone wanted to pummel him.

"You're lucky to be here," said Theo. "We were scrounging for medical supplies and stumbled across you in some room, out for the count. Someone was standing over you. I hope it was the guy who attacked you. He was armed. I didn't have a choice."

"Zubin," Welkin said thickly. He automatically touched his nose and discovered someone had reset it with permaheal.

"He's no longer with us, whoever he was."

Welkin looked at him quizzically.

"Well, I figured I had to shoot one of you and bring the other back here for questioning."

Welkin nodded slowly. "Tough choice."

"You're lucky I'm such a lousy shot. Popped the wrong one and, well, here you are."

Gillian spat into a cloth and dabbed around Welkin's nose. "You were all busted up," she said.

"Thanks. I'm glad somebody cares," Welkin mumbled, giving Gillian a look. She went on cleaning him up, giving nothing away. Maybe she *was* just being a good friend. He sighed. It was all too confusing.

Sarah brought him up-to-date. All the computer records and the stores of the virus itself had been utterly destroyed. Welkin smiled, wincing at the pain in his nose. He would give anything to see Jamieson's and Tobias's faces right about now.

"So even if they attempt to duplicate the program," said Theo, "it will take them a long time. It's even possible that we may have destroyed the original Marburg samples from which they engineered the killer virus."

All this was good news, in fact great news, yet Sarah's and Theo's faces weren't smiling. In fact, they seemed quite grim by the time they concluded their report.

"What is it?" he asked, feeling his sense of triumph draining away. He almost felt angry that his friends should deny him this moment. After all, he had started this crusade, if that's what it was. He'd found the top-secret program and helped destroy it. The Earthborn were safe again. Why couldn't they just enjoy it?

"You're holding out on me," he said finally.

Sarah looked at Theo, who dropped the charade and dug into his pocket. He held up a CRC. It was the size of dice. He slid it into a holovid. "One of my undercover Hawks, Hetti, just delivered this. Now we know why the elders got so excited a month back."

A field of stars appeared above the holo stage. Off to one side, Saturn—in all its ringed glory—floated in blackness.

"What am I supposed to be looking at?" Welkin asked.

Theo said, "Mag. 200." The hologram expanded and bled over the stage perimeter.

Now Welkin saw it. A bright metallic dot moving slowly against the background of stars.

At first he felt a rush of excitement; then the full implications hit. "It's another *Colony,* isn't it?" he said dully.

Sarah looked grave. "More trouble, returned from the stars . . ."

Theo said, very quietly, "Best estimate, it'll be here in three days."

The next few hours were spent discussing what they should do. Ferrik had told them about the satellite transmitter he'd found in a Lagrange orbit some weeks earlier and hazarded the guess that the skyship might be responding to that. Problem was, that would mean the newcomers had FTL drive and maybe much else.

"That's not possible," said Theo.

Welkin disagreed. "Who knows what they found out there? More advanced races, super technology . . . For all we know, we're the Neanderthals of the Galaxy."

"You're definitely a Neanderthal," said Harry. "Me, I'm from way classier stock."

After several people had thrown things at Harry, Welkin announced his plan, which involved him staying on board *Colony.* Theo vehemently opposed this as being suicidal. Clifford was ambivalent. He had faced death so many times that he seemed resigned to it.

He simply waited for Sarah and Gillian to comment.

Predictably, the two tried to dissuade Welkin at first but, knowing how obstinate he could be, soon realized they were wasting their time. Still, they voiced no objection when he left the meeting as he had done back at the farm, when this adventure began. They then set about Theo and Clifford. Sarah and her sister could be very persuasive.

Welkin returned to the large communal chamber where Harry was recuperating. Ferrik was in charge of mustering both Theo's and Clifford's people. The oddest thing about the gathering, Welkin mused, was that it contained both lower *and* upper deckers. And they weren't trying to kill each other. He voiced his thoughts to Ferrik.

"Something I thought would never happen," Ferrik agreed. "How'd the meeting go?"

Welkin stretched and yawned. "By the numbers," he said. "I could've told you the outcome before it started."

"You need a rest," Ferrik said. "Decisions made when you're running on empty are decisions bound for disaster."

"Patrol-speak?"

Ferrik shook his head. "No, Sarah-speak. I had to ask her what 'running on empty' meant."

Welkin smiled. The Skyborn had a lot of catching up to do so far as ancient colloquialisms were concerned. "You're right; I need to nap. Wake me when you have to, huh?"

"You've got it," Ferrik said.

Welkin woke from a deep sleep, feeling refreshed for the first time in days. Ferrik was waiting for him. "I would've let you sleep, but things are happening."

Welkin rubbed his face. "Good things or bad things?"

"See for yourself. But be warned: What you told the others earlier? About staying on here. I don't think Sarah or Gillian are happy with it."

Together they crossed the chamber and joined the "command desk," around which sat Sarah, Gillian, Theo, and Clifford. Hatch was off somewhere, securing their newly won territory.

"How goes it?" asked Welkin. Sarah looked up tiredly and smiled. She hadn't slept in twenty-four hours. Few of them had.

"Clifford says his people will be ready in an hour. Gillian and I will lead everyone out through the tunnels and back to the Merri Creek where we hid the cruisers. We figure there's safety in numbers. What's left of the Penitent, even the ferals and cavers, will think twice before taking on this lot."

She indicated the large group of people, packing and checking weaponry. "Gillian will take a cruiser and head for the family to let them know what to expect and prepare for the newcomers." Gillian made her view of this abundantly clear. "I'll guide them to the farm, taking the most direct route. I'm pretty sure *Colony* will have curtailed her sweeps for a time."

"Where'd all the equipment and medicines come from?" asked Welkin.

"We've scavenged everything we could," Theo said. "We'll need this stuff."

Sarah shouldered a knapsack. "On the way back down from upstairs it seemed a shame not to take advantage of the confusion caused by the darkness. We have enough medical supplies now to last us a couple of years." She sighed. "Providing we can read the labels; most of them are in double-Dutch." She rummaged around in the knapsack. "I know this one's for pain, says so in plain English. But the other vials . . ."

"I'll have one of my pharmacists write out a list," Clifford said. "Something you probably don't know, but these are concentrates. One tab, combined with a harmless base, will provide enough doses for more than a dozen patients. Together with all the other stuff you people got, it should last your family many years."

"That's great," Sarah said, delighted. "No one Earthside makes this stuff anymore; that's for sure." She tossed the vial back into the bag. "That's one more thing we aren't reliant on *Colony* for."

"We're really hitting the elders where it hurts," Welkin said.

Everyone agreed, but a shadow crossed Sarah's features and Gillian looked away for a moment. "You still determined to stay?" she asked Welkin.

"I am," he said. "I'm glad you're getting out of here. It's no place for Earthborn." He turned to Theo and Clifford. "You're in for a treat."

Theo stood up and clapped Welkin on the back. "Not yet I'm not. Ferrik and I will be staying here with you, Koda, too, and his colleagues Jazz and Hopper, making sure you don't get yourself in too much trouble."

"I'm up for it," said Hatch, on impulse. "I got a few bones to pick with this lot."

"Glad to have you on board," Welkin said. Then he eyed Theo. "How come you're staying when you don't think there's any hope?"

Theo scratched his scalp. "The elders will clamp down on *Colony* with a vengeance, but ultimately I believe you're right. We must make every attempt to contact this new ship. And we can't do that Earthside."

Welkin grinned. "So it's no longer a suicide mission?"

"I didn't say that. But if Ferrik hadn't told us about the space shuttles, I'd already be out of here. And just for the record, I still think it's crazy."

"The mission isn't crazy," said Ferrik. "But the idea that this new ship's elders are going to side with us *is.*"

"That's a chance we take," Welkin said, "but we can't assume the newcomers will support *Colony*'s elders, or their genocidal schemes. What happened on board this ship—the rebellion and the plague— was a unique set of events. It's just as possible that these other colonists will be on our side and not *Colony*'s."

"Anything is possible," Theo said, "and that's why we will stay and help you." He pulled Hatch closer to him. "Glad you're sticking with us, Hatch." He smiled fleetingly at Jazz and Hopper.

Theo's high spirits were infectious, but it did not make the leave-taking any easier. Gillian and Welkin were suddenly awkward again. Gillian wore a grim expression.

"Don't go getting yourself killed," she said gruffly.

"Wouldn't dream of it," said Welkin. While the others were busy he took a huge risk, grasping her hand in his. Miraculously, she didn't jerk it back. Then an idea occurred to him. "Mind you, there's always a chance something might happen to me. This might be our last chance to—"

She thumped him in the chest and actually laughed. "Gawd, you guys try it on, don't you?"

He shrugged. "You aren't giving me much to work with."

"I'm not, am I?"

"Nope."

"Well, work with this." She grabbed him by the ears and kissed him, full on. By the time she let him go he was dazed and wondered if steam was coming out of his ears.

Then she was gone into the bustling crowd. "Wow," he said softly.

It must have been contagious. Sarah muttered a brief goodbye to Theo, and turned to leave. He grabbed her roughly and pulled her back, crushing her in a huge embrace. She froze for a moment, then passionately returned his kiss.

Harry went to join the group and slapped Theo on the back. "Time enough later for that," he said. "People are watching."

"Let them," Theo mumbled back.

Harry looked from one couple to the other, then grumbled good-naturedly. "What have they got that I don't?" he asked nobody in particular.

The departing group was already filing into one of the tunnels. There were more hasty goodbyes. Sarah squeezed Welkin's shoulder. "Eyes open," she said, gently.

"You too," he said, and returned her quick hug.

Welkin, Theo, Hatch, and Ferrik waited till the last of them had filed through the gaping hole. Theo's handpicked team was already packing the equipment they would need.

"Let's get to work," Welkin said.

The departing group reached the tunnels without mishap. One of Clifford's people who had ventured out into the maze of underground passages more than once was able to show them an alternative route to Rat Highway. Several hours out they had a brief encounter with a band of ferals, but as Sarah predicted, they were intimidated by the group's sheer numbers and backed off after a brief encounter that left two of their number dead. It appeared that the mutant rats had swarmed and had their fill for the time being, because they weren't seen again. Those who were seen were the ordinary Earthborn variety and hardly a threat.

They reached the Merri Creek without further incident. Here the Skyborn—lower and upper deckers alike—stopped in awe and fear of the true Outside and the endless horizon. The subterranean passages, although eerie and different, were still essentially tunnels, not unlike the corridors of *Colony.* But this was different. As several of the Sky-born wailed, there was no *ceiling.* The sun was all-pervasive and they had the impression the Earth was turning fast. The vistas before them were almost nightmarish to their way of thinking. Some of them top-pled to the ground from temporary agoraphobia.

Sarah, Gillian, and Harry conferred. "This may take longer than we thought," said Sarah. The other two nodded. "I'd forgotten that they would have to go through some kind of acclimatization." She looked at Harry. "You going to be able to handle your side of this?"

"Don't see why not," Harry answered, self-consciously testing his wounded shoulder. "Most of Clifford's people are coping pretty well. We'll use them as sentries and flankers and I'll keep them on the move. Looks like we got some cloud cover sweeping in, so that should help with their giddiness."

"Good enough," Sarah said.

"Are you sure, Harry?" asked Gillian. "I could stay, if you like. Sarah can let the Committee know we're coming."

"Look, I'll be fine," said Harry. "Now beat it, huh?"

"He's right," Sarah said. "Let's stick to the plan." The truth was Sarah did not foresee significant problems moving through the coun-tryside with such a large force. *Colony's* defenses were under attack from within and their ability to wage war on any significant level was severely crippled—at least for now. She doubted they would even have surveillance patrols out, and certainly not on long-range sweeps.

Gillian raised her eyebrow. "What if I go on my own, then? It'll be faster."

"And more dangerous," Sarah countered. "Nope, little sister, you're riding pillion." She hauled out several large containers from her knapsack and handed them over to Harry. They contained the CRCs and some emergency medicines she had "liberated." "Keep this stuff with all the other equipment. It'll be a little safer."

"If you say so," Harry said.

Sarah pushed the ignition stud, and the cruiser purred into life. "Eyes open, Harry," she said. He grinned as Sarah and Gillian rose from the ground and soared away above the trees, with Gillian shooting a quick look back at the distant slumbering bulk of *Colony*. It was only then that Harry allowed himself to acknowledge the churning feeling in his stomach.

He immediately went through the group assessing people's agoraphobia. With Clifford's help, he also selected a group of deputies. This done, he brought them together and explained what was ahead of them. Most of the group were used to uneven ground, having experienced the crumpled lower decks; others, like Hetti, Theo's undercover computer virus expert, kept seesawing their arms to keep their balance.

Harry told them all about drowning in fast-moving rivers, dealing with wild animals, and how to avoid potential aerial Skyborn patrols. He took a last look at the remaining two cruisers. They were priceless to the Earthborn. "We'll leave them for Welkin and the others."

Within an hour, as the sky became helpfully overcast, the group was moving northward on the old Merri Creek bicycle path. It was barely visible, and overrun with weed, but it was still usable, and made better traveling than the rugged countryside. It was Harry's intention to stay on the path till they reached the now-barren Coburg Lake, then to strike eastward for the farm, keeping to open ground as much as possible. With their combined firepower he felt they were more than a match for any ground-based opposition.

On the first day, they lost two Skyborn to an accident that Harry had laboriously warned everyone about—they had stepped too close to a ravine and had fallen a hundred feet to their deaths—and a woman died from a snake bite. The deaths spooked the group, but it also helped in some ways. They realized that Harry knew what he was doing and the end result was that his authority was strengthened rather than questioned.

On the second day they met an Earthborn raiding party. Again their numbers proved too daunting for attack, and Harry flew a white flag and parleyed with the group. He warned them of the approaching skyworld and they decided to put as much distance between themselves and the old city as possible.

Harry and Clifford watched the small group disperse among the dense undergrowth. "I doubt the newcomers are actually going to land," Clifford said.

Harry looked skyward. "Not unless their vessel's in as bad condition as *Colony.*"

"It'd be asking too much of the Pleiades for it to crash-land on top of *Colony,* I suppose," Clifford said.

"Odds are astronomically against it. Still, one can always hope." Harry then said thoughtfully: "Under different circumstances I would've asked that party to join us." He slapped at a mosquito on his arm. He wasn't half as agitated as the other Skyborn who had not yet been Earthside. "But then we have our hands full with this lot as it is."

"Isn't that the truth?" Clifford said, watching the Skyborn overreact to the sudden swarms of mosquitoes. There was even some hysteria.

Harry cupped his hands and hollered, "It's okay; they're only insects. They won't kill you. Just slap them off like this . . ."

The day after the others had departed, Koda, a communications specialist, called Welkin over.

"Is there a problem?" Welkin asked. He had detailed Koda to go through all the logs recorded on a CRC Theo had retrieved.

"It seems the elders have already made contact with the newcomers," the comm. operator said. "I've found a number of communications between Elders Jamieson and Tobias and the captain of the *Crusader.*"

Welkin felt cheated. Just once, he wanted a break. "I'll need printouts," he said with some asperity.

Koda held up a sheaf of papers. "Already done it."

Welkin took them. "Thanks. I didn't mean to heavy you."

The operator grinned. "Forget it. You should see Theo when things don't go his way."

Welkin sat down and started to read. Before long he was frowning. Theo came and sat beside him.

"I've just heard. How bad is it?" he asked.

Welkin looked up from the pages, his brow creased in worry. "These exchanges . . . there's something odd about them."

"Such as?"

"I don't know," Welkin said slowly. "I can't quite put my finger on what's bothering me."

By mutual agreement, Sarah and Gillian flew low. They had no wish to advertise their passage or attract attention. The likelihood of encountering a *Colony* patrol was small, but neither wanted to take chances.

They made their approach to the farm mid-afternoon. Sarah flew once over the fields by way of announcing their arrival and was perplexed to see they had not been tended and no one was about. She dismissed the thought, deciding that the outlying guards had heard their cruiser and given them clear passage.

They landed near the hay barn. Sarah waited for the dust to settle before taking her feet off the runner. She signaled for Gillian to be cautious and quiet. The farm hadn't been deserted; that much was clear from the tools lying about the place, and the general feel of the yard and surrounds. Yet no one had come out to greet them.

Sarah fought against the urge to take flight. She indicated the Committee's shed to Gillian and they walked slowly over to it. A door banged in the wind and Gillian jumped. Her reaction increased Sarah's tension. She strode cautiously forward and swung open the door hoping to see everyone seated at the table, enjoying their joke on her.

Instead someone caught her in a headlock and dragged her to the ground.

She struggled, managing to grab hold of her assailant's hair, eliciting a scream. Then someone else joined the affray and smashed the back of her hand. She let go of the hair and grunted as her arms were pulled behind her back and tied. She was vaguely aware of a brief struggle outside, and knew that Gillian had been wrestled to the ground as well.

She was dragged upright and slammed against the wall. As she glared, the first figure she saw was Tolk. He motioned for his people to step back from Sarah. Gillian stumbled into her as her captors shoved her forward.

"So you decided to come back," he said. "It would have been better for you if you hadn't. But no matter. Put them with the others," he said.

Now Sarah realized that Fish and Angela were among those who had captured them, though Angela seemed to hang back, her expression unreadable.

The captives were dragged across the compound and thrown into the prison hut. Here they found the other Committee members. Efi came over at once and hugged them. "I'm so sorry," she said. Denton and several others huddled around. They seemed battered and bruised but otherwise okay.

"What happened?" Sarah demanded.

"It was just after you left," said Efi.

Sarah detected accusation in Efi's reply, but she said nothing, waiting for the girl to finish her story.

The overnight disappearance of most of the family's leadership had thrown the community into disarray, and a split had occurred. Nothing, said Efi, that they couldn't have patched up, given time. But that was just what they didn't get. Taking advantage of the confusion of leadership, Fish and a bunch of Tolk's people had broken into the weapons hut and armed themselves, and in an almost bloodless coup they had taken over the family, imprisoning all the Committee members.

"It was that easy," Efi said bitterly. "No one knew who was in authority."

Sarah grunted. "You're right to blame us for it," she said. Gillian looked down at her feet.

"No one's blaming anyone," Elab said, but Sarah knocked against the wall with her fist.

"It was my fault," she said emphatically. "I left a power vacuum at a time when we had strangers amongst us. That was bad leadership and that's all there is to it." She thought briefly of the CRC she had stolen and the wealth of information that Welkin and the others had obtained. She had come too close to her life's dream for it to end like this . . .

"I bet that was Tolk's intention all along. And we handed him the perfect opportunity on a platter," Gillian said.

Elab gazed at her. "It gets better. Tolk is the Prophet."

Sarah broke from her reverie and looked at Gillian. "When I screw up, I *really* screw up." She indicated Elab should continue.

"Apparently it's his standard strategy. His people pretend to be victims of the Prophet, then ask for asylum with some unsuspecting group. Once in, they wait for an opportunity to take over. Any dissenter gets dispatched pretty soon."

"Great. Just great," Gillian said. "Every instinct I had screamed out at me not to trust that lot, but I just went against everything I knew and chased after Welkin."

Elab shook his head. "They would have found a way no matter what you had done. Face it: The rest of us were taken in by them."

While Lucida and Mira untied Sarah and Gillian, Sarah looked around at the weary faces. The O'Shannesseys had been roughed up, although Sarah knew they would have dished out as much as they had received. The others had bruises and cuts as well. Budge had his arm in a sling. "How many did we lose?" she asked.

"Na-na none on tuh-tuh the Committee, but five good people," Budge said. "Suh-suh some of Tolk's people got trigger ha-happy at first. They fried anyone who moved. It-it happened so fassst."

Denton said, "They've already started indoctrination classes. No one's about to refuse to acknowledge the supreme leadership of the Prophet and his 'mission.' Word is that if his inner circle figures anyone's not worth the effort, they get taken into the bush and are never seen again."

"So we play along with him for now. But friend Tolk has got a big surprise coming this way," Sarah said with some satisfaction. Gillian nodded. Efi and the others wanted to know what she meant, but she would not go into details. She trusted the Committee dearly, but spies like Devon had infiltrated them before now, and she couldn't risk being betrayed, not this time.

She quickly briefed them on the general events of the past few days on board *Colony* and everybody was clearly impressed by their successes but also alarmed at the approach of the new skyworld. She said nothing about the large force of armed Skyborn heading this way under Harry's leadership.

It was getting late by the time she had brought the others up to speed. "We'd best get some rest," she said, and settled herself on the ground. "Any idea what's on the agenda for tomorrow?"

Lucida looked at her feet. "The rest of the Committee was put on trial. I use the term loosely. A real kangaroo court. You're guilty before it starts."

"Well, obviously you don't face the firing squad immediately after it," Sarah said, with little satisfaction. "And Lucida? Don't worry about your brother. Welkin's more than able to look after himself."

True to Lucida's prediction, "the trial" proved to be a euphemism for a sham court. Before breakfast, Sarah and Gillian were summoned to appear before the Prophet and give witness to their faith and loyalty.

Standing before Tolk, Sarah snorted in contempt.

Fish slapped her across the face. Sarah barely flinched. "You will show respect to the Prophet," he snapped.

Sarah glared stonily at the man. "You'll keep," she said.

Fish raised his fist for another strike, but Angela caught his hand. Tolk nodded. "Later," he said. "We want dear Sarah conscious, at least for the time being."

The Prophet stood on a low platform, dressed in some kind of ceremonial robe. His pale, gaunt features almost gave him an ethereal presence, but his broken, yellowed teeth dispelled much of the illusion of holiness.

A crowd of his own people was present, their faces rapt and oddly slack, as though in a permanent stupor.

Tolk folded his hands and launched into a fevered speech. "One hundred and fifty years ago this world was brought to its knees. In His infinite wisdom, the One humbled humanity, laid waste its arrogant achievements, and condemned humanity to virtual oblivion. Many have asked, why was He so angry?" On and on he droned, his tone swelling like a rising tide. "What had we done to deserve such punishment?"

Tolk paused, eyeing the shining faces of his people, their glittering eyes. "Perhaps we ask the wrong questions. Perhaps we should ask: Did we not worship false gods, such as money and pleasure? We sought, in our hubris, to deny the very nature of the One by celebrating that which is the antithesis of the One: our individuality. But know this now and forever: There is only one Individual. Only a single oneness."

He took stock of his congregation. All eyes focused on him.

"After the war, when the radiation levels had dropped, only one creature survived: the humble ant. The ant does not know the curse of individuality. It knows only the collective. By preserving the ant the One sent us a message. As clear as could be. We must be One. We must create a Cosmic Collective. Where no one individual counts, only the true One . . . the Collective."

He raised his arms, beckoning thunder from the sky. "All hail the Collective!"

Everybody sank to their knees in supplication. Sarah and Gillian were forced to theirs also. After a long time Tolk opened his eyes and stood up, a signal for the others to do likewise.

He gazed at his prisoners. "All who we conquer must join us or die. How do you plead?"

Sarah slowly raised her head from her shoulder, as though waking from a deep sleep. Many eyes flashed angrily at her, and a low murmur moved through the congregation.

"Join you?" Sarah said. "I would rather join a band of cockroaches. You may have your congregation here brainwashed, but I know self-righteous salvationist dogma when I hear it. And I know my history. Every time human beings have attempted any kind of social collectivity it has quickly been commandeered by a single individual who becomes a despot. Just like you, Tolk."

Sarah paused, waiting to be shouted down, but there wasn't a sound. It was almost as though Tolk wanted her to dig her own grave. She obliged, and continued. "You say everybody is equal in your egomaniacal dream, but as somebody once said, some are more equal than others. So you want to know how I plead? Go to space! That's how I plead."

Tolk smiled. "It is as I thought," he said. "You stand condemned from your own mouth. You are a heretic to the Collective. My judgment is final: death."

Gillian gasped.

"Fear not, Gillian," said Tolk. "Your life I will spare. You have a higher destiny to fulfill. Take them away. Perhaps they shall repent in isolation."

Sarah was hustled away. She called out to her sister, telling her to stay strong. Gillian was escorted to a hut on the outskirts of the settlement.

No sooner was Gillian left alone than she worked her way around the windowless shed. Thin shreds of light came through mismatched planks, but even with her eye up against the cracks, she could barely see anything. She tried to calculate how long it would take Harry to get here with what she was coming to think of as "reinforcements," but even her best estimate put it some days past being any good to them. Then again, they had two cruisers at their disposal. How would they use them? For aerial protection? Or would they ferry injured Skyborn to the farm on them?

"So this is solitary confinement," she said, and kicked at a chair. It splintered against the door and a guard responded by banging on the boarded-up window.

"Keep up your nonsense and we'll tie you down," he called. "Now shuddup."

Gillian grunted. She could jab-kick that door wide open if she had a long enough run up, only it wouldn't do her much good. Not with one or more guards outside.

She lay down in the corner of the hut and rested. Nervous energy wouldn't let her sleep despite her exhaustion. Hours later, she heard the creak of the door followed by the soft pad of footsteps. She lay perfectly still and forced herself to maintain the rhythm of her breathing.

Tolk was standing over her. *If I am going to escape, now is my only chance.*

He knelt down. A hand brushed her hair.

In a lightning-quick gesture, she twisted under him, grasped his arm in a judo hold, and jerked hard. Before Tolk had even registered what had happened she looped her arm around his neck and rammed his head against a solid beam. She heard his nose crack and he slumped across her.

Gillian tightened her grip around his neck, then slackened it. She should really put the man out of everybody's misery, but Sarah was always saying that if you stoop to the enemy's level, then you become the enemy. She settled for giving him a left hook to the jaw.

Gillian lay still a moment longer, listening. She had fully expected the guard to come charging through the door, but he hadn't. Tolk must have dismissed him. *Silly man. He must truly be drunk on his own power.*

She rolled to her feet, patted Tolk down, finding nothing more useful than a penknife. She pocketed that and moved to the door. Outside, the settlement seemed empty. She kept to the shadows of the wall and edged along slowly, trying to stem her ragged breathing.

So far so good. She didn't think she had long before a hue and cry went up. She had to get Sarah away from here before then. As for the others, well, they would come next. It still rankled with her that they hadn't escaped. Had they given up so easily?

She knew what Sarah would say, of course. When everything depends on you, save yourself first, then worry about the rest. If she was recaptured now there would be no hope for the others. And if Tolk found out from her that Harry was coming with reinforcements, then he could fall prey to an ambush, or at best, Tolk would pull up stakes and move base.

Gillian reached a point where the decision became geographically more urgent. To her left lay the prison hut holding the Committee members. Sarah was probably in the hut next to them, it being the only other lockable shed. To her right was the hay barn, which housed the family's remaining cruisers. She knew most of them to be faulty.

For a long moment she struggled silently with the pros and cons. She knew what she ought to do, but the thought of abandoning her sister set uneasily with her. She actually started in the direction of the prison cabin. Then she stopped. She could almost see Sarah's frown, the scolding shake of her head.

With a sigh, she turned back and made her way toward the hay barn. Had she just passed a test, a kind of rite of passage? In some indefinable sad way, she had just become a leader.

Sarah would be proud.

But Gillian didn't like it. She entered the hay barn from the rear. There was only one guard and she owed the ease of his dispatch entirely to Sarah's training. She wrapped her forearm around his throat in a sleeper hold and applied pressure, then let him flop gently to the ground.

Gillian opened the hayloft doors, sat astride a cruiser, and prayed that it would start immediately. It didn't. It coughed and spluttered. She stabbed the ignition stud several times, listening with growing dismay to the staccato noise of the rotors kicking over.

Someone called out. An oil lamp flared and bobbed in the dark, coming rapidly closer.

Gillian was about to climb off the cruiser and silence this new threat when the cruiser sighed into a stuttering purr.

Gillian almost collapsed with relief. She pushed the orbital tab, lifted off, and skimmed across the courtyard, kicking up a maelstrom of dust and detritus. The girl holding the oil lamp barely ducked to one side, avoiding the hurtling cruiser. She called out, and the oil lamp dropped and exploded.

That's all Gillian saw in the rear visuals as she darted between the gums.

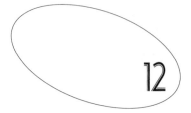

12

Welkin yanked the cable from his neural jack. Hatch and Ferrik looked up from the schematic of the skyworld they were studying.

"What's the latest?" Ferrik asked.

"It appears the elders are preparing a reception for their 'star brethren.' They seem to be officious, but chummy," he told them tightly.

Ferrik's face tightened. "Doesn't mean a thing," he said.

"I agree," said Hatch. Theo appeared and joined them, smiling. "Everything's set," he said. "Just say the word and we will attempt the impossible."

That night a bright new star appeared in a high orbit overhead.

Gillian stayed high, circling the upper canopy of the forest. It was dangerous to remain at such an altitude. *Colony's* radar could pinpoint her without much effort, nor would an enemy patrol take long to spot her. But she had to find the others and she had to find them fast.

Quartering all the possible approaches had taken time. Sarah had not asked which path Harry would take, but Gillian figured he would come the quickest way, counting on their numbers to deter opposition.

Then she saw it. A thin plume of smoke, which disappeared almost as fast as she spotted it.

She put the cruiser into a steep screaming dive and was among trees in a matter of seconds. Unfortunately, the cruiser's accelerator stuck. Her speed was too high. She tried to pull up, banked at the last second to kill her velocity, and plowed into a small clearing covered in range grass. The impact threw her fifteen feet through the air to land, breathless, on her back.

She lay there a long moment trying to get her lungs going again and hoping she hadn't broken anything. The moment she opened her eyes she knew one thing. It was better to keep them closed. Everything she saw was in montage. She stayed that way for some time, moving her toes, her ankles, checking her whole body section by section, fearing serious damage, but thankfully finding none.

Then she heard approaching footfalls through the long grass. She opened her eyes again and saw Harry's concerned face looking down at her.

"Are you dead?" he asked.

"I don't think so."

"Great landing. Suicidal, but great. You'll have to teach me it some time." Harry whistled and several people rushed forward. He bent down and helped Gillian get unsteadily to her feet.

Gillian staggered for a moment, and held on to Harry for support. "Something I have to tell you," she said.

"Sit back down," Harry said. "Whatever it is can wait."

Gillian pushed up onto her elbows. "I'm all right. But I have a headache you wouldn't believe."

Harry unslung his knapsack and fished out a leather pouch. He gave her a fragment of a tablet. "For headaches. Well, pain, really; they've helped my shoulder. Take three in case the first two don't work," he joked. "Have it with water. Here."

"You sure they're safe? I'd rather have some feverfew or lemon balm."

"Fresh out of herbs," Harry said. "This stuff's concentrate apparently. I hope you don't overdose." He gave her a piece the size of a pinhead.

Gillian suddenly blinked rapidly and took several deep breaths. "Harry, I've got to tell you this now in case I pass out," she said. "Tolk's taken over the family. He's got everything."

Harry stared at her. "What about Sarah? She's okay, isn't she?"

"No. They're going to execute her."

His eyes went wide. "What?" He helped her to her feet and she quickly filled him in on Tolk's coup at the farm. He smashed a fist into the palm of his hand. "What can we do?"

"How fast can you get there?"

He stared at her, running the numbers in his head. "It's not possible." He cleared his throat. "Even at a fast trot it would take two days."

Gillian bit her lip. "I'll have to do it alone."

"No," said Harry. "Go to Welkin. The other cruisers are still back there. With them you can launch a surprise attack from the air."

She shut her eyes tightly, then opened them. "Okay. What about you?"

"I'll get this lot moving as fast as they can go. You just delay Tolk and we'll be there, Gillian. Count on it." He paused. "We'd better make sure the cruiser is okay."

But the cruiser's gyros were stuck on high revs. After a debate, Harry yielded to Gillian's demand that he get the cavalcade moving, while she set about repairs.

Welkin and Ferrik gazed out through a grille matrix at a short length of corridor. Down the far end two heavies stood guard outside a reinforced bulkhead door. A third could be seen through the door's porthole. His job was to watch the corridor on *his* side of the door and keep an eye on the two guards. It could be expected that more heavies would be just beyond the door.

"They've got the place guarded like the cruise cabin," said Welkin.

"Must be something they don't want anybody to see," Ferrik mused.

"Or disturb."

"I guess that means—"

"That we should go in and disturb them," Welkin finished. He nudged Ferrik and they both squirmed back to where Theo and Hatch waited. Welkin outlined what they had seen.

"Doesn't sound good," Theo said. "A frontal assault is out."

Hatch patted his utility belt. "I'm fresh out of clusters."

"Relax," said Welkin. "This is no suicide mission. Ferrik says there's a way around. Sort of."

Theo stared at Ferrik. "Sort of? What does 'sort of' mean?"

"Now why don't I like the sound of that?" added Hatch.

"Because you won't," said Ferrik, smiling grimly. "Did you bring those gas masks?"

Hatch and Theo held laserlites at the ready, checking the corridor in both directions. Welkin and Ferrik were down on hands and knees, loosening recessed bolts from a floor plate. A moment later the last bolt came out and Ferrik jimmied what now appeared to be a kind of hatch that swung up on awkward hinges, screeching loudly.

They all jumped at the noise. "Shsssh," hissed Theo, grimacing.

"Okay, okay," said Welkin. "You first, Ferrik."

Ferrik squirmed through the hatch feetfirst, followed by the others. Welkin brought up the rear, pulling the hatch down flush with the floor. The others squatted around him, eyes wide and dark. Ferrik had switched on a powerpak, and its harsh light lit up a claustrophobically narrow crawl space lined with conduit and cables. Enormous strange shadows splayed across the walls and stretched into the distance as the light in Ferrik's hand moved about. Beneath their feet the floor curved concavely, dipping down on either side to sharp gutters.

Welkin rapped the floor. "Is this it?" he asked. Ferrik nodded.

"Is this what?" Hatch wanted to know.

"We need to find your namesake," Ferrik said. "Let's split up, check in both directions."

Welkin and Ferrik went one way, Theo and Hatch the other. They aimed the powerpak at the floor, checking the surface with painstaking care.

"You really used to play down here?" Welkin kept his voice down.

Ferrik thought back. "We used to play with the cleaner minibots," he said. "They're pretty cute when you stand them on their heads." He grinned at the memory. "Caused havoc with the sanitary crew."

"And I thought playing sick to get out of astronomy class was radical," Welkin said. He looked ahead into the dim recesses of the shaft. "Say we don't find this outlet?"

"Guess we go back to the frontal assault approach."

"Great," Welkin muttered.

For nearly an hour they inched along the crawl space checking the floor, growing tired and frustrated, and becoming sticky with perspiration.

"I don't understand," Ferrik said after a long stretch of silence. "I remember coming across heaps of outlet paneling."

"Sanitation might've sealed them all to stop your lot getting in here and wrecking their bots."

Ferrik slumped. "Anything's possible."

Suddenly, a distant whistle drew their attention. A dim light in the distance was making a circular motion. They scrambled around and hurried back as fast as they could in a low, awkward crouch. They passed the point at which they had entered the crawl space and hurried on, coming on the other two crouched over a section of flooring. It was a hatch.

Welkin grinned, slapping Ferrik on the back. Then they set to work trying to get it open, but it was a much tougher job than the previous panel. The edges had long ago fused with the surrounding metal. After struggling with this for a time Theo suggested they take a rest. They were all breathing heavily.

"This is useless," he said. "And we're making too much noise."

Welkin started adjusting the beam aperture on his laserlite. Ferrik saw what he was doing and reached out a hand to stop him. Welkin pushed his hand back. "I know the risks," he said. "You all move back. Give me thirty yards. Go on; move it."

They crawled backward and shortly Ferrik was lying with the other two, fretting silently. He had left the powerpak light with Welkin and now, off in the distance, almost swallowed by the squeezing darkness of the crawl space, he could barely see Welkin as he fired up the laserlite, producing a fine cutting beam. Then sparks began to fly as the beam ate into the fused metal.

Several minutes passed. Then came a sudden whooshing sound and a jet of flame erupted from the floor and consumed Welkin.

Ferrik and the others ducked instinctively; then Ferrik was scrambling back toward Welkin as fast as he could go, fearing what he would find.

As he came closer he could smell burnt hair and gas and hear a sharp hissing noise. Suddenly he saw a shape through the smoke. It coughed and waved at him.

"Seems you weren't quite right," came Welkin's voice, and Ferrik and the others sighed with relief.

"Thought you'd had it," said Theo.

"What in Space was that?" Hatch asked.

"Methane gas," said Ferrik, and Hatch frowned, glancing down at the curved floor. Then he said to Welkin, "How come you're still in one piece?"

"Sheer dumb luck," said Welkin. "If I'd removed the whole panel in one go I'd have blown us all sky-high. As it was I'd only opened up one small hole when it ignited. But I think I'm nearly through all the way around. A couple of good kicks should do it."

Ferrik stood up as best he could and beckoned Hatch to join him. They stamped their booted feet on the panel. Once, twice, then—with a wrenching screech—the panel gave way and dropped out of sight.

Instantly, they were assailed by a terrible smell. Racking coughs tore at their throats and they could hardly breathe.

"Masks!" gasped Welkin, fumbling for his. Tears streamed down his face and snot ran from his nose. The others donned their masks, too, sucking noisily at the scrubbers.

"What is that stink?" Hatch demanded, gazing around at the others.

"I told you: methane," said Ferrik.

"Well, what's methane?" asked Hatch, perplexed. "And what in Space is this we're squatting on?"

Welkin and Ferrik exchanged looks; then both burst out laughing.

Hatch said to Theo, "Permission to discipline impertinent cadets, sir?" Theo gestured his permission.

"Wait; wait," said Welkin, trying to stifle his laughter.

"Yeah, I'm waiting," said Hatch.

Ferrik said, "Hydroponics has been in trouble for a while. It's a makeshift sewer. Sanitation's been channeling this stuff down here since the beginning of the year."

"A sewer? Like the kind that carries raw sewage?"

"Yeah, that kind," said Welkin. "We're going to travel through it."

Hatch stared at him as if he was crazy. Theo shook his head. "Not on your life," he said. "I'm not going down there. You've got space fatigue, boy."

"Fatigue or not," said Welkin, "the elders would never expect us to approach the docking bay via the sewage canal. I got the idea from crawling underground Earthside."

Hatch shook his head in pity. "You've been outside with the savages for too long," he concluded. "No wonder Jazz and Hopper stayed behind."

Almost bent double, they progressed cautiously, feet barely clearing the lapping edges of the disgusting muck. Ferrik led the way, occasionally powering up a portable schematic map to check their location. The stink was pervasive, despite the protection of the nose filters. And there were *things* down there between their legs, living things that slipped and squirmed through the sewage, and sometimes broke the surface. The first time it happened Hatch yelped and almost lost his footing, swiveling his lasergun at the surface sludge. Welkin reached out and pushed the muzzle of the weapon up.

"Fire that in here and we're carbonized," he said. Hatch gulped and nodded. He conspicuously locked the safety tab.

"What do you think they are?" Theo asked, looking at the dark fluid.

"Rats," said Ferrik cheerfully. "And maybe Earth critters unknown. You do hear rumors."

"You're pretty safe if you slip," Hatch said good-naturedly. "There's not much meat on you."

They had been traveling for about half an hour when Ferrik signaled them to stop. "This should be it," he said, peering at the canal roof. Two permasteel rungs were fixed to the wall and led up to what must be another exit.

He handed his equipment to Theo and hauled himself up the ladder, then pressed his ear to the hatch. He was listening for sounds, but, more usefully, he was hoping to detect any vibrations that would indicate the passageway above was tenanted.

Ferrik heard nothing and felt nothing. He gave the others the okay signal, then, very slowly and cautiously, pushed at the hatch. To his surprise, it opened effortlessly. He took a deep breath and ripped out his nose filters, easing the hatch up just enough so he could peer out. Luckily, the hatch opened on a right angle to the corridor, so he could see both ways. It was clear.

He quickly flipped it open all the way and scrambled out. This was the riskiest part of the mission. The others knew this and popped out of the canal on high alert.

Theo coughed. "You guys are sure on the nose. If we're not seen, I reckon we'll be smelt."

Welkin sniffed. "It's not that bad. Purifiers will soon suck that out of us."

"I like optimists," Ferrik said. "Let's move it."

Within moments they were in the corridor and making for a maintenance access shaft clearly marked on Ferrik's schematic map. It was frizzing now, bleeding out at the edges into misty lines.

"It's not long for this world," Ferrik said. "C'mon, baby, get us to the spot marked X."

They found the access shaft easily enough. To their dismay it had been coded shut.

The farm was in uproar. Beacon fires had been lit and small squads of Tolk's people scoured the surrounding scrubland. Then an unconscious man was found and soon it was known that the infidel Gillian had added to her already heinous crimes against the Prophet by stealing a cruiser.

Tolk slammed his fist on a table and glared at his subordinates. He had comfrey plastered over his nose and jawline. "You will find her and bring her to me," he said. "She must be held accountable."

Angela and Fish nodded but said nothing. It did not pay to draw too much attention at times like this.

Tolk sought someone to vent his anger upon. "The blasphemer Sarah is still bound?"

Fish nodded again and ventured two words. "Sure is."

"Get going," Tolk grated. Someone would have to die for this blunder and he wondered whom he should pick.

Theo slammed his clenched fist into the barred door. "That tears it."

Welkin shook his head. "I'm not giving up that easily," he said. Then to Ferrik he said, "Find us another way in."

Ferrik closed his eyes in contemplation. The map was now an ether jungle, worm-like smoky lines interlacing one another. Useless. "There's only one other way into the maintenance system that accesses the docking bay."

"And you didn't mention it; why?"

"If you think trudging across sewage is bad . . ."

Welkin stared at him. "Exactly what is the problem?"

"*That* is the problem," said Ferrik. He pointed down into a four-story chamber that was some kind of cargo transfer hub. The area was filled with bustling Skyborn going about their assigned duties. It looked like an industrious ant's nest. There were no heavies in sight, but that was a minor comfort.

Ferrik pointed out the access to the maintenance network. Following his pointing finger, the others could make out a hatch on the far side of the compartment at their own level, reached by a narrow catwalk that ran along the farther wall but did not connect to the one on which they now crouched.

There was no way to bridge the gap. Or almost no way.

"You're not seriously proposing what I think you're seriously proposing, are you?" Welkin asked.

"I'm not proposing anything," said Ferrik.

Hatch stared at both of them, perplexed. "What are you two talking about?"

Theo sighed. "That," he said, indicating a crane gantry that spanned the width of the compartment. It was suspended from enormous tracks that ran lengthwise down the bay, allowing for the movement of gigantic cargo pallets with ease. The ends of the gantry were almost within reach of the catwalk at either end. The only good thing was that this entire upper section of the compartment was shrouded in gloom, as the main lights jutted from the walls beneath the catwalks and angled downward.

Hatch shook his head. "Uh-uh," he said. "I'm no trapeze artist."

"Then I guess that makes you the lookout man," said Theo. He eyed the perilous path they were intending to take and swallowed quietly. He wasn't that good with heights, either, but as a leader, he often had to do that which scared the life out of him. It was one of the many downsides of leadership.

Welkin sighed. "I'm going first. If I don't make it," he said to Theo, "it's over to you."

The end of the gantry was an arm's length from the guardrail of the catwalk. He could reach out and touch it, but that did not help. He would have to climb up on the railing, then take a death-defying step across empty space to the gantry, with nothing to hold or cling to. The first of a series of struts did not begin for several feet. One misstep and he would surely plunge to his death.

Well, we never did this in sims, Welkin thought as he clambered precariously up onto the rail, which itself suddenly did not seem very secure. Theo and Ferrik helped steady him from behind. He swayed slightly, feeling giddy when he looked down. Then he got his balance, took a deep breath, and stepped across onto the gantry, which was about a foot wide at this point. For a split second he nearly lost his footing. His arms seesawed wildly as he tried to regain equilibrium.

He made the mistake of looking down again, then teetered to the left. Miraculously, a laserlite rifle was shoved at him from behind, held tightly by Theo and Ferrik. He seized this, steadied himself, then lunged for the first of the struts. He clung tightly to it for several heart-pounding seconds.

Finally he looked over his shoulder and nodded to Ferrik, who was coming next. Welkin braced himself against the strut, his arms encircling it, and held out the laserlite to Ferrik to take hold of. But Ferrik had seen where Welkin had gone wrong. He no sooner stepped onto the end of the gantry than he squatted down and sat on it, a leg dangling on either side. Then, using his hands, he slid slowly along the beam in stops and starts until he reached the strut. Then, gingerly, he stood and carefully stepped around Welkin.

Theo came next, adopting the same strategy as Ferrik. They waved to Hatch, who climbed back into a maintenance shaft to await their return. He then started slowly across the gantry, trying not to look down and fearful of making a noise lest the workers below glance up and, despite the glare of the lights, see them.

In the center of the gantry the main structural beam split in two, forming a semi-circle, and they were forced to do another balancing act as they followed the beam around this arc without the aid of struts for handholds. Fortunately, directly beneath them was the supervisor's cabin for the autocrane, and this afforded them the illusion of only being a few feet off the ground. They made it to the other side of the circle and continued onto the end of the gantry.

Welkin and Ferrik made it across to the catwalk and stood on somewhat shaky legs, catching their breath, and waiting for Theo.

He came across confidently, it seemed, and then, stifling a cry, he fell. He barely managed to loop his arm around the beam, and then hung there, legs kicking in the air, some thirty feet above the heads of the cargo shifters below. If even one of them looked up, the game would be over.

Theo swung his left arm over the beam, but somehow his right arm was giving out on him. He shook his head frantically, indicating to Welkin and Ferrik that he couldn't hold on.

"Quick," said Welkin. "Hold me, brace your feet here." He leaned over the guardrail, Ferrik gripping him from behind. It was a precarious position and Ferrik could not get a solid brace against the rail. All he could do was hang on as Welkin leaned out as far as he could.

Even then it wasn't quite far enough. Theo would have to heft himself upward a few inches and twist at the same time, grabbing hold of Welkin's hands.

Sweat beaded on Theo's forehead. "My hands are slipping." He swung his legs to relieve the pressure on his arms, but even then knew he was going to fall.

"I'll catch you," Welkin whispered back, locking eyes with the Dove leader. "You can do it, Theo. Concentrate."

Theo went to hoist himself up. One hand, slicked with perspiration, lost its grip and for a second he was swinging wildly. His other hand started to give and his eyes went wide with fright. Then he managed to catch the edge of the beam again with his other hand. "Now," he wheezed, and did a sharp chin-up and twisted, flinging his left hand toward Welkin.

There was one awful moment when Welkin thought they would miss. Then Theo's hand locked tightly with his own and with Herculean effort, and Ferrik's help, he drew the man up and onto the catwalk.

Theo slumped against the rail, catching his breath. "I'm getting too old for this," he said. Welkin helped him to his feet and they crept the rest of the way to the maintenance shaft grille.

They squashed into a ventilation shaft that was barely three feet high and three feet wide. A soft thrumming ran the length of the shaft. Welkin edged forward on his belly, careful to make no noise above the background drone. He came to a grille set in the floor of the shaft and slowly slid forward till his eyes crested the first of the slats and he could look down into the area below.

"It's *Procyon*," Welkin said. Half a dozen Skyborn milled about the shuttle, two of them elders. Welkin recognized Jamieson and a flush of anger colored his cheeks. But the shuttle craft, long thought destroyed, distracted him.

"Looks like she's all loaded up with somewhere to go," Theo added. "Hey, Ferrik, didn't you say that was your baby?"

Ferrik squeezed in between them. "Until the heavies modified her." He stiffened suddenly, and Welkin nudged him to speak his mind.

"The heavies were fitting her with feeders to jettison the virus. I never had a chance to find out exactly what they were up to, but that's my conclusion after meeting the Earthborn. From what other crews told me, there have been adjustments back in the cargo hold."

"We've got to hurry." Welkin swung back to the grille.

For a moment Theo and Ferrik thought he was going to push the grille out and panic. Ferrik pulled him back just in case. "Ease up, Welkin," he said. "*Procyon*'s getting ready for space—not atmospheric. See the priming thrusters? That's heavy-duty procedure."

"You're sure?" Welkin said, eyes not leaving *Procyon*.

Ferrik let go of Welkin. "Sure I'm sure. I was the co-pilot, remember? And look at old Tobias and Jamieson. They're rigged for space, just like their gofers. *Procyon*'s about to ferry the top boys somewhere."

"Sorry," Welkin said, pulling back from the grille. "Why would they—"

"To meet *Crusader*," all three chimed together.

Welkin looked wistful. "If only we could smuggle aboard."

Ferrik clicked his fingers. "I think I'll grant that wish. Can't have someone else piloting my shuttle without me watching over them."

"Hold it; hold it," Theo said. "Are you guys space crazy? In case you haven't noticed, the place is crawling with personnel." He turned to Ferrik. "Even some of your former crew are down there, right? What if they see you?"

"They won't," Ferrik said. He had just seen Prath, Tox, and Sasha march off for their pre-flight plan. Thought of Arton made his heart thump hard. Where was he? Was he still alive? Just how did all this happen? The questions suffused one another, like colors in a kaleidoscope.

"How so?" Theo prompted.

Ferrik blinked. "They just left. We have about ten minutes before they come back and commence the pre-flight sequence. We either stow aboard now or we don't. What's it to be?"

Welkin and Theo were unanimous.

"What are we waiting for?" Ferrik said. He crawled backward out of the shaft. The others followed.

They reached the platform above the bay and stood by the gravity chute.

Theo held back Welkin, then motioned it was clear for him to drop down to the deck. The moment Welkin passed through the aperture, Ferrik followed him. By the time Theo hit the deck, the others were straightening their uniforms.

"Okay," Ferrik said. "Act as though you belong here. Chances are the techies and maintenance people won't remember me." He shrugged. "And if they do, so what? No one will know what happened to me. They probably think I got reassigned. Yeah?"

Theo took a deep breath. "Whatever you say, spaceboy. Let's hope we don't have to put that theory to the test."

Ferrik led the way. They passed several deckcrew, but as Ferrik said, no one questioned them. And why would they? They were high up in *Colony,* and no one, but no one, could infiltrate the inner sanctum of *Colony.*

Nonetheless, Ferrik took a quick inconspicuous look around the bay before pulling himself up into *Procyon.* He waited for Welkin and Theo to reach him, before leading them to the cargo hold where he hoped the virus canisters had been installed. They were there, all right, and the three stowed away beneath them, where the giant spray nozzles sat like squid suckers on the booster's burnished hull.

True to Ferrik's estimate, eight minutes later the crew returned to *Procyon.* Ferrik heard Plath's familiar voice: "Okay, fire her up and let's see what this beauty can do."

Welkin peered out and what he saw took his breath away. The navigator brought up their flight path schematic. As he watched, an image burned black and innumerable stars appeared like shining pinholes within the schematic sphere. A second later the perspective turned and the Earth, bulking hugely, appeared. It dropped away quickly, taking the viewer into space and their destination.

After several course changes a bright star appeared in the center of the schematic and quickly grew until it became a vast spherical object that filled the image and dwarfed the tiny, old-fashioned shuttle craft that darted around it powered by controlled bursts of antimatter explosion.

It was the new skyworld, *Crusader.* Unlike *Colony,* the sister ship seemed in pristine condition despite its long space journey.

Or maybe it hadn't traveled as far as *Colony,* Welkin thought. He slid back and closed his eyes. He hardly heard the banter between the crew, barely felt the shuttle leap from the deck and soar straight through the atmosphere and into the stratosphere. Ferrik and Theo similarly shut everything out. Their fate now was in the hands of the Pleiades and the rest of the sky gods.

Welkin woke from a restless sleep to a hand tugging his arm. Theo pointed forward. They were about to dock.

He eyed Theo. "Hatch was right. I am a lunatic."

"Maybe not," Theo countered. "You said you wanted to present your viewpoint to the newcomers. Well, now you can."

Welkin stared at him. "My mouth is always getting me into trouble." He pushed his eye up against the twin cylinders and watched the docking procedure. An hour passed before Ferrik deemed it safe to escape through a rear deck plate. He tugged at it, and it came away easily. *Crusader*'s deck was visible beneath the landing strut mechanism.

"It'll be tight," Ferrik said. "But I don't fancy going out through the bridge. This place is probably under tight security."

Welkin stayed him for a moment, and outlined a quick plan. Ferrik nodded slowly. "I guess if all else fails, I can order this baby to fly out of here." At Welkin's look of consternation, he added, "Just kidding. Now go for it."

With Theo holding his legs, Welkin lowered himself upside down till he could just see beneath the stubby wings of the shuttle craft and into the docking bay itself.

The place appeared empty. Here they left Ferrik. He would make sure their retreat was not cut off, but also, in the eventuality that the shuttle left before they returned, someone down on the planet would know where they were. Together, Welkin and Theo slid down one of the struts and crab-crawled to a section stacked with cargo pallets. From there they quickly gained entry to another maintenance tube.

Fortunately, both skyworlds had been built to an identical plan and Theo knew the rat holes and crawlways of these goliaths better than anybody since becoming a rebel on *Colony.*

A hundred yards from the docking bay was a reception chamber. It was intended to provide a place where ambassadorial parties could be received without undue risk to the entire ship. The original planners had tried to anticipate all eventualities. It had occurred to them that a hostile group of aliens might pretend to be of amicable character in order to gain access to the ship. What the aliens would not know, however, was that the docking bay and reception chamber could be completely sealed off from the rest of the ship and, in the most extreme of scenarios, actually jettisoned into space.

Welkin and Theo made their way carefully to the reception chamber. By the time they had squirmed and crawled through the equivalent of several hundred yards of tubes and shafts they were dusty, tired, and thirsty. But the sight that greeted them was worth the effort.

The crusaders did not stand on ceremony. Whereas the elders would no doubt have greeted other colonists or aliens with the kind of pomp and ritual reserved for Old Earth kings and popes, these crusaders had set up a large horseshoe-shaped conference table, as if debating was more to their style than public displays of status.

Welkin liked that. He could almost see the deflated expressions on the faces of Jamieson and Tobias.

The one ceremonial element that could not be avoided was the age-old exchange of ambassadors. Two designated "teams"—each comprising five men and women—met, chatted briefly, then simply swapped sides. The elders' team would remain, for now, with the crusaders, acting as a liaison group, and the crusaders' team would return in the shuttle craft to *Colony*.

"What are they saying?" Theo asked. There was only room at the metal grille for one, so Welkin had to perform a running commentary, though the truth was that he could make out little that was being said.

"You'll have to jack into their system," he said. Welkin did not answer. He was reluctant to connect his neural network into the skyworld's cybernetic one. There was no telling what alarms, booby-traps, or more subtle counter-measures were built into the computer's architecture. He also had an uneasy feeling. The crusaders seemed friendly enough and certainly there was no reason to assume they would be hostile to the elders or, for that matter, the Earthborn.

But he could not dispel the feeling that something was wrong. The "oddness" he had sensed in the communication exchanges between the elders and the newcomers gnawed at the back of his mind.

Perhaps the crusaders knew that the elders had become murderers and despots. Maybe they were simply being guarded in their exchanges with them.

"We need to get closer," Theo said. "I can't hear a thing they're saying."

Welkin nodded.

They wormed their way through more tubes, climbed up a ventilation shaft to a crawl space between the roof of the reception chamber and the bulkhead floor of the compartment above. As they crawled across this "roof" they noted the various devices and machinery designed to seal off the reception chamber and eject it into space.

They found a large matrix grille directly above the horseshoe table. Voices rose to greet them.

Elder Jamieson broached a subject dear to his heart. "It may have come to your attention that the mother planet is inhabited by hostiles."

The man he was speaking to was a broad-shouldered individual in his mid-fifties. He was artificially tanned, ruggedly handsome, and direct. Probably the skyworld's captain. The crusaders either had no elder hierarchy or were not willing to commit them at this stage.

"There are remnants of civilization?" he asked.

"In a manner of speaking, yes," said Jamieson.

"Their level of deterioration?"

"Barbaric," said Jamieson. "Barely out of the Stone Age."

"To have regressed so far . . . Is this important to you?"

"We were wondering if you . . . ah . . . have any specific policy with regard to these sub-human leftovers?" Tobias said bluntly.

"I shouldn't expect so," said the captain. "We will assess the situation for ourselves, then devise an appropriate policy."

Welkin felt his heart clamp, and saw Theo scowl. Genocide was just a word to them, to be tossed around carelessly.

Jamieson visibly relaxed. Tobias said, "Good. That's very good . . ."

"Doesn't mean anything," Theo whispered. "I mean, it was a noncommittal answer. Nor would he say otherwise if their sympathies were actually with the Earthborn."

"They must have knowledge of the situation on Earth," Welkin said.

"Agreed." Theo thought for a second. "They would have been picking up radio signals a long way out. Wouldn't take a genius to work out what was going on."

"We have to remember that these people have developed independently of us," Welkin pointed out.

"Which means we still don't know the score."

Welkin glared at Theo. "If you're hinting that I should interface with the ship's computer, I'm still thinking about it, okay?"

"Take your time. Only there's not much of it left."

Jamieson was speaking. "The situation is somewhat dire. The Earthborn—I'm afraid that is what they call themselves—are a pestilence." The elder seemed to be watching the *Crusader* captain like a poker player second-guessing his opponent. "We feel that they are a plague upon the mother world."

The captain cocked his head. "How so?"

Jamieson exchanged a quick look with Tobias. "Why, they carry diseases of course. But worse than that, they are rebels. They hate and fear harmonious society. They believe civilization is their enemy."

"Barbarians often see it so," said the captain evenly.

"True, true," said Jamieson, oddly uneasy in the face of this stranger's frank yet expressionless manner. "But we do feel the Earthborn are a serious threat."

"You wish our help in exterminating them?"

There. It was said. Twenty feet above them, Welkin held his breath. Theo just stared down at the tableau below.

Jamieson swallowed. "We . . . ah . . . would like to know your feelings on this matter."

The captain flicked his hand carelessly. "It is nothing to us," he said. "If you wish to exterminate them, feel free to do so. As mentioned, we will study the situation, but not hinder your activities."

Jamieson breathed out, a great sigh of relief. He smiled at Tobias beside him and both men beamed at their host.

"That's wonderful," said Tobias, bowing low. The captain returned the bow.

"Perhaps you would like a tour of *Crusader* before you return to the planet? After three hundred years, I'm sure our vessels differ somewhat."

Jamieson and Tobias nodded enthusiastically. Moments later, they and their entourage were escorted from the chamber.

High up in the ceiling crawlway Welkin and Theo sat for a moment pondering what they had heard. "It seems," said Welkin, dejectedly, "that our problems have just doubled."

"Just when I was thinking things couldn't possibly get worse."

They reconnoitered. Moving about the ship's network of maintenance corridors and shafts was relatively easy, since nobody was trying to stop them. Nor, as Theo remarked, were there any surveillance cameras. They didn't dare use the crew corridors as neither of them had *Crusader* uniforms. Instead, in order to gather as much information as possible, they headed for the main mess hall and found a ventilation duct that allowed them to listen in on conversations.

The only problem was that there weren't any conversations. The mess hall was half full, normal for this time of the "night," but it was deadly silent. Crew members sat around the tables, almost rubbing elbows, but no words were spoken. Nor was there piped music, or background noises. The crew of *Crusader* moved with quiet economy and sureness. They did not drop things. They did not stub their toes on chair legs and curse softly under their breath. They did none of these things.

"What's going on?" Welkin mused aloud.

"Beats me," Theo said. "Unless . . ."

"Unless what?"

"Well, some ships are tighter than others. You know, captain has a broomstick up his butt . . . Disciplinarian . . . I don't know."

Welkin stared down at the silent rows of crew, all eating and drinking with the same methodical and perfunctory movements. "It's spooky," he said. Then he gripped Theo's arm. "That's it. Take a look at their uniforms."

"They're all the same class," Theo said, thinking it through. "Khaki coveralls." Then he said, "Got it. No one's wearing class insignia. Not one of them. It's as though . . ."

"There are no superiors. Like working bees, each with the same single focus. Which explains the absence of elders."

"Let's not get too carried away," Theo said uneasily. "There's bound to be a logical explanation for this."

"We're out of here," Welkin said.

"Back to the shuttle?"

Welkin hesitated. They had come all this way and so far had little to show for it. He still hadn't decided if he would interface with the ship's computer, but he knew they needed better Intel than they had gathered so far.

"Let's see if they let their hair down in private," he said. They moved off through the maze of shafts and access corridors.

Some time later they peered into a small crew apartment, designed for two people. The room was sparse, utilitarian, with two cots and little else. The cots, however, were odd. One of them was occupied by a woman who appeared to be sleeping. The other, empty, drew Welkin's attention. At the head of the cot, where the pillow should be, was a small raised section with a dark cavity to the side. While Welkin was trying to puzzle this out the door opened and a man entered. He went straight to the cot and lay down, placing his head and neck on the elevated part. There was a soft hum. Some kind of mechanism moved on the side away from him. All Welkin could see was an eerie glow that outlined the man's profile.

Instantly, the crewman went rigid and his eyes closed.

Welkin signed for Theo to move back the way they had come. When they had reached a safe distance from the vent Welkin described what he had seen. Theo had no more idea of what was going on than Welkin did, but they both agreed they wanted to take a closer look at one of those augmented cots.

They found an empty apartment, neutralized the grille matrix, and went to the cots. Something metallic gleamed in the hole adjacent to the raised portion. Neither of them wanted to insert fingers to find out exactly what it was. Instead, Welkin lay down on the cot and put his head down beside the cavity. Almost immediately, a thin spike of metal rose up out of the hole and a needle shot out sideways from the top, accompanied by an intense blue glow. Welkin yelped and only just managed to snap his head away. If he hadn't, the needle would have perforated his eardrum. Trying to hide his fright from Theo, he peered closely at the needle. Suddenly, a shower of tiny filaments shot from the hollow tip, questing about like tiny worms. At the same time a red viscous fluid seeped from the hollow tip.

Welkin involuntarily rubbed his ear, feeling squeamish.

Theo stepped back in disgust. The syringe remained extended for about fifteen seconds, then retracted. Welkin climbed off the cot.

"What in Space is *that*?" Theo asked. Even in this light, Welkin could see that he was pale.

"Do you think it's some kind of neural connection, like our jacks?"

"Through the *ear*?"

Welkin shrugged. "If it is, then they're all jacked into the ship's system."

"What's the red Jell-O for?"

"Beats me," said Welkin, oddly uneasy. "Maybe it's recreational."

"Like the way we use neural sims for training?"

"Maybe they use them for dreaming," Welkin said. "They plug in and order up whatever nirvana they want, like we order up a vid."

"One big pleasure cruise," Theo said. "Why'd my ancestors get stuck with *Colony*?"

"I'm not sure we missed anything," Welkin said seriously.

"Maybe not," said Theo. "I've never seen a more docile lot. They act like they're drugged or something."

"Maybe they are. Maybe they're overdosing on neurotransmitters, serotonin reuptake inhibitors, hallucinogens. You name it."

"Could be that's the way their elders like it. You know, a satisfied crew is a happy crew."

Welkin's face suddenly blanched. "What if they're part of the ship's neural network? I mean, an extension of the ship's computer?"

"Enhancing it?"

A shadow crossed Welkin's face. "Or being enhanced by *it*. I don't know."

A noise from the outside corridor interrupted them. They scrambled back into the vent, replaced the grille, and remained very still, holding their breath. But no one entered, though footsteps went past the apartment and they heard the door to the adjacent apartment opening and closing. They actually heard the hum of the neural jack—if that's what it was—being activated.

"And we have another satisfied spaceman," said Theo with heavy irony.

"I think we should get back to the shuttle."

"Works for me."

They were nearing the docking bay when Welkin made up his mind. He stopped suddenly and Theo, following along behind, bumped into him.

"Hey, give a guy some warning."

"You go on ahead," Welkin said.

Theo looked at him. "What are you going to do?"

"I'm going to jack in."

"Then I'm staying."

"Theo, there's no need for both of us to take the risk. If I set off some kind of alarm it's not going to take them long to get here. One of us needs to make it back to Earth and warn the others."

"You're absolutely right," said Theo. "But I'm still not budging."

Despite his scowl, Welkin felt relief. "You're as stubborn as an elder."

"Thank you. I think."

They moved into the docking bay, which was still empty, and found an isolated comm. panel. Welkin paused for a long moment, took a deep breath, and jacked in.

There was a hurtling instant of mind-numbing cold, then a barrage of images and sensations that he had never experienced before. He tried to scream, but he had no voice now. He tried to rip out the jack, but his hands didn't respond.

Then he experienced nothing more.

With a hoarse sucking gasp he lunged up into a sitting position and his hands flew to the back of his head to yank out the jack, but nothing was there. He stared around, panting. Theo and Ferrik stared back at him.

"Where am I?" he gasped. Theo pushed him back down and he realized he was lying in the cargo hold on some packing-fab.

"You're back on the shuttle."

Welkin looked around. He could feel the familiar vibration of flight. "We're heading back down to *Colony*?" he asked.

Theo nodded. "We thought we'd lost you." He was pale and tense. Ferrik was looking from one to the other. Obviously Theo hadn't had time to fill him in yet.

Welkin sat up groggily. "What happened?"

"You tell me," said Theo. "You jacked in, went rigid as a board, then collapsed. The whole thing must have lasted three seconds. I unjacked you and went and got Ferrik and between us we managed to carry you back here."

"You don't remember anything?" Ferrik asked.

Welkin frowned, trying to recall something. But he had no memory of what had happened, nor did he know if he had succeeded in downloading anything from the skyship. He tried to force some memory to surface, but all he got for his trouble was strange flashes of light and jags of pain, like some crunching migraine.

"Nothing," he said. "Not a thing."

"Maybe something will come back to you later," suggested Ferrik.

Welkin sighed heavily, closing his eyes. "Maybe," he said.

"So what else happened?" Ferrik prompted. Theo quickly brought him up-to-date on everything they had seen and heard. When he got to the part about the augmented cots and the strange neural jacks, Ferrik's eyes went wide.

"What's the matter?" Theo asked. "You act like you've seen one of those cots before."

"I have."

Welkin opened his eyes. "On *Colony*?" he asked.

"No. Here, on the shuttle." Ferrik told them that while they were away he had explored the shuttle. He had soon regretted his action, as he was very nearly discovered. He had entered one of the rear compartments when two of the *Crusader* crew had arrived from the other side. Fortunately for Ferrik, they had come in backward, carrying some elongated object. Before they discovered him, Ferrik ducked out of sight. That was when he saw that the object being carried was a cot.

It seemed a strange thing to bring on board, so he followed them to see where they were taking it.

Theo said, "Must be for the exchange group, the ambassadors."

Ferrik shook his head. "They installed it in Jamieson's cabin," he said. "I hid in the ventilation shaft and verified it. Then I had a look into Tobias's quarters. Same thing, except while I was looking he suddenly came back and lay down. There was this weird glow and a humming noise and he went rigid as a slab of plastisteel. And while you were trying to rouse Welkin, I went and checked the bridge. Apparently Jamieson went straight to his cabin when he returned and didn't come out. The bridge crew have gone quiet. Something weird's happening. Plath wouldn't shut up if you flesh-welded his lips."

"So what are we supposed to make of that?" Theo asked. "These people are some kind of cosmic drug pushers, selling neural nirvana?"

Welkin shook his head. "Let's think this through," he said. "It's got to be part of something bigger."

"How do you know? I thought you said you didn't get anything out of the ship's computer."

"I said I didn't remember anything, but I seem to . . . it's hard to describe," said Welkin, his brow creasing. "I seem to *know* things . . ."

"What do you know?" Theo asked.

"I know when something fits. And when it doesn't."

"I suppose there's no point asking how?" Theo looked at Welkin hopefully, but Welkin just stared blankly. "Great," said Theo.

"Curiouser and curiouser," said Ferrik.

"Freakin' thing!"

Gillian hit the command unit, and hurt her thumb. Her eyes watered from the stinging pain, but it soon subsided. She kicked the cruiser for good measure and turned around. Then to the cruiser she said, "Give me any more trouble and I'll turn you into scrap."

She mounted the vehicle, flicked the ignition, and throttled up. It worked first time. "Now that's a miracle," she muttered to herself.

Seconds later the cruiser lifted out of the clearing and swept away across the forest, the slipstream whipping the treetops into a frenzy.

She nailed the throttle and streaked away, heading southwest. Before long she came to the Merri Creek and followed it down till it met the Yarra River. She was taking risks, flying at blurring speed only a few feet above the water. Trees and riverbanks swept past.

She was within three miles of *Colony* when the blast hit her. The cruiser bucked and yawed wildly and nearly threw her from the saddle. She managed to get the gyrating machine under control and looked up as a space shuttle roared overhead, braking rapidly. Gillian swerved into and through a derelict building to shield her from prying eyes. She found a section of the building that had fallen away some ninety feet from the ground and took the cruiser inside, landing hurriedly. Jumping off, she ran to a window in time to see the shuttle glide gracefully into one of the docking bays on *Colony*'s upper surface.

What in blazes was that all about? she wondered.

It was the waiting that taxed their patience. Welkin, Theo, and Ferrik had to stay in their hidey-hole for nearly an hour after *Procyon* docked till they considered it safe to leave. Not until the last of the maintenance crew departed did Ferrik sign for them to disembark.

Welkin was still weak from his experience on board the new skyship. Helping him through the maintenance corridors and shafts wasn't too difficult, but crossing the gantry taxed their ingenuity. Fortunately, Ferrik came up with the idea of using a spar, held at each end by himself and Theo, with Welkin in the middle. They were helped by the fact that for some reason the cargo chamber was empty. Later, they discovered that Jamieson and Tobias had called a ship-wide meeting, a very rare event aboard *Colony*.

Seeing their plight and their slow, painful journey over the gantry, even Hatch battled his fear of heights to crawl out and help them the rest of the way.

In this way, they eventually made it back to Theo's sanctuary, empty now except for Koda, Jazz, and Hopper, who had volunteered to remain behind to monitor all internal communications and to offer some kind of rudimentary support, if the need arose.

Welkin, Ferrik, and Theo were exhausted by the time they got back and immediately lay down and slept for two hours, before being roused by the others as Theo had directed. They then ate and everybody was brought up-to-date.

"What's the news from *Colony?*" Theo asked.

For answer Koda flipped a switch on a CRC device and Elder Tobias's voice boomed out: ". . . must thank our star brothers for their hospitality and for their cooperation in the great enterprise that awaits us. The Pleiades willing, together we will build a new Earth. We will forge a future such as this planet has never seen. United, we will finally eliminate the Earthborn who seek to annihilate us, and who desire to destroy our destiny. With the help of our new friends we will prevail. Captain Cortez of *Crusader* has personally assured me that they have the means—gathered upon some alien world—to rid Earth of its foul pestilence. To facilitate this, *Crusader* will join with us, physically and spiritually, to do battle and we will give them every assistance known to us. Further, we have decided that for the duration of this war we will appoint Captain Cortez as our battle commander . . ."

Koda flipped it off. "There's a whole lot more," he said, "but it's all in the same vein. That went out about an hour ago, while you were sleeping. There's something big planned for the afternoon. Everybody's supposed to watch their holovids."

Theo thanked the team for their vigilance, then noticed that Welkin was frowning. "What's up?"

Welkin looked up at him. "I don't need some alien neural network in my head to tell me something is rotten in the state of Denmark."

Hatch looked momentarily bewildered. Ferrik leaned close and said, "Shakespeare. An ancient Earth writer."

"You see it, too, don't you?" asked Welkin, looking at both Theo and Ferrik.

Ferrik answered. "You think there's no way the elders would willingly share power with the *Crusader* crew?"

"Exactly," said Welkin. "Even I know that once you give up a little bit of power you'll soon bleed dry. Like cutting an artery. And from Tobias's little speech, it seems we're helping *Crusader,* not the other way around."

"So why'd they do it?" Hatch wanted to know.

"Brainwashed," said Theo. "That's what those sleep time jacks are about."

"Makes sense," said Ferrik.

"Does that mean the entire crew of *Crusader* is brainwashed?" Welkin asked.

"Would certainly solve the problem of disagreement." Theo grinned. "The beauty of it is, it's almost humane. No dissent, no dissenters, no punishment. Everybody's just one big happy family. Lots of hugs and kisses. That kind of thing."

Hatch looked at Theo dubiously. "I don't like hugs and kisses," he said.

Theo put his arm around Hatch's massive shoulders. "Of course you don't," he said. "That's why they recruited you into the heavies."

Welkin thought of Gillian but just as quickly pushed it away. He would have loved to hug her right there and then. "Whatever the reason or the method, the fact remains that anybody as ruthless and treacherous as Jamieson and Tobias would not give up any part of their power. Which means either they are, as Theo says, brainwashed, or—"

Ferrik jumped in. "They're planning an ambush."

"Affirmative," said Welkin. "Betrayal is second nature to them. If that's so, then that might be our 'in' with the newcomers."

"We'd need proof," said Theo, stroking his wispy beard.

"There is another consideration," said Welkin. "We could all leave. Get out of here now. Head back to the farm, build defenses, get ready."

Everyone started speaking at once and Theo waved them down to have his say. "You guys can do what you will. But I'm committed to fighting this war here."

Hatch and the others nodded agreement, but Ferrik remained uncommitted.

"I'm not saying we should go," Welkin said hurriedly. "Fact is, I don't think we should. But you've got to admit we've been pushing our luck. It's only a matter of time before *Colony* flushes us out. Stars, they could seal off the entire bottom quadrant, release a twenty-four-hour virus, and wipe everyone out down here." He had to hold his hand out to stop Theo from interrupting. "Outside will only get harder, especially if they really do join forces with *Crusader*. But I think it's only fair that we consider leaving. Staying here may be a suicide mission."

"What I said before stands," Theo said. "I haven't watched my friends die around me just to flee. We might never get in here again."

"That's settled then," Welkin said. "We stay."

That afternoon, at precisely 1300 hours, a notification went out on the central comm.band urging everybody on *Colony* to get to a holovid. Koda set up a small deck in one corner of the sanctuary and at the designated time Welkin and Theo and Ferrik and the others were all crowded around it.

The holovid powered up precisely on schedule. At first there was blackness, and it took some time before the watchers realized they were staring at star-strewn space. A speck of light grew until it took on the gigantic proportions of *Crusader*. A commentary accompanied all this, but Theo had the audio turned down low.

For a long time nothing happened. The great sphere hung in the blackness of space like a Christmas decoration, dotted with tiny portholes lit from within. Then, suddenly, as they watched, puffs of vapor appeared around the sphere's "equator" and with vast and ponderous slowness the bottom half or hemisphere of the skyship began to "unscrew."

The whole process, which must have taken some time in reality, was speeded up for the benefit of the earthbound audience. A short time later, jetting more vapor and fluids and trailing a sea of cables and pipes, the lower hemisphere detached itself completely and immediately started to drop down toward the Earth.

The view shifted suddenly, a lurching movement that was almost sickening. Then they were gazing up at the sky from atop *Colony* as the hemisphere entered the atmosphere high overhead and streaked across the sky like a meteor, coming closer and closer.

The hemisphere grew in size till it almost filled the sky, then came to a hovering stop a mile above the ground. From there cannons pulverized the ground. The noise was thunderous. Their vision obliterated by dust and hurtling rock and detritus, the hologram seemed to jump ahead until the picture cleared and *Crusader* came through clearly.

The homeworld's stabilizers pulsated and the craft dropped, to settle gently as a feather less than a hundred yards away from *Colony*. The ship, gleaming and new in contrast to *Colony,* was an awesome sight.

Several minutes passed with nothing happening. Then a port opened and a tubular bridge protruded, telescoping out from the side of the ship and across to *Colony,* where it docked with a similar but rusted portal.

The two ships were now joined. The commentary, even turned down low, was filled with the sound of cheering masses and trumpets, as if the physical joining of the two homeworlds symbolized two alien cultures becoming one.

"This is a new beginning, and the end of life as we know it," Welkin said, expressing all their thoughts.

From her concealed perch high in the ruined building, Gillian watched the hemispherical skyship descend, pummeling everything beneath it with all the might of a tornado. Within seconds, hurtling debris forced her back behind the wall. Half an hour later she sneaked a look and saw the worm-like tube extending from *Crusader*. She knew in principle what was happening, but the sight of the two ships being joined gave her a sense of foreboding far greater than the one she had felt about Tolk and his people. And the thought that Welkin was in the middle of all that shook her.

She just hoped that this time her pessimism was wrong.

13

Not knowing was the worst. The hours dragged and no one came to her prison, other than to bring food, and that youth did not speak, except in grunts. Sarah had heard the uproar earlier in the day; in the midst of that someone knocked lightly on the door and Sarah, still bound hand and foot, had hobbled across and pressed her face to the small wooden grille.

"Who's there?" she asked.

"It's Efi," came the sibilant reply. "*Siopi tora.* I can't stay. Gillian has escaped on a cruiser." Then the shadow outside the door was gone and since then, there had been nothing. No news. Yet no news was definitely good news. If Tolk and his band of cutthroats had found Gillian there would have been some kind of celebration, some noisy display, an execution even.

So Gillian had eluded capture, and she hadn't risked rescuing Sarah. Good girl. Maybe some of Sarah's strategic thinking was at last rubbing off on her kid sister. But Gillian was free. Sarah kept coming back to that thought. What did that mean for *her* and her predicament? There wasn't anything Gillian could do on her own; she would have to get help. Harry would be closest, but Sarah could do the math. Even at a dog trot, which would be impossible for such a large and inexperienced group, Harry could not reach the farm until the day after her execution, not without the cruisers, which Harry would have left for Welkin's party.

But Gillian would know that. She would find Harry if only to warn him about the changed circumstances at the farm and to urge him to hurry. But that would not be enough. Okay. That meant Gillian would head back to the city and *Colony,* and what? It had taken five of them days to infiltrate *Colony* the first time and they had been lucky. Worse, Clifford's people were no longer on the lower decks to facilitate her passage to the domain of the Skyborn.

No, any way Sarah looked at it, she realized there was nothing Gillian could do, other than exact a fitting revenge, and Sarah had no doubt that Tolk would rue the day he had set sight on the farm, and most especially Gillian. The thought brought a ghost of a smile to Sarah's lips. She did not want to die, but if she must then at least let her be avenged.

Sarah laughed at herself. *There's a little of the primitive in us all,* she thought.

That night she mentally prepared herself for the next day. She wasn't afraid to admit that she was frightened.

Late in the evening there was a soft sound at the door. Sarah looked up. She was sitting on the prison cot, chanting sub-vocally. The door opened and Angela entered. She carried a flask of water. Sarah's jaws worked when she saw it; her mouth was so dry she could not even summon up some spit. Angela placed the flask to Sarah's lips, let her drink her fill.

"Thanks," she said.

Angela got up without saying anything, then hesitated. "He will make you an offer," she said. "If you accept it, you will live."

"And if I don't?"

She remained silent.

Sarah shrugged.

Angela took a small vial from her pocket. She dug a hole in the far corner of the room with her knife, placed the vial in it, and covered it over. "The bottle contains a fast-acting poison. It will make things . . . easier. I am sorry I can do no more for you."

An hour later Tolk entered, alone.

She said nothing and he did not speak at first but prowled silently around the room, as if seeing it for the first time. Finally he said, "Do you pray?"

"That's none of your business."

"Pray to me and I might let you live."

Sarah laughed with derision. "Pray to you? You must be mad."

"Why do you seek to anger me?" he asked, sounding more like a forlorn sixteen-year-old than at any other time since she had known him. "We could be friends."

"As much as an owl and a mouse, I imagine."

He frowned. His face darkened with resolve. "We could unite the bands, your people and mine. We could do this."

Sarah swung her feet down from the bed. She suddenly saw that here was a chance to delay her death, perhaps just long enough for Harry's force to reach her. She took a deep breath and pushed the feeling of disgust away and let a slight hesitant smile play across her lips.

"I thought you wanted me dead," she said.

"There are things that are more important than my personal feelings."

"Such as?"

"The politics of state."

"You don't think you can cow my people."

"In time, anything can be achieved. But there would be much discord, much resentment, if—"

"If I die."

"Yes. There will be others. There will have to be others. They will also die."

"More resentment."

"Indeed, more resentment."

"Wasting your energies, deflecting your mission."

He met her eyes for the first time. "See? You do understand. You were born for this. You were born to rule."

"To rule, Tolk? Or to be ruled *by* you. Alongside you?"

He shrugged frankly. "Does it matter? You will be my queen. It is a generous offer. Give me your answer."

"I want my people freed."

Tolk frowned, considering. Then, he smiled magnanimously. "It is done."

"Something else."

He let out his breath, exasperated. "What is it?"

"My people do not have to pray to you."

Tolk stamped his foot in anger. "You ask too much!" he shouted.

Sarah gave him a placating look. Tolk gazed at her, relenting. "You will make a great queen. All right. Done. But you are pressing my patience."

"A pardon for my sister."

"Done. After all, she will be my sister-in-law. Do we have a deal?"

"We have a deal." *A deal with the devil,* Sarah thought to herself. "Now what about removing these straps?" She held out her bound wrists. Tolk removed a knife from his belt. He pulled Sarah to her feet. He leaded closer.

Sarah brought her bound wrists up sharply, catching him hard under the jaw. He staggered. Sarah dropped back onto the cot and kicked out with her feet.

With a strangled yelp Tolk collapsed in a heap, whimpering in quick spurts. Sarah lunged for the knife.

She hobbled back to the cot, and placed the hilt of the knife between her knees, clamping it there as tightly as she could, its blade pointing straight up. She began to saw the straps binding her wrists.

Seconds later the straps fell away and she massaged her bruised and torn wrists. Then she grabbed the knife. At the same instant a foot kicked out, smashing her fingers. She dropped the weapon, then surged to her feet and made a dive for it, but her fettered legs betrayed her and she fell on her face. Tolk got to the knife first. He snatched it up, then seized her by the hair with his other hand. His face was twisted in pain and hate. The knife stabbed down at her; she cried out in reflex, but he stopped the blade inches from her throat.

"You would have killed me," he spat. "Me? Fish warned me you couldn't be trusted, but I didn't listen. I won't make that mistake a second time."

He rebound her wrists, this time behind her back. Then he howled in anger and in a sudden and terrifying rage he started stabbing and slashing everything in the room. The hessian bedding, the eating utensils, even the hard, packed ground. Sarah lay facedown, her eyes shut, blanking out this almost elemental insanity.

She didn't open them till Tolk slammed the door behind him.

Eventually Sarah fell into a fitful sleep but woke suddenly to find someone bending over her. The horror of the attack came back in a flood and she tried to squirm away, but gentle hands restrained her and a soft voice said, "Sarah. *Eisai se kala heria.* Be still. It's me, Efi."

It took Sarah a long moment to realize that it was in fact Efi. She glanced at the door and Efi understood her query and shook her head. "Give him five minutes max," she whispered.

Sarah frowned, then remembered her facial injuries and winced.

"Just lie still and keep quiet. We won't have time for this later. Hold still." Efi washed and tended Sarah's injuries. She had overheard Tolk describing the next day's execution, and how Sarah had tried to jump him. She had come as soon as she had devised a plan. Being the only trained medical person in the community gave her a measure of freedom that few of the others enjoyed.

"I must get you out of here," Efi told her. She finished dabbing raw aloe vera into the puffiness around Sarah's face. "Tolk means to go ahead with the execution, now more than ever. He hates you, Sarah. I've never seen so much hate in one person."

The beginnings of a dark bruise filled one side of Sarah's face. Efi reached out and gently touched it. Her eyes filled with tears. "It could have been much worse, I guess."

Sarah nodded. She was trying to ignore the pain and think strategically again. Any moment she expected Tolk to return, and then Efi's fate would be sealed alongside hers. "You should get going," she said around swollen lips.

Efi smacked her own forehead—a familiar habit. "I'm going senile." She picked up the saucepan and plucked out a knife from the hollow handle. "Patrick's idea." She deftly cut Sarah's bindings.

"Remind me to thank him when it's all over," Sarah said. "The guard?"

Efi put a finger to her lips. "I think he's out of the picture. *Ande re!* Come on, you."

The guard outside was slumped on the ground, the remains of

cake spilled on the ground. "He's just sleeping," Efi said. She nudged him self-consciously. Too much of her valerian infusion and he wouldn't wake. She had witnessed many brutal deaths, but never had a hand in any of them.

"I'm glad you're not the cook," Sarah said despite herself.

They slid into the shadows, making their way slowly around the compound. Efi silently pointed out where guard posts had been set up. They avoided these with relative ease, but making it to the forest would not be easy and stealing a cruiser, since Gillian's escape, was out of the question. "I think he was more upset about losing the cruiser than losing Gillian," Efi said when Sarah suggested trying for one of the sky vehicles.

After tense minutes of quiet maneuvering, they reached a crude rock and wood "wall" Tolk had had the family members build, ostensibly to protect them from marauding bands. The popular opinion was that the only marauders in these parts were Tolk's people themselves. Ready humor was all that had kept some of them going.

They picked their way through the palisade of sharpened poles and climbed the wall slowly, careful where they placed each hand and foot, afraid they would make some noise that would give them away. But they needn't have worried. As they stepped down on the other side, powerpaks flared all around them and a dozen of Tolk's hunters emerged from the forest in front of them.

It was a trap. Tolk himself stepped out of the trees, grinning. "That was fun," he said. "Pity we can't do it again. Tie them both up."

"No!" Efi squealed, but she was knocked to the ground and was buried beneath three of Tolk's people. Sarah snapped a kick to one kid's leg. The blow toppled him and he cried out.

Stepping back, Sarah caught her next opponent with a well-judged front kick. He, too, buckled over. But there were too many of them. She was grabbed from behind and lifted off her feet. She tried head-butting her captor, and it worked, only he held on to her while others barreled into the pair. Arms flailing, they went down, and like Efi, Sarah disappeared beneath scrabbling kids.

"Hold on to her," Tolk said.

By the time Sarah could see clearly, her left arm had been wrenched behind her back and someone had a sleeper hold on her neck. She thought she was going to pass out.

"Haul 'em up and bring them over here," Tolk said.

They were dragged back over the wall and shackled to a post in the main square.

Tolk squatted beside them. He looked at Efi and shook his head sadly. "Now you, I will miss. You amuse me. All those fancy foreign words you keep sprouting like you're hanging on to the past." He hawked a wad of phlegm at the ground. "There is no past. Only future, Greek Girl. And I can't have you going around poisoning my people."

"I didn't poison him," Efi said dully.

"Well," Tolk said, straightening. "You took up with the wrong leader in any event." He stalked off to where Fish and several kids were driving a second pole into the ground. Several faggots of wood were heaped around the base of each pole.

It seemed Sarah would not be dying alone tomorrow.

"Efi, I'm so sorry," Sarah said.

Efi slumped against the pole. "I tried, Sarah. I should have guessed they'd expect us to try something."

Sarah looked up at the sky. "Maybe it'll rain tomorrow," she said.

Efi sucked at the blood forming in her mouth. "And maybe Gillian will return at the head of an army and rescue us."

But in the face of the two grim poles their lightened spirits faded and they leaned against each other for moral support. It would be a long night.

The floor rocked and for a moment Welkin thought that he was having a nightmare. He woke as his body lurched from the cot he was sleeping on and sprawled to the floor. The deck shook again and Welkin tried to dig his fingers into it, to hang on, and make it stop.

When the deck slowed to a tremble, he looked up. Theo was hanging on tightly to his cot; Ferrik was a few feet away with a bloodied face; Hatch was at the door, trying to open it. The others were climbing slowly to their feet. Evidence of similar damage and the sibilant sound of laser fire was muffled by the intervening walls.

"What in deep space is going on out there?" said Theo, eyes wide and alert.

Hatch pulled his head back in from the corridor. "It's started," he said.

"The elders," Ferrik said. "It's got to be them. They've sprung some kind of trap on the crusaders."

Everyone crowded around Welkin as he jacked into a comm.link. Three nail-biting minutes later he unjacked. "Nothing," he said. "Not a thing. All frequencies are jammed."

Ferrik frowned. "Why would the elders jam the entire comm. system?"

Theo collected his laserlite from a cot. "They wouldn't be able to coordinate their own forces, let alone respond to new threats."

Welkin fetched his own laserlite. "Why don't we go and find out," he said. "Before curiosity kills us."

"Follow me," Theo told Welkin and Ferrik. He ordered the others to take up defensive positions. If they didn't come back they were to try to exit *Colony* and make their way to the Earthborns' farm, away to the north-east in the Dandenong Ranges.

Theo led them into an access shaft that led underneath several passageways in which they could hear frantic voices and the heavy tread of running feet. In one corridor they heard screams and a strange hissing noise followed by complete silence. They followed the access shaft for more than a hundred yards, then climbed into a vertical shaft that took them up several levels to what appeared to be an abandoned security room. It was filled with monitoring holovids and other hardware designed for internal ship surveillance.

Welkin and Ferrik stared about. "You never told us about this."

The door irised closed behind them. "That's because we don't come here. This system is separate from the one being jammed and it's booby-trapped. It's designed to alert the elders the instant anyone tries to access it."

"So what use is it to us?" asked Ferrik.

"I figure whatever's going on out there, the elders are way too busy to worry about us. And it might just be safer than sticking our noses out in public."

"Providing the AI firewall doesn't fry any infiltrator's brain," Ferrik said, taking an unnecessary step back from the console.

Undeterred, Theo sat down at the comm. panel and waved his hands, initiating a coded sequence. Within moments, several of the holovids came to life, displaying sharp images of corridors and compartments within *Colony.*

Theo's fingers danced across holo icons, and another bank of holovids lit up.

The virtual images matched up with the sounds of mayhem they had heard, though they saw no more explosions and never discovered their source.

"What the—?" Ferrik said, almost to himself, as he stared at the main stage. It showed a broad hallway filled with stampeding people, men, women, and children. The similarity of the image to that of animals fleeing *en masse* from some danger or predator was hard to escape, even for men like themselves who had grown up on board a skyship. The sounds of desperation and horror made Theo order the sound down.

The hallway was choked with smoke, and some kind of alarm beacon was flashing in the background. As yet, though, the cause of the stampede was not readily evident.

Suddenly, half a dozen of the crusaders in their unadorned khaki coveralls came crashing into view from the farther bend. They moved like sharks closing for the kill, calm and calculated. They fanned out and brought strange ugly snout-shaped weapons to bear on the fleeing colonists.

"But they're just civilians," Welkin said breathlessly as the guns spat their loads. He almost didn't look, expecting to see dozens of casualties. But no bullets flew. What erupted from the muzzles was not high-velocity pulses of rationalized light, but a dark cloud of almost invisible particles, so fine that they could be seen only by their volume.

When they struck their victims no terrible wounds opened up, no bodies were shredded. Instead, a faint peppering of the skin was apparent, but this only lasted for the blink of an eye; then that, too, was gone. But almost immediately those struck stiffened into rigidity, frozen in the act of running, dodging, or shielding someone else. One or two toppled to the floor, as still and stiff as statues.

"Have they poisoned them?" Ferrik asked, horrified.

"I don't think so," said Welkin, starting to get a really bad feeling.

Theo pulled several stages into a tighter focus. Faces sprang from the holo images as though they were in the room with them.

"You're right; they're not," Theo said. "Look at those guys," he added, pointing. "They're still breathing."

The crusaders made their way with uniform precision and without haste among the frozen statues and disappeared off holo. Theo picked them up on another stage.

The same scene was being repeated all over *Colony,* though everywhere the rout was not the same. Some colonists fought back, bringing heavy weapons to bear on the crusaders who, as strange in death as in life, made no effort to find cover or to shield themselves from the spray of laserlite fire. The crusaders died quietly and seemingly without fear, yet the colonists they felled didn't die.

Welkin's skin itched with unease.

"What in deep space is that?" Theo said suddenly, pointing at the main deck, where a gaggle of crusaders appeared, each towing a kind of cart. The carts contained a pile of weapons and, next to that, a large cylinder filled with red viscous liquid.

As the crusaders came to bodies they rolled the still-breathing Skyborn onto their stomachs, turned their heads to the side, exposing their ears, then reached into the cylinder of red Jell-O. Their arms came out holding a small greenish object that pulsed faintly. It was the size of a large man's thumb and about the same shape and looked for all the world like a nerve ganglion, with a "tail" that ended in hundreds of incredibly tiny filaments, all of which were writhing and squirming like a medusa.

Even before he saw what happened next, Welkin began to feel sick. "I know what they're doing," he said, almost to himself.

They all watched as one after the other the crusaders held the ganglions above the exposed ears of the unconscious Skyborn. The creatures—whatever they were—seemed to have been waiting for this. Theo cranked up the zoom, and though they didn't believe it, they plainly saw what happened next.

The creature produced a kind of probe, which stabbed into the ear, burrowing inward. Moments later, after the probe had anchored itself inside, the entire creature, pulpy and rubbery as it was, was swiftly drawn into the ear till there was nothing to be seen, other than the merest hint of tiny waving filaments.

Immediately, the body of each Skyborn affected stiffened. They were rolled onto their backs and seconds later their eyes snapped open. A few more and they sat up, blinking.

Then they got to their feet, looked briefly at the other crusaders; then, without any direction from them, they went to the nearest cart and pulled out one of the snout-shaped weapons. Without awaiting instructions they marched off down the corridor, just like all the others.

"They've gone to find more victims," said Ferrik in a small voice.

Theo tore his eyes away from the image and looked at Welkin. "Tell me what just happened," he said, his eyes dark and frightened. "What the hell are those *things*?"

"You don't want to know."

"I want to know. I want to know what's going on."

"They're aliens," said Welkin. "Symbiotes. Parasites. They live inside host species. Controlling them. Adapting to their lives. They attach themselves to the brain and take control of the higher functions. They think of themselves as . . . gods. They think they're bringing peace to the Galaxy."

"By turning us all into zombies?" Ferrik asked, staring at Welkin.

"And just how do you know all this?" Theo asked.

"I told you. I know things. Only I don't know that I know it. I can't just call up the memory. As soon as I saw those things . . ." He shuddered. His eyes were wide, all whites, staring into space as if he didn't dare gaze into his own mind, for fear of what he might find there.

"So they're all like that?" Ferrik asked. "Everybody on *Crusader* is like that?"

"Looks like it," Welkin said.

Theo got up and started to pace. "So how in deep space does this fit into your pattern, Welkin? Huh? Can you tell me that? How does this fit into your ruddy pattern?"

"I don't know," Welkin told him gently. "We need more information."

Theo stopped pacing. "Fine," he said. "Let's grab one of those automata. I will personally take great pleasure in persuading him to talk."

"Wait a minute," said Ferrik. "Is this a good idea? We're the only ones who know what is happening. If we get caught . . . or . . . changed . . . then the others won't have any idea what's coming for them."

Theo stopped, eyes blazing, but he wasn't angry at Ferrik, just at his impeccable logic. "Deep space! We need better Intel on these things," he said. "We may never get another chance like this. In all this carnage."

"You're both right," said Welkin. He beckoned Ferrik over and spoke quietly into his ear. Ferrik's face soured, as if what he was hearing left a nasty taste in his mouth. But he straightened and nodded, slowly.

"What was all that about?" Theo demanded.

"I asked Ferrik to get off *Colony* and make his way to the farm and alert everybody. Just in case we get separated. He isn't exactly pleased with the idea."

"I can see that, and I'm in complete agreement, but why the secrecy? Don't you trust me?"

"From now on I don't think we can trust anyone. Which is why Ferrik's going to tell Hatch the plan shortly, in private."

"You're not making sense," Theo growled.

"Calm down. I don't trust me, either. In fact, I trust you more than I trust myself. You don't know how Ferrik and Hatch are getting off the ship, but I do. That means you can't tell anyone anything. But if I get caught, I can. So you know what you have to do, no matter what."

Theo stared, flinching slightly. Another tasteless bit of truth. He gave a single hard nod. "I know what we both have to do."

"Good, 'cause *I* couldn't do it, if our positions were reversed."

"You might have to."

"Noblesse oblige?"

"Yeah," said Theo. *"Noblesse* bloody *oblige.* Comes with the territory, I suppose. Let's get out of here."

Welkin and Theo lay in wait, hiding out in a storeroom off a main intersection. It was in a part of the ship already swept clear by the crusaders, but they hoped to pick up a straggler, or one of the newly converted.

They did not have long to wait.

A lone crusader came down the corridor. He was making adjustments to his spray weapon. It appeared there was something wrong with it. A second after he passed the storeroom the colonists leapt out after him. The crusader turned but showed no surprise or alarm, nor did he try to fire at them.

Welkin seized him by the wrist and bent it, immobilizing him. He put up no resistance. They hustled him quickly along the corridor and into another small side passage that led to an access shaft. They had barely turned into this corridor when they heard pounding feet behind them. Their prisoner suddenly sat down and refused to budge. It was an effective tactic. Welkin could not carry him and, judging by the approaching noise, they were about to be outnumbered.

"Come on," Theo shouted. "Leave him."

Welkin snatched up the crusader's spray weapon and they sprinted for the next intersection. They barely made it before a hail of particles hissed past like a horde of angry wasps. They kept going, but there was no pursuit.

An hour later, having dropped the exotic weapon off with Hatch and Ferrik in the sanctuary, they tried again. The same thing happened. Within a couple of minutes of seizing their prisoner they heard the sound of boots approaching fast.

Once again, they abandoned their prisoner and ran for it. This time their escape was an even closer shave than before. Winded, they holed up in a deserted staff room till the coast was clear.

"They must be wired to send out a distress signal," Welkin guessed. "Unless they're hijacking *Colony's* own comm.system."

"Maybe the little buggers are telepathic," Theo said grimly.

"Don't even think that."

They made their way back to sanctuary. Hatch was waiting for them. He had a disgusted look on his face.

"This weapon doesn't make sense," he said, throwing it on a cot. "I can't even figure how it fires anything. Best I can see, it uses some kind of miniature linear accelerator with a modifiable induction field, but it's something I'm guessing by general theory only, if you know what I mean."

"I, for one, don't," said Theo, "but we'll have it looked at later when there's more time."

"If there is a 'later,' " said Welkin.

"Just what's going on?" Ferrik said.

"We're not sure," Welkin said. "But they're obviously able to call for help. We don't know if that's a purely local process, or if it's something else."

"Guess that's why they're not exactly chatterboxes, either," Theo mused, remembering the silent mess hall up on *Crusader.*

Welkin said to Hatch, "If they are using some radio frequency, is there any way to jam it?"

Hatch looked at the crusader weapon. "I could rig a jammer. Mind you, without knowing the exact frequency I'd have to put together a broad-spectrum job. Wouldn't be much good except close up."

"How close up?" Welkin asked.

"Oh, fifteen feet or thereabouts."

"That'll do us," said Theo. "Get on it, Hatch."

"You got it, Boss." Hatch retrieved the crusader weapon and huddled over the comm.board. Before long he was carefully dismantling the weapon.

Two hours later Welkin and Theo grabbed another crusader. He gave them a startled look and that reaction told them all they needed to know. Whatever signal he had beamed out to his buddies hadn't gone through. He was effectively "blind."

Must be kind of scary, thought Welkin. If you lived your entire life in a vast fraternity and were suddenly cut off . . . what would that do to you? Ordinary human beings cracked under far less trauma sometimes.

They slipped a hood over the crusader's head and led him back to sanctuary. At least he wouldn't be able to "tell" his friends where he had been, in the event he escaped.

They tied him to a chair, positioning the jamming device very carefully nearby and a lot closer than fifteen feet. Theo wasn't taking any chances.

They peered into his ear and saw nothing. Theo fetched a light and aimed the beam inside and only then could they see the telltale filaments, hardly distinguishable from a middle-aged man's natural growth of ear hair. It was into the middle of this that one of the cot needles would undoubtedly penetrate to deliver its ooze of red Jell-O. And perhaps more.

Welkin suddenly got a thoughtful look on his face. He had an idea about those tiny squirmy filaments that had emerged from the end of the syringe.

"Now," Theo said, "it's time to talk. You understand 'talk'?"

The crusader stared back at him, impassive now. He didn't so much as blink. Welkin frowned. Maybe it was an absence of self, he thought. He looked more intently at the bound youth. There seemed no one in there to react.

Half an hour later a frustrated and angry Theo leaned down close to the prisoner's ear, growling. "You'll talk or I'll push your head into the nearest plasma conduit."

For the first time the crusader's eyes cleared. His calm, stoic expression never changed. "Please do with this body as you wish," the youth said. "And understand that we will harbor no ill will toward you and your kind."

Theo threw up his hands. "What's this about 'our kind'? We are your kind!" he spat.

"We're wasting time, Welkin. We could slice him up piece by piece and he wouldn't talk."

Welkin plucked at Theo's sleeve and pulled him away. "Then I guess we need to try something different."

"He's all yours," Theo said in exasperation.

Welkin grabbed a medkit and removed a syringe gun from it and filled it with a pale yellow fluid from a vial. He then faced the prisoner.

"I'm going to inject the organism concealed inside your auditory canal."

The youth suddenly looked concerned. "You mustn't do that," he said.

"This will only put it to sleep."

Hatch readied his laserlite. The youth seemed agitated now.

Theo held the prisoner's head and Welkin inserted the gun's funnel into his left ear, probing for what he felt sure would be a pulpy resistance. He found it. Instantly the prisoner stiffened, but then for several seconds nothing else happened.

Then the prisoner went into an epileptic-like seizure, started to relax, and, "Look out!" Ferrik warned. The prisoner lunged from his chair, his bonds broken, and threw himself bodily at the jamming device. Hatch squeezed off two shots, one of which lifted the crusader into the air, crashing him into the jammer.

The youth did not die immediately. Something like a beatific smile played about his lips and he managed to croak two words before he died. "Join us."

Theo dragged the body off the panel, revealing the shattered remains of the jamming device.

"All right, everybody, grab your gear," Theo shouted. "We've got one minute to evacuate."

14

Dawn was breaking. Gillian roused herself, feeling sick in the pit of her stomach. Today her sister would die and there was almost nothing she could do about it. Nor had she found any way to contact Welkin or Theo inside *Colony*. She felt so impotent, so angry, she wanted to break something; everything that could go wrong had.

She chewed her lower lip, wondering what to do. Racked by guilt over Sarah, she was also torn in other ways. She had a terrible vise-like fear that something bad had happened to Welkin and that she would never see him again, never get a chance to to tell him things he needed to hear.

But there was scant time for such thoughts. Since the landing of the new skyship the area around the two had become a hotbed of activity.

The crusaders had sent out aerial patrols, which methodically combed the area like angry bees. She watched in a mixture of frustration and awe as the crusaders picked off ragtag escapees from *Colony*. But they weren't being killed. Somehow they were being paralyzed, then revived. Each colonist was then handed a weapon before returning to the skyship. Gillian chewed her nails raw. Were they being sent back as suicide agents? Had they been hypnotized? Bribed? What? After working through several more scenarios, she gave up on the puzzle.

In the last few hours everything had gone very still. It was as if nothing was left alive in a five-mile radius, or if it was, it was holding its breath.

Gillian scraped the sleep from her eyes. She could not stay there. Thermal ranging would pinpoint her position; she was surprised she had not realized that earlier. Mounting the cruiser, she was about to power up when all around her erupted a tumult of noise: screams, shouts, and a strange hissing sound.

She pushed up against a jagged tear in the wall and looked down on a scene of utter mayhem.

Colonists were fleeing their homeworld. A few had commandeered cruisers like her own, but most were on foot, carrying or half dragging loved ones. At first she could not make out what pursued them; then she saw the phalanx of armed crusaders, dressed in what looked like dung-colored coveralls. They were firing indiscriminately at anything that moved.

The wholesale slaughter jarred Gillian into action. She needed to get out of there, and fast. She jumped on the cruiser and pushed the ignition stud. She jabbed it frantically, but the gyros remained silent.

Sarah was shaken awake. She looked up into the face of Fish, who ordered her to get up. She expected to see the habitual hatred in the man's eyes, but it was oddly absent this morning. Perhaps the impending execution had soothed his need to despise others, at least temporarily.

Good to know my death will accomplish something, Sarah mused, smiling to herself. Fish saw the smile and frowned.

"I don't know what you're so happy about," he said. "Don't you know what's waiting for you?"

"Oh, I know all right," said Sarah. Efi was jerked to her feet by a woman and the two were led to the community's bathhouse.

"The ritual cleaning before death," sneered Fish. "Let me know if you need any help."

"Go to space," snarled Sarah.

Welkin and the others crammed into a small, disused room. They had managed to put a fair distance between themselves and sanctuary.

They had heard the crusaders break in even before they were out of earshot. Hatch's last clutch of cluster bombs exploded five seconds after the door was opened.

Theo licked a finger. "One to us," he scored. "But that'll be about our only tally while we remain trapped here. We need to get off *Colony* now."

Welkin shook his head. "Not through the lower decks," he said, second-guessing Theo's escape rout. "They know about the breach and the tunnels through caver and Penitent territory. The *Crusader* computer nexus got that much Intel from me before I could seal the memory leak. There's another way."

Hatch tightened his grip on the laserlite. "It'd better be good."

"I have to tell you what I know," Welkin said.

"Can't it wait?" Theo asked.

"No. Something might happen to me," Welkin told them. "I'm remembering things. When I jacked into the system on *Crusader*, I downloaded a lot more than I thought. And you all need to know what we are up against in case any of us fall."

It was over a hundred years ago, out on the fringes of Orion's Belt, when the skyworld *Crusader* came across an Earth-like world and went into orbit about it.

In due time they sent down exploratory probes and, later, shuttles.

At first they believed the world was empty, but soon they discovered a race of beings on one of the smaller continents. They made contact and were invited to join what appeared to be an advanced agrarian society.

And join them they did. The beings were the puppets of a hive race, a strange parasite: a single being with a million minds and bodies. The being was incredibly ancient, almost immortal; its parts could wither and die to be endlessly replaced by the newborn, but the single burning consciousness that existed could never be extinguished, except by some unforeseen planet-wide catastrophe.

The creature, or consciousness, whatever it was, called itself the Hive, or that's how Welkin translated it into English. The entity had enormous patience. It waited. When the opportunity came—a passing starship—it moved to another race and drew them into the warm embrace of its vast collective mind.

Its destiny was to spread through the known Galaxy and beyond, absorbing all intelligent life, bringing coherency and unity where before there was separateness and discord. The creature understood that it was engaged upon a kind of religious mission and that it could not fail. Only time stood in its path, and time meant nothing to *it*.

Some of the *Crusader* crew stayed on the new world out in Orion's Belt, but most reembarked and headed back for Earth. Headed back to a whole new world just waiting to be absorbed into the cosmic community of Oneness.

The team stared mutely at Welkin. As he described what he had downloaded from the ship it was as if they could see it for themselves, as if vast vistas of time were unfolding in their mind's eye, giving them a glimpse perhaps of their own destiny—of the end of the human race.

"They intend to absorb every human being on the planet," Welkin told them, "convert everybody into *it*. One being, one mind . . . forever." He paused before adding, "There's much more. It's all in my head, but it's hard to make sense of it yet. It's like having a jigsaw puzzle in a million pieces. I need time."

"Which we don't have," Theo reminded him.

"You said they know we're on board," Hatch pointed out. "They'll have sealed off any way we could possibly get off. And I bet you anything you like they're waiting outside, too, converting anyone who manages to get out."

Welkin held up his hand for quiet and looked pensive. There were only seven of them. A small enough team to carry out this plan. "There just might be a way . . ."

But it was hard for Welkin to think straight. It wasn't lost on him that the crusaders' ideals were uncannily similar to those of Tolk. Was the Prophet a crusader spy? Were his people right now consuming the family into the Hive?

. . .

Tolk mounted the crude wooden steps to his throne. He was robed in white, embroidered with sequins and colored thread. He sat down on his throne and regarded his people. His face appeared impassive, but the features were twisted with repressed fury.

"Light the torches, my children," he intoned. "It is time for the heretics to die."

Six torchbearers trooped dutifully over to the fire that was kept burning at all times and thrust their tar and tallow clubs into it. They ignited instantly. The acolytes then held the burning torches aloft and a hush fell upon the assemblage, though here and there some disbelievers swooned and moaned.

He raised his arms to the sky.

Welkin and the others made it all the way to the docking bay unmolested. They did not need to go via the sewer. The ship was strangely deserted. Hatch reminded them that many on *Colony* must have fled outside and the crusaders had followed.

Whatever the case, it worked to their advantage. Until they reached the docking bay.

They burst in, lulled into a false sense of security by the empty corridors and checkpoints. Welkin cursed aloud when he saw them. A dozen crusaders were transferring supplies and equipment from one of their own newly arrived shuttles.

"Okay, Ferrik, Hatch, away you go. Koda and Jazz, you follow them. Theo and Hopper, this way," Welkin said.

Theo's people looked at him for guidance. "Do as the guy says," he said. "This is his show."

The crusaders saw Welkin's team at the same instant and went for their weapons. Theo opened up and the crusaders returned fire.

"Get to *Procyon*," Welkin yelled.

"You sure you can fly her?" Theo shouted back.

"I think so."

"You *think* so?"

They raced for the open hatch of the shuttle. Welkin and Theo backed toward it, firing nonstop. Hopper stood by the ramp and kept cover. More than half the crusaders were down and the remainder was too far away for their spray guns to be effective. Despite the withering fire, they marched inexorably closer.

"In you go," Theo ordered as they reached the hatch. "Fire her up!" Accelerated mist smacked into the hull as the hatch slid shut.

Welkin jumped into the pilot's chair. He had never flown a shuttle in real life, and even the sims he had trained in were a long way in the past. He fervently hoped that the synapses of his brain remembered what he was suddenly realizing were somewhat foggy memories.

He scanned the control panel, and relaxed. It was all pretty straight-forward. He worked through the checklist that obediently presented itself in his mind and instructed the ship's computers. As the engines hummed he called back to Theo and Hopper to hold tight.

He heard a yell and took it to mean they were secure. Theo burst onto the bridge and took the co-pilot's seat. "Hurry," he said. "They're bringing up artillery."

Welkin activated the forward holovid. More crusaders were pouring into the docking bay. Several were setting up and positioning a gravity-amplifying cannon. One direct hit from that and the shuttle would compact into an obscene sardine can.

Welkin raised the shuttle several feet from the deck and rotated it. "Hey," Theo shouted. "Too far. The exit's back over there."

"I don't know how I know this, but I'm not arguing," Welkin said. He brought the nose around a little more, then flipped a safety cover and depressed the tab beneath it. A laser pulse blasted from the forward guns of the shuttle and seared oxygen over the heads of the gravity cannon team. They didn't even duck. Welkin adjusted the computer's aim and fired again. Direct hit. The attackers' weapon exploded in a small, colorful mushroom.

"There are more of 'em," said Theo. Two more teams were methodically positioning a gravity cannon, but they would not be ready for at least a minute, maybe more.

"Let's get out of here, huh?" Theo said. He squinted. "Ferrik's firing up, too."

"One more chore," said Welkin. He rotated the shuttle a few more degrees. The crusaders' shuttle came into view. Welkin ordered the "fire without cease" command. A rain of pulses leapt across the intervening space and knifed into the other machine. He kept rotating his own ship and the pulses practically cut the other in half. He then swung the nose a little more and did the same to the third *Colony* shuttle. Within moments it, too, was a smoking ruin.

"Are you finished?" Theo asked. "Oh, in case you didn't notice, they shut the bay door."

Calling the enormous armored docking hatch a "door" seemed ludicrously inappropriate. Welkin said, "Open sesame."

He gunned the throttle. The shuttle moved forward, picking up speed, straight for the hatchway. Still a hundred yards off he changed the setting on the weapons console and fired. A wide beam fanned out, vaporizing most of the hatchway in a soundless explosion.

The shuttle shot through the opening. Something hit the rear of the vehicle but did not stop them or do serious damage.

"They're right behind us," Theo said, watching Ferrik maneuver *Capella* through the maelstrom.

Then they were both outside and rising. Theo whooped in delight. They had pulled off the impossible, or so it seemed.

"What's that?" Theo asked, pointing. A mile away to the north there was a swarm of cruisers and the quick sharp flashes of laserlite fire.

Gillian had left her departure too long.

After tinkering with the cruiser for thirty long, frustrating minutes she discovered she had a squashed power line. By the time she had spliced it an hour had passed since she had seen the Skyborn fleeing *Colony* and being disabled by the crusaders.

She mounted the cruiser, powered up, and swung it about. Pausing just long enough to check that the coast was clear, she throttled hard and rocketed out of her position, heading north-east. Within seconds a dozen cruisers were on her tail.

"Catch me if you can," she said, zigzagging through the ruined cityscape.

Either they had known her rough position and had lain in wait for her to make a move or else it was sheer dumb luck. Either way she was outnumbered and outgunned, as she quickly discovered when a laser-lite beam flashed past her left ear.

She banked the cruiser hard and threw it into a dive but just as suddenly pulled out of it and clawed for height. Her only advantage was that she was more or less headed into the sun, which might throw off their shooting a little; too, she had Earthside experience, whereas the crusaders were only sim-trained.

More pulses bolted past. The first few were wide, but they were quickly compensating for her erratic maneuvers and the vagaries of accelerated flight. And they were good.

She banked again but this time pulled a one-eighty and shot back at them, firing on wide beam. Not enough to kill but enough to give anybody caught in the beam an unhealthy case of sunburn.

She took out two cruisers before she looped over and nailed the throttle again. Now she needed speed and the best damn evasive tactics of her short life.

More laser pulses swept past her. They were getting her range far too quickly. By now any normal Skyborn would have been so flustered by her unpredictable tactics that they would be firing wide. But not these johnnies. They were getting better.

The beams were coming so close now she could hear the air sizzle and smell the sharp tang of ozone. She tried more crazy tactics, but nothing shook them from her tail. There were just too many of them and they worked too well as a team. She had screwed up again, left things too late. Now Sarah would die because she, her dumb sister, couldn't curb her stupid curiosity.

A pulse hit the port nacelle of her cruiser, throwing her into a yawing dive. She pulled out and got the machine back under control, but something was wrong with it. She didn't have the same acceleration as before and its stabilizers seemed to be on the fritz.

I'm going to ditch, she realized. *But I'll take at least one of these guys with me.* She shot a look over her shoulder just as one of the cruisers behind her, moving into a direct firing line, suddenly exploded in a raging fireball. A second later another of the cruisers exploded, then another. Soon there were only a couple left and they suddenly swerved aside and retreated.

Gillian glanced behind again and gulped as a huge shuttle bore down upon her as if it meant to ram her out of the sky. At the last second it veered to the left and pulled alongside. Gillian was hyperventilating when she realized the pilot was waving at her.

She shaded her eyes with one hand and squinted, and did a double take. It was Welkin, and beside him was Theo, both waving crazily and grinning like mad.

She thought she must be going crazy, but Welkin blew her a kiss and indicated she pull around behind the shuttle. Laughing, crying, not knowing what to make of all this, she did as she was bid and found an open cruiser bay.

Maneuvering a now-erratic cruiser into the bay against the slipstream of the larger craft took real precision flying. She pulled out of the first two attempts, then nailed it on her third, though she crashed into the forward wall of the bay hard enough to dislodge her from the saddle.

Then a door burst open and she was in Welkin's arms.

Welkin—confused—pulled back and stared at Gillian. "But . . . I thought . . . what about . . . you know . . . you just wanted to be friends."

Gillian grinned. "Just shut up, Welkin. Okay?" Then she kissed him.

A distant panicky voice came through the door. "You're not going to leave us up here by ourselves, are you? I tell you we don't know how to fly this thing!"

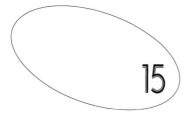

15

In a gesture of mercy, Tolk decreed that the heretic Efi would be spared.

The crowd roared with approval. But no mercy would be shown to the heretic Sarah, he thundered. The crowd roared its approval.

Sarah made no outward sign of the pain in her wrists as they lashed her tightly to the pole.

The crowd fell silent as Tolk descended from his throne and walked across to Sarah. He smiled. "The day of reckoning has come, Sarah," he said. "Do you have anything to say in your defense?"

Sarah took a deep breath. She could barely hear what Tolk was saying over the loud beating of her heart. "You talk about the one and not the individual. But you act like you think you are God. I have a better name for you."

"Really?" he smirked. "And what was that?"

"A psychotic."

Tolk stared at her, flushed with fury. "As you wish." He scowled.

Tolk waved the torchbearers into positions. "The blasphemer will now be cleansed by the purity of fire," he cried.

Suddenly there was a series of muffled explosions. People screamed as intense pulses of light exploded through the crowd. They were being attacked!

Tolk stared about wildly. He shaded his eyes and looked up. Two dark shapes swept out of the sun and hovered above them. More jagged pulses sliced down, picking off his congregation with uncanny precision. They came from two huge space shuttles, which blocked out the light of day and cast a deep gloom over the scene below.

Then an unnaturally amplified voice boomed out. "This is Welkin, a member of the family's Committee. Tolk, tell your people to lay down their weapons."

With that the family became an angry mob. They swept over the remainder of Tolk's followers. Others rushed to the fire and quickly put it out.

Tolk batted aside his fleeing congregation. With a muttered curse, he, too, took flight, using the confusion as camouflage. He was followed by Fish. Angela darted away, seeking her little brother. Tolk called after her, but she ignored him. Youths with newly captured laserlites fired volleys of pulses after Tolk and his aides.

Sarah's burns had been tended and she was able to sit up in bed and hear the full story of all that had happened. Her recovery seemed nothing short of miraculous but owed more to Efi's tender ministrations as well as the large stock of medicines the raiders had "liberated" from *Colony*. More had been found on both *Procyon* and *Capella*, including a complement of long-range cruisers, laserlites, body armor, and more. Under Gillian's guidance, Welkin and Ferrik had also ferried Harry and his followers from their location a day's hard march to the west.

The Committee was now gathered about Sarah's sickbed while outside a feast was being prepared. Farther afield, teams of hunters were scouring the nearby forest and mountain slopes for any of Tolk's people who had escaped. Tolk himself had not been found, though Fish, who had been discovered hiding in a rotted tree trunk, swore that the Prophet had died while trying to cross a flooded mountain stream.

There were many questions and not always enough answers. Ferrik learned that his old friend and fellow co-pilot, Arton, was only a few huts away and he rushed to see him as Arton left the infirmary. Their meeting after so much upheaval involved a lot of back thumping, and talking over each other.

Theo held Sarah's hand and she smiled back at him. Theo had not left her bedside for a second since the shuttle had touched down. Nor did Gillian leave Welkin's side, and their hands were locked tightly together where all could see.

At the end of an hour Harry summed up everybody's chief question. "Now what?"

The next morning, everybody gathered in the main square. The dais on which Tolk's throne had sat was still standing, though the "chair" had been removed. Welkin, hand in hand with Gillian, mounted the steps and looked down at the sea of faces. Many bore the scars and marks of Tolk's brutal but mercifully brief regime.

"We have learned much," Welkin told them. "We have learned that we have a new enemy and that we must stay alert. Our survival depends on this. Yet Tolk was right in one thing: There is safety in numbers.

"Our world has changed," he went on. "Our old enemy, *Colony*, is no more. But a far deadlier adversary has replaced it, one against which there can be no appeasement, no treaty, no mercy. In their eyes, I believe, they bring us a great gift. The gift of peace. Peace and brotherhood and harmony. But humans were not meant to live like ants or bees, to be insignificant parts of a hive. The Hiveborn don't hate us as *Colony* did, but that is only because they don't have feelings. They have a monstrous destiny and they are implacable. They will not stop until every human being on this planet is absorbed into their collective, extinguishing the very spark of humanity that we cherish—that we *must* cherish."

He paused to take a breath, looking around at their faces. "We must leave this place," he said. "We must leave and find a home that can be defended. A *home*, not a hidey-hole. A place to raise children, a place to build the future of our species." He pulled Gillian close and kissed her, then looked around again. "We have long-range shuttles now, and the pilots to fly them. We can go anywhere on Earth. But wherever we go we must go quickly, leaving no trail. And we must never stop looking over our shoulders, because they will come after us. The Hiveborn will never stop until we are theirs . . ."

Lal nodded agreement. "I never worked on the virus myself," he said. "But we all heard rumors. Some kind of selective viral agent . . . but nobody said anything about deploying it against Earthborn. We heard it was a sterilizing agent."

"And that's okay?" Gillian asked heatedly. "Most of us are dead by the time we're twenty-one."

"Gillian," Sarah snapped. She handed the baby back to her mother.

"So the Earthborn *are* diseased," someone said. Suddenly everyone was speaking.

"QUIET!" Clifford shouted. "Longevity and all that stuff is in the genes. Space, have you lot forgotten *everything* you ever learnt?"

Lal waved at Gillian for her attention. "Sure, sterilization's okay when it's personally fatal to ask questions about the elders' business." The way he said it released the sudden tension and made them all laugh. Even Gillian seemed to unwind.

"Trust me," Lal continued more seriously. "We all minded our own business."

"How long ago was this?" Welkin wanted to know.

Lal calculated, closing his eyes. "I've been down here about two weeks. We heard they were having problems with the junk DNA and also the delivery system. But really, I don't have a clue. It was all rumor and fragment. We didn't really know what to believe."

"And Jamieson's daughter didn't tell you anything?" asked Harry.

Lal snorted. "We didn't do a lot of talking."

Laughter erupted. When it died down, Clifford said, "We can get you past level five. There are ruptures they've never found, though we don't do much raiding up that way anymore. There are too few of us to take unnecessary risks."

Gillian frowned. "Don't you need to raid for food and weapons?"

Clifford nodded. "Weapons, yes. But food . . . we've discovered a new food supply. Sort of what you might call a symbiotic trade . . ."

Welkin stared. "You mean rats?"

"I mean mutant rats. Taste pretty good, too. Wait till you try some."

Welkin and Harry grimaced. Sarah and Gillian, never having had the luxury of trying out Skyborn cuisine, had no problem with eating rats. Earthborn did what they had to to stay alive.

"I don't want to stay hidden," said Gillian angrily. "I didn't come on this mission to *hide*."

"You're not hiding," Welkin tried to placate her. "Somebody has to organize Clifford's people and get them ready for the journey Earthside. Neither you nor Sarah can go into the upper decks. You don't know the customs, you don't know the lingo, and you definitely don't look like Skyborn. You have freckles for a start. So give it a rest, okay? You have your orders."

Gillian's eyes blazed for a moment. "My 'orders,' " she said numbly. "I have my 'orders'?"

Welkin reached out to touch her, but she flinched back. "Drop dead, Welkin," she said, and pushed her way past Clifford and Sarah.

Welkin almost jumped when Harry slapped a hand on his shoulder. "Life at the top isn't always easy, *Boss*," he joked.

Welkin scowled. "What did I say wrong? She couldn't come with us any more than Sarah could."

Harry coughed politely. "You said nothing wrong. You just put someone in her place who doesn't like being told what to do." He winked. "Matter of fact I think you did remarkably well. If anyone else had reminded her to take orders she would've thrown a left hook. She's got a mean temper when riled."

"Don't I know it," Welkin said, shaking his head. He turned to Ferrik. "I'd really like to have you with us. Do you think you're up for it?"

"My uniform's a mess, but unless we come across other heavies or elders, we should be okay. And even if we do, we say that you're the sole survivor of a reconnaissance team. You're reporting directly to Elder Stevens on level fourteen. We can refuse to give any further information unless they provide specific security clearance."

"And if that doesn't work?" Sarah asked.

"It won't matter anymore," Ferrik said simply.

Clifford and two other lower deckers, all well armed, led the family to level five. After some torturous belly-crawling along collapsed corridors they came to a ruptured ventilation shaft. Here Clifford and Sarah set up a temporary camp with food and water and bedding. Only the Skyborn would go past this point and only Welkin, Harry, and Ferrik would initially penetrate the upper decks. Their mission was, first, to reconnoiter and, second, to obtain suitable uniforms. The decision to use Ferrik had been debated hotly, and in private. Gillian had been most against him while Welkin had come round completely to trusting him. The disagreement had fueled the ever-growing distance between the pair.

In the end, Sarah sided with Welkin. Ferrik had recent up-to-date experience of *Colony*. A lot could have changed since Welkin and Harry were last on board. They couldn't take that chance.

Sarah hugged them all. "Don't be long," she said. "And don't take unnecessary risks, okay? We need intelligence, not heroics."

Welkin smiled. "I already feel like a rabbit going into a wolf's den. First sign of danger and I bolt."

Sarah knew that wasn't true. "Go to it, Welkin."

He, Harry, and Ferrik squirmed into the ventilation shaft. Here a ladder, missing several rungs and bolts, led up into enemy territory.

They started to climb.

Welkin stepped out of the shaft entrance. He was in a part of *Colony* he didn't immediately recognize. He turned to Ferrik. "You'd better lead the way. First thing we need are uniforms." He looked down at himself. They had each been outfitted with barely passable clothing. It was faded and full of small tears sewn neatly, but not invisibly so. "I don't think this outfit is going to get me past too much scrutiny."

"Let's hope we don't get too much," said Ferrik.

"Looks like *Colony*'s on some kind of power rationing," Harry observed. "Good news for us of course."

They had only traveled the length of a corridor when a group of maintenance workers came into view.

The family moved deliberately up the corridor toward them, did not meet their eyes, but stared coolly past them. Ferrik strode out in front and bored straight through the other group, which split to either side of him as they passed. Welkin and Harry stayed close behind him.

The *Colony* personnel kept going. Their conversation lulled briefly as they passed, then started up again seconds later, as if nothing untoward had happened.

Feeling more confident, they started searching for their second objective. Ferrik led them up two decks. They had one close call. A sub-elder and his assistant passed them and suddenly called out to them. Already in the act of turning a corner, the family kept going, hoping the sub-elder would think they had merely not heard him. It all depended on how important the summons had been. They breathed a sigh of relief when, a few moments later, it was clear the official's gofer was not pursuing them.

That had been close. Welkin noticed that Ferrik's hand had strayed to his laserlite pistol and stayed there.

They turned another corner and Welkin came to a sudden stop. His face did a complete change of expression. Harry went on a little way before realizing he was alone; then he turned and looked back. Welkin was white-faced. Ferrik seemed uncomfortable.

"Welkin?"

Welkin didn't seem to hear him. He stood in front of a door that looked like all the other non-descript anonymous doors in this long grey corridor, and reached out to activate the opening switch. But his hand stopped halfway, frozen.

He stood thus for some time. Harry came slowly back and stood beside Welkin.

"Welkin, what is it?"

Welkin swallowed but said nothing. Harry carefully reached around him and activated the door. It slid open with a dry rusty *whoosh* and a cloud of stale air enveloped them. Inside were cramped living quarters for a small unit. The place was covered in dust and had obviously been abandoned a long time ago.

"I visited here," said Welkin, stepping cautiously inside and taking a long slow look around. He seemed to be coming out of his